THE CHINA LOVER

═The═
CHINA LOVER

IAN BURUMA

Atlantic Books
LONDON

First published in the United States in 2008 by The Penguin Press,
75 Hudson Street, New York, NY 10014.

First published in hardback and export and airside trade paperback in
Great Britain in 2008 by Atlantic Books, an imprint of Grove Atlantic Ltd.

1 3 5 7 9 10 8 6 4 2

A CIP catalogue record for this book is available from the British Library.

Hardback ISBN: 978 1 84354 904 8
Export and Airside ISBN: 978 1 84354 546 0

Designed by Sophie Huntwork

Printed and bound in the UK by
CPI Mackays, Chatham ME5 8TD

Atlantic Books
An imprint of Grove Atlantic Ltd.
Ormond House
26–27 Boswell Street
London WC1N 3JZ

www.atlantic-books.co.uk

For Eri

PART ONE

THERE WAS A time, hard to imagine now, when the Japanese fell in love with China. Well, not all Japanese, of course, but enough to be able to speak of a China Boom. Like all such crazes in my country, the China Boom was only a fleeting thing; here today and gone tomorrow. But it was spectacular while it lasted. The boom hit the country in the autumn of 1940, just as our foolish army was getting trapped in a quagmire of its own making. Nanking had fallen a few years before. Our bombers were roughing up Chungking. But all to no purpose. Frankly, we were like a tuna fish trying to eat a whale.

Back in Tokyo, the humid summer heat lingered unpleasantly. Asakusa, usually so full of life, looked exhausted, as though people no longer had the energy to enjoy themselves. Most of the action had moved west anyway, to the Ginza area, but even there a gloomy atmosphere hung heavily in the sultry air: the coffeehouses were half empty; bars had fallen on hard times; the food in the restaurants didn't taste as good as before. Joy was in any case, if not yet strictly forbidden, officially discouraged, as "unpatriotic."

Then came that crazy China Boom, like a rainbow in a dark gray sky. Films set in China were suddenly the rage. And all the girls wanted to look like Ri Koran, the Manchurian movie star. You would see them strolling down the Ginza, their short legs, like plump white daikon radishes, squeezed into tight silk dresses. Cosmetics were used to make their eyes look more slanting, more exotic, more Chinese. "China Nights," Ri Koran's hit song, evoking the louche glamour of nocturnal Shanghai, was played on the wireless all day long. The girls would hum its lilting tune, closing their eyes in rapture, gently swaying, like tropical flowers. A coffee bar in Sukiyabashi, named China Nights, employed Ri Koran look-alikes. Not that they really looked like her. Their crooked teeth and stocky build betrayed them immediately as Japanese country girls. But there they were, wrapped in a bit of garish silk, with a flower in their hair. That was enough. The men went crazy over them.

Perhaps the drabness of the home front made the Asian continent seem alluring by contrast. And it is not as if this boom was the first of its kind. As I said, we Japanese often catch collective bugs, which cause temporary fevers for this or that. You might say it's in our blood. But perhaps the real reason was more mundane. Listening to Ri Koran's song allowed people to forget, if only for a short while, about wars, economic slumps, and soldiers slogging through the mud of a blood-soaked land. Instead of being a place of a thousand sorrows, sucking us into worse and worse horrors, China became a place of glamor, promising untold pleasures.

It all seems so long ago now, as I contemplate the wreckage of our foolish dreams. China Nights is long gone. The Ginza a ruin. Japan a country of ruins. I'm a ruin. Anyway, just a year after it erupted, the China Boom was all over. After Pearl Harbor, victory over the Anglo-American barbarians was all people thought about. It proved to be just another one of our dreams, a mirage in the desert toward which we, a thirsty people, crawled in the vain hope that we would quench our thirst for a little justice and respect.

But before getting ahead of my story, I should like to explain my own love for China, which was not at all like that superficial China Boom of 1940. To understand my feelings, I have to take you back to the 1920s, to my native village near Aomori, a small place in a narrow-minded province of a small country, whose people held the narrow views of frogs stuck in a dark well. To me, China, with its vast spaces, its teeming cities, and its five thousand years of civilization, always represented an escape from the well. I was one little frog that got away.

Where I grew up, loving China was not exactly viewed with approval. There was old Matsumoto-sensei, of course, a thin man in a faded blue kimono and tortoiseshell glasses, whose long white hair floated around his shriveled neck like a tangle of cobwebs. But the China he loved stopped somewhere in the twelfth century. He lived in a world of musty Confucian classics, whose wisdom he attempted to impart to us with scant success. I can still picture him, his head almost touching the pages of the Analects, a half-smile playing on his cracked lips, as he traced the Chinese characters with the long brown fingernail of his right index finger, oblivious to the sniggers of his pupils. Even now, when I hear the names of Kōshi (Confucius) or Mōshi (Mencius), the image of Matsumoto-sensei comes back to me, with the burnt-milk smell of an old man's breath.

My father, Sato Yukichi, had actually been to China as a soldier in 1895. But there was no love lost between him and the country of his former enemies. He didn't mention the Sino-Japanese War often. I even wonder whether he ever had more than the haziest idea of what it was all about. Just once in a while, when he had drunk too much saké, he would throw back his head and burst into a marching song, cupping his hand to his mouth imitating the sound of a trumpet. He would then bore us with stories about Commander Koga rescuing the imperial flag, or some such act of derring-do. Or he went on about the weather in Manchuria, which, as he never tired of telling us, was colder even than our snow country in winter, so cold that your piss froze solid, like an icicle, from the tip of your penis to the frozen ground. Mother would always withdraw at this point and make clattering noises as she busied herself in the kitchen.

One day, when I was still a boy, I discovered a lacquer box among my father's books, which contained some woodcuts of famous battle scenes set in landscapes covered in thick snow. Since the pictures had hardly ever been exposed to daylight, the colors were still as crisp and true as when they were first printed—fiery reds and yellows of gunfire; the dark blues of wintry nights. The horses, in pretty checkered padding from their necks to their ankles, were so vividly drawn that you could almost sense them shivering in the snow. I can still remember the titles: *Hard Fight of Captain Asakawa, Banzai for Japan: Victory Song of Pyongyang*. And the Chinese? They were depicted as cringing, yellow, ratlike creatures, with slitty eyes and pigtails, either writhing in terror or prostrated under the boots of our triumphant soldiers. The Japanese, looking splendid in their black Prussian-style uniforms, were much taller than these dead Chinese rodents. They looked almost like Europeans. This didn't strike me as particularly odd at the time. Nor can I say that it filled me with pride. I couldn't help wondering why beating such pathetic enemies should be presented as something so glorious.

These pictures were my first glimpse of a wider world, far away from our village near Aomori. But they were not what made me dream of leaving the old place. I think, now I look back, that such dreams were nurtured by something more artistic. I've always thought of myself as an artist at heart, a man of the theater. This began at a very early age. Not that we had the opportunity of visiting anything so grand as a Kabuki theater. You had to go to Aomori for that. Our village was too remote even for the travelling players, offering a bawdier and much inferior form of drama. And even if they had graced us with their temporary presence, my father would never have let me go anywhere near such entertainments anyway. As the village schoolmaster, he prided himself on his respectability. Men of substance, in his view, did not go to see performing riffraff.

Entertainment, where I grew up, consisted of one man only, the estimable Mr. Yamazaki Tetsuzo, candyman and "paper theater" performer. He would arrive, on festival days, on his old Fuji bicycle, carrying a wooden contraption rather like a portable set of drawers that contained a box of candies, a paper screen, and a stack of pictures, which he would pass in front of the screen one by one, while mimicking the voices of characters shown in the pictures. Since our village was buried in thick snow during the winter season, Yamazaki could only reach us in spring and summer. We always knew he was coming as soon as we heard the sound of wooden clappers, which he knocked together to announce his arrival. Before the show began, he would sell candy. Those lucky enough to have money to buy it were allowed to sit right in front of the screen. I was never that fortunate. My father, though rarely expressly forbidding my attendance at the candyman's theater, certainly didn't approve of spending any money. Aside from anything else, he declared that such candy was unhygienic. He may have been right, but it wasn't the candy that provided the main attraction.

Mr. Yamazaki wasn't much to look at, a skinny, bespectacled man with a few licks of well-greased hair swept across his shining pate. Though he told the same stories over and over, he allowed himself room for improvisation. When he spoke in the falsetto voice of a beautiful woman, you almost believed that the skinny old candyman, as if by magic, had been transformed into a great beauty. And when the beauty turned out to be a ghost, who slunk off at the end of the story as a malevolent fox, his impersonation of the animal trickster made us break out in a cold sweat. His sound effects were as important as the lurid illustrations of brave boy heroes and demon foxes. He was especially good at such dramatic touches as rolling thunderstorms, the *clip-clop* of wooden sandals, and the clashing of samurai swords. But his *pièce de résistance*, most popular with us, his most devoted fans, who

7

would anticipate its coming like true connoisseurs of the theater, was the extraordinary honking fart, emitted by the pompous lord in a well-worn story called *Snake Princess*. On and on he went, like a human trombone, for what seemed like minutes without pause, his face getting redder and redder, veins bulging on his forehead, as though he were about to explode. We were in hysterics, no matter how many times we'd seen this remarkable performance. But then, suddenly, like a pricked balloon, his face quickly regained its normal shape, and he stopped the show, even though the story was still far from reaching its conclusion. He wrapped up his pictures, and folded the makeshift stage, neatly stacking it on his Fuji bike. "More, more!" we'd shout. But to no avail. We had to be patient until the next time we heard the noise of his wooden clappers announcing his arrival.

I have seen many great performances since, from far more famous entertainers than this humble candyman, but first impressions are precious as gold. Nothing would ever compare with the magic of Mr. Yamazaki's paper theater productions. I quite lost myself in his stories, which painted a world that was so much more attractive than the dreary everyday life of our village; not just more attractive, but in a way more real. In the same way that one can feel resentful at having woken up from a particularly vivid dream, I hated it when Mr. Yamazaki's stories ended in mid-flow. I was hungry for the next episode, even though I already knew exactly what was in store.

There was no reason for Mr. Yamazaki to pay any special attention to me, a fawning, stagestruck little boy, who never bought any candy. But after many days of following him around like a homeless puppy, offering to polish his bicycle, asking him to take me on as his apprentice (as though my father would have let me), he finally deigned to speak to me. It was a hot afternoon. He squatted down by the dusty roadside, mopping his brow with a cotton handkerchief and sipping cold barley tea from his flask. Squinting through the smoke of his cigarette, he asked me what I wanted to do when I grew up. I said I wanted to be like him, travel around and put on theater performances. I begged him to be my teacher. He didn't laugh or mock me, but slowly shook his head, and said that it was a hard life, being a performer. He did it because he had no other choice. But I looked like a clever little boy. I could do much better than him. And he had no need for an apprentice, anyway. I must have shown my disappointment, for as a kind of consolation, he reached into his candy bag, fished out a picture book, and handed it to me as a gift.

It was a more precious gift than the candyman could possibly have imagined. I would go so far as to say that it changed my life. For this was my introduction to *Suikoden* or *All Men Are Brothers*, my favorite book of all time, my Bible, as it were, whose stories about Chinese swordfighters released into the world during the fourteenth century as demons I learned to recite word for word. I could tell you the stories of all of them, all one hundred and eight heroes: Shishin, the warrior with the nine dragons tattooed on his back; Roshi Ensei; Saijinki Kakusei; and on and on. These immortal warriors, battling in the marshes of central China, were so far removed from the twisted yellow creatures in my father's woodblock prints that they seemed to be from a different species altogether. They were giants, not cowering dwarfs. They had style, these fighters for justice and honor, and they were free. Perhaps that was the main thing, their sense of unlimited possibility. The *Suikoden* heroes could only have existed in a vast place like China. Compared to them, Japanese warriors were bumpkins with small dreams, constrained by the narrow boundaries of our small island country.

I read the book over and over until the cheap paper wore so thin that it began to fall apart. Alone, in the yard of our house, I wielded my bamboo sword in imaginary battles against wicked rulers, striking poses I knew from the pictures, putting myself in the roles of Nine-

Dragon Shishin or Welcome Rain, the dusky outlaw with his phoenix eyes. We Japanese prize loyalty and honor, but we copied these virtues from the ancient Chinese. Reading *All Men Are Brothers* made me wonder, even as a child, about the fate of that great nation. How could it have allowed its people to fall so low? I knew better than to ask my father, who had nothing but contempt for "the Chinks." So I posed the question to Mr. Yamazaki, who tilted his head and sucked in his breath. "I don't know about such difficult matters," he said, and told me to study hard, so that one day I would know the answers to all my questions. But even though he was unable to enlighten me on the sad fate of China, he did make room for me in the front row, right under the screen perched on his bicycle, in spite of the fact that I was never able to buy any candy.

2

I FIRST SAW Yamaguchi Yoshiko perform in the great city of Mukden in October 1933. Mukden, which we called Hoten, was the busi-
est, most cosmopolitan city in Manchuria, more modern even than
Tokyo in its best days, before our capital city was turned into a smol-
dering ruin by the American B-29s.

It was her eyes that left the deepest impression. They were unusually large for an Oriental woman. She didn't look typically Japanese,
nor typically Chinese. There was something of the Silk Road in her, of
the caravans and spice markets of Samarkand. No one would have
guessed that she was just an ordinary Japanese girl born in Manchuria.

Before we Japanese arrived, Manchuria was a wild and terrifying
place, located perilously in the border areas of Russia and China, which
didn't belong to anyone. Once the seat of the great Qing Dynasty emperors, Manchuria fell on hard times after the emperors had moved
south to Peking. Warlords did as they liked, looting this vast region of
its treasures, while pitting their bandit armies against one another,
causing terrible misery to the impoverished people who were unfortunate enough to get in their way. Women were taken as slaves, and men
were killed or forced to join the bandits, who swept through the villages like a swarm of locusts. The poor, long-suffering people of Manchuria ate nothing but bitterness for hundreds of years. Those few
brave souls who tried to resist would end up hanging upside down

from the trees, their intestines spilling out like broken wires, as terrible examples to others who might have similar ideas. Order was eventually restored, however, and not a minute too soon, when the great state of Manchukuo was founded under our tutelage.

Manchukuo was a truly Asian empire, ruled by the last scion of the Qing Dynasty, Emperor Pu Yi. But it was also a cosmopolitan empire, where all races mixed and were treated equally. Each of the five main races, Japanese, Manchu, Chinese, Korean, and Mongolian, had its own color on the national flag: mustard yellow with stripes of red, white, black, and blue. Then there were Russians, in Harbin, Dairen, and Mukden, and Jews, as well as other foreigners from all corners of the world. Arriving at the port of Dairen, at the southern tip of Manchuria, to me felt like arriving in the great wide world. Even Tokyo felt narrow and provincial in comparison. Cosmopolitanism was in the very air. Apart from coal dust and cooking oil, you could pick up the pungent melange of pickled Korean cabbages, steaming Russian pierogis, barbecued Manchu mutton, Japanese miso soup, and fried Peking dumplings.

And the women! The Mukden women were the most beautiful north of Shanghai: the Chinese girls, lithe and nimble as eels in their tight *qi pao* dresses; the kimonoed Japanese beauties, perched like finely plumed birds in their rickshaws bound for the teahouses behind the Yokohama Specie Bank; the perfumed Russian and European ladies taking tea at Smirnoff's in feathered hats and furs. Verily, Mukden was paradise for a young wolf on the loose. Since I was a fit young man, always well turned out, I had no reason to complain of a lack of female attention.

Every autumn since the early 1920s, Madame Ignatieva, who had once sung *Madama Butterfly* in St. Petersburg for the Czar and Czarina, would perform in the ballroom of the Yamato Hotel, a grand but rather forbidding establishment, whose turrets and castellated walls had the air more of a fortress than a hotel. Madame Ignatieva and her husband, a White Russian nobleman, had fled from the Communists in 1917 and lived in Mukden ever since. The count, always impeccably dressed in his old army uniform complete with the Cross of St. George bestowed on him personally by the Czar, ran a boardinghouse near the railway station.

The highlight of Madame Ignatieva's artistry was the "Habanera" from *Carmen*. She also sang arias from *Tosca* and *Madama Butterfly*, but *Carmen* was considered by music lovers to be her finest piece. The hall was packed. The crystal chandeliers cast a sparkling light on the gilded chairs and the medals pinned to long rows of uniformed chests. Everyone of any consequence in Mukden was there, and some people had come down especially from Shinkyo, the capital city of Manchukuo: General Itagaki of the Kanto Army, our garrison force in China, sat in front, with Hashimoto Toranosuke, head Shinto priest of Manchukuo, and Captain Amakasu Masahiko, president of the Japan-Manchukuo Friendship Association. I spotted General Li, chairman of the Shenyang Bank, looking martial in his Kaiser Wilhelm mustache; and Mr. Abraham Kaufman, head of the Jewish community, sitting in the back row, trying to stay out of the way of Konstantin Rodzaevsky, an ill-mannered ruffian who was always pestering us to "clean out" the Jews.

And there, bathed in the spotlight, was the splendid figure of Madame Ignatieva herself, dressed in a long black gown, with a shawl of black lace trailing along the floor. She smiled as she strode to the center of the stage, a red rose in her right hand, her chin held high, acknowledging the applause with curt little nods to all sides, like a haughty pigeon. "Strode" is actually not the right word; she undulated, voluptuously, in the way large Western women do. And right behind her was her star pupil, a sweet young Japanese girl in a long-sleeved purple kimono with a pattern of white cranes. She was like a delicate flower, just before its moment of bloom, radiating a childlike innocence as well as a kind of exotic elegance not normally seen in Japanese girls. Perhaps she was a little nervous, for just as Madame Ignatieva was about to take her place at center stage, the girl stepped on the tip of the long black shawl, stopping her teacher in her tracks. For an instant the smile vanished from Madame Ignatieva's face, but she immediately recovered and opened her throat for the "Habanera." The girl's dark eyes widened as if to plead for our forgiveness and she blushed most prettily.

It was, as I said, those wide eyes that left an indelible impression on me. Though not beautiful in any conventional sense, and rather too large for her small face, almost fishlike even, they nonetheless expressed a delightful vulnerability. There was no more trace of nervousness when she launched into her first song, following the performance of Madame Ignatieva. I remember "Moonlight at the Ruined Castle," a Japanese song which made us all weep; then Beethoven's "Ich Liebe Dich," then a folk song in Chinese, then a Russian song whose title I can't remember, and finally a charming rendering of Schubert's "Serenade." It was quite clear, even at her tender age, that Yoshiko was not like the provincial warblers who can make concerts in Japan such a torment. Her command of languages and grasp of different national styles was extraordinary. Only the cosmopolitan soil of Manchukuo could have yielded such a treasure. I know it is easy to say in hindsight, but I knew then that Yoshiko, at the tender age of thirteen, was something very special indeed.

Yoshiko was born in 1920. Her father was the kind of adventurer we called *tairiku ronin,* or continental drifter, a Sinophile who roamed across the Manchurian plains in search of fortune. This, alas, remained elusive. For the most part, he made a precarious living teaching the Chinese language to Japanese employees of the South Manchurian Railway Company. Precarious, that is, not because he was especially poorly paid, but because he had a weakness for gambling. One of his pupils, at one point, was me. Before she was adopted by a Chinese general, Yoshiko lived the typical life of a Japanese child on the continent, mixing freely with children of other races, even as she received the strict education of a proper young Japanese.

The year of Yoshiko's birth was just a decade before the birth of Manchukuo. Or perhaps one should say just eleven years before the conception of Manchukuo. For this happened with a big bang, on September 13, 1931, when a bomb exploded on the railway tracks just outside Mukden. Quite who the culprits were was not made clear at the time. Let us assume it was from a Sino-Japanese one-night stand that Manchukuo was eventually born. Our Kanto Army quickly secured all the towns along the South Manchurian Railway and the territory was effectively ours—except at night, when local bandits still made a safe passage along the railroad impossible. Less than a year later, the former Manchu kingdom, which had gone rotten like an abandoned old mansion and become a refuge for the worst ruffians in China, became a modern state.

But I'm a romantic, so I prefer an alternative date for the birth of Manchukuo. On the dawn of March 1, 1934, Pu Yi, the last scion of the Manchu Dynasty, dressed in the yellow silk robes of his imperial ancestors, prayed to the sun in the garden behind his palace in Shinkyo, and was officially reborn as the Emperor of Manchukuo. The moment he emerged from his audience with the sun, the new state had become an empire. I was obviously not allowed to attend this ceremony, which had to be carried out by him alone. But I shall never forget the sight of Emperor Pu Yi later that day, in his magnificent double-breasted uniform, with gold epaulettes streaming down his narrow but hallowed shoulders and a gold helmet sprouting red-tinted ostrich feathers. The band played the Manchukuo anthem, as the Emperor goose-stepped along a red carpet to his throne, escorted by Prince Chichibu, three officers of the Kanto Army, and ten Manchurian pageboys from a local orphanage. His trousers were too long, his bespecta-cled head almost disappeared into his feathered helmet, and his goose steps made him look a bit like a puppet on strings. Frankly, the cere-mony was not entirely devoid of comedy. And yet there was an unmis-takable sense of grandeur about the occasion. People need spectacles to nurture their dreams, give them something to believe in, foster a sense of belonging. The Chinese and Manchu people, demoralized by more than a hundred years of anarchy and Western domination, needed it more than most. And—although people tend to forget this now—we Japanese gave it to them; we gave them something larger than them-selves, a great and noble goal to live and die for.

It was altogether a good time to be alive, for those of us who had big dreams for Asia and Manchukuo. It was certainly the best of times for me personally. After years of drifting from job to job—a private teacher in Dairen, a researcher at the Manchurian Railway Company, during which time I studied the Chinese language, and an indepen-dent consultant on native affairs to the Military Police in Mukden— I had finally landed the perfect job. Quite frankly, in Japan I had been a failure. I failed as a student of economics in Tokyo, because I barely ever saw the sunlight. My life was spent in the cinemas of Ueno and Asakusa. This is where all my money went. The walls of my tiny room were covered with pictures of my favorite stars, which I stole from the local picture palace at night. I would love to have worked in the mov-ies, even as a humble assistant director. But in Japan you needed con-nections, and I had none. For who was I? An obscure dreamer from a village in Aomori prefecture.

In Mukden, however, under the auspices of the Kanto Army, I, Sato Daisuke, was able to open my own office: the Sato Special Services Bu-reau for New Asian Culture. The services I offered were somewhat di-verse, and subject to a certain degree of discretion. Let us say my business was information, finding out things, some of them of a delicate political nature. This took a certain theatrical talent. To blend into the local scene, I had to learn how to speak and behave like a local. Luckily I am blessed with an excellent ear. Friends sometimes joked that I was a human parrot. When I'm with a stammerer, I stammer; with someone with a thick Kansai accent, I speak like an Osaka merchant. That is why I picked up Chinese with relative ease, astonishing other Japanese. To my compatriots I remained plain Sato Daisuke, sometimes dressed in Western suits, sometimes in Japanese kimonos, sometimes in a Kanto Army uniform. With the Manchus and Chinese, I was Wang Tai, and I chose the best Chinese clothes, made of the finest silk by the most reputable tailor in Shanghai. Politics was part of my job, but culture was my real domain; and by far the most pleasant task, certainly for me the most important, was to find local talent for Manchukuo broadcasting and motion picture companies. This is how my own modest gifts found their perfect application.

The problem with Japanese entertainment in Manchukuo was not the lack of money or goodwill. Since the picture studios, as well as the broadcasting stations, were funded by the Japanese government, there was plenty of cash to spend on the best equipment money could buy, from Japan, but also from Germany and even the United States. The Manchuria Motion Picture Association had superb studios. And though some of the money (and most of the native actresses) stuck to the hands of Kanto Army officers, there was still plenty to spare for making top-notch films. The Mukden Broadcasting Corporation too was entirely up-to-date, with the latest soundproofed recording studios, some of which had room for an entire symphony orchestra. Artists visiting from Japan could not believe their eyes; they had never seen anything like it. People sometimes forget this when they criticize us for what happened later. But it is a plain fact that in Manchukuo we dragged Asia into the modern world. This enterprise, so often misunderstood, was surely something we can still be proud of.

To raise the morale of the native population and make them understand what we were fighting for, it was no good just shouting the usual slogans about Japanese-Manchukuo friendship. Nor could we hope to appeal to the natives by showing films of Japanese pioneers building schools or designing bridges. These things just bored them to tears. And, frankly, who could blame them? They bored me, too. The Manchu mind was, in any case, much too sophisticated for our regular propaganda, and at the same time almost childlike in its craving for comic entertainment. We needed to enlighten and educate, naturally, but also amuse. We wanted to make good movies; not just good movies, but the best, better than the pictures made in Tokyo, pictures that would embody the spirit of the New Asia. This couldn't be done without top native performers who could sing and act in Chinese, as well as understand our cause, and speak enough Japanese to communicate with the directors and cameramen, who came from our homeland. Finding such people was my headache, often alleviated, it is true, by the company of some lovely Manchurian actresses, whose talents were estimable, though not always quite what was required by the Mukden Broadcasting Corporation.

The man in charge of our propaganda in Manchukuo was an odd fellow, with a finger in many pies, named Amakasu Masahiko, a captain in the Kanto Army. A born fixer, who knew all the powerful people in Tokyo, Shanghai, and Manchukuo, both respectable and not so respectable, Amakasu was like a spider in a giant web. There was nothing in Manchukuo that escaped his attention: the opium trade went through his office, as did other discreet enterprises necessary for the state to function properly and efficiently. Apart from everything else, Amakasu combined the tasks of supervising the security of Emperor Pu Yi and presiding over various important cultural and political institutions, such as the Shinkyo Symphony Orchestra and the Concordia Association, to promote racial harmony and social order in Manchukuo.

Although he was a figure of great cultural refinement, Amakasu had a somewhat fearsome reputation. Room 202, his suite in the Yamato Hotel in Shinkyo, was guarded day and night by heavily armed soldiers from the Kanto Army. But Amakasu was not a man to leave anything to chance. He always slept with a pistol by his side, a black German Mauser C96. There were many people who would have been happy to see him dead. And even those who would not were afraid of him. The odd thing was that he didn't look at all imposing. A trim little man with a shaved head, shaped a bit like a peanut, and round tortoise-shell glasses, he rarely smiled and almost never raised his voice above a breathy murmur. To look at him, he could have been an accountant or the manager of a drugstore. But looks are deceiving. Amakasu was feared for good reasons. We all knew that he had spent time in prison back in Japan for murdering a Communist, as well as the Red's wife and young nephew. Amakasu was a lieutenant in the Kempeitai at the time, our Military Police, and he strangled the entire family with his own bare hands.

A strange bird, as I say. But I liked him. We shared a love of the arts. Amakasu adored classical music and would sit in his room listening to his phonograph for hours on end. And like me, Amakasu was a great reader of *All Men Are Brothers;* a copy always lay by his bedside, next to his Mauser C96. We sometimes discussed the merits of various heroes. His favorite character was Riki, also known as the Black Whirlwind, the hard-drinking warrior who wielded two axes in battle, and who, rather than live in shame, preferred to commit suicide after his band of brothers was defeated. Like his hero, Amakasu was loyal to his friends and a sincere patriot. What endeared him to me most, however, was not his patriotism, which I never doubted, but his unfailing courtesy to the native people. Often, when Japanese officials spoke of "harmony among the five races," they were just mouthing official words. One of the great tragedies of Manchukuo was that those who most loudly proclaimed our ideals so rarely managed to live up to them. But not Captain Amakasu. He really meant it. I have reason to know this from personal experience. Let me relate just one example.

Most of Amakasu's business was transacted in his hotel suite, but once in a while he would entertain at a Japanese restaurant nearby, called the South Lake Pavilion, a place frequented mostly by Kanto Army officers. I attended a party there in the winter of 1939. It was a bitterly cold night. The streets were frozen solid. Even the slight mist that hung over the city seemed to have hardened into a cloud of pins and needles. A full moon shone through the haze like a milky fluorescent light.

Amakasu sat on the tatami floor at the head of the long rosewood table, with a straight back, as though a steel rod had been inserted into his spine. Dressed in an olive green uniform, he gazed silently through his round spectacles, drinking his usual White Horse Whiskey. He barely touched the food, even as his guests, including a senior Kempeitai officer and a burly Kanto Army colonel, became increasingly merry on the saké, poured for them by several gorgeous actresses from Manchuria Motion Pictures, who made up for their linguistic deficiencies by being absolutely charming. However, Amakasu was not in a sociable mood. Something was bothering him. An occasional grunt was all that escaped from his lips when anyone addressed him directly.

At one point a surgeon, by the name of Ozaki, an important figure in the Japanese-Manchukuo Friendship Association, raised his cup and proposed a toast to the harmonious relations between the five races. A fat, grinning, red-faced man, the type who fancies himself the life and soul of every party, Ozaki was an egregious example of those who spoke of harmony without sincerity. In any case, Amakasu raised his glass too, and Ozaki, who had a surprisingly mellifluous voice for such a coarse individual, launched into an army song, jerking his short little arms back and forth, like a tortoise turned on its back, and the others followed suit. Even though the actresses didn't know the words, they humored the men by smiling and clapping along as well.

Ozaki then proposed an egg race. Clambering down on all fours, not an easy thing to do for a corpulent man in his inebriated state, he ordered one of the actresses to do the same. When she hesitated to take part in the childish game of blowing an egg across the matted floor, a slap on her silk-clad bottom, provoking much laughter from the other guests, forced her onto her knees. One of the men slipped his hand up the skirt of MeiLing, then Manchukuo's leading actress, and told her to top up his saké cup. Conviviality swiftly descended to lewdness, with cries to hold a "Miss Manchukuo" contest. The Kempeitai officer ordered one of the women to balance a saké bottle on her head, then made her drink from a cup on the floor, like a cat. When she failed to keep the bottle from falling off her head, the lecherous colonel demanded a striptease.

I shall never forget what happened next. Amakasu, already ramrod-straight, stiffened even more. His face had gone very pale, like the moon outside, and his eyes glinted behind his spectacles as though they were catching fire. "Enough!" he rasped in that breathy voice of his, as though he had a permanently sore throat. "Enough! Actresses are not geisha, they are artists." Nodding toward the girls, he continued: "I demand respect for the artists of the Manchuria Motion Picture Association, and hereby wish to apologize for the behavior of my boorish countrymen."

Although there were several men in the room who outranked Amakasu, his words had an instant effect. There was no need for him to shout. The fact that he had spoken at all was sufficient to impose instant obedience. The actresses bowed their heads and fixed their eyes on the floor. Ozaki realized he had overstepped a dangerous mark and kept quiet for the rest of the evening. The men started to pay respect to the Manchurian ladies, some even offering to pour saké for *them*. The reason I can still vividly recall this incident is that it showed another side of this much-feared and indeed maligned man that has not received its due attention. Amakasu may have strangled a family of Reds, but he was also a Japanese gentleman of the greatest sincerity.

It was Amakasu, at any rate, who asked me to find a local singer who could speak sufficiently good Japanese to work with us on a new radio show to be called *Manchukuo Rhapsody*. "The independence and unity of our state cannot be taken for granted," he told me. "Education through entertainment should be our motto. Our message must be sweet, even if our aims demand sacrifice, rigor and perseverance." This is the way he usually spoke, when he spoke at all: in clipped sentences, like a man who has no time to waste.

After giving this much thought, and conducting a few auditions in my office with some extremely attractive ladies, which produced nothing in the way of musical or indeed linguistic talent, but were perfectly agreeable otherwise, I hit upon an idea that was so obvious that I couldn't understand why I hadn't thought of it before: the girl singer at the Yamato Hotel. Her Chinese was fluent, and since she was in fact Japanese, she could obviously speak in her native tongue. In short, she was just what we were looking for. Age might be the only issue, but that could be accommodated. "Go and talk to the parents," said Amakasu, whose thin lips curled into a rare hint of a smile. "I'm sure we can come to a mutually beneficial agreement."

3

EVERY MAN HAS his weaknesses. Mine was young women, especially Chinese women, and most especially Chinese actresses. I say Chinese, but could have said Manchus. We Japanese liked to pretend that most Chinese in Manchukuo were Manchus. In fact, there was little distinction between the two races. Chinese or Manchu, I adored making love to them. They had none of that giggly, schoolgirlish coyness of Japanese women. Their erotic attraction was like Chinese poetry—refined, romantic, and elusive. There is something particularly alluring, too, about the Chinese body, which matches the Chinese mind in its subtlety and finesse: the long elegant legs, the pert, round bottom, the perfect breasts, not too small, not too big. Where the Western woman is large and coarse, like an overripe fruit, and the Japanese woman is small, shapeless, and bland, like cold beancurd, the Chinese woman is a banquet of flavors, spicy, sweet and sour, bitter; she is the finest specimen of a racial selection that found its perfect form after more than five thousand years of civilization. And the feeling that she was mine, all mine, afforded a pleasure that was more than just sexual. I would go so far as to say it was spiritual.

Miss Yamaguchi's father, Yamaguchi Fumio, had a different weakness, which was, as I mentioned earlier, gambling. To look at him, he was an inoffensive type, slight of build and sporting a pair of owlish spectacles. But he was actually a bit of a rogue. Once in a while we would visit a brothel in Mukden, stocked with fine Manchurian girls, but this wasn't really to his taste; he would always be waiting for me, nervously sipping tea in the reception room, long before I was ready to leave. He much preferred the *click-clack* of mah-jong tiles, the rustle of playing cards, or even the chattering sound of fighting crickets, anything indeed that was worth a gamble. The problem with his particular vice was financial. He was always in debt, and relied on the likes of General Li of the Shenyang Bank to bail him out of trouble.

To be frank, Li was a former warlord from Shantung, who took our side in the early 1930s, and was made chairman of the Shenyang Bank as a token of our friendship. The old warhorse had taken a liking to the Japanese gambler and proposed a fair exchange. The Yamaguchi family would have a free place to live in the General's compound, if Mrs. Yamaguchi would teach the General's concubine proper European table manners. A somewhat peculiar arrangement, perhaps, but Yamaguchi found the company of the General, with his Kaiser Wilhelm mustache, his dark blue Rolls-Royce, and his liking for mah-jong games, which he invariably lost, thus enabling Yamaguchi to recoup some of his debts, congenial. And instructing his number two wife in the art of eating green peas with a knife and fork, or lifting her little finger when drinking Indian tea, was not too strenuous a task for Mrs. Yamaguchi, who was a modern, educated woman with very fine manners, acquired at a first-rate Catholic school in Nagasaki.

General Li's compound was in the diplomatic quarter of Mukden, a quiet area with large brick mansions in the European style—Baroque, Renaissance, Rococo, or whatnot—standing in the shade of fragrant apricot trees and sweet-smelling acacias. Many wealthy Chinese, friendly to our cause, lived there. The poorer natives dwelled in the walled Chinese city, a lively but rather unhygienic place of dark alleys that reeked of charcoal, garlic, and human excrement. Japanese tended to congregate around Heian Avenue, a big wide boulevard leading to the main railway station, up-to-date and clean, lined with department stores that could stand comparison to the best stores in London or New York. General Li's house, not too far from there, was a modern structure in white stucco with a wide entrance flanked by a portico of lime-colored columns.

The Yamaguchi family lived in a redbrick house that used to be occupied by one of the General's older concubines. Before moving there, they had lived in a comfortable but less romantic part of the city, in the kind of clean, modest house designated for middle-ranking Japanese company men. Though Yoshiko was brought up to be a proper Japanese girl, her father made sure she spoke good standard Chinese, a highly irregular thing to do, but he was, after all, an admirer of all things Chinese, and sought to impart this to his daughter. Other Japanese did not always look kindly on such enthusiasms, so a certain discretion was in order, not only to shield little Yoshiko from teasing at school, but also Yamaguchi himself from the unwelcome attentions of our Kempeitai. He had the excuse of being a Chinese teacher, to be sure, but one still had to be careful not to catch "a case of jaundice," as the Japanese in Manchukuo used to say.

Nothing of the sort was called for in General Li's compound, which is why Mr. Yamaguchi, though not necessarily his wife, was so happy to move there. He could indulge in his Chinese passions as much as he liked. The household routine proceeded like clockwork: twice a week the General would come down from the main house, lose a game or two of mah-jong with Mr. Yamaguchi, have Yoshiko prepare his opium pipes, and retire with his favorite concubine—a tiny woman hobbling around the compound in her tightly bound feet, who was probably relieved not to have to spear any more peas on her silver fork.

According to my information, there were few visitors to the Yamaguchi family quarters. But there was a young Jewess, a school friend of Yoshiko's, named Masha, who would come round regularly. It was she,

I believe, who introduced Yoshiko to her singing teacher, Madame Ignatieva. Since she attended the same Japanese school as Yoshiko, her Japanese was fluent. I checked out her parents and found nothing remiss. Her father, who owned a bakery near the railway station, was a loyal member of the Japanese-Jewish Friendship Association.

The General was so fond of Yoshiko that he decided to adopt her as his unofficial daughter. This would have been in 1934, round about the time of Emperor Pu Yi's inauguration. Ceremony is very important to the Manchu mind. Particular care is taken over family rituals. So to be adopted by a Manchu family should be considered a great honor. And I was greatly honored to be invited to witness the ceremony in General Li's compound.

Kneeling in front of the Li ancestral tablets, Yoshiko was given her Chinese name, Li Xianglan, or Ri Koran in Japanese, and was officially received into her second family. The ceremony was attended by both her parents, as well as the General and his wife and five concubines, who were all dressed in splendid Manchu robes. The girl acquitted herself of her task quite beautifully. First she bowed to her new Manchu father, then to his ancestral tablets, and thanked the General in beautiful Chinese for the honor of bearing his name. This was followed by a banquet, attended by everyone in the household, including all the General's concubines, who tittered charmingly behind their ivory fans. I was tempted to deepen my acquaintance with one or two of them, but knew better than to reach for these forbidden fruits. We were served at least one hundred dishes, including, this being winter, a superb dogmeat stew, a specialty of the Manchu cuisine.

As his favorite daughter, Yoshiko spent most of her free time in the General's rooms. Since he got ill-tempered whenever she was not on hand to serve him, she would rush to his villa as soon as she came back from school, to prepare his pipes and make sure he was comfortable. She could not leave to get on with her homework until he had fallen asleep, which, after a pipe or two, usually occurred with merciful swiftness.

Mr. Yamaguchi was not best pleased with the suggestion of putting his daughter in a wireless broadcast. "We are a respectable family," he protested, "and my daughter is not a showgirl." Mrs. Yamaguchi served us Japanese tea and remained silent. Yoshiko looked up at me with those big luminous eyes of hers, pleading with me to help her out of her dilemma. She was not averse to singing but hated to upset her father. I asked her mother what she thought. "Well," she replied after some hesitation, "Yoshiko does love to sing . . ." I added that it was "for the sake of our country," thinking that a dose of patriotism might help. Besides, it would earn Mr. Yamaguchi some much-needed protection from prying officials. "Well, yes, that is as may be, but . . ." And so it went on for some time, until the question of gambling debts was carefully broached and the matter was concluded to the satisfaction of all, including General Li, who was tickled to have her perform under his family name. Henceforth, Yamaguchi Yoshiko would appear on the *Manchukuo Rhapsody* radio show as the young Manchurian singer Li Xianglan, or Ri Koran.

4

TIENTSIN COULD NOT have been more different from Mukden. First of all it was in China, not Manchukuo. A wide avenue cut right across the foreign concessions like an open sore, the symbol of China's submission to Western colonial powers. On the south side of the White River (actually black with filth, carrying bits of rotten fruit in its sluggish stream, as well as driftwood, dead cats and dogs, and sometimes human remains) were the Americans, British, French, and Italians. The Russians and the Belgians were on the other side of the avenue, which changed its name as it passed through the various foreign concessions, starting off as Woodrow Wilson Boulevard, and ending as the via d'Italia by way of Victoria Road and rue de Paris.

Tientsin was a city wreathed in smiles, most of them phony. The privileges enjoyed by the white race in their concessions were like dark stains on the honor of all Asiatics. They did as they liked and literally got away with murder. One of the most highly respected Chinese officials, in charge of Tientsin Customs, was assassinated in a cinema by gangsters hired by the British. Like me, he loved the movies, and was peacefully watching *Gunga Din* when he was brutally gunned down. Since the British refused to hand over their hired killers to the police, and Customs affairs were handled by us Japanese, we had no other choice but to blockade the concessions. For this brief period—until we restored full Asian sovereignty a few years later—we could feel proud of ourselves.

Despite such outrages, some contemptible Japanese wished to behave like the Europeans, angling for invitations to the Tientsin Club, where they might be allowed in as "honorary whites" if accompanied by their British hosts. Such people, in my view, were not only contemptible but absurd, looking like monkeys in their ill-fitting tropical suits. You would see them, eating rich cakes at the Kiesling Café, hoping to catch the eye of the British consul, or some other long-nosed bigwig. The most they got, I believe, was a severe case of indigestion.

As for myself, I always thought that Chinese dress was more becoming to my trim Asian physique. Most people took me for a Chinaman and that suited me fine. Indeed, I felt flattered, for I much preferred the company of Asians, who were so much more civilized than the Western riffraff that floated, like scum, on the surface of local society. Tientsin, to me, reeked too much of butter. Before we managed to bring him to his senses and remind him of his duties, Emperor Pu Yi, too, was part of that buttery world, frittering away his time on the tennis court and drinking tea with foreigners. He lived in an old Chinese mansion on Asahi Avenue, where we could watch him as he held court to a variety of European charlatans. One used to come across him also at the Empire Cinema, especially when they showed Charlie Chaplin films. He seemed utterly mesmerized by the little American tramp. I never once saw him laugh, but his fascination never waned. Even after we had restored him to the throne in Manchukuo, Emperor Pu Yi had to be kept entertained in his private cinema at the old Salt Palace with Chaplin movies. He sat through them no matter how many times he had seen them already until, finally, the films were worn out, and new copies had to be ordered from Shanghai. I recognized, in my humble way, a kindred spirit in him, even though I didn't share his particular passion for Charlie Chaplin.

There was one place in Tientsin where I was able to escape from the stifling atmosphere of the concessions, and forget the shabby intrigues and general skulduggery that took place there. It was an unassuming establishment behind a crimson gate, on the edge of the Native City, named East Garden. They knew me so well there that my pipes were always prepared without a word needing to be said. All I required was a cup of green tea and my pipe, and I was off into a world of my own. Stretched out in that room filled with the smell of sweet dreams, I quite forgot the war-ravaged country with its stench of blood and excrement, its poverty and degradation, its humiliating submission to the rapacious imperialists. When I closed my eyes, I just let my mind drift, without imposing my will, and the inside of my skull would be filled with images of incomparable beauty. I saw Song Dynasty Chinese landscapes, with soaring mountains and rushing rivers, and boatmen fishing in the mist of dawn. I saw the roofs of Peking, glowing in the dusk of a late spring evening, red and gold and yellow, and I saw the blue hills of Manchukuo, stretching far into the horizon. And I saw my lover, Eastern Jewel, walking toward me, as though in a motion picture, against the backdrop of a garden in Hangzhou. She beckoned me to come to her, as the pan-pipes of a court orchestra keened on the sound track of my mind.

To call Eastern Jewel pretty would be an injustice. She looked much too unconventional for that. Her pale moon face, radiating soft light, combined the fresh beauty of a young boy with the yielding loveliness of a young girl, like those Tang Dynasty sculptures of Kannon, the Goddess of Mercy. Her body was that of a gorgeous woman, but she had the aristocratic bearing of a young prince. She lived in a handsome gabled villa in the Japanese Concession, not far from the Chang Garden. She, too, went by the name of Yoshiko, or Princess Yoshiko, to be precise. But to me she was always Chin, as in To Chin, or Eastern Jewel, and she called me not Sato, but by my Chinese name, Wang.

Her Japanese was so fluent that many people took her for a native of my country. But in fact, Eastern Jewel was the daughter of Prince

Su, tenth in line for the Manchu throne. Alas, the prince died young, and Eastern Jewel was adopted by a Japanese patron of the Manchu cause, a provincial worthy named Kawashima Naniwa. Renamed Kawashima Yoshiko, she grew up in Japan, where at the tender age of seventeen she was seduced by her fifty-nine-year-old stepfather, who declared that she, as a Manchu princess, had inherited great benevolence, whereas he, the scion of an ancient samurai clan, was imbued with natural courage, so it was their duty under heaven to produce a child of benevolence and courage. Fortunately, a child was not born from that union. To promote the liberation of Mongolia, and perhaps to ward off scandalous gossip, Yoshiko was married off to a plump young Mongolian prince, whom she detested so much that she fled to Shanghai, where she had a passionate liaison with Major General Tanaka, chief of our Secret Service.

Eastern Jewel was particularly useful to us because of her close relationship with Emperor Pu Yi, and more particularly with one of his wives, who had given her the run of her mansion in Tientsin, and later in Shinkyo. Tired, perhaps, of being confined to the grounds of his palace in Shinkyo, impatient to occupy, once more, the dragon throne that was rightfully his in Peking's Forbidden City, the Emperor sometimes behaved like a willful child, refusing to attend official ceremonies or receive official guests from Tokyo. I could understand his feelings. The officials from Tokyo could be very dull company. But an emperor must do his duty, no matter how tedious. However, after a visit from my Eastern Jewel, who knew just how to dose our demands with the right amount of Manchu flattery, he would invariably decide to behave in the manner of his station. I would then report back to Captain Amakasu in Room 202.

Yet to see my Jewel as a Japanese agent, or even as a spy, as some people still do, is to misunderstand her completely. She was loyal to one cause only, the restoration of the Manchu Dynasty. For that noble goal, she would have been proud to sacrifice everything, even her own life. Far from being anti-China, she was dedicated to the future of her country, but not under the rule of Chiang Kai-shek and his shabby gang of money-grubbing officials. Her aim, like mine, was to restore China to its former greatness.

Eastern Jewel rarely rose before four or five in the afternoon. Her first act, before rising from her bed, was to drink a glass of champagne and feed a handful of nuts to the two pet monkeys who jumped onto her bed from the yellow velvet curtains. These daily rituals always took place in the presence of at least two or three of her young female companions, whom she called her "Chrysanthemums." Her dependence on them was total. Without her Chrysanthemums, Eastern Jewel wouldn't rise from her bed. After her glass of champagne, she would retire to the bathroom, attended by the Chrysanthemums. She would reemerge an hour later, smelling sweeter than a Chinese orchid. On most nights, she wore a male army tunic of her own design, in military khaki or black, with a pair of riding britches, a thick brown leather belt, shiny black boots, a peaked army cap, and a long samurai sword. On other occasions, when she was in a less martial mood, a simple black male Chinese mandarin robe with a silk cap would suffice. When she had finished her toilette, she would examine herself in the mirror, striking poses this way and that, leaning on her sword, as though for an official photograph, sometimes with a monkey perched on her shoulder.

Eastern Jewel had one other peculiar habit. At various stages of an evening, she would sit down, usually in full view of whoever happened to be there for her amusement—myself, her Chrysanthemums, or perhaps one of her favorite Chinese Opera performers—take down her britches or hike up her robe, and stick a needle into her soft eggshell white thigh. It was a gesture of shocking transgression, as though she were taking a knife to a beautiful work of art, and at the same time of delicious sensuality; the sheen of her pale flesh, begging to be touched and kissed, the penetration of the silver needle, the crimson beads of blood, like rubies on white satin. My passion for her was such that I was in a constant state of desire. I was hungry for her love, a slave to her caresses. Just to hear her voice on the telephone would conjure up visions of pleasure, the nature of which delicacy forbids me to repeat in these pages. The baring of her thigh for the injections she craved took place in a private room in the restaurant she owned near Asahi Avenue, staffed by her former Mongolian bodyguards, or indeed anywhere she felt she was among friends. She called her drug "my little sister," the morphine without which, she often told me, she would surely die.

Since we shared a passion for dancing, we would frequent her favorite nightclubs on the rue de Paris, and after that, if we felt the urge, an opium den, not my usual one but a smaller place just outside the Native City. Or we would go to a brothel in the early hours of the morning on the rue Pétain in the French Concession, where we paid the owner, a fat Lithuanian Jew, to let us watch through a peephole as White Russian girls were being ravished by Japanese officers, a spectacle that Eastern Jewel found particularly arousing, especially if the men were a bit rough in their amorous attentions. She marveled at the beauty of the Russian skin. "So white," she would whisper in my ear, as she gripped my hand, "so perfectly white, like Siberian snow." I was struck less by the whiteness of the Russian skin than by the fact that the officers remained fully clothed, apart from their legs, exposed after they lowered their trousers, as though in a lavatory. Were they ashamed to show their dark Asian skin, I wondered, even to a Russian prostitute?

Eastern Jewel wanted her nights to last forever. The early hours of the morning, when the city was still in deep slumber, and the only sounds were of the creaking wheels of the night soil collectors' carts, had a tonic effect on her. That is when she was most fully alive, and allowed me to make love to her. Even though the jibbering monkeys could be rather a distraction, making love to Eastern Jewel was unlike possessing any other woman—and I had had plenty of them. She was skilled in all the erotic arts, as one would expect from such a worldly creature, but that was not what made loving her so peculiarly exciting. I don't quite know how to put this, but once this proud Manchu princess had discarded her military uniform, taken off her black shiny boots, put aside her sword and cap, she was so soft, so yielding, so vulnerable, so womanly, and yet so mysterious. No matter how much she tried to pose as a Japanese named Kawashima Yoshiko, when I made love to Eastern Jewel, I felt as though I were penetrating the flesh of China. Alas, however, the feeling was as fleeting as a bolt of lightning, for after we had made love, it was as if she were no longer there, out of my grasp, like the fox woman in a ghost story. I loved her more than any woman before, or since. But I never really felt that I knew her at all.

Until one day in the late fall of 1937. We were attending a function together at the mansion of Baron Mitaka, an amiable old nobleman, who represented our government as consul general in Tientsin. We didn't actually arrive together, since we had to be discreet. Emperor Pu Yi was one of the guests, along with the ambassadors of all the major Western powers. Eastern Jewel and I kept apart for the most part, but she happened to be standing next to me when the baron was handed a scroll by one of his staff members, a nervous young man with thin red hands. The baron's many decorations twinkled like stars in a bright winter night. He held the scroll in his outstretched arms, in the old-fashioned manner, and read his speech about our peaceful intentions in Asia. "His Imperial Highness, the Japanese Emperor," he began, standing to attention as the words rolled off his tongue, "whose benevolent intentions have never been in doubt, desires nothing less than eternal peace and prosperity for all under his celestial roof . . ."

As the baron spoke in his pompous English accent acquired during a stint in London, I tried to read the expressions on the faces of our guests. Emperor Pu Yi blinked his eyes without betraying any emotion. The foreign diplomats tried to look superior, as was their habit in the company of Asians, but I couldn't read anything more in their inscrutable European faces. Our Chinese friends, including Emperor Pu Yi's court chamberlain, and the governor of the Tientsin Bank, nodded as the baron spoke of "the common culture of our yellow races" and "our ancient spiritual traditions," "China, our great teacher," "samurai spirit" . . . "Sun Goddess" . . . "Peace . . ." But when the baron was still speaking forty-five minutes after he began, even the attention of our closest friends showed signs of flagging. "The zest for hard work and the natural sense of mutual cooperation nurtured by our rice-growing civilization," went the baron, and I could see the British ambassador whispering in the ear of his French colleague, laughing in his supercilious European way, laughing at us, no doubt, for being "uncivilized," I daresay. The baron, however, showed no sign of coming to a close. I tried to see how much more there was on his scroll. "Five thousand years of civilization . . . reinvigorated by the discipline and youthful energy of modern Japan . . . Asia will rise . . ."

As I listened to the words, I felt a hand lightly brush mine. Eastern Jewel looked into my eyes with a tenderness that made my heart leap. "You are one of us," she whispered. I was so moved that I had to restrain myself from taking her hand into mine and kissing it. "Of course I am," I whispered back. "We are one, you and I."

"I always knew you were different from them," she said softly.

"Yes," I said. "I'm yours, only yours."

"A glorious future for a New Asia . . ." went the baron.

"Come to our side," whispered Eastern Jewel into my ear.

"I already am," I replied. "I'll always be with you."

She nodded briefly and turned away.

"A toast to His Imperial Highness . . ."

5

I N 1938, NOT long after the Fall of Nanking, Eastern Jewel asked
me to introduce her to her namesake, the other Yoshiko, who by that
time had made quite a name for herself. Most Japanese in China knew
Ri Koran's songs by heart ("Ah, Our Manchuria!," "Chrysanthemums
and Peonies," and so on) but no one knew that she was then also a student at a Chinese mission school in Tientsin. Her father, as always, had
gotten himself into a financial scrape (too much money on the wrong
horse at the Mukden Jockey Club), and had been obliged to put his
daughter in the care of another of his Chinese friends. Her new surro-
gate father, Mr. Pan, was a businessman of immense wealth, who had
studied in Tokyo, and was friendly to us. He had many concubines and
a private army, and was high on the list of pro-Japanese Chinamen
whom our enemies would like to dispose of. He called Yoshiko his favorite "daughter," and had her painted by a celebrated Japanese artist
as a typical young Chinese beauty in a silk dress.

Whenever I was in Tientsin, I kept an eye on Yoshiko, as I still
called her, to make sure she was all right. I even gave her pocket money
from time to time, pretending, for her sake, that it was from her father,
who was in no position to provide for her in any way at all.

You could say I was her official mentor, but I looked on her more as
my daughter. One day, during her summer holidays, at one of our reg-

ular lunches, she opened her heart to me. She was dressed simply in her light blue Chinese school uniform, looking adorable as usual, her eyes radiating young innocence, as she puckered her plump little mouth to receive a sweet dumpling from my chopsticks. But I could tell from a slight frown that something was troubling her on this occasion. We normally spoke in Japanese, but Yoshiko sometimes switched to Chinese, if the Japanese word did not come to her readily.

"I'm so confused, Uncle Sato," she said.

"What about, my precious?"

"I keep hearing rumors at school about bad things we Japanese do to the Chinese."

"What bad things, my sweet?"

"They say we are invading their country and killing many Chinese patriots."

I tried to reassure her, explaining that rumors were not to be trusted. There were so many rumors, almost all untrue. A few had some basis in fact, to be sure. But how could I make this darling girl understand that painful medicine was sometimes required to cure serious ills? So I told her, in all sincerity, that we were in China to help the Chinese people, that we aimed to liberate Asia. But as I spoke, I realized that these words might have sounded hollow, like the slogans on Manchukuo Radio. She didn't look entirely convinced. It was hard, she said, for her to know what was true. I felt for her, for it was indeed sometimes hard to tell truth from falsehood in China. Even I, whose business it was to find the truth, sometimes felt as though I were sliding along the icy surface of a lake in the middle of a moonless night.

"I love China," she said. "I've never even been to Japan. But my Chinese mother scolds me for behaving too much like a Japanese. She tells me how to move like a Chinese, striking me when I bow in the Japanese manner. Then, when I go back to Mukden, my mother scolds me for not behaving like a proper Japanese girl. Please, Uncle Wang, tell me what to do."

She was both, I said, this time with more conviction. She was a child of Manchukuo. We were living at the birth of a New Asia, I explained. One day, in a better world, without stupid prejudices—a world without war and greed and imperialism, a peaceful world in which all races would be treated as equals—then and only then would people appreciate her for who she was.

However, the poor thing still looked confused. Why did she have to conceal that she was Japanese? How could she explain to her schoolmates that her Chinese stepfather, whom they called a traitor just because he had Japanese friends, was really a kind and decent man? How was she to behave when all the others went off to march in a demonstration against Japan? Her childlike purity of heart moved me profoundly. As I looked into her moist dark eyes, I wanted to do something to comfort her, dry her tears, and put her mind at rest. But how could she possibly understand adult society and its political complexities? She was, really, too good for this world.

So I counseled patience. History cannot be made overnight. Chinese wisdom tells us to take the long view. Future generations would understand our good intentions. We had to work together to overcome cultural misunderstandings. But I realized then that she should not be allowed to stay at her Chinese school for much longer, or indeed with her Chinese family. It was far too dangerous. She could easily end up being consumed by the anti-Japanese flames fanned by agitators.

And, besides, I wasn't at all sure I liked the idea of the two Yoshikos meeting. My young protégée seemed too innocent of the ways of the world to be exposed quite yet to Eastern Jewel's particular brand of sophistication. No one was more devoted to Eastern Jewel than I, but she was too complicated. Their meeting might lead to all kinds of misunderstandings. Yoshiko knew so little, and Eastern Jewel so much. I sensed danger, and so I kept delaying my promised introduction. But I couldn't watch her day and night. I was her minder, not her bodyguard.

I suppose it was inevitable. They were introduced by Colonel Aizawa, the military attaché, at a party in Eastern Jewel's restaurant. Apparently, my Jewel, dressed on that particular night in one of her black mandarin robes, looked Yoshiko up and down approvingly, after they had been introduced, and said: "So, you're Japanese after all. But how utterly charming." She then took her arm, and said: "From now on, I want you to think of me as your big brother."

Yoshiko received phone calls almost daily from then on, usually from one of the Chrysanthemums, to meet Eastern Jewel at the restaurant, or at some unsuitable nightclub in the foreign concessions. And the seventeen-year-old girl, no doubt flattered by the attention of this great seductress, became an adoring pupil. She was given several Chinese qi paos by Eastern Jewel, who loved to dress her up as though she were a doll, made for her "brother's" personal amusement. I was furious, for I still felt responsible for the child.

One night, close and thundery, I found myself in one of my least favorite places, the ballroom of the Astor House Hotel, where foreigners pretended to be in London or Vienna, dancing in their stiff evening clothes and looking down their noses at the few Orientals who were no doubt supposed to feel privileged to be there. Well, I did not. My presence was entirely professional, to do with a small business matter with the German military attaché. And then I saw them, on the dance floor, in the midst of the Britishers and their powdered wives, who looked like shuffling white ghosts, as the lights flickered every time lightning struck in the skies outside. Eastern Jewel in a military uniform, a monkey on her shoulder, and dear little Yoshiko in a mandarin robe were dancing the waltz together. Round and round they went, staring into one another's eyes like two young lovers, oblivious to the foreigners, who sniggered quite brazenly.

I made up my mind there and then that this rot would have to be stopped. I would have to get Yoshiko back to Manchukuo, if only to protect her purity, which was, for some reason I barely understood myself, more precious to me than anything.

6

SHINKYO, THE CAPITAL of Manchukuo, was everything that Tientsin was not. Built from scratch on the foundations of a small Manchurian trading town which the Chinese used to call Changchun, it may have been lacking in pseudo-Western glamour, compared to Tientsin or Shanghai, but that was precisely its virtue. Wherever they go, Westerners impose their own architecture. Just look at the Bund in Shanghai. It's nothing but a stage set, trying to resemble London or Chicago. Shinkyo was nothing like that. For Shinkyo was actually an anti-colonial city, a counter-Western metropolis, the capital of a multiracial Asian state. And there was nothing quaint about it, either. Planned by the most progressive architects and engineers from Japan, Shinkyo was a marvel of mathematical precision; its straight boulevards laid out like sun rays from Great Unity Square, in the center of town, which had perfect views of the Kanto Army headquarters with its traditional Japanese roof, the Kempeitai building and the head office of the Municipal Police. At one end of Great Unity Avenue was the Shinkyo Yamato Hotel, and at the other South Lake, with the brand-new Manchuria Motion Picture Association Studios on its shore. Shinkyo had the finest new department stores, first-class hospitals, and spacious new homes equipped with flush toilets which made even Japanese from Tokyo marvel at their modern efficiency. Shinkyo was spotless, the cleanest city in the world. Whenever a person was caught littering or spitting, he would be arrested. This might seem a bit heavy-handed, and I confess that I sometimes missed the greater liveliness of Mukden, but civilization can only come as the result of education, and softhearted educators are seldom effective. I was proud of Shinkyo. We had achieved something unique there, the beginning of a modern Asian Renaissance.

But civilization is fragile, and there were many obstacles to overcome before such a Renaissance could be completed. Topping modern buildings with Chinese, Japanese, or Mongolian roofs was not enough. Language, for example, remained a serious hurdle on the road to Asian unity. I spoke Chinese, but none of the Japanese directors, camera operators, art directors, or scriptwriters at Manchuria Motion Pictures did. Since the actors and actresses were all natives who spoke, as yet, very little Japanese, this was proving to be a difficulty. Some things, like the calisthenics at the beginning of each day led by Amakasu himself, in his capacity as studio chief, required no language skills. But Amakasu wanted the native staff to be instructed by Japanese experts in the art of film acting. This was proving to be an uphill task.

Endo Saburo, one of the most seasoned experts ever to work at the Shinkyo studios, had been a famous performer in Japan. Trained as a Kabuki actor, he switched as a young man to a Western-style theater, where he created a sensation in the 1910s with such bold modern innovations as playing Hamlet while riding a bicycle on stage. His most celebrated role in the cinema was that of General Ulysses S. Grant, whom he managed to resemble so perfectly that some people thought he had to be at least half foreign. Tired of playing foreigners in wigs and long wax noses, however, Endo had been persuaded to come to Manchukuo to establish a new, uniquely Asian style of acting.

The problem was that no one had a very clear idea as to what this style should be, except possibly Endo himself. But how was he going to convey it to Manchurian actors who didn't even speak Japanese? Our translators were not really up to the task. I was in the studio one day when Endo had assembled the full cast of a new film for a lesson in motion picture acting. He used various modern Japanese film scripts as his teaching material. Since his audience couldn't understand the words, he acted out, with all the skill of his early Kabuki training, anger, sorrow, love, and so forth, while the translator did his best to explain. Endo acted female roles as well as male ones, which he did to brilliant effect. Alas, however, the translator failed to keep pace, so the translated words no longer matched the actor's mimicry. Ferocious words of rage came through in translation just as the master was fluttering his eyes in the manner of a love-struck young girl, which made the Manchurians giggle—and me, too, if the truth be told, but I had to try and control myself, since it would not do to let such an illustrious person lose face. Our rude response to his artistry put him into a rage, which, though entirely genuine, was sadly mistaken by his audience as part of his act, while the translator, having just caught up with the previous scene, paraphrased words of sweet love.

And this is why, after a little scheming by my good self, dear little Yoshiko was met on a cold autumn evening at Shinkyo North Railway Station by Amakasu, surrounded by his bodyguards, and a military brass band of the Kanto Army playing the tunes she had made famous on the radio, with the yellow, red, blue, white, and black Manchukuo flag snapping proudly in the evening breeze. Amakasu made a speech on the spot, saying that Asians had proved their mettle in terms of military and economic power. Now it was time, as he put it, to show "Asian artistic power." An odd choice of words, I thought, even though I entirely agreed with the sentiment.

Yoshiko was perfect from our point of view: a native who would appeal to the natives, and yet she was one of us. Besides, she had already proved her mettle on the wireless. The arrangement, carefully worked out by Amakasu, was that Yoshiko would receive a monthly salary of

250 yen, which was about four times as much as her Manchurian colleagues, but then she was to be the biggest star in Asia. A suite was prepared for her at the Shinkyo Yamato Hotel, on the same floor as Amakasu's Room 202. Every morning, a chauffeur would pick her up to drive her to the studio, which was only ten minutes away. A Japanese chaperone was employed to take care of all her needs. But all this hinged on one condition, which could not be broken under any circumstances: Her Japanese nationality had to remain a state secret. From now on Yamaguchi Yoshiko was to be referred to only as Ri Koran, or Li Xianglan, Fragrant Orchid of Manchuria.

Persuading Yoshiko to go along with our plans had been a little trickier than anticipated. I had already told her in Tientsin that she would be very well paid. This made no impression. What about her poor father, I persisted, at the risk of being blunt. She would be able to help him pay off his debts. This just made her weep, the tender-hearted child. She had made up her mind to be a journalist, she said, with a firmness that surprised me in one so young. "I want to write the truth, and fight against all the stupid prejudices in this world. If only the Japanese and the Chinese understood each other better, they would no longer be enemies."

I put it to her that we weren't enemies. "But we are fighting a war," she said. "Not a war," I said. "Some people are trying to stop us from helping China. They don't want us to succeed in making China free." She asked me why those people should want us to fail. I tried to explain, but she fell into a sullen silence. Clearly my words weren't having much effect.

"So was he one of those people?" she suddenly asked, with a flash of childish anger.

"Who was one of those people? What kind of people?"

"One night, when I couldn't sleep, I heard people shouting outside our house in Mukden. I looked out the window and saw a Chinese man tied to a tree"—at this point the poor girl started sobbing—"they were beating him with rods. Japanese soldiers were beating him with rods. There was blood all over his body. He was screaming. I hid under my bedclothes and cried myself to sleep. The next morning, I tried not to look out the window, afraid of what I might see. But I looked anyway, and he was gone. I thought I might have dreamed it all, that it was just a nightmare. I wanted to believe that. But when I went out, I noticed dried blood under the tree—" She started crying again, her little shoulders heaving. I patted her. She withdrew.

"That man . . . I knew him. Mr. Cheng. He'd been our caretaker. He was always kind to me. When I asked my father what had happened to him, he said nothing. When I insisted, he said there were things I didn't understand."

I didn't know what to say. Young children should never be allowed to be exposed to such scenes. So I stopped trying to explain politics to her. Instead I tried a different tack. I told her she was right. She did have an important role to play in fostering mutual understanding. That was precisely what the Manchuria Motion Picture Association was trying to do. We wanted to give the Chinese a favorable impression of Japan, and the Japanese a favorable impression of China. Friendship and peace were the whole point of the films we would produce. And she, Ri Koran, was the only person in the entire world who could do it, who could bridge the gap in mutual understanding. She should think of herself not just as an actress but as an ambassadress of peace. She would be famous, I said, not only in Manchukuo but in Japan, and all over China, and indeed in the rest of Asia, for being a peacemaker.

I could see that my words were having some effect. "Really?" she asked, gazing at me with a guilelessness that touched my heart. "Really," I confirmed. And what is more, I meant it.

It is always easy to be a critic in hindsight. Maybe we were too naive, but one has to think of this in the context of the times we were living in. To be sure, there were plenty of bad Japanese in China. We had made errors, and caused a great deal of inconvenience to the Chinese people. But that is inevitable in times of great historical change. Curing an ancient civilization of its ills is a tough enterprise, bound to be messy at times. The main thing to keep in mind is that our ideals were sound. Our principles were right. And if we don't act according to the right principles, cynicism takes over, and life is no longer worth living. If we hadn't stuck to our ideals, we would have been no better than the selfish Western imperialists. So I took pride in playing my humble part in launching the career of Ri Koran.

I wish I could say otherwise, but Ri's debut film, called *Honeymoon Express,* was not a success. A hackneyed remake of a Japanese comedy, translated into awkward Chinese, directed by a man who could not speak to the actors in their own language, was bound to end in failure. It just wasn't very amusing, no matter how much the director, Mr. Makino, screamed at his actors to bring out the humor. "Joke!" he would shout in the few words of Chinese he knew. "Act the joke, act the joke!"

The Manchurians failed to see the joke, and Ri was in despair. She would never do another film, she cried, stamping her tiny feet. The director had been an absolute beast, telling her in front of all her colleagues that she was no good. She had never wanted to be an actress anyway. And on, and on.

I did not witness this myself, but the commercial failure of *Honeymoon Express* had upset Amakasu so much that he went into one of his periodic drunken rages. Smashing his whiskey bottle on the table at the South Lake Pavilion, he raged at Makino, and at the scriptwriters, the cameraman, and the producers. While the Japanese staff listened in silence, heads bowed, Amakasu virtually ripped the room apart, crashing his fist through the paper screens, upsetting the rosewood table, and trampling the broken glass into the tatami floor. He raged on about "sabotage," about "Reds" trying to undermine Japanese policy, about "letting down the people of Manchukuo."

And that might have been the end of Ri's career in the movies, if it hadn't been for one of those unforeseen consequences that so often change the world in ways we cannot possibly foresee. In one of the key scenes, on a railway platform in Shinkyo, Ri as the young lover, doubting her fiancé's devotion, sings a song, entitled "If Only." It isn't a great song; she has done far better ones since. The melody is too cloying, like a sticky sweet. And so are the words: / "If only you would love me, if only you'd be true, / If only you would dream my dream . . ."

The popular imagination is as fickle as it is mysterious. But Ri's song managed to catch it in a big way, heralding the China Boom. "If Only," sung in Chinese and Japanese, became a surprise hit, first among the Japanese in Manchukuo, then in the Japanese homeland. Perhaps Ri's voice had the exotic ring of distant lands. Possibly it was a light diversion in anxious times. Whatever the reason, it spread like a bush fire—or rather, given the gallons and gallon of tears it produced, a flood—in cafés, in dance halls, in the variety shows of Asakusa, indeed in any place where Japanese was spoken, from Harbin to Hokkaido. Ri Koran was now launched as a star.

7

JUST AS RI Koran's reputation as an exotic Manchurian singer began to spread in Japan, an actor at the top of his fame opened the door of his Packard on the lot of his studio south of Tokyo, and walked slowly toward his dressing room. Perhaps he was already rehearsing his lines, or maybe he had other things on his mind, having just moved to a new movie company, but Hasegawa never saw the gangster coming, who, quick as a flash, sliced his left cheek with a razor. It was as though a vandal had plunged a knife into a great painting. Hasegawa Kazuo, a former actor of women's roles in the Kabuki theater, was famous for his great beauty, both as a woman on stage and as a young romantic male lead in the cinema. Now his celebrated profile would be scarred forever, courtesy of the bosses of his former studio, who did not take kindly to acts of disloyalty, especially among their most lucrative stars.

In fact, however, the incident made Hasegawa into an even bigger star. It added an element of masculine panache to his persona (as well as his face, which was rather too sweet anyway), and women warmed to his vulnerability. Nonetheless, he tried to make sure, whenever he could, to present only his right profile to the cameras, and when he couldn't, a thick layer of greasepaint was applied to cover the scar, which ran from the corner of his mouth to his earlobe.

The reason I mention this is that Amakasu had the brilliant idea of bringing Hasegawa Kazuo over to Manchukuo to star with Ri Koran in a Japanese-Manchurian co-production. The romantic coupling of the most famous, most handsome, most dashing male actor in Japan to the most beautiful, most exotic female star in Manchukuo would do wonders for our cause. It was one of Amakasu's most inspired schemes, a pairing made in heaven. But as with all schemes, the results were neither straightforward nor predictable.

The story of their first collaboration was a simple melodrama, entitled *Song of the White Orchid.* He (Hasegawa) is a young Japanese engineer building an extension to the South Manchurian railway line. She (Ri) is a Mongolian music student in Mukden. They fall in love, even though the hero is expected to marry his boss's daughter in Tokyo. Because of this unfortunate obligation, he tells the Mongolian girl that their love is impossible. She returns to her family of anti-Japanese bandits and threatens to blow up his precious railway line. Realizing that love cannot be denied, he goes back to her, and declares his true feelings. She melts into his arms. The railway line is preserved and our people are united.

Some might call this cheap propaganda. So it was, propaganda, but it wasn't cheap, for it was for a good, progressive cause. We all wanted to build a better world than the one we were living in, where millions of innocent, hardworking Asians were ruined by the ruthless competition of Anglo-American capitalism. Americans make films to show *their* way of life in the best possible light. Why shouldn't we have done the same? Besides, how often do you see Hollywood films celebrating the love between people of different races? In their lily white entertainments, dark people perform only as servants or dancing clowns. In that respect, we were well ahead of them.

While this picture was in production, I noticed something unusual about Ri. It was as if she had forgotten about her earlier resistance to being a movie star. She reveled in it now, like a child who suddenly finds herself being the most popular girl in school. I would even say she was growing addicted to the perquisites of the little diva's life: the hotel suite, the chauffeur-driven car, the explosions of magnesium flash powder whenever she appeared in public. But in the presence of the great Hasegawa, she still looked overawed. She followed him around like an adoring puppy, begging him to teach her how to be a better actress. He teased her that a Chinese woman would never understand the ways of a Japanese. She would first have to become a Japanese, he said, before she could act like one.

Much of *Song of the White Orchid* was shot on location, outside a village near the South Manchurian railway line. Security provided by Kanto Army soldiers had to be tight because of bandit activity in the area. Several times the shooting was interrupted by gunfire, and we had to rush for cover inside a brick barn. It was during these moments of enforced idleness that Hasegawa taught Ri the art of female seduction. Ri was all eyes, as Hasegawa transformed himself into a traditional Japanese beauty. He showed her how to glance coquettishly from the corner of her eyes, and reveal, just for an instant, the nape of her neck, by a subtle inclination of the head. In the murky light of our shabby place of refuge, his soft round face took on a sweet femininity that was quite uncanny. We all watched in awed silence as he moved his hands, and eyes, and neck, like a beautiful courtesan. Foreigners' sex appeal, he instructed Ri, was frank and straightforward, while Japanese ways were always indirect, just hinting at sensuality without ever flaunting it. Ri would imitate the master's womanly gestures over and over, the glances, the little pigeon-toed steps, like a man practicing his golf strokes, until she felt she had got it right. Hasegawa just smiled, like an indulgent parent, repeating that she would first have to become Japanese before she could fully master his art.

8

NOT LONG AFTER the success of "If Only," Amakasu decided to start a Ri Koran Fan Club. He, Captain Amakasu, would be the president of this illustrious society, whose members included industrialists, bureaucrats, and Kanto Army generals. The fan club actually played an important role in the tragic history of Manchukuo, so I shall relate my few brushes with it.

Once a month, the members met in a private dining room at the Yamato Hotel to discuss affairs of state, while listening to recordings of Ri's songs. I can still picture the room, filled with heavy wooden chairs, set around a long oak table under a brass chandelier. Deer antlers were attached to the doorways, giving the place a vaguely Germanic air. The beige silk wallpaper was decorated with spring orchids. Amakasu was drinking his usual White Horse Whiskey. I recognized most of the people there. Who wouldn't? Everyone knew these men in those days. They counted some of our top leaders, including Colonel Yoshioka, adviser to Emperor Pu Yi, and Kishi Nobusuke, the minister of industry. Kishi was not exactly good-looking. His suit was slack like a flag on a windless day, and his scrawny neck made the collar of his shirt look several sizes too big. His teeth stuck out and his eyes bulged. But they were the eyes of a shrewd man, and held a hint of menace. Amakasu often said that Kishi would go far, maybe one day as far as prime minister. Kishi bared his moist red gums when Amakasu talked like that, but he never made any attempt to contradict him.

Yoshioka cut an equally unpleasant figure. Known as "the Wasp" for his trim physique, made to look even trimmer by the brown belt strapped extra tight around his waist, he laughed a lot without betraying the slightest evidence of humor. His face was marked by a prominent nose with wide nostrils, like dark holes, which widened when he was ingratiating himself with someone more powerful, or amused by the misfortunes of someone less powerful.

One man in the room was unknown to me. Dressed in a blue suit, which accentuated his narrow, slightly pockmarked face, he looked unremarkable except for a pair of diaphanous silk socks, which revealed unusually thin ankles, protruding from a pair of shiny black lacquered pumps. Only later did I realize who he was: Muramatsu Seiji, boss of the Muramatsu gang, a much-feared outfit with branches in several Manchurian cities. Getting in trouble with them was like catching a death sentence, except that the victim never knew when it would be carried out. Sometimes the execution came long after the poor wretch had forgotten what he had done wrong. Muramatsu was not much seen in public and spent most of his time up north in Harbin.

I was asked some questions about the state of culture, and whether our message was getting through to the native people. I tried to be as positive as I could, but said that we needed more time. Various pet schemes of the Kanto Army were discussed, including, rather to my astonishment, a plan to assassinate Charlie Chaplin. Evidently the plan had been around for some time, for all the men were familiar with it. The aim was to demoralize the American people by killing one of their favorite idols. Unfortunately, it would have demoralized His Majesty Emperor Pu Yi as well. But Amakasu, who took a personal interest in this project, thought that could be handled. Certain practical obstacles were mentioned. The fact that Chaplin had not visited Japan since 1932, and did not seem inclined to do so again soon, was one of them. Then Kishi, I think it was him, casting a quick glance at me, changed the subject with a slight cough. I should have realized that one could never be too careful in Manchukuo.

Kishi calculated for us how much money was needed to keep the army in Manchukuo afloat, and explained that extra resources were an absolute necessity. Colonel Yoshioka, an expert on native affairs, added that Manchurians and Chinese were excitable races, who needed regular doses of opium to calm them down. Supplying them with the drug had several benefits. Apart from keeping the natives quiet, it would provide much-needed revenue for our troops. The problem was that Chinese gangsters in Harbin were trying to get a piece of the action. A Jewish businessman was also said to be involved. His flaw was his love for his only son, an artist of some kind. Perhaps some pressure could be applied by taking care of the son. All eyes were on Muramatsu, who gave an almost imperceptible nod and growled in a soft low voice, like a dog who has been tossed a meaty bone. Since there were no servants at these meetings, to avoid unnecessary gossip, Amakasu got up to change the record on the phonograph himself. I don't recall what else was discussed, but I do have a distinct memory of hearing Ri's sweet voice warbling "Spring Rain in Mukden" as we listened in silence. It was yet another demonstration that Amakasu was more than a martinet. He reached for his handkerchief, removed his glasses, and wiped a tear from his eye.

9

THE NEXT FILM pairing Ri with Hasegawa, called *China Nights,* was the one indisputable masterpiece to emerge from the Manchuria Motion Picture Association Studios. But for her it almost became a personal tragedy.

Ri plays a wild Chinese girl, named Ki Ran, whose village has been destroyed by the Japanese Imperial Army. Hasegawa plays Hase-san, a Japanese ship's captain in Shanghai, who picks her up in the street, hoping to save her from destitution. She is treated with typical Japanese hospitality by the Captain and his friends in a Shanghai boardinghouse, but Ki Ran can't forget that Japanese soldiers killed her parents. When she is offered a cup of tea by the Captain's Japanese landlady, she knocks it out of her hands. That is when it happens, the scene that made Ri a detested figure in China: Hase-san slaps Ki Ran in the face—a shocking moment, but also an intensely moving one, for it shows the heart of a man in love. Hase-san's slap is really a sign of his kindness. Ki Ran understands his true feelings, and falls into his arms.

To any Japanese, the scene makes total sense. But we are not all alike in this wide world of ours. Ri had tried to warn the director that this episode might not be properly understood in China. Alas, the director, a new arrival from Tokyo, wouldn't listen. Ri turned out to be right, of course. This romantic encounter, which moved every Japanese to tears, had the opposite effect on the Chinese, who misunderstood totally, and regarded "the slap" as a blow to their pride. They couldn't understand that we Japanese sometimes use force against women and children to show that we care about them. Ri was not forgiven. Henceforth she became notorious as the Chinese actress who collaborated in a deliberate insult to the Chinese race.

China Nights truly is a picture of endless riches, however. Every time I see this masterpiece, I notice yet another beautiful detail I missed before. "The slap" is followed by Hase-san and Ki Ran's honeymoon trip to Suzhou, and China has never looked more ravishing; Suzhou is a vision of heaven, with its gorgeous canals, its ancient bridges, and classical Chinese gardens. It is here, in this paradise, worthy of a classical ink drawing, that the Sino-Japanese union is consummated. Then something astonishing happens. Those who have an eye for these things will note that the Chinese girl not only turns out to speak Japanese, but makes the coquettish moves of the traditional Japanese woman, the sidelong glances, the tilt of the head, just as Hasegawa had taught her. In this love scene, so full of tenderness, Ri Koran is the purest fusion of all that is best in the Chinese and Japanese races.

But that's not the last of the picture's many unforgettable moments. Ki Ran's uncle is the leader of anti-Japanese bandits, who plan an attack on Hase-san's ship. When the ship fails to return to Shanghai one day, Ki Ran knows that her husband must have been killed by her uncle's men. In a scene of incomparable beauty, she returns to Suzhou to drown herself in the river where she had just spent her honeymoon. Whispering the words of a Japanese poem which her husband had taught her, she wades into the water and is slowly submerged, her silk Chinese dress billowing above the surface, the melody of "China Nights" softly playing in the background. I can never contain my tears at this point, and they don't stop flowing until well after the picture has ended.

But for once the director listened to good advice. Although Ki Ran dies for her love in the Japanese version of *China Nights,* a different ending was contrived especially for the Chinese public. Instead of meeting an untimely death as she wades into the river, Ki Ran hears her name being called, over and over. It is him! He has survived. In the last scene, the most handsome man in Japan and the most beautiful woman in China sit side by side in a boat, gliding toward the rise of a new dawn. He pulls a cigarette from his case and she, in a moment of great feminine delicacy, lights it for him.

It isn't simply the story that makes the picture so touching. The magic of cinema isn't usually in the plot, but in the chemistry between the leading actors, which is conveyed through the eyes. The camera detects something the naked eye can't see. I would almost call it magic— no wonder primitive people speak of the evil eye. Both Hasegawa and Ri look more gorgeous in each other's presence, and through some mysterious process the camera manages to capture this. More than anything, it was *China Nights* that made the Japanese fall in love with China. And this was largely due to the purity of Ri Koran's performance. Her eyes are like pools of light, filled with exquisite melancholy, as she faces her tragic death.

Shooting *China Nights* was not without its moments of danger. Suzhou was no problem, since we had secured the city a few years before, but getting there was another matter. One late afternoon, as we rattled across the northern plains in the train heading south, Ri suddenly cried out: "Look at all the red flowers! They're gorgeous." Bored with the bland scenery of northern China, we all peered out the window. At first I thought it was the setting sun that cast everything in a blood red glow. But as the train slowed down, we could make out people lying all over the place, like broken dolls. Some were huddled in small groups or sitting alone, but more were sprawled on the ground, and others still were rushing about, carrying white bundles stained in red. There must have been hundreds of men littering the landscape, dressed in bloody rags and brown uniforms. The train stopped with a jolt, as though it were shivering. I noticed Ri turning away from the window.

Orders were barked. The doors opened with a clanking noise. A wounded man—the first of many—passed by our window. All I could see of his bandaged face was his mouth, opened wide as if he were about to scream. Hasegawa, in a fit of anger, tugged at the curtain of our compartment, but didn't manage to close it properly. The noise of men crying and moaning got steadily louder. Some were howling in pain, some begging for water. A harsh voice told them to shut up. I saw a man who had lost a leg and both his arms. Another was twitching uncontrollably, like a fish. A young doctor was trying to staunch a fresh wound by pressing a white rag into the chest of a soldier, whose blood kept oozing through the cloth. A hand from a passing stretcher left a red smear on our window. The stench was unbelievable—rotting flesh, excrement, and filthy feet. One of the soldiers, staring into our compartment, suddenly became animated and pointed at Hasegawa. Others followed, pressing their blackened faces against the glass. At last, after frantically tugging at the curtain, Hasegawa managed to shut them out from our view.

An officer opened the door and sat down heavily. He removed his cap and stuck his finger under his collar to wipe the sweat off his neck. There were bloodstains on his boots and trousers, rather like a butcher's. I asked him what had happened. He looked at me suspiciously. "Chink bandits," he said, baring his crooked brown teeth. "Had to clean out the whole village. The way these savages fight . . . even a three-year-old kid is capable of murder. It's either them or us." Ri looked astonished. "Clean out?" Since she was dressed in Chinese clothes, the officer turned to us in disgust: "What the devil is this Chink bitch doing here?" Hasegawa introduced himself and politely explained that she was Ri Koran, the movie star. "Aah," the officer replied. "'Spring Rain in Mukden.' Well, I never," he said, scratching the back of his neck, bobbing his head up and down in the direction of Hasegawa. "Well, well! Hasegawa Kazuo! Ri Koran! Well, well." Perhaps Hasegawa-san could say a few words to the troops, and Ri could sing a song: "That'll cheer the boys up."

Once more the door to the corridor was opened and another officer was pushed inside by a medical orderly. He was young and handsome, but seemed incapable of speech. The orderly pointed to his head and said: "Doesn't even know who he is." We tried to make him speak by asking his name and where he was from. All we got was a blank stare. "Your mother must miss you," Hasegawa said, thinking this might provoke a response. It seemed to have some effect. The young officer's mouth began to work. "M-O-TH-E-R," he mumbled slowly, "m-o-th-er . . . mother . . . mother." But that was all, the same word repeated over and over. His eyes were wide open, but they didn't appear to see a thing.

It was dark outside when the train lurched into action. After a mile or so, we came to another halt. Several men got off the train. "Well," said the officer, "this is it for the night. Better make ourselves comfortable." Guards took up their positions along the side of the train. The smell inside was still overpowering. We opened the window, but the late autumn air was too chilly, so Ri asked us to close it. "Why the hell can't we keep going?" asked Hasegawa, who was not used to being held up. "Bandits," said the officer, who pulled a flask of saké from his tunic, took a swig, and slipped it back into his pocket.

"So what about a song, then?" the officer persisted. Ri told him that would be impossible. In the middle of the night, without a stage, or a microphone, or any light at all. "My, your Japanese is good," said the officer and hissed politely through his teeth.

Soon all the lights were turned off inside the compartments and we were in the dark, with nothing but the sound of moaning and coughing men, and once in a while a disembodied scream. Sleep was impossible. Several officers came in with torches and asked for autographs. One of them insisted that Ri should sing. It would comfort the men, remind them of home, get them through the night. He would provide her with a torch, which she could shine on her face. Hasegawa instructed her that she should always think of her fans. At last, she shrugged her shoulders and relented.

But this was easier said than done, for there were bodies everywhere in the corridor, some barely alive. I followed Ri through the train to protect her. We kept treading on arms and legs, as she sang, eliciting soft moans and the occasional curse. At first she was almost inaudible. The sounds of distress, the bodies, and the darkness were unnerving. But as she slowly made her way, from compartment to compartment, her torchlit face the only visible spot in the entire train, something magical happened: her voice gained strength and the moaning stopped. It was as though an angel had stepped into this hellish place. "China nights, ah China nights . . . the junk floating upstream, the ship of dreams, China nights, nights of our dreams . . ." Then "If Only," and the men sang softly with her, a ghostly chorus in the dark: "If only you would love me, if only you'd be true . . ." And then, the unforgettable sound of hundreds of grown men sobbing.

10

THERE WAS NOTHING wrong with the first part of our trip to To-kyo. Ri, Meng Hua, Menchukuo's second biggest star, and myself boarded the train at Shinkyo Station, where the Manchurian studio staff gave us a wonderful send-off. All the actors and actresses were there, as well as the technical staff, dressed in their uniforms, waving little Japanese and Manchukuo flags, shouting words of encourage-ment, as a brass band played songs of farewell. In the middle of the station hall Amakasu stepped onto a wooden podium, festooned with the Manchukuo colors, and gave a speech, in that hoarse voice of his, which was difficult to hear over the din of hissing steam and people singing songs of farewell. I remember that he mentioned his great personal pride in sending the finest flowers of Manchukuo to our im-perial homeland as "the ambassadresses of friendship."

Ri was so excited about the prospect of visiting her ancestral coun-try for the first time that she could barely sit still all the way to Pusan. The train was not as comfortable as the silver-clad Asia Express, and considerably slower, but unless it had to stop for snowdrifts or bandit raids, at least it was always on time. I tried to catch some sleep after we passed Ando and crossed the frozen Yalu River into the Korean penin-sula. It was dark outside. All we saw of Ando were a few flickering lights far in the distance. The train's whistle sounded lonely, like a wander-ing ghost. But Ri was wide awake, her eyes shining with anticipation.

She couldn't stop talking, about the Nichigeki Theater, where she would star in a gala performance celebrating Manchukuo-Japanese friendship, and the sights of Tokyo, and the various entertainments to be laid on by famous figures of the literary and cinematic worlds, whom she had met when they passed through Manchukuo. She asked me about the most fashionable restaurants and cafés, where the most stylish people were to be seen. A new word had entered her vocabulary: "knowable." Whenever I mentioned some celebrated figure, her first question would be: "Is he knowable?" Even though she was a movie star herself, and knew many famous Japanese already, Ri was still like an overexcited child on the eve of her birthday. I had not been back to Tokyo for several years, and certainly didn't know everyone who was "knowable." I tried to answer her queries as best I could, but she wasn't really listening. Her mind had already arrived at our destination before we even reached Pusan.

Amakasu, despite his rousing speech at Shinkyo Station, had not actually been in favor of this trip. He took a paternal view of his actresses and their personal lives were a constant worry to him. He regarded the artistic world in the metropolis as dangerously frivolous and bad for our morale. An added complication was that the Nichigeki gala concert was organized by the Oriental Peace Entertainment Company, and not by the Manchuria Motion Picture Association. Oriental Peace was backed by the Japanese Ministry of Foreign Affairs, which Amakasu despised as soft and buttery. But even the Kanto Army was powerless in this case. Amakasu warned me that I should be held responsible if anything should happen to the actresses that would reflect badly on the superior reputation of the Manchuria Motion Picture Association.

Sleep was impossible even on the second night of our voyage, aboard the ferry from Pusan to Shimonoseki. Meng Hua, a typical beauty of the north, tall and creamy, with a delightful beauty spot on her left knee, shared a cabin with Ri. I wouldn't have minded a little fun with her, but business was business. I couldn't afford any trouble on this trip. Like Yoshiko, she had never been to Japan before, but the prospect put her in a state of apprehension more than excitement, and she retired to her cabin alone, while Ri talked and talked in a wild mixture of Japanese and Chinese, determined to be awake at the first sight of the Japanese isles. When dawn finally broke, we were wrapped in a thick fog. The ship's horn moaned like a wounded animal. Ri pressed her face to the window, trying to see through the dense gray soup. Nothing. And yet, at 7:30 a.m. sharp a woman's voice announced through the ship's loudspeaker that we were approaching our "beloved imperial homeland." The voice continued: "If you look to the starboard side you will see the port of Shimonoseki, renamed as such in 1904, before which time it was known as Akamagasaki, a place famous for its natural beauty and redolent of our glorious national history, the site of the famous battle between Heike and Genji in 1185 . . ." On and on it went in this vein, as all faces turned to starboard, where dense fog was still all there was to be seen. Our national anthem was played through the loudspeaker, and everyone, including the Chinese and Koreans, jumped to attention.

It was only just before the ship berthed that we could make out the outlines of the city, an ugly jumble of godowns, cranes, and warehouses, hardly the glamorous introduction that Ri had been hoping for. The maritime police boarded our ship with an air of immense importance. A thick black rope was strung across the main lounge next to the gangway, and a plump little man with a Charlie Chaplin mustache sat down behind a desk, with an attendant behind his chair whose duty it was to breathe on the stamps before handing them to the mustachioed official, who pressed them onto our documents after careful and lengthy examination. How I loathed the officiousness of my fellow countrymen! Japanese nationals were ordered to line up in front of the rope and foreigners to stay behind. Ri was the first to rush into line. I could see a look of bewilderment on Meng Hua's face. It was the first time she realized that Ri was a Japanese national, and not simply a half-breed, as was widely suspected among the native staff of the Manchurian studios.

Ri's passport was duly stamped. She turned to Meng Hua and told her in Chinese that she would wait for her in the Customs hall. But the official had second thoughts and ordered her back. Inspecting her with a look of disgust, he barked: "Aren't you a Japanese?" Ri nodded and cast her eyes at the floor. "So what are you doing in that ridiculous Chinese garb? You should be ashamed of yourself, gibbering in that Chink language. Don't you realize that we are a first-class people!"

I tried to intervene by telling the officer, as discreetly as I could, that she was a famous film star, on her way to Tokyo to celebrate Manchukuo-Japanese friendship. He was not in the least impressed and told me to mind my own business. Discretion clearly was not working, so I informed him of my affiliation with the Kanto Army and mentioned the name of Amakasu. The wretched fellow instantly straightened up and his fleshy lips curled in a hideous grin. "Please," he said, "I didn't realize . . . Welcome home, welcome home."

There was nothing I could do to speed up procedures for Meng Hua, however, and it was many hours later that we sat in the cramped compartment of our eastbound train. The fog had lifted but the sky was still smudged with dark clouds, like wet gray rags, casting a gloomy atmosphere over our homecoming journey. The air smelled of damp clothes and pickled horseradish. Few words were spoken in our compartment. Meng Hua was still put out by the hours of questioning she had had to endure, and puzzled by Ri's status. But she was too discreet to probe. So we looked out the window in heavy silence at a succession of provincial towns, filled with small, shabby wooden houses, densely built as though huddled together in fear of the outside world. The clammy oppressiveness that had prompted me to leave for the Chinese continent came back to me instantly. I was already longing for the wide-open spaces of my beloved China and Manchuria. This was no country for a man who prized his freedom.

11

I HAVE A favorite walk in Tokyo, in a district I have frequented ever since I came to the capital as a student. It is an area quite without modern glamour. In fact, it has little to recommend itself at all. Most Japanese shun the place, because of its unwholesome reputation. People say that it is haunted by ghosts. My nocturnal wandering usually starts at the old execution ground in Senju, guarded by a statue of Jizo, the holy patron of souls suffering in hell. Here he is known as "Chopped-neck Jizo," for this is where thousands of people literally lost their heads. Old bones are still found in this dark, forgotten corner of the city. Nezumi Kozo, the legendary burglar, was buried here. And so was Yoshida Shoin, the samurai scholar and revolutionary, who believed that we could only stop the Western barbarians from invading Japan by studying their ways. Imprisoned in a cage by the Shogun's men after he attempted to board an American ship in 1854, Master Shoin wrote the immortal lines: "When a hero fails in his purpose, his acts are then regarded as those of a villain and robber." He was beheaded in 1859 for his loyalty to the Emperor in opposition to the Shogun. Of all our historic figures, I admired him the most.

After paying my respects to Master Shoin, and others, now long forgotten by our fickle countrymen, I walk along the Sanya Canal toward Yoshiwara, the old Edo pleasure district. It is now a sadly neglected place with ugly Western-style buildings, which look as flimsy and provisional as sets in a movie studio. Gone is the refined style of Edo men of pleasure who knew how to woo the great courtesans with their cleverness and wit. Gone, too, is the more plebeian but still spirited revelry of the 1920s.

In the winter of 1940, many of the dance reviews of Asakusa had already been closed down, and so had most houses of pleasure in Yoshiwara. The few that were still open looked so forlorn that they might as well have been closed. Still, I found, much to my surprise, that one establishment I used to visit in my student days, a brothel that featured a popular girl made up to look like Clara Bow (the owner, a gruff man with the face of a bloodhound, was a movie fan), was still there. Since Hollywood films were now officially frowned upon as decadent, the place had changed its decor into something more Oriental, with a stucco facade made up to resemble a Chinese mansion. One of the pimps, a thin young lad with a bad case of acne, tugged my arm and whispered in my ear: "Master, you'll like it here. We have a girl who's the spitting image of Ri Koran." My first instinct was to smash his face. I thought better of it, but walked away with a feeling of utter revulsion.

12

'M AFRAID I can't boast of having been much good as a chaperone for our ambassadresses of friendship. Meng Hua was in a funk and only emerged from the Imperial Hotel for official functions. And Ri was being squired around town by the son of the foreign minister, which put my mind at rest, that is, until I realized that his attentions went further than the rules of hospitality strictly required. Ri didn't seem to mind one bit. Perhaps she was still too naive to understand his true intentions. She seemed flattered by the reception she received in our imperial capital, meeting this famous writer or that celebrated actor, all totally "knowable" to her now. She had even been introduced to the foreign minister himself, a man with a rather brutal reputation, whom she declared, in the theatrical language she had begun to pick up, "an absolute sweetie." It put me in an awkward spot, for I hated lecturing her. The dear child, disguised as a woman of the world, wouldn't have listened to me anyway.

In her interviews for the Japanese press, however, Ri played her part to perfection. Beautifully turned out in silk Chinese dresses, she answered a variety of inane questions in flawless Japanese (naturally), which elicited a great deal of favorable comment. What did she think of Japan? Who was her favorite male Japanese film star? Had she eaten Japanese raw fish yet? What about Japanese baths, and Japanese beds, and Japanese chopsticks? Weren't they hard to handle if you were used to those long Chinese chopsticks? She put up with it all, telling the reporters what they wished to hear, including the fact that Japanese chopsticks may be shorter, but were far more beautifully shaped.

Only one newspaper, mercifully with a small circulation, dared to suggest that Ri might actually not be a Manchurian at all. This article was ignored by the mainstream press, to my great relief, for Amakasu would have been furious if the rumor had gone any further. But there were threats to Ri's reputation that were more dangerous than this press report. I was approached one morning at the hotel by an obsequious young man from the Oriental Peace Entertainment Company. After much bowing and mopping of his brow with a white handkerchief, the young man came to the point, not at all delicately. The president of the company, Mr. Nagai, a man notorious for his voracious appetite for young women, was interested in getting to know Ri Koran a little more intimately. I was handed a business card with the name of a well-known Tokyo hotel and a room number scribbled on the back.

Even I, with my known weakness for the female sex, was shocked by the coarseness of this approach. All my relations with women were based on the premise of mutual pleasure. And if I may say so myself, I know how to give satisfaction. Women are always free to turn me down. In fact, I prize women's freedom very highly. I am, indeed, a feminist in my way. Nagai was treating Ri like a common prostitute, Ri, who, despite her occasional childishness, was the embodiment of all that was good and pure. So I sent the young flunky on his way, instructing him to thank his boss for the kind invitation, but to convey the message that Ri Koran, alas, was indisposed. Since I knew this wouldn't be the end of the affair, I also asked for a personal appointment.

Nagai's office in Marunouchi was large and comfortable, with wood-paneled walls, leather chairs, an open fireplace, and a large empty desk. A whiff of stale cigar smoke lingered in the air. Nagai was a short man, pressed into an expensive-looking double-breasted suit. His dyed black hair shone brightly in the light of a large chandelier, upon whose polished brass branches cherubs frolicked and angels played on trumpets. Nagai sat down behind his desk, shifting his ample rump in the soft leather seat, lit his cigar, and asked me in the familiar tone reserved for children and social inferiors what I had come to see him about.

"About Ri Koran," I said.

"Yes?"

"You know she is from a good Japanese family?"

"You don't say."

"We cannot afford any hint of scandal."

"I'm not sure what you're implying, but whatever it is, I don't think I like it. If it weren't for me, she would be just another common starlet. I'm going to make her world-famous."

I knew this was not strictly true, but let it pass. I said, as politely as I could, that I had strict instructions from Captain Amakasu himself to the effect that the activities of Ri Koran in Japan should be of a strictly professional nature.

Nagai's face flushed. I could smell his expensive cologne. I was gratified to see little beads of sweat appear on his brow.

"Very well then, I'll have the other girl, the Manchu one."

Again, I was taken aback by the sheer vulgarity of the man, and was about to make an excuse to protect Meng Hua. But he had regained some of his composure and moistened his cigar by rolling his tongue around the tip. "Or do you want me to inform the press—after the concert, of course—that we have all been duped, and that we now have it on the authority of her personal minder, Sato Daisuke, that Miss Ri Koran has been performing under an assumed identity?"

I found it hard to believe that Nagai would take such a risk just to satisfy his sexual urges. He might have been bluffing. But I couldn't afford any mistakes. My first duty was to make absolutely sure that Ri was safe from this predatory beast. If the Oriental Peace Entertainment Company had muscle, Manchuria Motion Pictures too was not without resources. Our man in Tokyo, an old friend of Amakasu's from his policing days, had gangster connections. He was a trifle uncouth, but effective. When I explained the problem to him, he first threatened to have Nagai "rubbed out." Since this was not practical, he said he would provide Ri with guards, but Meng would have to take care of herself.

At first, Meng didn't understand. Why did she have to go and entertain the company boss? I explained to her that he was a very powerful figure in Tokyo. His goodwill was vital to the success of our tour. Perhaps there might be a future role for her in a major Japanese picture. I was speaking too fast, and felt like a heel. She had been around powerful Japanese men in Manchukuo long enough to suspect what might be required of her. But she didn't even speak proper Japanese, she said. When she realized that was no impediment, she began beating my chest, screaming in her northern dialect, before breaking down in sobs. I tried to comfort her, stroking her back, telling her that greater things than movies were at stake, that sometimes sacrifices had to be made for a good cause, that there were certain things in life that were beyond our control, that if she would agree just this once to meet Mr. Nagai, she would be rewarded back in Shinkyo, that I would never forget her courage and devotion. It was one of the most difficult moments in my career. Neither she nor I mentioned this unfortunate incident ever again.

13

THE NICHIGEKI GALA concert was a triumph. The date was auspicious, for it fell on February 11, the 2600th anniversary day of our nation's foundation by Emperor Jinmu. Emperor Pu Yi had come to Tokyo especially for the occasion. Despite the cold weather, thousands of people lined up in front of the Imperial Palace to bow to our Emperor—and perhaps catch a glimpse of Emperor Pu Yi too, about whom there had been much written in the papers. Little did they know what I knew—that the Emperor of Manchukuo spent most of his time smoking opium and watching Charlie Chaplin movies. This was just one of the satisfactions of being in the information business. I knew things that ordinary people couldn't even imagine, not in a million years.

The scenes around the palace were nothing, however, compared to what was going on around the Nichigeki Theater. People had been out there all night, wrapped in overcoats and blankets, waiting for the box office to open. By nine o'clock in the morning there were three lines coiled round the building. By ten, it was five. And by the time the concert started at eleven, seven lines of people packed together in the freezing cold surrounded the theater. There was not an inch of room to move. The concert almost didn't begin at all, for Ri and her bodyguards couldn't get through the lines, which were like a solid wall of humanity. Policemen had to be called in to help the guards beat their way through with truncheons, and hustle poor Ri, who was hiding her face under the collar of her fur coat, into the stage door.

The show was magnificent. I knew Meng Hua could be depended on. She was a tough Manchu, who could sing like an angel. The applause was generous. There were even cries of "Manchukuo Banzai!" But no matter how well Meng Hua sang, Ri was the star attraction. It was she whom everyone had come to see. Half the curtain was in the colors of Manchukuo, and the other half showed the red beams of our rising sun. Across the top, printed in gold letters, were the characters: *Harmony among the Five Races* and *Peace in the Orient.* When the curtain rose, the stage was dark except for a small spotlight that picked up Ri, dressed in Chinese rags, just like in the famous street scene at the beginning of *China Nights.* She cursed in Chinese, and the more she cursed, the more the audience loved it. The light dimmed, the theater went dark. No one knew what to expect. Softly, the melody of "China Nights" began to fill the hall. Some people clapped in anticipation. The music grew louder. A spotlight revealed a solitary figure, dressed this time in a shimmering gold Chinese dress, her face hidden behind a large fan in the Manchukuo colors. The fan came down, and Ri, with a smile that could melt an iceberg, sang her famous song.

The audience went wild. I had never heard anything like it. People were hooting, screaming, stamping, even dancing on their chairs. The frenzy was such that the Nichigeki security staff panicked and ran into the hall ordering people to sit down. Some were slapped in the face, or kicked. Girls were fainting with excitement, and rowdy students were dragged out of the hall. The music just kept going: "Suzhou Creek," "Ah, Our Manchuria!" Ri, all alone in the spotlights, with the band drowning out all other sound, had no idea what she had unleashed. I shall never forget the acrid smell of urine and sweat that hung in the empty hall after the concert was over.

We didn't know this at the time, but even more riotous scenes had been going on outside. Only about two lines out of those seven and a half that ringed the theater ever managed to get through the door, and the people who didn't, after having suffered for hours in the cold, did not take kindly to their exclusion. Japanese are an obedient race and not prone to causing disturbances, especially not at a time when the military were keeping such strict control, but the disappointment of missing Ri Koran at the height of the China Boom was too much to endure. What followed was the one and only riot to take place in Japan between 1940 and our defeat. The press was instructed to ignore it, but word got around anyway: the large black staff cars outside the Asahi Newspaper Building were rocked and the windows smashed. The mounted police charged into the crowd on their horses. A young woman in a Ri Koran haircut got crushed under a horse's hooves. A policeman was lynched and barely breathing when relief finally came in the form of auxiliary police forces, who attacked the riotous young fans with great ferocity. By the time we emerged into the night, men in dark blue uniforms were busy hosing down the streets, causing streaks of cold dark water to swill around our feet as we stepped into the cars waiting for us outside the theater.

14

THE YEAR 1941 was a magnificent one, but it did not begin auspiciously. I had rented an apartment at Broadway Mansions in Shanghai, a city more suited to the task of penetrating the artistic circles of China than my old haunts in Manchukuo. I had always liked Shanghai, despite its rancid smell of Western imperialism. It gave me a peculiar satisfaction to stroll past the British consulate on the other side of the creek, with its huge lawn kept smooth as a billiard table by teams of natives straining to pull an iron roller so the English could play their game of cricket. In the spring I would listen to the sound of arrogant English voices rising over their teacups, and I would say to myself: It is our turn now. They had lorded it over the Asians for too long. This time we were in charge. They had to bow to us, even to the lowliest Japanese policeman, if they wished to go anywhere outside their wretched concession.

However, I'm getting ahead of the story. New Year's Day, 1941. After handing the doorman of Broadway Mansions his New Year's tip, I walked into my bedroom to get changed for an evening I had been looking forward to all week. Bai Yu, a budding young actress, was going to be my guest at the premiere of a new film at the Cathay Theater. She was a charmer, with a saucy smile and the kind of Chinese legs, long, firm, slender, that drive me crazy. Her young breasts stood up proudly to attention. Her peachy bottom was just begging to be caressed by a man of experience.

So I wanted to look my very best. After a long soak in the bath, thinking of all the things I would do with that little minx, I opened my closet. And there, to my horror, was a scene of total devastation. Every single item of my clothing—my silk Chinese robes, my summer kimonos, my Kanto Army uniforms, my white sharkskin suit made by C. C. Lau, the finest tailor in Shanghai, my shirts from Charvet, even my Italian neckties—had been cut to shreds. Strips of linen, worsted, and silk were spilled all over the floor, as though a wild animal had been rampaging in my closet. What kind of maniac could have done this? I looked for a clue, but found nothing. I switched on the bathroom light to splash cold water on my face, and then I saw it—how could I have missed it before? Daubed in powerful, rather masculine, but extremely elegant Chinese characters, in lipstick, on the bathroom mirror: "There cannot be two Yoshikos in your life. You have chosen the wrong one."

I was more than used to female temper tantrums. Chinese girls, especially, were given to thunderous rages. I had seen it all: crying, screaming, cursing, running away with my money. But this was the first time my entire wardrobe had fallen victim to a jealous fury. What made this especially irritating was that this act of wanton destruction was based on a complete fantasy. I may have spread my affections around a little liberally at times, having my pleasure where I could find it. I was a man, after all. But I couldn't feel guilty about something I had not done. And this was the woman who knew me better than anyone, including my mother. How could she have misjudged me so badly? I could only put it down to the madness of true love.

15

SHINKYO WAS FREEZING as usual in March. Snowdrifts kept even the Asia Express from arriving on time. And this, I can tell you, was a very rare occurrence. So rare, indeed, that this little story had a sad ending. The driver of our train took personal responsibility for our tardy arrival and threw himself in front of the express train from Dairen. At least he was given the posthumous satisfaction of an honorable mention in the next day's papers. Perhaps this accident affected me more deeply than I thought, but my mind was not at ease.

Amakasu had summoned me to Shinkyo for a meeting. Normally, I would have been happy to visit the Manchurian studios and catch up on the latest gossip. But this time I felt something particularly oppressive in the wintry air. Compared to Shanghai, the wide avenues of the Manchukuo capital looked deserted. It was as if only policemen and soldiers ventured out into the cold, loitering in drunken groups at night. The natives stayed in their homes on the outskirts of town.

It was the second time I attended a meeting of the Ri Koran Fan Club. On this occasion there were more people in the large, overheated room at the Yamato Hotel. The usual members, including Kishi and Yoshioka, were there, rubbing their hands around the fireplace in large, overstuffed leather chairs, but also a high-ranking officer of the Kempeitai, whom I didn't recognize. I'm not, as a rule, fond of our military policemen. We all lived in fear of them, even if we were in the Kanto Army. This young fellow, named Toda, looked particularly smug, pulling at the crease of his trousers and patting his brown leather boots with a look that managed to convey impatience and limitless self-satisfaction.

I knew I had to have been called in for a reason, but the gentlemen took their time to come to the point. Kishi spoke about the usual humdrum business of state: the need for harsher measures to raise the production in our factories and mines, to crack down on banditry, and so on and on. Colonel Yoshioka was asked how the Emperor was doing. Very well, he said, laughing for no apparent reason. Except that His Majesty had been showing unfortunate yearnings to leave his compound. He was bored. His wives were a constant source of irritation. And he couldn't very well watch Charlie Chaplin films all day. Thank goodness for the poppy, said Yoshioka, for His Majesty could always be pacified after a pipe or two. "Courtesy of the Manchukuo government, I trust?" offered Kishi, baring his prominent teeth in a grin that looked more like a snarl. Yoshioka's nostrils widened alarmingly.

Amakasu got up from his chair to change the record, and offered me a drink. Peering into his own whiskey glass, he said he had to broach an embarrassing topic. All eyes were now on me. I braced myself. "It has been brought to our attention," he said, "that you are having an affair with Ri Koran." I began to protest, but he held up his hand. "No need," he said, "no need. We know you wouldn't do anything so foolish. The information comes from an unreliable source, indeed from a woman who is giving us nothing but trouble, a woman with whom, I believe, you do enjoy intimate relations."

I was astounded that my Eastern Jewel would go so far to do me damage. Wrecking my clothes was one thing, but this could have ruined me. The Kempeitai officer, who spoke in a provincial Kansai accent, began to lecture me. His hand had shifted from his trousers to his belt buckle, as though to check whether it was still there. He puffed out his chest like a pigeon. I couldn't bear the man. But there was nothing I could do. I had to listen to this youngster telling me that my liaisons with native actresses were lowering the tone of our mission in Asia. Every man was entitled to a bit of fun, he declaimed, but intimate affairs were a different matter. We Japanese had to be seen to be above that kind of beastliness. We had responsibilities, after all. We were not here for our pleasure, but to offer leadership and discipline. All the while, the sweet voice of Ri was crooning away in the background. "China nights, nights of our dreams . . ."

Much to my relief, Amakasu changed the subject. But the relief was only temporary. Kawashima Yoshiko, Amakasu said, was becoming a problem for us, a real menace in fact. Apart from her lies about Ri Koran, she had been causing trouble in other ways. It seemed that she had been blabbering about politics in a most inconvenient manner, shooting her mouth off about us Japanese forcing opium on the Chinese people, and so forth. She had even approached some deluded Japanese idealists about starting a party in favor of Chinese independence. This was a most delicate time for our mission in Asia, and it went without saying that we had to put a stop to this kind of thing. "We will have to get rid of her," said the Kempeitai officer, who had shifted his attention to the shiny tips of his boots, turning them this way and that. "And since you know her better than anyone," he continued, "and you have to make up for your unfortunate behavior, we have chosen you to take care of our problem." An unpleasant grin lit up his face. "After all, you have a bone to pick with her now. So it shouldn't be too hard for you to get your own back, now would it?"

I looked at Amakasu, who refused to return my gaze. Kishi and Yoshioka were softly talking to one another about something else. I was beside myself. A refusal was out of the question. And yet the idea of murdering someone I loved so dearly, even though she had tried to do me harm, was unconscionable. Now that the official business had been concluded, the members of the Ri Koran Fan Club decided to have some gaiety. More drinks were ordered and the men sang a song celebrating the beauties of Suzhou. Sometime after midnight, Amakasu, red-faced and roaring drunk, conducted with his chopsticks, as the rest of us, standing on the long dinner table, sang "Coo Coo Goes the Pigeon." It was one of the most unpleasant evenings of my life.

I was not a fool. I could see the hypocrisy around me. Eastern Jewel was speaking the truth about our opium trade. But she failed to see the big picture. I still believed in our mission, despite men like Kishi or the Kempeitai officer. Even when I wore Chinese clothes, I was still a Japanese. I loved China, perhaps more than I loved Japan, but I knew that my country offered the only hope for a better Asia. Even if I disagreed with some Japanese policies, or the petty little officials entrusted to carry them out, my duty was clear.

And yet I couldn't do it. I lacked the moral courage to kill a woman I loved. I didn't even have the guts to pay someone else to do the job. And so I did nothing. Back in Shanghai, I canceled all my social engagements and neglected my professional duties. For three days and three nights I dropped out of our sordid world and stretched out on a comfortable bed in an obscure corner of the French Concession, trying to focus my gaze on a slender Chinese girl with melancholy eyes cooking the black, sticky stuff of my dreams over a bright blue flame, before placing it with her expert fingers into the bowl of my pipe to take me to the sweet land of oblivion.

16

THERE WAS A man in Peking, a born fixer. I had had dealings with him before, and did not care for him. A petty gangster in the 1920s, Taneguchi Yoshio had worked himself up ten years later as the self-appointed head of the Japanese Fascist Party and had even contrived to have a meeting with Mussolini in Rome. The photograph of him, beaming like a schoolboy in his black uniform, shaking hands with the Duce, had been printed in all the Japanese papers. He was unscrupulous, greedy, rough with the local women, just the kind of Japanese I despised. But he did know his way around China. If you needed to smuggle antiques, diamonds, or weapons, Taneguchi was your man. If someone needed to be eliminated, quickly and without fuss, Taneguchi would get the job done. If secret meetings between people who couldn't afford to be seen together had to be arranged, Taneguchi would manage it. There were even rumors that he, Taneguchi, was the liaison man between the Japanese army and General Chiang Kai-shek, our arch enemy. Taneguchi, in short, knew everything and everyone, including Eastern Jewel, who had been his lover at one time. I had reason to believe he still viewed her with some affection and was hoping that he might see a way out of my dilemma. I knew the risk of taking this man into my confidence, and found it humiliating to ask him for favors, but at that dire moment in my life I didn't know where else to turn.

Taneguchi's compound in the center of Peking, in a short alley between Wang Fu Jing and the Forbidden City, was guarded by White Russians. He trusted them for some reason. I believe he spoke a bit of Russian. I was ushered into his office by a young Japanese who packed two pistols under his armpits. Taneguchi, dressed in a blue suit and a tie pinned to his white shirt with a fat shiny pearl, was on the phone. He was a short man, with thick lips and tiny eyes, which tended to disappear from view entirely after he had had a few drinks. His small stature was accentuated by the fact that he seemed to have no neck; his round pink face emerged straight from his narrow shoulders, like a turtle's head. He didn't so much speak on the phone as grunt. The entire conversation consisted of grunts. Behind his desk, on the wall, was a gold-framed calligraphy in bold, showy, masculine brushstrokes. They were the Chinese characters for sincerity, loyalty, and benevolence. On the opposite wall, behind my chair, as though about to leap at my neck, was the stuffed head of a tiger.

I thanked Taneguchi politely for the meeting. He told the young man with the pistols to bring us two cups of green tea. The young man padded off to the kitchen in a pair of light blue woolly house slippers. After I had told Taneguchi my story, he cocked his head and said, more to himself than to me, and not without a hint of fondness: "She's a troublemaker, that one." All I was asking of him was to get her out of the country. A leering smile creased his fat face. "So she's getting in the way of your love life?" No, I said, that wasn't the point. He waved away my objection with his right hand, which looked surprisingly dainty for someone so stout. "Yes, well," he said, "we might still need her one day." He couldn't promise anything, but mentioned a place in Kyushu where she might lie low. It would buy her some time. He had friends. They would protect her, at least for a while. I would be in his debt forever, I said. "Yes, you will be," he replied, sizing me up like a shrewd peasant at a country market. As soon as I returned to my hotel room, I ran a hot bath and soaked in it for a long time, as though I were covered in slime.

17

B ECAUSE OF THE war, the outskirts of Shanghai were reduced to rubble. From the window of my train it resembled a huge garbage dump. But human resilience is an amazing thing. The people of China are used to living with catastrophe. Out of bits of straw, scraps of corrugated iron, the odd brick, or whatever remained of what once had been a densely populated area, people had fashioned housing of a kind. Rows and rows of straw huts, no more than shoulder-high, leaned against the banks of a stinking canal filled with every kind of waste that humans and animals can produce: excrement, dead dogs, bloody rags, and cans filled with toxic waste from a nearby chemical factory. Even from a moving train, I could see the bloated rats, as well as stray dogs, rooting in the filth. Families cooking their scraps of food kicked away the rats only when they upset the children, and sometimes they couldn't be bothered even then. Some people were dressed in old newspapers. Kids ran along the tracks with nothing but bits of straw wrapped around their blackened feet. They were lucky to have both feet. Some people were scuttling around on their stomachs, propelling themselves forward with their arms, like crabs. When we stopped for a short while near the North Railway Station, I noticed, to my surprise, a young girl dressed in fur, scratching my window, begging for food. At least, I *thought* it was fur, until I took a closer look, and realized she was naked under a matted curtain of her own hair. She would not have survived for very long, and is probably happier dead than alive.

But that's China, where life always goes on, like the Yellow River, relentlessly, slowing down here and there almost to the point of stagnation, only to gush forth again in bursts of violent activity. Such scenes of misery as I saw from the train put me in a melancholy mood, for they gave me a sense of great weariness. Trying to change China seemed as futile as attempting to push an ocean liner off course with one's bare hands. Any such endeavor is bound to end in failure. That is the grandeur of China; and the terrible burden of five thousand years of history. China shows up the puniness of all human aspirations, including our own mission to build a New Asia. I took no pleasure in such thoughts. I desperately wanted us to succeed. For chaos and bloodshed would be our only legacy, if we failed.

Our police had at least restored order in the center of Shanghai, reducing crime, making it safe for people to go about their daily business. Films still opened at the Grand. Dancing went on all night at the Park Hotel. People still gambled away their money at the Race Club. Whatever happened in the world, the hedonistic spirit of Shanghai was irrepressible.

My main guide and companion in Shanghai was a man who was in every sense the opposite of Taneguchi. Kawamura Keizo, boss of the Asian Pictures Company, was a man of culture, who spoke many languages, including fluent German and French, and was respected by the Chinese. Asian Pictures was Japanese-owned, but specialized in high-quality local films made by the finest Chinese directors. It was, in so many ways, what Manchuria Motion Pictures should have been. Films made by Asians for Asians, which actually appealed to local audiences. They had a lightness of touch sorely lacking in the heavy-handed propaganda pictures favored by Amakasu, who, not surprisingly, did not like Kawamura at all. Of all Japanese I knew in those years, Kawamura came closest to understanding the Chinese mind.

A tall, handsome fellow, with a shock of wavy hair and a taste for fine English suits, Kawamura was intimately acquainted with every pleasure the city had to offer. Quickly bored with official business, he would call me in the afternoons to meet at the Great World tower for some relaxation.

The Great World on Yangjingbang West Street was a giant pagoda of pleasure. At the bottom of the tower was a cinema with room for one thousand people. Pretty whores in *qi pao*s with slits up to their armpits lingered in the lobby from morning till late at night. We started on the first floor, feasting on Shanghainese dumplings, and slowly began our ascent up to "paradise," as the locals called the summit, sampling the delights of every floor: bathing in scented steam on the first; foot massage and earwax-picking on the second; acrobats, tightrope walkers, and musicians on the third; peepshows of naked girls and theatrical performances of an indelicate nature accompanied by delicious Suzhou pastries on the fourth; exquisite stimulations by expert young girls, various games of chance, and a store specializing in "rubber goods" on the fifth; and so on, up to the top, where Chinese beauties offered every imaginable pleasure, while an orchestra played film tunes, including, I am pleased to recall, some of Ri Koran's songs. Chinese visitors to this palace of delights, who had been unable to resist the temptation to spend all their money on girls or games of chance, would sometimes jump from "paradise" all the way into the teeming streets below. Locals called the steps leading to a wooden platform jutting out from the top of the tower "the stairway to heaven."

Though Kawamura had made films with most of the top Chinese movie stars, his greatest wish was to entice Ri to work for his Shanghai studios. He wanted to make her as popular in China as she was in Japan. Naturally, Amakasu was highly reluctant to let her go, even for one film. In a fit of unforgivable rashness, I agreed to see what I could do for my friend to change Amakasu's mind.

Just when the cold spell was finally breaking in April, Ri arrived in Shanghai from Japan, where she had been shooting scenes for a new picture, entitled *Suzhou Nights*. We met in my favorite restaurant on Hankow Road, where we had a luncheon of fried eel and hairy crabs. I noticed that she kept stooping to scratch her legs. "Oh, that," she said, when I enquired about it; "a little souvenir from the homeland." They had been shooting a scene in a pond near Tokyo, which bore a passing resemblance to the lakes of Suzhou. The director was well known as a hard taskmaster. Poor Ri had spent hours standing up to her waist in the pond, waiting for the camera to roll, and had been set upon by leeches. She also brought another piece of news, which was much more startling. She had had an encounter with the other Yo-shiko, my Jewel. When I heard this, it was as if a block of ice slid down my spine.

While staying at a hotel in Kyushu, Ri received a phone call: "Your big brother needs to see you." Worried by the tone of Jewel's voice, she agreed to meet her at once. Jewel came over dressed in a man's ki-mono. Looking frantic, she reached into her bag and handed over a sheaf of papers, bound in silk, and covered in her handwriting. "Please read it," she said. "This is my life. Only you understand me. So you must play me. This must be your next film." Ri was so taken aback that she had no idea what to say. She had never seen Eastern Jewel like that, twitching with anxiety. "Please," she said, "I beg of you. You must do it. It's my last chance." Before Ri was able to hand back the manu-script, Jewel was gone. Listening to the account, I silently thanked Taneguchi. At least Eastern Jewel was safe for the time being. The thing is, despite what she had done, I still loved her. The film was of course never made. Ri quickly handed over the manuscript to me, as though it were scorching her hands. And I consigned it to my fireplace. It was an act of love, not betrayal. For I could well imagine Eastern Jewel's fate if those pages had fallen into the wrong hands.

Kawamura's parties were legendary in Shanghai. He lived in a large comfortable villa just off the Avenue Joffre, furnished in the European style. Many people had passed through those rooms, including Marlene Dietrich, with whom he was rumored to have had an affair, even though her Jewish lover, Josef von Sternberg, had been his guest in the same house. Kawamura worshipped von Sternberg. He pointed at the chair in his study on which the great director had once sat. Before lowering himself on that hallowed seat himself, Kawamura lovingly polished the shiny leather surface with his handkerchief. "The master," he murmured, like a priest in prayer.

So when Kawamura invited me to a party when Ri was in town, it seemed like a good opportunity to introduce them. The sitting room was already full of Chinese when we arrived. Zhang Shequan, head of the Ming Xing Studios, was there with his latest mistress, a young hussy named Jiang Qing, who later joined the Communists in the caves of Yanan. Bu Wancang, the famous director, was talking to Ding Ling, the novelist. And Xu Yen, the playwright who had been cautioned by our censors on many occasions, was in a corner, laughing at Zhao Dan's jokes. Zhao, surrounded by a group of admirers, did an imitation of a typical Japanese army officer, barking orders in mock Japanese. The one who laughed loudest was Kawamura. But I noticed how the laughter died on everyone's lips as soon as I approached with Ri. Memories of the "slapping scene" had not yet faded. It was highly awkward, not because I felt embarrassed by the malicious mimicry, but because of Ri. Politics always confused her. And she took rejection so badly.

People were openly complaining about the pettifogging ways of Japanese censors and the many restrictions on life in the city under Japanese control. None of this fazed Kawamura as he went about the room, beaming at his guests, making sure everyone was comfortable. It seemed to me that he was actually encouraging this kind of talk. I had heard Chinese speak like this before, of course, and couldn't help agreeing with some of their complaints, but I didn't think it was advisable to expose Ri to this kind of thing. She had suffered enough as a student in Peking. Besides, she might be compromised. I decided that we should leave, despite Kawamura's offer of more champagne and assurances that "we are among friends." When I insisted, he leaned toward me, with a faint odor of alcohol and cigar smoke on his breath, and said: "My dear fellow, our people have no idea how much we Japanese are loathed here. It's all our own fault, you know."

I was startled by Kawamura's cynicism. Not that he was entirely wrong. But I still believed in our ideals. Without faith in what is right, life becomes as meaningless as a permanent cocktail party. So I dragged Ri away from Zhao Dan and Zhang Shequan, who seemed to have overcome their reservations and were crowding her into a corner, like two tomcats waiting to jump on their prey. She was enjoying the attention too much, the poor child. For her own sake, I had to bring this to a close.

I never said anything to Amakasu about the party, or about Kawamura's behavior, because he was a good man, who genuinely cared about China. Every basket of peaches contains some rotten ones, and it's those few who spoil everything for the rest. So it was in China. I felt this keenly whenever I saw a bunch of Kempeitei officers swagger into a Chinese shop and take what they wanted without paying. I felt it every time I crossed the Garden Bridge to Broadway Mansions, and saw the natives being forced to stand in long lines for hours and hours on frosty winter days, in the pouring rain or steaming summer heat, only to be beaten up for the smallest infringement of rules they barely understood. When an old man was slapped in the face in front of his own family for failing to bow deeply enough to one of our soldiers, the Chinese said nothing, but I could see the loathing in their eyes. I saw a small boy in rags being whipped by two soldiers because he tried to hide a sweet potato, just one, to feed his hunger. He was just an urchin, no more than five years old. A few Japanese civilians hurried along the bridge, pretending not to see anything. I could hear the pitiful screams of the boy's mother, but I did nothing, for I too hurried along to the other side.

It was at moments like this that I tried to think of the many good Japanese who loved China as dearly as I did. Men like Kawamura, whose films were the building bricks for a new Asian civilization. Or Ri's father, the old gambler, whose heart was still in the right place, despite his vice. Or even Amakasu, who may have had iron running through his veins, but whose dedication to a New Asia I never doubted. And of course Ri herself, whose trust in humanity could still lift my heart. She didn't know this, but in moments of despair just thinking about her gave me the courage to carry on. For she had a pure heart, this young Japanese woman who lived and performed under a Chinese name. She restored my faith in Japan, and in our mission in Asia. But love needs to be reciprocated if it is to bear fruit. We badly needed the trust of our Chinese friends. And here I have to say that Kawamura was right. Their trust was constantly undermined by the stupidity of our own people.

And yet, for a brief and blissful time, I thought that all would turn out well after all. In the early morning of December 8, 1941, as I came down from breakfast, I noticed immediately that something was up. A Japanese businessman living at Broadway Mansions asked me whether I had heard the news. Someone told the Chinese receptionist to turn up the volume of the wireless. It was a special news bulletin on our military broadcasting station, repeated every fifteen minutes. Even the announcer sounded excited. I can still recall his exact words: "Early this morning our Imperial Army and Navy launched an attack in the western Pacific. From this morning we are at war with the United States and Britain." I couldn't believe my ears. But there was more. "Our Imperial Navy destroyed five enemy battleships, three destroyers, and three cruisers. No loss has been reported on our side . . ."

Over the sound of the wireless I could hear loud explosions coming from the direction of the Bund. Surely it was too early for fireworks. Rushing outside, I was just in time to see a British gunboat go up in flames. It was a typically crisp Shanghai morning, but to me it was as though the wintry clouds that darkened our hearts for so long had been driven away by warm rays of sunlight. The arrogant white man had been given a bloody nose at last. Now we were fighting the war we should have been fighting from the beginning. I knew it wouldn't be easy, but I felt sure that victory would be ours in the end, for we were fighting for justice and freedom, while the imperialists were just defending their selfish interests, like thieves trespassing on a continent that wasn't theirs. No longer would we bow to their self-serving treaties. This was the moment that marked the end of the white man's rule in Asia, and it was good to be alive to see it. You might say, in hindsight, that we should have been more cautious. But that's not the point. This was not a question of cold strategy. We did the right thing. That is why we rejoiced on December 8, 1941, which will remain a glorious date in our history.

You should have seen the faces of the Europeans when we booted them out of their Shanghai Club. They couldn't believe what was happening to them. It was as if the world had been turned upside down. No longer would the famous Long Bar be closed to Asians. No longer would we have to put up with signs on Asian territory barring "dogs and Chinese." Shanghai now belonged to us. I choked back my tears when I watched the British flag come down and our flag rise over the Hongkong & Shanghai Bank. What a splendid sight! What a glorious moment! Later that night, when fireworks lit up the sky from the roof of the Cathay Hotel, I cheered and cheered, like a madman. The Bund was filled with Chinese crowds. Perhaps they were still shell-shocked from all the fighting, and not quite sure of what lay in store. Some even looked fearful. I went over to a group of men in long winter gowns and told them not to be afraid. This wasn't gunfire, but a celebration. Even though they were too shy to share my joy, I knew that one day they would understand that this was the moment of their liberation.

18

THE ANNUAL DINNER celebrating the friendship between Japan and the Jewish people at the Hotel Moderne in Harbin was always held in March. Who knows why? But it had become a tradition. In the year 1942 it happened to fall on March 8. I never cared much for Harbin, with its Russian Orthodox churches, horse carriages, and beggars. Harbin was a treacherous place. One always felt spied upon. The one-eyed Greek, skulking in the lobby of the Hotel Moderne, was a spy, though exactly for whom was not clear. That was the thing about Harbin. You never knew who your friends were. The Bolsheviks had spies everywhere. So did the Chinese Reds and Chiang Kai-shek's rebels. We had our own spies, of course. But we weren't very good at it. To be effective, a spy has to be able to blend in, speak more languages than one, be omnipresent and invisible. The Jews are natural spies. We Japanese stick out like sore thumbs in foreign company.

But we were not stupid. Of course we knew very well that the Jews owned the world's biggest banks, that they had infiltrated the British government, and ran Washington like their own puppet show. It was no coincidence that Roosevelt was a Jew, and that Rothschild was his banker. We were also aware that no outsider could possibly penetrate the international Jewish networks. But attacking them with force was as useless as hitting at cobwebs; you destroyed one and another was built just as fast. No, unlike the Germans, we Japanese had the wit to understand that we should keep the Jews on our side.

The Hotel Moderne was owned by a Russian Jew named Ellinger. The former owner, another Jew, had gone mad. One of his children had been snatched away, by Russian Bolsheviks most likely. This was as common in Harbin as snowstorms in winter. Even after the establishment of Manchukuo, kidnappings were accepted as an inevitable part of life. Golfers in Harbin would not set foot on the links without armed guards. Every restaurant aspiring to attract a decent class of people had guards. You couldn't enter the Harbin Opera, or a public park, without several armed men to protect you. Most rich Chinese had their private armies. The victims of the kidnappers were very often rich Jews, for they were usually too stingy to pay for their own protection and, besides, the Russians hated the Jews. At any rate, Ellinger was a very rich and influential man, who owned several theaters in town. Music was his passion, especially music by the great German composers. In the course of my duties, I became quite close to Ellinger, even though I knew I could never totally trust him.

Ellinger had one weakness: his son, an opera singer trained in Paris, whom he treasured above anything else in this world. This boy, named Max, was a handsome tenor, with the melancholy eyes and hooked nose typical of his race. He wore a monocle, which often popped out of his eye when he became excited. Large, pink, sensitive ears were his other prominent feature.

On the occasion of our annual friendship dinner, Max was back in town to visit his father. Max too had a weakness: girls, especially tall Russian girls. His indulgent father tolerated this. A young buck must have his pleasures, and so forth. But the old man was worried about his son's carelessness. Max would be out in the streets after dark without bodyguards, carousing in this nightclub or that, as if he were in Paris.

I often came upon father and son in the midst of a terrible row. They shouted so much that even the opera music booming from the phonograph couldn't drown out the noise.

Since the boy wouldn't listen to his father, Ellinger, sick with worry, asked me to talk sense to him. Much though I liked my friend, this was an imposition I could have done without. I was not disposed to like Max. As far as I was concerned, he was a spoiled young man, whose Chinese was worse than his father's. But Ellinger begged me to see him, so, rather against my better judgment, I agreed.

They say that first impressions are usually right. Perhaps I am a bad judge of character, for this is not my experience. Once I got to know Max, I realized that he was a sweet, gentle soul, who lived for his music. The girls were a hobby, an outlet, and his behavior could hardly be described as wild. He just liked to watch them, walking by, parading naked at brothels, making love to other men. He watched, openmouthed, softly whimpering like a young dog. "Father worries about me too much," he said to me, when we had our first little tête-à-tête. He smiled: "Jewish fathers. They always worry too much."

"But he is right to worry," I said. "You must be careful. This is a dangerous town."

"Why would anyone want to harm me?" he replied.

"Your father is a very wealthy man," I said. "Just be careful. Don't go out without a guard."

"What about you?" he said.

"I don't need a guard."

"No, I mean why don't you come out with me?"

The best way to make friends with a man is to visit a brothel together. We must have visited at least a dozen, Max and I. He watched and watched, through peepholes specially provided for men of his taste, while I gave a proper account of myself. Russian brothels, Chinese brothels, and even on one occasion an establishment stocked with mature Jewesses, who had the reputation of being the hottest lovers in town. Though I prefer Asians, a man needs a change of diet once in a while. Max was not so keen on this place, however. I think he felt embarrassed.

He told me about his mother, who had died when he was still a child. He carried a picture of her in a locket around his neck. He took it off once to show me. A small, round face, with Max's sweet smile. He told me more: about his music, and his life in Paris, and his loneliness. It was my turn to feel embarrassed. I don't normally like hearing confessions from men. And yet Max moved me. I felt a tenderness I had never felt before for a man, especially a white man. I had never known a white man like him before. In fact, I'd never known anyone like him before. He was too gentle for this world, and most certainly for the rough and tumble of Harbin. And so I adopted him, as it were, as my charge.

On the occasion of the dinner celebrating Japanese-Jewish friendship, Ellinger glowed with paternal pride as he introduced his son to the various Japanese dignitaries. Among them were Kobayashi Tetsu, chairman of the Yokohama Specie Bank; Honda Chozo, adviser to the mayor of Harbin; and Nakamura Shunji, chief of the Kempeitai. I also noticed among the Japanese guests the pockmarked face of Muramatsu Seiji, boss of the Muramatsu gang, whom I had met only once before at my first Ri Koran Fan Club meeting in Shinkyo. His face betrayed no knowledge of me when I made a polite bow in his direction. I hadn't much liked the look of him the first time. I liked him even less now. A sinister fellow.

Though food was becoming scarce in 1943, Ellinger had managed to rustle up some excellent Russian caviar, superb beef, and fine French wines to wash it all down. The banquet hall was nicely decorated with banners printed with the Jewish star linked in fraternal love to the colors of Japan and Manchukuo. Speeches were made and toasts to our deep and enduring friendship exchanged. The banker, Kobayashi, spoke eloquently about the many things we shared: our ancient cultures, our love of hard work, and the sad necessity for both our peoples to fight for our survival in a hostile world. Ellinger then rose to thank the Japanese for protecting the Jews at a time of great peril. And to top off the evening, Max agreed to sing for us. His first song was in Russian. Then parts of Schubert's *Winterreise,* and finally, as a surprise, Ri Koran's "Spring Rain Over Mukden," which moved us all to tears. Even Muramatsu, not a demonstrative man, applauded vigorously.

Ellinger's banquet, however, splendid though it was, would not have been a sufficient reason to keep me in Harbin. There was another reason for my extended visit. In the spring, Ri's latest picture was slated to be made on location there. It was a highly unusual work, entitled *My Nightingale,* produced by Manchuria Motion Pictures, despite Amakasu's reservations about the project. The background to this picture is complicated and requires some explanation.

Ri was more than a little infatuated with the man who planned the movie, a former Tokyo movie critic named Hotta Nobuo. I blamed myself for this unfortunate affair, for I had actually introduced them. Ri was easily impressed by bookish intellectuals with a gift for the gab and fine-sounding ideals. Hotta was of that type: a thin fellow with long hair, who wrote flowery essays about "people's art" and "proletarian culture." He was one of those Russophiles one used to find in Ginza cafés, reading difficult novels, and quoting Soviet theories about the cinema. This kind of mumbo-jumbo deeply impressed Ri, who thought it all very profound. And Hotta was no less taken by Ri. Apparently, while he served time in a Japanese prison for spouting anti-patriotic propaganda, he heard Ri singing "China Nights" on the wireless, which helped him to get through his ordeal. This, at any rate, is how he related his experience to Ri.

In fact, Hotta grossly exaggerated his hardships. What actually happened was far less heroic. He was arrested by the Thought Police, that much is true. Having refused at first to renounce his Marxist views, he spent some time in a solitary cell, and eventually came to his senses. I was never a Marxist myself, but found it impossible to trust these spoiled young men who renounced their opinions after a few days of bad food and cold baths. To be sure, he got knocked about a bit. What can you expect? But he looked a little too pleased with himself when he showed the scar on his face, as though he were some kind of resistance hero. One might well wonder how such a man ended up producing films in Manchukuo. But Amakasu liked idealists, even ones with a Red past. He was strange that way. Or perhaps he was shrewder than many thought. Employing these rascals was the best way to control them. So he offered Hotta a job as producer at the Manchuria Motion Picture Company in Shinkyo.

Somewhat miraculously, Hotta had managed to persuade Amakasu to back a musical film shot almost entirely in Russian. Ri played the part of a Japanese girl who was adopted by a Russian opera singer. So she had to learn to speak Russian, sing in Russian, and act like a young Russian woman. Her model, she told me, was Masha, her Jewish friend in Mukden. Despite my misgivings about this project, I was fascinated by the way she acquired the mannerisms of a typical Russian girl by practicing in front of a mirror in her room at the Hotel Moderne: how to pour tea from a samovar, how to greet her Russian stepfather, how to walk and talk and dance and sleep, just like a damned Russian. It was an extraordinary and to me rather nauseating spectacle. One had to admire her skill and dedication, though, if not the end to which these were put.

Shimizu Toru, the director of the film, was another shifty character with a reddish background. He was on loan from a Tokyo film studio. I suspected fraudulence as soon as I saw the man. So when I was asked by Amakasu to keep an eye on him, as well as on Hotta, I had no hesitation. It wasn't a question of spying so much as of saving Ri from getting into trouble. She was much too gullible and prone to fall under the spell of clever men with a plausible manner.

The story of *My Nightingale* takes place in the 1920s, when Chinese warlords and Russian Bolsheviks were running amok in Manchuria. The Japanese girl loses both her parents in an attack by Chinese bandits, and is saved in Harbin by a Russian opera singer. He refuses to sing any longer himself, after his performances are disrupted by Bolshevik saboteurs, but teaches his adopted daughter. When the same Chinese bandits who robbed the girl of her parents threaten to take over Harbin, the Russian refugees are terrified. But all is well in the end when the Japanese army restores order in 1931 and offers protection to the poor Russian refugees. The girl's stepfather agrees at long last to sing Mephistopheles in a performance of *Faust*, but becomes fatally ill, and collapses on stage. This would have been one way to end this sorry little melodrama. But there is another twist. They learn that the girl's real father has survived, after all. When he hears that his daughter is safe in Harbin, he allows her to tend to her sick Russian stepfather until he finally dies in a harrowing last scene, designed to squeeze the public's tear ducts like a lemon.

Life on the set was fraught from the beginning, and relations quickly descended into a war of old goats. Like Helen in the old Greek myth, Ri became the object of masculine warfare. Shimizu could not bear to let her out of his sight, especially when Hotta was hovering around. But Ri couldn't resist the attentions of a famous Japanese actor who flew in from Tokyo to play the part of her father. And the Russian baritone of the Harbin Opera Company, Dimitri something or other, who played her stepfather, was so smitten that he howled with rage whenever Ri went out for dinner with one of her Japanese admirers. She was so trusting, so eager to learn from these men, to whom she foolishly looked up, that she was an easy mark for their beastly ends.

And then there was Max, poor, foolish Max. It was my fault. I should never have introduced him to Ri. But I thought he would enjoy watching how a movie was made. He had expressed an interest. He loved movies, he said. It was just puppy love, no doubt, and he was too timid for any physical relations, but he wouldn't stay away, following Ri around the set, insisting on taking her out for dinner, calling her at the hotel, until I had to put a stop to it. I'm afraid I got angry with him and told him in no uncertain terms not to go anywhere near Ri ever again. He went white as a ghost and said very softly: "You were my friend." Then he turned round and disappeared. I stopped hearing from him, which made me feel bad. But what could I do? I wanted to protect him, but my main duty was to protect Ri.

That's why I had to keep a close watch on Hotta and Shimizu. This involved many nights of heavy drinking in the bar of the Moderne. I heard a great deal of lovesick whining and tearful complaints about the difficulty of making good films in troubled times. But they were too clever to divulge any truly dangerous thoughts. Only once did Hotta's caution slip, and that was after a monumental bout of drinking. He had fallen asleep with his head on the table. Just as I was ready to go up to my room, he raised his head, trained his bloodshot eyes on me, and slurred: "You know, Sato . . . We're going to lose this war. That's for sure. We'll lose, because we're just a poor, small island country and America is too big and powerful. But even though we'll lose, I want to show the world that we can make a musical film that's just as good as theirs. No, it'll be better, better than Hollywood. At least we'll have accomplished that. This'll be the best musical film ever . . ."

19

ONE DAY, AS I was sitting alone in my hotel room while the crew was out shooting on location, I heard someone calling, or rather shouting, my name and banging on the door. It was Ellinger, wild-eyed and uttering strange animal-like sounds. I got him to sit down and gave him a glass of water. He finally managed to stammer something in his broken Japanese. "They've kidnapped him!" He fell on his knees, sobbing like a woman. I was confused at first. Kidnapped whom? Why? Where? I could not help feeling contempt for Ellinger's lack of composure. That is the other side of the Jew: take away the protective cloak of money and you find a miserable heap of sniveling humanity.

But I was shocked too, when I realized it was Max. I should have looked out for the boy. He was too trusting. Perhaps I had been too harsh on him. But of course, Ellinger himself was partly to blame. He had gone around bragging about his precious Max, his talent as a singer, his good looks, his success in Paris, and so on. He had broken the golden Harbin rule: Never attract attention.

I asked Ellinger whether anyone had demanded a ransom. No, he hadn't heard anything yet. Had he been aware of any particular threats? He shook his head. I decided to talk to the one-eyed Greek, who was perched at his usual spot in the lobby, squinting at a newspaper without any interest in its contents. A cowering little wretch, one felt soiled even talking to him. He said he knew nothing, had seen nothing, and heard nothing. He was just minding his own business, drinking his morning coffee. All he could offer was a tip to check the Russian papers. "If they're Russians, they'll state their price in the personal advertisements," he said. Ellinger could hardly bear to touch, let alone read these "anti-Semitic rags." In any case, there was nothing in the papers that day.

The following afternoon, by which time Ellinger had been reduced to a gibbering wreck, I received a message to come and see Captain Nakamura at the Kempeitai headquarters on Bolshoi Prospect. The building, known to locals as "Devil's House," used to be a Russian bank. It had a large steel door behind a row of massive columns. On quiet days, it was claimed, you could hear screams coming from the basement cells, which were obscured from the street by thick iron bars. Nakamura's office was up a flight of marble stairs on the first floor. Apart from a map of Manchukuo, the office was bare of any ornament. A round-faced man with plump, pinkish hands, and a toothbrush mustache above a tight little scar of a mouth, Nakamura didn't bother to get up from his desk when I entered. Somewhat to my surprise I saw Muramatsu sitting in a comfortable chair. "You know one another?" Nakamura enquired. I said we had met. Muramatsu turned his pale, pockmarked face toward me and said nothing.

Nakamura did all the talking, in his vulgar Hiroshima accent. Fighting the American imperialists, he said, was proving to be a drain on our economic resources, and the strain was felt in Manchukuo, too. To finance our necessary presence here, and keep up the war effort, we needed every cent we could get. The Jews, whose lives we protected with much inconvenience to ourselves, had been typically reluctant to help us out, so it was decided that we should, as he put it, "shake a few coins from that Jewish money tree." Proud of his way with words, he revealed a perfect row of gold teeth, which caught the light of his desk

lamp. I must have noticed, he continued, the unfortunate disappearance of Ellinger's son. Listening to his words, I felt a sudden chill.
Sweat began to pour down my neck. I had paid no special attention to
it at the time. It was just one of those things one overheard, the kind
of rough talk one grew accustomed to in Manchukuo. But now it came
back to me with a horrifying clarity: the Ri Koran Fan Club. Colonel
Yoshioka and Muramatsu, the transparent silk stockings, the artist son
of a Harbin Jew.

"He's in the hands of our friends the Russians," Nakamura continued. "They know how to treat the rich Jews." A grayish tongue flicked
his little mustache, as he glanced across to Muramatsu. Then back to
me: "You are a friend of Ellinger's, and we have observed that you
have been out on the town with the boy." I felt sick, and could only
hope that it didn't show. "A ransom will soon be demanded. It would
be in your interest, as well as ours, if you persuaded the Jew to cough
up. And this time, don't slip up."

Even though he was smiling, I realized that this was a serious
threat. My failure to get rid of Eastern Jewel had not gone unnoticed.
I loathed the arrogant tone of this horrible little man, but I had no
choice. It was the only chance of getting Max out of trouble. Even
with the backing of Amakasu, I had the forces of the Kempeitai and
organized crime stacked against me. I later discovered that the man
who informed our Military Police of Max Ellinger's movements was
none other than the one-eyed Greek. I would have been happy to stran-
gle him, but that would have been most unwise in the circumstances.

So when, a day or two later, a notice appeared in *Nash Put*, the Russian Fascist newspaper, demanding fifty thousand dollars for Max's release, I told my friend that he should pay up immediately. Ellinger,
however, wouldn't hear of it. "How dare they!" he cried. "Why should
I, a humble man of business, who never did harm to a fly, bankrupt
myself for these gangsters? It is an outrage! An outrage!" I agreed, of

course, but tried to persuade him that he had little choice. I didn't give him any details, but hinted that I knew whom he was up against. But Max was a French citizen, Ellinger shouted; he would go to the French consulate. I said that that might make things worse. Still the old man wouldn't budge. Two days later a package arrived at the Hotel Moderne. Inside, wrapped in a piece of paper torn from *Nash Put*, was a finger, reddish, like a small sausage.

Amidst all this commotion, I still had to keep an eye on Ri, whose relations with Hotta were becoming uncomfortably close. On and on she went about Hotta-san this and Hotta-san that, how clever he was, how much he knew, how well he understood her feelings. She repeated, in her childlike way, Hotta's political views on American capitalism and the Asian proletariat. These conversations usually took place in the Victoria coffee shop on Kitaskaya Avenue, where she stuffed herself with Russian pastries, licking the cream off her fingers while telling me all about Five-Year Plans, as well as her troubles with men. Shimizu was so kind to her, she said. She just had to accept his dinner invitations. At the same time, however, Abe Shin, the actor playing her Japanese father, was so suave and attentive, and promised her anything she wanted if only she would go back with him to Tokyo. She shook her head as she adjusted the fur collar around her neck, like a pretty little bird. "Ah, men," she sighed. "I try to give them what they want, but then they become so . . . so . . . ." I watched and said nothing as she removed a fleck of cream from her upper lip.

While Ellinger was secluded in his rooms, not willing to talk to anyone, the film crew had taken over part of the hotel. The main bridal suite had been transformed into the apartment of the Russian baritone and his Japanese daughter. Shimizu was directing a distinguished Russian actress named Anna Bronsky through an interpreter, a disreputable-looking fellow, who scribbled away in a little notebook when he thought no one was looking. Heaven only knows to whom he was reporting. Behind the director sat Nakamura, a frequent visitor to the set. The scene took place during an attack by Chinese brigands. "Oh!" the Russian woman cried. "We are just helpless refugees without protection. Where are the Japanese?" The baritone, looking rather frantic himself, patted her shoulder and told her that everything would be all right. Ri clutched her stepfather's arm and whimpered. Her facility to cry on call was a source of constant wonder. One moment she would be merry, laughing along with one of the actors. Then, as soon as the director said, "Start!" her face crumpled in a look of utter helplessness and the tears began to flow. "Papa," she cried, "Papa!" as the baritone embraced her a little too tightly. Tears even welled up in Nakamura's piggy eyes. For he, too, was one of Ri's ardent fans.

"Cut!" cried the director, his face crimson with anger. "Tell him not to hold Ri like that," he shouted at the interpreter. "But I'm her father," boomed Dimitri, a picture of innocence. "I don't give a damn," shouted Shimizu. "It won't do in Japan." Dimitri: "But I'm Russian." Shimizu, screaming: "But she's Japanese!" Dimitri stomped off the set, the interpreter rushing after him with his little black notebook. Russian voices, one pleading, the other petulant, could be heard on the other side of the wall. Poor Ri was sobbing on Hotta's shoulder, as though he could intervene in the Russian contretemps. I know I should have paid more attention to all these dramas, but my mind was elsewhere, on Max, on the stubbornness of Ellinger, who refused to do what was necessary to get his son released. I didn't even want to imagine what they might do to the boy.

Just then a Chinese fellow from the reception desk tried to enter the room, but was barred by our Japanese security guards. Apparently he wanted to see me. For this, he received a slap in the face. I had no idea what was going on. But eventually a message was passed to me anyway. Ellinger asked me to come to his room at once. At first, I couldn't make him out in the dark. I just heard a succession of moans, like those of a wounded animal.

"What is it?" I asked, reaching for the light switch. His eyes were red from crying. He threw up his arms, as though in supplication to his Hebrew God. I looked around the room and on the table was a note with a piece of paper, stained with streaks of red. Neatly wrapped inside was a large ear, shriveled like the petals of a dead rose.

"Tell the Jew that if he pays up half the ransom, he can see his precious son." Nakamura looked away, as he spoke from behind his desk, and worked on his fingernails with a small silver file. "The second half after he's released." He was clearly displeased with my inability to persuade Ellinger. But I felt a wave of hope. At least Max was still alive. I said I'd do my best. Nakamura dismissed me with a grunt. "I'll talk to the Russians, as soon as he coughs up. Then you go with Ellinger. And under no circumstances will you even think of uttering my name."

Ellinger, after much persuasion, finally realized that he would never see his son again if he didn't pay the money. We were driven in a car for what seemed like more than an hour. It was night, so I couldn't make out where we were going, except that our destination was far from the center of town. Ellinger was shivering in a thick winter coat. The driver was Chinese. An armed Russian with vodka and garlic on his breath sat next to him in the front seat. We stopped at an unremarkable gabled house, the kind of place reserved for middle-ranking Japanese bureaucrats, with a modest front garden, covered in a layer of hard, crunchy snow. Another Russian quickly let us in. Five men were sitting around a table, listening to a recording of sentimental Russian songs. Three looked Russian and two were Japanese, of the worst type, the kind of tattooed thugs who made one feel ashamed of one's country. Several empty vodka bottles stood on the table. One was broken in half, its jagged edges pointing toward us. There was no sign of Max. One of the Japanese was working his teeth with a toothpick.

"Let's see the cash," said the Japanese, who had a crudely fashioned image of the Goddess of Mercy carved into his upper arm. I told him that we had to see Max first, as we had been promised. "Who are you," asked one of the Russians in Japanese, "the Jew's lawyer?" This made the other men snigger, as though it were a capital joke. "Bring out the boy," said the other Japanese, an odd-looking brute with eyebrows tattooed onto his forehead. The Russian got up lazily from his chair and left the room. Ellinger could barely contain himself. After a few minutes, the door opened, and the Russian appeared, dragging a human figure by a rope. A single lamp shining onto the table made it hard to see more than shadows, since the men were standing in the dark. Ellinger wanted to rush toward his son, but the Russian ordered him to sit down.

The Japanese with the false eyebrows grabbed the lamp and shone it into the prisoner's face. It was impossible to tell whether it was Max. His eyes were hidden under a swollen mess of pulpy tissue, his skin was a patchwork of yellow and blue, and his mouth a great gash crusted with dried blood. Unable to stand by himself, his head was held up by his hair. I recognized the dark curls, and a dark scab where his right ear should have been. Perhaps he was trying to tell us something, but all we could hear was a high-pitched moan. Bubbles appeared from what looked like a toothless mouth. "I'm afraid he won't be able to do much warbling any longer," said the Japanese with the Goddess of Mercy on his arm. The men giggled. One of the Russians pointed to a pretty glass jug, standing on a side table. In it a purplish piece of flesh floated obscenely. "He'd seen a little too much for his own good. Now pay up if you want him back."

I turned toward my friend, who opened his mouth wide and howled, and kept on howling, louder and louder, until he stopped and slumped over unconscious. It was the last sound he ever made, poor Ellinger. For he never regained consciousness, which was probably just as well, for Max, too, did not survive much longer. His corpse was found in the rubbish dump near the river, half eaten by stray dogs. There were no obituaries. The French consul protested. The Japanese police deplored the rise in violent crime and said they had done everything to save the young Parisian singer. And when I next saw Nakamura, he waved his pudgy hand dismissively and said: "It can't be helped. You know what they're like, those barbarous Russians. They always go too far. We Japanese will never understand their hatred of the Jews. A cultural difference, you know."

I could no longer stand being around the movie set. I hated the whole enterprise with a passion. But it was my duty to be there. So I watched without really taking anything in. All I could see in my mind's eye was the bloody mess that once was Max. But what could I have done? Ellinger should not have been such a braggart.

The last scene was set in a hospital room, re-created in the kitchens of the Hotel Moderne, where the Russian stepfather was dying with his stepdaughter by his side. "It's time to go back to your real father," he croaked. "Japan is a beautiful country, a great country, the country of the gods. You must return to your own soil." Ri burst into tears, crying, "Papa . . . Papa . . . Papa!" Shimizu, overcome with emotion, dabbed at his eyes with the sleeve of his coat. Dimitri, when it was all over, took the young girl in his arms. Ri did a girlish little twirl and smiled, proud of her performance.

The wrap-up party was held in the hotel ballroom. I was not in a festive mood. The hotel now bore the smell of death. But Ri, the director, Hotta, and the Russian cast were excited about the prospects of their musical film. Rivalries seemed to have melted away, as everyone sang sentimental Japanese and Russian songs. Dimitri sang an aria from *Faust*, and Ri gave a rendition of "My Nightingale" in Russian, and then "Ah, Our Manchuria!" Speeches were made about international solidarity and a new world order, and Ri expressed her hope that we could all live in peace.

The film was never shown. Our government censors decided that a Russian musical, entirely lacking in fighting spirit, was not suitable for distribution at a time when our empire was fighting for its survival. As the censors put it in their official document: "Stress on individual happiness goes against the wartime regulations laid down by our Imperial Government." I found this profoundly silly, but was not entirely displeased with the verdict. Ri should never have wasted her time on this wretched picture. As for the others involved in this disaster, I hated the lot of them.

I sympathized with her, of course. There were just too many stupid people in this world, and a large number of them happened to be running around in China. I told her to be patient. Things would be all right. But I wasn't even convinced of this myself. "I can't take it anymore," she cried. "I have to come clean, tell my public that I'm Japanese and quit the Manchuria Motion Picture Association. That's the only way, Uncle Wang, the only way. I'll have a press conference, and then I can be myself again, just plain Yamaguchi Yoshiko."

I patted her arm. There was more at stake here than the feelings of an innocent young woman. The end of Ri Koran would be a disaster for our war effort. So I told her not to let down all her fans, all the people who paid their hard-earned money to see her perform, the millions of Asians who believed in her. Just imagine the consequences if they knew that she had tricked them. It was too late to turn back now. She had to carry on. Without her, what hope would there be for some goodness to come out of our mission in Asia? No, no, no, she said, stamping her foot on the wooden floor so hard that it stopped the mah-jong game. I was worried that we were attracting unwelcome attention. No, she repeated, she was sick and tired of being a fake Manchurian star. She would go to Shinkyo, talk to Amakasu, and resign. Hotta would help her. He always knew what was best for her.

It was as if she had stuck a knife in my heart. I told her that Hotta was a dangerous man, a subversive element. She lifted her hand from my knee. It was the first time I had seen her so cross, and with me of all people, her trusted adviser. "What about you?" she hissed. What about me? "Don't you know that you're a marked man, that they no longer trust you, either? I'm always being asked questions about you, ever since that business with Yoshiko . . ."

I didn't want to discuss this any further, perhaps because I was shocked that she knew so much, or perhaps because she was right and I didn't want to face the truth. So I switched the subject back to Ri's career. I had an idea, I said. And I must confess it was a good one. Why not stay here, in Shanghai, the real center of Chinese films? Why not join a Shanghai studio and be an authentic Chinese movie star, not a phony one? I would talk to my friend Kawamura. He would cast her in his films. Indeed, he had already said as much. And no one accused him of producing propaganda films. It would be quite different from working in Manchukuo, or Japan. Ri Koran, or rather Li Xianglan, would be famous all over China as a patriotic star. Shanghai would be at her feet.

Ri's sobbing slowly subsided. Her big eyes lit up in the way I had always adored, so full of hope and goodness. "I want to meet Mr. Kawamura again," she said, suddenly determined. And so you shall, I assured her. "When, when?" It could be arranged very easily, I replied. She looked worried. But what about the contract with Manchuria Motion Pictures? What about Amakasu? I said that I'd go to Shinkyo and take care of that personally. "Thank you, Uncle Wang, thank you. I knew I could depend on you. You're the only one who understands my feelings. You're the only one." In that instant, despite all my problems, I felt something like perfect happiness.

To say that Amakasu was furious would be an understatement. He got drunker than I had ever seen him. The waitresses at the South Lake Pavilion fled in terror as he overturned the table, sending food and drink crashing to the tatami floor. Stumbling round the room like a crazed beast, he punched the walls with his fists and smashed every piece of crockery in sight. "I'll shoot that bastard Kawamura," he screamed, "and I'll take care of you too!" But despite all his huffing and puffing Amakasu knew he was beaten. The government in Tokyo had already approved of a film production to commemorate the 100th anniversary of the Opium War. The Asian Pictures Company was going to produce it, and Ri Koran's casting had the backing of General Tojo himself. A film about the Opium War would help to convince the

Chinese that we were joined together in the same battle for survival against the white race. Besides, there was no greater admirer of Ri Koran than General Tojo. He even talked about setting up a Ri Koran Fan Club in Tokyo to rival the one in Shinkyo. Tojo had never liked Amakasu, anyway. And there was nothing Amakasu or the Kanto Army could do to reverse his decision.

Amakasu's rage had left him exhausted. He revealed a side of his character I had not seen before. With tears in his eyes, he began to whimper, as though oblivious to my presence in the room: "How could she? After all I've done for her! Don't young people understand the concept of loyalty anymore?" I told him, as best I could, that this wasn't a matter of betrayal, but a way to help our dream of Ri Koran survive. She needed to move on to a bigger stage. I don't know whether my words had any effect, but he slumped to the floor, groaning in self-pity: "But her stage is here, here in Manchukuo. We're building the New Asia, right here, in Shinkyo, this is the big stage." I left him sprawled on the tatami floor. There was nothing more to be said. I could still hear his moans in my ears as I walked into the cold morning air outside the South Lake Pavilion. I felt pity for him. His heart was sincere, but he didn't realize there was a wider world out there. In the end, he too was a frog in a well. He never could see that Ri Koran was bigger than either of us and would be remembered long after Amakasu, or I, had slipped away into the long dark night.

21

PERHAPS I SHOULD have seen it coming, but one never does, I suppose. The loud knock on the door when one least expects it, men in civilian clothes going through one's things, dropping books on the floor, ripping through the furniture, confiscating letters, while I stood by helplessly, and after that was over and done, the bundling into an unmarked car with the engine running. I should have been terrified. In fact, absurdly, I thought of the fresh flowers I had just arranged in my living room, and of Mei Fan, a lovely new actress from Dairen, with a tight little bottom. She was going to think that I stood her up for our dinner appointment, I who had never stood up a beautiful woman in my life.

My cell, which I shared with two other Japanese, was at least kept a bit cleaner than the cells for natives and foreigners. Our daily ration of watery gruel was served in tin bowls, rather than thrown onto the cells to amuse the guards, who took turns to watch the spectacle of desperate natives licking bits of broth from the filthy floor. Even though we were not alone, we were not allowed to talk, and were forced to sit all day on our knees. I never found out who my cellmates were. Black marketeers, perhaps, or subversives of some kind.

Interrogation came almost as a relief, were it not for the stupidity of the interrogators. Nothing is worse than extreme physical pain. I had seen with my own eyes what the men of our Special Higher Police could do to people. If their victims survived at all, their lives were no longer worth living. I was in the hands of the Thought Section of the Special Higher Police. My interrogator was a handsome brute with slicked-back hair, the type of man who in different circumstances might have run a moderately successful brothel. I feared the worst, but in fact, apart from frequent smacks or thumps in my face, I was not physically harmed, at least not at first. More than anything else, my interrogations were unbelievably tedious.

Imagine being stuck with a crashing bore in a train compartment, not for an hour or two but for days on end, a simpleton who bores relentlessly, on and on, and who has total power over you, every second of the day and night. I had to listen to this moron, this jumped-up pimp, lecturing me about patriotism and moral behavior. His main purpose was to make me confess to things I could not possibly have done. To be accused of "decadent behavior" that was "contrary to military ethics" was one thing. I had no trouble writing a confession on that score. But I couldn't confess to "spying for the enemy" or "conspiring to undermine the mission of our national polity." Whenever I asked for proof of my spying activities, I got a smack and was told that I should know the details of that better than anyone. This game, to which there could be no conclusion, went on for hour after hour after hour.

Once in a while, he rose from his desk, came to where I was tied to the chair, and screamed in my ear: "Which side are you on? Are you Japanese or a Chink? Who the fuck do you think you are! You fucking Chink spy! You fucking puppet of the stinking Chinks! You degenerate drug addict and whoremonger! You're a scandal to the Japanese race. How can we fight a war with perverts like you?"

I said: "I'm Japanese and I'm fighting for the unity of Asia." His fist hit my already swollen mouth. Blood was streaming down my chin. "Shut up!" he screamed. "Shut the fuck up!" And he hit me again, and

again. As much as the beating, it was the constant screaming that became unbearable. "Unity of Asia! Those are just fancy words. You're a
liar, a fucking liar!" I still had just enough strength left to contradict
him. "They're not lies, it's our imperial mission. You're contradicting
the orders of our Imperial Majesty." Another blow to my head: "Fucking liar, fucking Chink spy! Either you're a Japanese, or you're with
them. Confess that you're with them!"

When the brute got tired of trying to extract a confession, he was
replaced by another man, a schoolmasterly type in glasses, who chain-
smoked cigarettes. He had big feet and wore large brown shoes with
thick rubber soles that squeaked when he stood up. There was no
shouting this time. He said little and waited for me to talk, striking me
only when I was about to lose consciousness. When you have been tied
to a chair for a day and a night, without any sleep, with a lamp shining
in your face, eventually your mind rebels. At first you feel like crying.
Then your vision starts playing tricks with you; you no longer know
what is real. And you feel humiliated because you are no longer in
control of your bodily functions, and finally, reduced to a wreck, you
no longer know where or who you are. Only the pain feels real.

I craved sleep in the way a parched man craves a drop of water. I
would do anything, even write a confession, tell them anything they
wanted, just to be able to close my eyes without being woken by a slap
in my face. A few minutes' rest was all I wanted. The schoolmaster
handed me a piece of paper and a pen. My hand was shaking so much
that I could barely write. But I managed to put down that I had been
decadent, had fraternized with our enemies, and leaked secrets. I returned the paper, desperate to close my eyes. The schoolmaster took
his time, smoothing the paper in the fastidious manner of a railway
clerk, adjusting his glasses, moving his lips as he read my words. He
slowly pushed it back to me. "It's no good playing tricks with us. We're
not stupid. We can tell when you're just writing words to please us. We

want more conviction. You have to believe what you confess. Until you do, I'm afraid we'll have to continue this interrogation." I wanted to howl but no longer had enough strength even for that.

I was woken up, after several hours, or perhaps less, I don't know, in my cell by a bucketful of cold foul-smelling water, and ordered to sit up straight and reflect on my crimes. The water quickly froze on the wooden floor and the extreme cold was the one thing that stopped me from falling asleep again immediately, that and the ever vigilant guards who beat me with a bamboo cane whenever I so much as moved. I tried to meditate, as if I were a monk instead of a prisoner, but my mind was a whirl of incoherent and sometimes terrifying images. I just couldn't think straight. I thought I was hearing voices of people I had known, some of them calling my name, telling me to confess. I could hear screams, but didn't know whether they were just in my own head.

I don't know when it was, or how long I had been in prison, but it was after I had written many drafts of my confession, all turned down for being "insincere," that I thought I heard Ri, singing in Chinese, something about selling candy, "tasting sweet, so sweet." Perhaps I had lost my mind and was imagining things, but I didn't care anymore—it was the most beautiful thing I had ever heard, the voice of my very own Goddess of Mercy. Only later did I realize that it had in fact been her song playing on the wireless, somewhere in the prison. It was called "The Candy Girl," from her latest film, *Opium War*. While I was locked away, this song had made her famous all over China, just as I had predicted. We didn't realize it then, but everyone knew it, from Canton to Harbin, in the areas under Japanese occupation as well as the Red strongholds and the provinces under Nationalist control. Chiang Kai-shek must have heard it, and so must Mao Zedong. It penetrated even the walls of the basement cells at the Special Higher Police Headquarters in Shinkyo. I think, perhaps, it was only Ri's sweet voice that kept me from going insane.

But I knew I couldn't hold out for much longer. One day, or night, I had no idea which, I was dragged out of my cell for what I thought would be another session with the schoolmaster, or the brute. I was pushed into an interrogation room. The rooms had all looked more or less the same, but this one was different. I hadn't been there before. It was more like an office, with framed images on the wall of the Manchukuo and Japanese flags. Even more astonishing was the cup of barley tea that was held to my lips, which I gulped down so fast I was convulsed with hiccups. I tried to focus my eyes on the man sitting on the other side of the table. He had a familiar face: the tiny eyes, the fat lips, the short, rubbery neck.

"I told you we'd meet again, my friend," he said with a dry chuckle, "though I'd hoped it might have been under more comfortable circumstances." He laughed out loud, as though sharing a good joke. That voice, the laugh. Then something clicked in my mind: it was Taneguchi! Still smiling: "A good deed never goes unpunished. Didn't you know that?" I was stupefied. What the hell was he doing here? My hiccups made me feel even more vulnerable, and faintly ridiculous. "You should have killed our little Yoshiko when you still had a chance. Now she has made some powerful friends in Tokyo." My mind wasn't working properly. For a moment I thought he was talking about Ri. Why should I have killed her? Who were these powerful friends? "I'm afraid she's up to her old mischief, our little Yoshiko. She's denounced you to her friends as a Chinese spy. And I'm sorry to say that was just what your enemies in Shinkyo wanted to hear." Gradually it dawned on me. I had been betrayed by the vengeful spirit of a Manchu princess. But who were my enemies?

Taneguchi called out for more tea. "Something to eat?" he asked me solicitously, as if we were in some pleasant restaurant. Before I had a chance to answer, he told the guard to bring us a plate of steamed buns. Even though I loved nothing more than steamed buns, I was baffled by this treatment. I was glad not to be slapped for a change, but not at all reassured by Taneguchi's brand of good cheer.

He watched as I gobbled up my bun. He left his untouched on the plate. I was dying to grab it. He must have noticed but just let it sit there. "Now let's get down to business," he said. "I'm sure you'll agree with me that our Special Higher Police officers are doing a splendid job protecting our imperial mission from spies and traitors. But I shouldn't be surprised if you were ready for a break from their hospitality. A change of diet, a touch of fresh air. Am I wrong? What?" He seemed to be enjoying himself. Still eyeing his bun sitting on the plate, a treasure carelessly abandoned, I waited for him to come to the point. "Now, you're lucky that you still have some friends left in Shinkyo. They have instructed me to make you a little proposition, which would be of great benefit to all of us. Our friends have become increasingly vexed by the activities of Mr. Kawamura in Shanghai. I hardly need to spell out to you what they are. Suffice it to say that our sacred mission would be much better off without him. Unfortunately, he is cautious and well protected. So we need someone he trusts, preferably a friend, to do what is necessary. Our friends don't care how you do it, as long as the job is done. This is your chance, your only chance, if I may say so, to make up for past errors." I tried to say something, but he held up his hand. "No need for an instant answer. Sleep on it. But whatever you decide, there is no backing out this time."

There may be nothing worse than physical pain, but Taneguchi's words came as a bigger blow than a fist in my face. He was a man of pure evil. It was he, not Kawamura, who had betrayed our mission in Asia. It was because of people like him that the Chinese hated us. I could just about forgive Eastern Jewel. She couldn't have known that I'd saved her life. Even I didn't know how she was bundled out of Manchukuo. Taneguchi would have left no tracks. But Eastern Jewel was misguided, not evil. The vengeance of a Manchu princess was terrible but forgivable. Taneguchi was a devil.

My treatment improved over the next few days. I was given sorghum to eat and a blanket, to stop me from freezing. I was moved to a better cell, where I was joined by another prisoner, a bony Japanese with purplish lips, whom obviously I couldn't trust. They might have planted him to trap me into an indiscretion. Even though he didn't say much, I was on my guard. There were red scars across his pale face, but they may have been there just to trick me. His reticence, too, could have been part of their strategy, to allay my suspicions. Sleep was impossible now. I kept waking up in a cold sweat. The only way to save my life was to kill a friend, but even if I succeeded, what would my life be worth after that?

Ri's sweet voice was playing once more, somewhere in the prison, on the floor above ours, more loudly this time. I listened to the words: "I am the candy girl, the candy girl . . . my candies taste so sweet. Please taste one of my candies Before you go to sleep . . ." It stopped and was repeated. Someone kept playing the same record. This went on for about an hour, over and over again, until even I grew tired of hearing her sweet voice singing the same tune. There was also a sound of stamping feet, as though people were dancing. Was I just hearing things? Was my mind still unstable? I looked at my cellmate. He shrugged and whispered: "They're giving someone the full treatment. Poor bastard." I still can't listen to that song without feeling sick.

I decided to agree to Taneguchi's proposition. Anything to get out of that hellish place. I'd figure out what to do once I was out, breathing fresh air, thinking more clearly. I might disguise myself as a Chinese, and slip away into the unoccupied zones. My Chinese was good enough to survive, I thought. Taneguchi was pleased with my decision. He knew I'd come to my senses. I'd done the right thing, he said, smiling as though he had just wanted the best for me.

22

AFTER MY RELEASE, Amakasu organized a dinner party for Taneguchi at the South Lake Pavilion. If truth be told, I no longer knew whether he was my friend or my enemy. I'd try to find out. All the regulars of the Ri Koran Fan Club were there, but Ri's name was never mentioned. She no longer existed for Amakasu, who was drinking heavily—whiskey, beer, saké. Jokes were made about my weight loss, and I was encouraged to eat more food. Amakasu stood up unsteadily, clutching the table for support, and proposed a toast to our final victory. His eyes were bloodshot and unfocused. Taneguchi wrapped a napkin around his head and did a country dance, while the others sang and banged their saké cups with their chopsticks. I pretended to be drunk and sang along, praying for the evening to come to an end.

Kishi, whose political star had risen even faster than Amakasu predicted, never missed a Ri Koran Fan Club meeting, even now that he was a cabinet minister in the imperial capital and unable to spend much time in Manchukuo anymore. The club was one place where he could relax among trusted friends. His eyes bulging as though he had a fever, he held forth about the final showdown with the white race. We might even have to fight the Germans, he said, for the pull of blood would prove to be stronger than any temporary alliances. We were lucky to be alive at this historic moment, for the fate of the world lay in our hands. Amakasu nodded, splashing whiskey on the table as he aimed for his glass. After acknowledging Amakasu, Kishi resumed his discourse. It would be a hard struggle, he said, but we Japanese would prevail because of our superior fighting spirit. Look at the brave people of Tokyo. Much of the city had been destroyed in one night by the cowardly American bombers. But would the Japanese people give up? "Never," cried Amakasu. "We will fight to the end," said Kishi, staring like a mad rabbit. "To the end," we all agreed, and lurched to our feet to give three cheers to our Imperial Majesty. Amakasu started a song I hadn't heard since my primary school days: "If you're a happy little boy, Then clap your hands . . ." We all clapped. "If you're a happy little boy, Then sing a song . . ." I closed my eyes and pretended to fall asleep. But a sharp prod from a chopstick in my side made me sit up instantly. I was gazing into the florid face of Taneguchi: "Don't shirk your duty this time, Sato, my friend. And don't try to escape, for we will find you, and when we do, you'll regret still being alive." He patted me on the shoulder, and smiled. "Cheer up, my friend. Life isn't so bad. After all, you'll be doing your bit for our victory and the future glory of Asia." Soon after that, mercifully, the party was over.

23

I WOULDN'T HAVE thought it possible, but Shanghai was looking even more battered than the last time I saw it. The Americans had bombed Honkew, where the European Jews had found refuge under our protection. The roof had been blown off Broadway Cinema on Wayside Road. Ripped movie posters were strewn across the street. And there was a gaping hole, filled with waterlogged rubbish, where Siegfried's Bakery had been. Unsightly sandbags and wire mesh fences were packed around the Cathay Hotel and other buildings on the Bund. Even Broadway Mansions resembled a military fortress more than an apartment building. I was relieved to hear that Kawamura was on business in Peking. At least that would give me some respite. I was less pleased to hear that Ri had moved into his apartment on Ferry Road. Not that I suspected anything untoward. Kawamura was a gentleman. But the last thing I wanted was for the Special Higher Police to get on her tail as well.

The heat was insufferable, even for a Shanghai summer. No sooner did I step outside my building than I felt like dashing back in for a bath and a change of linen. But even to get a decent bar of soap you needed special contacts now. A foul-smelling vapor hung over Suzhou Creek. The smell of death and decay was so strong it seeped into one's clothes. I called some of my Chinese friends, but failed to get hold of any of them. They were out of town, or busy, or made some other excuse. Even my old friend Zhang Songren, editor of *New Horizons*, who had always welcomed me with a Chinese meal at the Park Hotel, left a message that he was indisposed and couldn't meet me this time. Old Zhou's bar, my usual refuge in the old French Concession, was closed. Old Zhou, I was told, had gone back to his hometown in Shandong.

The Good Friend on Yuyuen Road was still open. I attended a party there for "Count" Takami's latest mistress, an Indian princess, or so she claimed. People claimed all kinds of things in Shanghai. Rumor had it that she was in fact a bar girl from Bombay, picked up one night by a drunken English merchant, who was so taken by her charms that he married her on the spot, and took her to Shanghai, where, after six months of conjugal life, she linked up with a Russian aristocrat who ran a gambling joint on Jessfield Road. "Count" Takami, whose title was as bogus as his girlfriend's, was an old rogue from Hawaii who made his money selling drugs of dubious quality to the Chinese.

People were dancing to American Negro music, forbidden in Japan, but played on our English-language radio stations to make the Americans feel homesick, one of those absurd ideas cooked up by our propaganda people. Takami, dressed in a white suit, was lurching around the dance floor with his "Indian princess." Perhaps it was the opium, or the bootleg vodka, or too many nights in Badlands nightclubs, but she looked a fright. Her face was bloated and splotched with gray. I waved at her. She looked in my direction, fluttering her hands to the rhythm of the music, without appearing to see me.

The music was intolerably loud. I never understood this American love for jungle drums. Negroes are treated like savages, yet the whites dance to their music. Captain Pick, the Russian expert on Jewish affairs, had lipstick smudged all over his mouth and chin and was dressed in a woman's ballgown. His eyes gleamed, as though he was in a trance. I noticed the same glazed look on the faces of other people at the party. Four of the five Japanese military officers had taken their jackets off and were sitting around a table with some Russian girls. One of the soldiers had a thick wad of what looked like old Russian money sticking from his waistband. The girl on his knee shrieked and threw back her head as one of his companions pulled down the top of her dress and splashed drink all over her naked breasts, as if watering a flowerbed. I tried to talk to Takami, but couldn't get a sensible word out of him. "Hot Peanuts!" he shouted. "Hot Peanuts!" I had no idea what he was talking about, and I shouldn't think that he did either.

The news got worse by the day. Even though people were not allowed to listen to enemy stations, they all did, and I noticed a change in the Chinese, who no longer cowered like dogs about to get a beating whenever they saw a Japanese uniform. They knew that our game was up. I could understand their feelings. Who could blame them? I would have felt the same way if I had been Chinese. I sometimes wished that I were, but I was Japanese, and there was nothing I could do about that. Native blood, like the lines on one's hand, cannot be faked. The Chinese had suffered for too long. It was time to make peace. We should never have been at war with China in the first place. That was our great historical error. If we had done a better job of convincing the Chinese that we were on their side, we might still have salvaged something from our common dreams; but our military leaders thought they knew better. They had decided to fight on to the last man, woman, and child. And we Japanese have always been bad at explaining ourselves, part of being frogs in a well, I guess. Kawamura was right. The Chinese hated us now, and it was our own fault.

What can I say about August 6? Murdering all those innocent people of Hiroshima, who had no part in the war, was the single worst act of inhumanity ever committed by man. This was not a battle but a massacre, as though Japanese humans were no better than rats. The American pilots never even saw their victims. Only a rootless nation without a shred of humanity could have committed such an atrocity.

Our soldiers did many bad things in the war, but never anything remotely as base as that.

On that terrible night of August 6, Ri gave a concert at the Grand
Theater. *A Musical Fantasia* was the title. It was to be her last performance, though we didn't know this at the time. The hall was packed,
mostly with Chinese, who had come to see the star from *Opium War*.
Even the most patriotic Chinese had forgiven Ri for her Manchukuo
past. To them, she was just the Candy Girl now.

The sight of Ri, looking so small and vulnerable in the silvery spotlight, dressed in a beautiful white *qi pao* printed with lotus flowers,
was like a magic potion that made us forget, for an hour or two, about
all the horrors going on outside. The Shanghai Symphony Orchestra,
a motley group of Russians, Jews, Germans, and Chinese, had never
sounded better. Ri sang a selection of Chinese songs: "Orchids Are
Sweet," "The Fragrant Garden," "Moon Over the West Lake." The
applause was like thunder. For the second part of the concert Ri
changed into a red evening gown and sang jazz numbers, wriggling
her behind like a Negress. I don't know how she got away with it. This
was clearly "enemy music," which would never have passed our censors before. I guess it was as good a sign as any that the end of our
dreams was near.

Ri changed yet again for the third and final part of the concert.
When the red velvet curtain rose, she appeared in a Chinese dress of
shimmering blue silk with a pattern of silver birds. She sang a song
from *The Merry Widow*. There was a pause, as the conductor prepared
the orchestra for the second number. It was hot under the spotlights.
Little pearls of perspiration were clearly visible on Ri's brow, despite
her thick makeup. She had sung the first bars of the next song when
the sound of an air-raid siren cut in. Perhaps she couldn't hear it over
the noise of the orchestra, for she carried on singing. The American
bombers must have been flying directly overhead, for there was a loud

rumble like a thunderstorm. The crowd cheered, even though we could all have been killed. This time Ri stopped, startled by the noise. Ushers rushed into the hall ordering us to run for the air-raid shelter.

To steady our nerves after the raid she and I had a drink in her dressing room. We spoke softly in Japanese. I insisted that she should leave the city at once. There was no telling what the Americans might do once they reached Shanghai. No Japanese woman would be safe. I told her to join her parents in the north. There would still be enough time to get out through Manchukuo. I would accompany her, if she wished. But for once she absolutely refused to listen to my advice. She had done enough for her parents, she said. Almost every penny she earned had gone to her hopeless father. She would wait in Shanghai for Kawamura to come back. He would protect her. I told her not to rely on that. The Americans would surely arrest him. But nothing I said could change her mind. Her face was set in a look of total resolve. "I will stay here," she said, switching to Chinese. "This is where I belong. Didn't you see how much the audience loved me tonight? This is my home."

Tears still spring to my eyes when I think of her, so alone and helpless in that stuffy dressing room, smelling of greasepaint and perspiration. Several times the room went dark, when the electricity cut out. I felt that she was slipping away, beyond my reach. Because of the war, and the circumstances of our birth, a gulf had opened up between us, which I could no longer bridge. I wasn't Chinese, not even born in China. But there was nothing waiting for me in Japan either. I, too, would stay in China, but not in Shanghai or Peking. I would go back to Manchuria, where my adventures began. I would confess the failure of my mission to Amakasu. I doubt whether anything would happen to me. What could they do? Kill me? Put me in prison again? It was too late for that. I knew it was all over for us Japanese, as soon as the clumsy agent sent by Taneguchi to spy on me disappeared one day, probably to be out of harm's way when the Americans came. No, I would put myself at the mercy of my Chinese friends. I had never done anything to harm the Chinese. I had always been on their side. I knew that they would understand my feelings.

Now I realize that we were both foolish dreamers, Ri and I. What could my Chinese friends possibly have done for me? It took some time to sink into our hearts, even after we knew it in our minds. We were defeated. And those who had been our friends were rounded up by the victors, or else they made sure to keep their heads down. None of them would have anything to do with me. And Ri, poor sweet innocent Ri, was granted her wish. She did become a Chinese, and she shared their fate. As soon as the Americans took Shanghai, the Chinese Nationalists charged her with treason. Like the other Yoshiko, more foolish even than we were, returning to China in the last days of the war, hoping to join the partisans, she was awaiting her trial in a Shanghai jail, and her inevitable execution.

I arrived in Shinkyo, exhausted, after I don't know how many hours on a train that was subject to constant delays. "Troop movements" was the usual explanation from harassed railway officials. In Shinkyo, I saw what those troop movements were. Every carriage of the Asia Express was filled with Japanese military brass and their loot; one compartment stuffed with Chinese lacquer, another with valuable paintings, yet another with gold, and bags of rice, or crates filled with precious porcelain. Men I recognized as Kempeitai officers were feasting on saké and food inside the train, while a Kanto Army colonel, looking very annoyed, pulled down the blinds of his compartment to block out the tumult on the platform. Japanese civilians with bundles strapped to their backs fought to get near the train, hoping against hope for a place on board. Low-ranking soldiers held them off using their rifles as clubs. I saw Japanese children being trampled underfoot, as their parents pleaded with the soldiers. A loudspeaker announced in

Japanese that there would be no more trains to Dairen, due to necessary troop movements. This message was repeated several times, until
the Asia Express slowly slunk out of the station in a cloud of steam.
Some civilians, in a fit of rage, attacked the soldiers, but they were
clubbed to the ground and left bleeding on the platform. Most just
milled around the station, immobilized by panic, not knowing where
to turn.

I walked to the Yamato Hotel, only to be told by the receptionist,
Old Chen, whom I had known for years, that there was no more room.
The lobby was filled with trunks waiting to be shipped off to Japan.
Ozaki, the surgeon, whom I had always detested, was frantically trying
to arrange transport for himself and his family. He was screaming at
another Japanese, a bureaucrat of some kind, that he, Ozaki, as the
chairman of the Japanese-Manchukuo Friendship Association, should
be the first in line. Both men fell silent, however, when a Kanto Army
colonel pushed them both aside and ordered a soldier to load up his
luggage in the car claimed by Ozaki, who, his face turned almost scarlet with anger, sputtered in protest. The colonel turned round and
roared: "Don't you dare address an officer of the Imperial Japanese
Army like that, you insolent bastard!" I decided it was time to leave.

The film studios, where I was bound to find some friendly face,
seemed my best bet. Great Unity Boulevard was swarming with Japanese civilians, carrying their belongings in pushcarts or on their backs,
like a flood tide rolling in the direction of the station. It was no use
telling these people that there would be no more trains, at least not for
them. Who would have believed me? Even a hopeless task is sometimes better than doing nothing at all. Furious honking sounded from
the direction of the army headquarters. The crowd scrambled to make
way for a convoy of military trucks and black staff cars racing toward
the station. Several people were nearly run over, as the convoy left us
choking in a cloud of dust. An elderly man waved his fist at the sol-

diers and shouted that they were a disgrace to our country. I could have told him so long before this unseemly end to our presence in China.

My clothes, which I had worn since I left Shanghai, were heavy with dirt and perspiration. I longed to take a bath. Normally a place full of hustle and bustle, with costumed extras running to this sound-stage or that, the studio buildings appeared to have been abandoned. One or two nervous-looking clerks scurried down a corridor with bags containing who knows what. I didn't see anyone I knew, and was about to find a place to lie down and get some rest, when a familiar voice called my name: "Well, well, if it isn't Sato, coming back to roost in his old nest."

Amakasu, neatly dressed in his usual green uniform, looked positively friendly. I hadn't often seen him smile, and certainly wouldn't have expected to see him doing so at this grim hour. It was as if nothing had ever happened between us. "What about going to the lake for a spot of fishing, eh?" He put his hand on my back and steered me outside. I was so astonished that I followed him, meek as a child. The South Lake looked peaceful in the afternoon sun, like a Chinese painting, with white herons poking about in the bamboo groves, and water gently lapping on the shore. Amakasu gazed fondly at the New Asian—style roofs rising above the trees of the South Lake Park, and said: "Look, Sato, at the sun shining over our beautiful city, radiant as the destiny of this great land." I wasn't sure what he was talking about. "We both loved this country, didn't we, Sato? Factories, mines, railroads, they were Kishi's creation, and grand projects they were too, vital to the survival of our empire, no doubt. Our work was different, though, wasn't it, Sato? But no less important. Not at all. I like to think that our contribution was to put a smile on the faces of the people of Manchukuo. And you know what, Sato? Even as we Japanese fade away from this great land, those smiles will remain as a testament to my work."

He felt a tug on his fishing rod and gently eased a plump fish out of the water. It was a beautiful white carp with patches of red, glistening in the sunlight. Amakasu turned to me with the look of a proud young boy, joyful and innocent.

I saw him once more, very briefly, on the afternoon of the next day. I don't know why I was still hanging around the deserted studio. But I had nowhere else to go, and found some comfort in revisiting my memories. As I strolled through the empty soundstages, I recognized bits of old sets from Ri's first films: the interior of a train from *Honeymoon Express*, the facade of a Buddhist temple from *Suzhou Nights*. And I thought of all the great movies, and the labor that went into them, by Japanese, Chinese, Manchus. There is nothing more wonderful than people working together to create a thing of beauty. Here at least, in the Manchuria Motion Pictures Studios, we made no distinctions in race or nationality; only talent counted. I wept as I walked, for the last time, through the door of Stage 3, and entered the hall that led to Amakasu's office. Perhaps he had heard my footsteps. He emerged from his room, smiling, and stuck out his hand like a Westerner. I was surprised to see him in the full dress uniform of the Concordia Association, with the characters for "harmony among the five races" stitched on his lapels. It was the kind of thing he would only have worn at official functions. I thought it looked clownish. He shook my hand and said: "We had a grand time in Manchukuo, didn't we, Sato?"

After that, he turned back into his office and softly closed the door. Seconds later I heard a loud bang, which echoed down the corridor. With the shot still ringing in my ear, I knocked on Amakasu's door, calling his name. I don't know why I did this. It was absurd, now I think about it. Anyway, the door was locked. When I finally managed to break in, I saw him slumped over his desk, blood dripping onto the Persian carpet. I rather wish that I had had the courage then to follow his example.

Instead, I rushed from the scene to find help. But where? The police stations were abandoned, and the hospitals had their hands full coping with Japanese refugees camping out in every room, terrified of what might be in store for them. Everywhere I went I heard fearful stories of Chinese brigands raping Japanese women and taking the children off as slaves. So I went back to bury Amakasu myself, in the garden of the studio he had built. It was the least I could do for this often misunderstood man, whom history will surely treat more kindly than some of his contemporaries did.

A stroke of luck rescued me from having to share the hospital floor with a mass of filthy, hysterical refugees. On my way back from the studio I ran into Liu, an old Manchu friend. He had worked as an interpreter at the Manchukuo Broadcasting Corporation, first in Mukden, later in Shinkyo. Our friendship went back to the early days of the *Manchukuo Rhapsody* programs. Unlike all the others, he still valued our friendship and offered to put me up for a few days. I have no way of finding out what has happened to him since, but I wish to pay tribute to his spirit of kindness and courage.

Liu was a learned man, who had studied literature in Peking before the war. Books were his only passion. His small house in Shinkyo, not far from Great Unity Avenue, was like a bookstore, with books piled high in every room. There was nothing he hadn't read in Japanese as well as Chinese literature. He was certainly much better read than me. But we shared a passion for *All Men Are Brothers*. So we spent the next few days reciting our favorite stories, Liu in Chinese and me in Japanese. His favorite hero was Wu Song, the drunken hero, who takes revenge for the murder of his brother. My preference went out to Soko, the great leader with the phoenix eyes. "But he betrayed his men in the end," said Liu, gently mocking me with his laughter. "He joined the government forces," Liu continued, with feigned indignation. I defended my hero, claiming that this was part of his strategy. Soko was always on the side of justice. On and on we went, arguing back and forth, drinking our way through Liu's last supply of rice wine. We were like brothers in that small apartment filled with stories. For a few days, amidst the mayhem, I felt as if I were at home.

Perhaps it was on the fourth day of my stay with Liu, or possibly even the fifth, but whichever it was, around noon we heard a tremendous racket going on outside. It came from Great Unity Avenue, the sound of screaming and the music of a brass band. Liu went pale and told me to stay inside and have another drink. But I couldn't contain my curiosity. I joined the crowd running toward the main street. Army trucks were parked randomly in the middle of the road near the entrance of Mitsukoshi, the department store, which had been abandoned when the Japanese took flight. It was immediately clear that the trucks weren't ours. They had red stars on the sides. Large foreign men in untidy military uniforms were rushing in and out of the stores carrying as much as they could: women's dresses, table lamps, clocks, shoes, curtain materials, brass fittings, chairs, bottles of saké, anything that caught their fancy. I saw a man with four pocketwatches dangling from his neck, and another with a stuffed bird borne on his head like a lady's hat. Soldiers were not so much marching as roaming along the avenue, staring at the stores, most of which looked as though they had been struck by a hurricane, and at the women, wondering which one to take first. More trucks arrived from the direction of the South Lake. The soldiers, obviously drunk, looked quite insane. They were hollering like beasts and decked out in the strangest assortment of clothes. There were men wearing traditional Chinese robes, and Japanese women's kimonos, and bowler hats. Two soldiers were fencing, one with a Chinese sword and the other with a fake rifle. Another, tottering on his feet, was wearing a Chinese emperor's hat and a women's dress of silk.

It took me a while to make sense of this crazy spectacle. But then I understood. They had looted the film studios and were running amok with our costumes and props. One of those Chinese dresses might actually have been worn by Ri Koran. I thought of poor Ri, waiting for her cruel fate in a Shanghai jail, and Amakasu, buried in the hard Manchurian soil, and Eastern Jewel, forever caught between her native and adopted countries. Our cowardly troops had left us to the mercy of these savages. The barbarians had looted our dreams.

PART TWO

1

W E ALL KNEW the rules back then, in the summer of 1946: NFWIP, No Fraternization with Indigenous Personnel. The penalties for infringements were severe. If you were caught one too many times in an off-limits restaurant, bar, or movie theater, it meant a one-way ticket back home, and "home" was the last place I wanted to be. Fraternization still went on, of course. Most officers had a "kimono girl" tucked away for their own amusement. Not that I was particularly interested in that kind of thing, but a man could pick up a girl behind Yurakucho Station and have his way with her in Hibiya Park for a packet of Camels. However, that same man would be punished for attending a performance at the Kabuki Theater, which was off-limits, and God, or General MacArthur, only knew why.

The good thing was that the U.S. Military Police were rather like modern tourists, parochial and incurious. They watched a few places like hawks, mostly around the Ginza area, but stayed away from lesser known parts of Tokyo, the bombed-out plebeian districts near the Sumida River, where street markets, fairgrounds, burlesque joints, and moviehouses had sprung to life as soon as the war was over. Those were my illicit stamping grounds, where adventure beckoned around every corner, in the grounds of every broken shrine, along every rank-smelling garbage-filled canal, in every movie theater when the lights were dimmed. Ueno was already famous in Hokusai's days for its boy brothels. Some of them catered to Kabuki actors. Others were said to be frequented by lovers of young monks. For me, the park on the lake, carpeted with water lilies, was the setting for many an unexpected encounter.

Summer, when the cicadas rasp in the steaming heat, is my favorite season in Tokyo. It is then that the Japanese seem most natural, most themselves. In those early, less inhibited days after the war, strong workingmen emerged freshly scrubbed from the public baths, often in nothing but their white *fundoshi* neatly wrapped around their loins, leaving very little to the imagination. Tokyo, my Tokyo, the Tokyo of the common people, in August, was a banquet of honeyed curves and soft skin, displayed not to show off, but innocently, unself-consciously. I stood and watched the world go by, an invisible observer in the Garden of Eden, entranced by what I saw, even if that garden was still a landscape of ruins stretching all the way to Mount Fuji, whose pale cone is no longer visible now, but still rose in those days majestically over the scorched earth. I wasn't literally invisible, of course, but as a foreigner I was ignored. The Japanese never see what they choose not to see. So they pretended that I wasn't there. And that's just how I liked it.

This feeling was most acute when I entered one of the moviehouses, strictly off-limits, of course, but even the most hawk-eyed MP would never have had the imagination to come and snoop around in the Asakusa Rokko or the Ueno Nikkatsu. Tokyo, in those days, was full of movie theaters, almost as many as there were public baths. Some of them had just about survived the bombings and retained some of their prewar glitter, like old prostitutes with thick layers of makeup, cracking at the edges. Many more were jerry-built, and looked as flimsy as movie sets. There were cinemas in the basements of wrecked department stores, cinemas clustered around the railway stations, and cinemas tucked away in obscure back alleys that were hard even to stumble across by accident. People were just crazy for the movies. Day and night you would see the Japanese lining up for another show. It was as if a kind of movie madness had been dropped into the water supply. The whole nation was seeking to escape into a world of celluloid dreams.

And so, on those hot Tokyo nights, I would slip inside a packed movie theater and stand in the crowd that gave off a sweet smell of rice sweat and camellia oil, flesh pressing against flesh, my eyes trained on the screen in rapture as scene after incomprehensible scene demanded my full attention. I tried to make sense of the family dramas featuring suffering daughters-in-law and war veterans drowning their memories in drink. Even though the stories mostly escaped me, the emotions that swept across the audience like rays from the flickering screen affected me deeply. I wept with the men and women around me, who were so much like the men and women on the screen. The Japanese didn't want to see movie stars living more glamorous lives than they did; no, they came to see the lives of people just like themselves. Instead of wallowing in their own wretchedness, they cried for the misfortunes of imaginary characters, misery redeemed by art. Odd though it may sound, it was in these cinemas, surrounded by people whose language was still a mystery to me, that I felt totally at home.

2

NOT THAT THE idea of home meant much to me. For where was home? Bowling Green, Ohio, is where I had the misfortune of being born, in a small white suburban house near Route 6, halfway between Napoleon and Venice. My dear mama, Florence, had grown up in a suburb of Chicago and I think she felt trapped in Bowling Green, and even more in her marriage with my father, Richard Vanoven, who hated all the things she loved, like listening to music on the radio or reading books. I was named Sidney, after my father's elder brother who died in the war in France. If there was one thing I couldn't stand, it was being called "Sid," but "Sid" it was, alas, until much later in life, when I was old enough to assert my right to be called by my proper name, and even then the dreadful "Sid" would crop up with annoying regularity.

I can still hear the *tick-tock* of our Swiss wall clock (yes, it had a cuckoo announcing the time of day with a grating mechanical sound) and the rustling of my father's newspaper as the only sounds to break the heavy silence in our living room. Mama would be itching to turn on the radio to listen to one of her favorite bands, Ted Weems on the *Johnson's Wax Show*, or Paul Whiteman, or her absolute favorite, Ben Bernie and his magic violin. (Classical music had not yet reached Bowling Green, I'm sorry to say.) But she knew that the merest attempt to reach for the radio would be met by a growled order to "leave that damned noise off."

As long as I can remember, I realized that some awful mistake had been made and that I didn't belong there. Quite where I did belong was unclear. But in my earliest dreams, inspired by books about Aladdin or Peter Pan, I was forever flying to some Never-Never Land as far away as possible from Bowling Green, Ohio. I often imagined that I could be one of the characters in these stories—Aladdin himself, of course, but I would also have been perfectly content to have been one of the pirates serving under Captain Hook. Indeed, I might have preferred it, for I secretly adored Captain Hook. Aladdin I envied for his jeweled turban and his magic lamp. The idea of calling up miraculous adventures just by rubbing a lamp was too marvelous for words. And there was something about Aladdin's fairy-tale world of soukhs and djinns and minarets that held a deep and mysterious allure.

As I grew older, travelling vicariously with Aladdin or Peter Pan no longer sufficed as a viable escape and life became more and more intolerable. Barely on speaking terms with my father, I found it harder to understand Mama's stoic endurance. The only time I saw her really happy, almost as if she had grown ten years younger by the rub of a magic lamp, was during a visit to the Chicago World's Fair with her sister, my Aunt Betsy. I must have been about eight or nine at the time. It was as if God had opened up a treasure chest and dropped its contents onto the shores of Lake Michigan just for us: a Moroccan Village, with turbaned sheikhs and wandering nomads in long colorful robes; a Japanese Pavilion, with the Seven Geisha Girls performing arcane ceremonies with a teapot; an Italian Hall shaped like a sleek modern airliner; and a real German Beer Hall, with men in leather shorts. Mama never touched any alcohol at home, since my father disapproved of it. Yet there they were, Mama and Aunt Betsy, lifting huge steins to their lips, giggling like young girls. I asked Mama why we couldn't stay there forever, if not at the World's Fair, then at least in Chicago, with Aunt Betsy. She laughed. What about Dad? she said. Well, what about him? I replied.

I might not have survived my childhood in Bowling Green, Ohio, if it hadn't been for two things: my Aunt Tess and the Luxor Playhouse. Aunt Tess was my father's elder sister. I can still conjure up her room in my mind: the maroon-colored walls, instead of the usual drab off-white; the reproduction of a Renoir painting, hanging in the front parlor, of people dancing in a Parisian music hall; the old Persian rugs, the Chinese landscapes in silk, and all the other souvenirs from Uncle Frank's travels. Her room was like a cave full of strange delights, where one could hide from the ugliness of the world outside. Uncle Frank I only knew from stories. I was three when he died in a car accident on Route 7 on his way to Lima. But my aunt would show me pictures of Uncle Frank in various exotic places where he traveled to meet the suppliers for his tea business, which stopped flourishing in the late 1920s and went bust in the crash on Wall Street. Much later, in a moment of indiscretion on Mama's part, I learned that he had been drinking when his car overturned on the route to Lima.

Those photo albums, bound in dark green leather, were an endless source of daydreaming. No matter how often I scrutinized the sepia pictures of Uncle Frank posing in front of a Chinese temple or a teahouse in Assam, the magic never wore off. I would pester Aunt Tess with questions about these enchanting scenes. What she didn't know, she made up, and I didn't mind it one bit. We invent stories in order to live. Once in a while, these half-fictional memories seemed to distress her. She stopped talking and silently stroked my hair, softly repeating my name: "Sid, Sid, oh dear, oh dear . . ." Sensing that something was wrong, but not quite what, I asked her whether she was hungry. I found comfort in her French perfume that stuck to my clothes, to the disgust of my father, who complained that I "stank like a bordello" every time I returned from his elder sister's house. I had no idea what a bordello was, but my father's condemnation made it sound very attractive. I associated it with the Moroccan Village at the Chicago World's Fair. It sounded pleasantly foreign, like the food at the home of Frankie, my best friend at school. His parents were Italian. They ate garlic, which disgusted my father almost as much as Aunt Tess's French perfume.

The Luxor was one of two moviehouses in Bowling Green. It was located on the corner of Wooster and Main. When I was small, Mama or Aunt Tess would take me to the other cinema, the Rialto, farther up on Main Street, where I saw Harold Lloyd hanging from that great clock and Dolores Del Rio dance with Gene Raymond in Brazil. But the Luxor was the more glamorous, with its bronze relief of Egyptian dancers in the lobby. The connection between Egypt and the movies still escapes me, but it seemed right at the time. As soon as Mr. Ray Cohn's luminous Wurlitzer sank into the pit, and the titles of the first film (one movie was good, but a double bill was heaven) came on, I entered the lives of Clark Gable, Norma Shearer, Lewis Stone. I can still see in my mind's eye that slap in the face of Norma that made Clark into a star. And *Grand Hotel*. Those opening words: "Grand Hotel. Always the same. People come, people go. Nothing ever happens." Well, nothing except for jewel heists and movie premieres and doomed love affairs! The imaginary lives of John Barrymore and Greta Garbo meant so much more to me than my own drab existence. I spent hours imagining that I was Baron Felix von Gaigern, or Peter Standish. What small amounts of pocket money I received from my father, who always gave grudgingly as if parting with his last savings, was spent on the movies. Mother knew, but never told my father. When I was obliged to buy a present for my father's birthday, she would slip me a few dollars. I always bought him a new necktie. I never saw him wear them.

The Luxor is also where I had my first erotic encounter. I never knew the man who gave me my first taste of adult pleasure. I can't even recall precisely what he looked like, but I remember the moment quite vividly. I had gone to the movies alone, a habit I retained all my life. It was *The Scarlet Pimpernel,* with Leslie Howard and Merle Oberon. They were sailing from France and just as they spotted the white cliffs of Dover, I felt a hand brushing my right thigh. I still wore shorts. The hand felt warm. I was surprised, but did nothing to discourage this sudden invasion, thinking it might be an accident. It soon became clear that it was no accident. The hand, more confidently now, made its way up higher, feeling my thigh as if to test its firmness. When the desired goal was reached, I felt a sensation that was utterly new to me. Instinctively, I opened my legs to allow more room. I heard the man next to me breathing and glanced at him from the corner of my eye. He was just a middle-aged man in a suit, giving off a slight whiff of hair oil. His eyes were fixed on the screen. Merle Oberon spoke the famous words: "England, at last!" The hand relaxed and was pulled away as quickly as it had arrived a few minutes earlier. I never saw the man again. Nor did I ever have a similar experience in the Luxor. Though not exactly losing my flower, it was the beginning of something that would become a major part of my life, the pursuit of pleasure in encounters with strangers.

3

I ALWAYS THINK of that bus trip to Los Angeles in the summer of 1944 as my first Great Escape. Fresh out of high school, but just too young for the draft, I had no idea what I wanted to do, but one thing was for sure, whatever it was I ended up doing, it wasn't going to be in Bowling Green, Ohio. My father was so disgusted with me that he had even stopped calling me "a damned sissy." Mama looked permanently worried since she found me one day pulling faces in the mirror while uttering Marlene's famous words: "It took more than one man to change my name to Shanghai Lily." Spending the summer jerking sodas at Lou's Drugstore was not really an option, as far as I was concerned. My sexual life was all in my own head, leaving me feeling exhausted as well as ashamed whenever I found temporary release in the privacy of the restroom. I thought I might go mad if I stayed home one moment longer.

A fortune-teller once told me that I was blessed with good luck. It was an easy thing for her to say. We all need reassurance. But I believe it might be true. I think I have a guardian angel who steps in whenever things become too desperate. My Great Escape in the summer of '44 was made possible by my Aunt Betsy in Chicago, who had a friend, who was married to a businessman, who knew a man in motion pictures, named Warren Z. Noakes. Noakes worked for the distribution office in Chicago for the Twentieth Century Studios in Hollywood. After a lot of to-ing and fro-ing this angelic figure, whom I never actually met, managed to get me a job as a gofer in the research unit of a movie to be made in Hollywood by the great Frank Capra. Mama wept when I finally left Bowling Green. My father was just glad to get rid of me.

My direct boss was named Walter West, a large man of few words, who happened to be blessed with an extraordinary eye for photographic images. He didn't just watch film; he devoured it, greedily, with an appetite that was impossible to satisfy. Walter spent most of his life in the dark, like a bat, with his red-rimmed eyes trained on the end of the projected beam. Nothing excited him more than the sight of a stack of film reels. When I say that Walter was large, I really mean very large. I rarely saw him without a doughnut or some other confection in his pudgy hand, spilling sugary powder like dandruff all over his jacket. But he was a glutton for celluloid. Walter would work his way through the stacks in record speed to find that one nugget of cinematic gold that everyone else had overlooked. Our assignment for Mr. Capra (God forbid that I should have called him "Frank," let alone "Frankie," or "Chief," as some of the older studio hands did) was to select a compilation of images from Japan—anything from Japanese newsreels to Japanese feature films—that would be used for a movie, commissioned by the U.S. government, entitled *Know Your Enemy*.

We worked in an office that was a far cry from my Hollywood dreams. I had expected to be in the midst of great splendor, with famous stars descending from marble stairs in white gloves, with imperious directors in riding boots and black-suited waiters hovering with silver plates offering glasses of champagne. I had never imagined all the hard work that went into producing the movies, all the hustle on the soundstages, all the shouting and screaming amidst the chaos of electric cables, microphones, camera boxes, makeup women, continuity girls, best boys, first assistants, second assistants, lighting cameramen, soundmen, and whatnot.

But even the movie sets, of which I only caught occasional glimpses, passing through the studios when the red lights were off, were alluring compared to our shabby little office in a neglected building in the Western Avenue Twentieth Century Studios. There were two projectors, one for sound, the other for image, ripped out of their concrete casings in the cooling tower. A worn old table, piled high with film cans, and two or three rickety chairs made up the furniture. This is where Walter performed his magic, watching reel after reel and picking the cherries that Mr. Capra was looking for. Once in a while, the great man himself would appear, in an expensive double-breasted suit and a fedora hat, trailing cigar smoke and cologne. "Walt," he would shout, "what's old Santa got in the can for me today?"

Since it was my job to run errands for Walter, or anyone higher up the pecking order than me, which is to say, everyone, I rarely had the chance to watch the movies with them. But what I did manage to see was a revelation. The images selected by Walter were sliced together by Capra, with graphics supplied by the Disney studio, and commentary spoken by John Huston. It was pure propaganda, of course, to show our boys in the Pacific what we were up against: a nation of robotic, fanatical, modern-day samurai programmed to kill and die for their Emperor. Pictures of Japanese bowing en masse in the direction of the Imperial Palace, or blowing up Chinese cities, or marching across the Manchurian plains, were cut together with scenes from Japanese features. It was all most effective, I am sure, but I was less interested in the overall effect of the finished film than in the material we discovered in the process. It was the most marvelous introduction to Japanese film, and it didn't take long for me to see, even in the crudest swordfight pictures, that we were dealing with a vast source of treasures.

One, in particular, caught our fancy. Made in 1940, it was called *China Nights*. Walter was equally captivated, so much so that he immediately sent me off to fetch Mr. Capra. At first Mr. Capra failed to see the point, especially of the main actor, who much later I realized was the great Hasegawa Kazuo. "What can we do with this?" he asked, waving his cigar impatiently. "This guy looks like a damned girl." But gradually he got pulled into the movie. He and Walter were so mesmerized by the end of it that they forgot to send me away on an errand and I was able to watch the whole film with them. Since there were no subtitles, much of the story escaped us. It was the natural flow of the images, the beautifully timed cuts, and the camerawork, which was intimate without being intrusive. There were few close-ups, and no false glamor. Here was life itself being discreetly yet closely observed. I shall never forget the sight of Mr. Capra as the credits rolled after the last scene when the Chinese girl, who was about to drown herself in a river, is saved by her Japanese husband. Tears dropped on his carefully tailored suit as Mr. Capra heaved with emotion. Rubbing his eyes with both hands, he brushed his right cheek with his burnt-out cigar, leaving a dark smudge like running mascara. "The Japs are way ahead of us," he said. "We can't make movies like that here in America. The public wouldn't have it. And that girl, Walt, who is that little Chinese girl?" Walt didn't know, but promised to find out. Her name, we discovered, was Ri Koran.

I watched other Japanese films with Walt, some of them long and without interest, but many were almost as compelling as *China Nights*. I have no idea what we saw. Some of Mizoguchi's masterpieces, perhaps, or Naruse's? We wouldn't have known what they were, anyway. It's all a blur now. But the Chinese girl stayed with me. Walter and I used to hum Ri's song with that lilting Chinese melody. Like Aladdin's lamp, it conjured up images in my mind of an enchanted world beyond anything I could imagine, that promised Never-Never Land I had yearned for from the moment I could speak.

By the time I was ready to be called up for military service, we dropped the big ones on Hiroshima and Nagasaki. I hate to say it, but this, too, felt like the brush of a wing of my guardian angel. The horror of an invasion of Japan does not bear thinking about. Besides, I was hardly cut out for soldiering. What saved me from that ghastly fate and precipitated my second Great Escape was a letter from Mr. Capra to a friend of his, a big shot at General MacArthur's GHQ in Tokyo. His name was Major General Charles Willoughby. "Charles'll take care of you," promised Mr. Capra, as he slipped me a Havana from his coat pocket. I later tried to smoke this great thing and ended up feeling sick.

Actually, things were not quite as simple as Mr. Capra thought. Charles may have been able to take care of me once I was in Japan, but first I had to apply to the Foreign Service in Cleveland. And they would only take me on if I had some skill they required. Since I had no languages, apart from English, and no work experience besides being a gofer for Walter West, I was not an obvious candidate for an overseas posting. I could only come up with two skills that might be of any use: I could type like lightning (Champion Typist in the Ohio Schools Contest of 1941), and I had learned to take shorthand from Mama, who had once worked as a secretary for an insurance company in Chicago.

An agonizing month was spent in Bowling Green, most of it at the Luxor, out of sheer boredom, and hoping, I guess, for some adventure in the dark, which never materialized, I'm sorry to say. But I did see *Bring On the Girls* with Veronica Lake at least six times. The only alternative at the time was *Christmas in Connecticut* with Barbara Stanwyck, playing at the other theater, but after sitting through that twice I turned back to Veronica Lake with relief. I had also, by then, discovered the solace of literature. My taste was untutored and thus indiscriminate. We had no books at home, but the Bowling Green librarian, a middle-aged man with thick glasses and an overpowering smell of talcum powder, was a guide of sorts. He introduced me to Thornton Wilder. When I said I'd like to read something more foreign, European perhaps, he suggested Jane Austen. When I had exhausted the stock of her works, I asked him for something else. He peered at me carefully through his owlish spectacles, as though about to divulge a risky secret, and ventured that I might wish to start on the French writer Marcel Proust.

When the letter finally came through, telling me to report in Philadelphia for embarkation to Japan, I was so happy I could almost have hugged my father. Instead, I did a wild improvised tango through the living room with Mama, which prompted my father to flee in disgust. He could call me a damned sissy for the rest of his life, for all I cared. Next stop was Tokyo!

4

MY FIRST DAYS in Japan were not promising. I was put up with other Americans in a gloomy office building that had once been the headquarters of a soy sauce company and now bore the grand name of Continental Hotel. Most of the inmates of this grim institution worked in one way or another for the Supreme Commander of Allied Forces in the Pacific, also known as SCAP, or "The Old Man," or "Susan," in the less reverential coinage of my friend Carl. Carl was a fellow movie maven, whose knowledge of motion pictures was even greater than mine (he grew up in New York). "Susan" was a rather abstruse reference to a Joan Crawford movie, entitled *Susan and God.* Carl maintained that General MacArthur bore an uncanny resemblance to Joan Crawford in the title role of that picture. I can't say I saw the likeness myself, but I was amused by the name, so it stuck, at least between us.

I didn't yet have the benefit of Carl's congenial company in those early days, however, so I felt lonesome in my billet, living on a steady diet of Spam and powdered potatoes. But since most Japanese would have given their left eyes to share this life of splendor, I knew I shouldn't complain. When I wasn't tap-tapping away in the typing pool of the Allied Removals and Transportation Division, I spent most of my time wandering around in the charred ruins of the Ginza. I've always regarded shyness as a vulgar vice. So I'd strike up conversations in my few words of Japanese with young men on construction sites, and sometimes even traffic cops, if they looked approachable, or market traders. I spent endless time trawling through the black markets, where everything was sold from cigarettes to old bloodstained hospital blankets. Hawkers shouted themselves hoarse: "Fist-class American blankets! You'll sleep like babies!" "Delicious pork meat! Just like mother used to make it!" Well, maybe it was pork. Old ladies stirred with long wooden chopsticks in great bowls of pig's offal. Fights broke out over the price of a turnip or a pair of old socks. Young toughs in Hawaiian shirts and army boots kept a semblance of order in this pandemonium and took most of what they needed for free. I would love to have talked to them, but my fumbling attempts to do so did not, on the whole, meet with much encouragement. I once tried to talk to a man dressed as Charlie Chaplin to promote a picture featuring Deanna Durbin. He was friendly enough, in his toothless way, but our conversation ran dry rather quickly.

When I was tired of wandering, I would rest at various landmarks that stuck out of the ruins like rocks in a desert. At the Hattori Building, now the Wako department store, then the PX, I observed the sad transactions between large Americans in crisp uniforms, dispensing bars of soap or crackers or indeed anything remotely edible to the young men in Hawaiian shirts, who would no doubt make a handsome profit on these vital goods at the black markets. A crippled young woman sat in her usual place outside the PX with a little wooden box that served as a platform for American boots, which she polished to a perfect sheen, while repeating one of the few English phrases she had managed to pick up: "Japanese, no fucking good."

Much of what I saw on my solitary walks made me feel embarrassed to be an American: the speeding jeeps forcing Japanese to jump out of the way; the laughing GIs throwing sticks of chewing gum at emaciated street kids, shoeless and filthy, who followed every American around with pleas for more, "gimme more, gimme more"; the "pan-pan girls" *clip-clopping* in their wooden heels behind Yurakucho Station, puckering their crimson lips, throwing kisses at any foreigner with a few bucks to spare, or a packet of crackers, or a pair of stockings. Periodically, our MPs would round them all up, together with anyone else, female and Japanese, who happened to stray into their net, and transport them in trucks to an army clinic for compulsory VD checks. Perhaps the hardest thing to bear was the glum silence with which other Japanese observed these signs of their country's degradation. I would swiftly move on, trying not to look any Japanese in the eyes. And yet, as I got used to these daily spectacles of collective humiliation, embarrassment gradually made way for something else. I grew to admire these stoic people who, no matter how impoverished, always retained their dignity. Nobody begged for food, or asked for our pity. They may no longer have had a decent roof over their heads, or enough money to feed their families, or proper clothes to wear, but respectability was still insisted upon. Men emerged from jerry-built hovels, in wooden sandals and frayed army surplus pants, but always with a clean white shirt and a tie. Even the homeless, bombed out of their homes, who had found a temporary shelter in the squalid subway stations, smiled at us, as though we were valued guests in their country instead of members of a conquering army.

I was longing to get closer. I wanted to see more Japanese movies, and visit the Kabuki, but such entertainments were still off-limits for Allied personnel. Instead, we could see Hollywood pictures at the old Takarazuka Theater, or the Ernie Pyle, as we then knew it. On Saturday nights there would sometimes be special theater performances on at the Ernie Pyle, and very peculiar some of them were, too. I recall with particular affection a *Swan Lake* with Japanese dancers in blond wigs baring their gums in show dancers' smiles as they gamely produced a version of the ballet that left me feeling rather exhausted.

The Japanese were not allowed inside the Ernie Pyle, but an exception was sometimes made for the people working for us. So I decided to take Nobu, the roomboy at the Continental Hotel, to attend a performance of *The Mikado*. Nobu was a pale youth, with longish black hair and the wiry body of a flyweight boxer. He cleaned our rooms and polished our shoes, always making sure they were deposited outside our doors first thing in the morning, but he was in fact a remarkable young man who had been studying French literature at Tokyo Imperial University, before joining a squadron of kamikaze pilots in the summer of 1945. Two of his best friends had already died in suicide attacks off Okinawa, so he felt he had no choice but to follow their example. His life was saved only by the Japanese surrender, a point we rarely discussed, for it made him feel awkward. Nobu much preferred to talk about our shared passion for Marcel Proust, whom he read in French.

I had only seen *The Mikado* once before, in the movie version with Dennis Day as Nanki Poo. This was at the Luxor in Bowling Green, of course, which seemed awfully remote from the world of Gilbert and Sullivan. But nothing, I mean *nothing* in my wildest dreams, had prepared me for the lavishness of *The Mikado* at the Ernie Pyle. The Mikado himself, a tall and very stout British major, appeared against a backdrop of bright pink cherry blossoms dangling over a golden bridge, and was decked out in long trailing pantaloons made up of gold and blue panels. Pooh-Bah, Ko-Ko, and Pish-Tush, played by British and Canadian officers, were dressed in kimonos rented from the imperial court. Clearly designed for shorter men, the kimonos only reached down to their sturdy calves, revealing a rather long expanse of bright pink tights. The choruses were made up of men and women from the Japanese Bach Choir, who had never sung Gilbert and Sullivan in their lives before, and brought to *The Mikado* the solemnity of a Christian Passion, which was interesting, though perhaps not entirely appropriate. The leading players could barely sing at all, except for Nanki-Poo, who shrieked in an arresting falsetto, and the acting certainly failed to match the standards of their costumes. But the audience was ready to applaud anything from the moment the Japanese nobles dropped their outlandish fans and launched into "If You Want to Know Who We Are":

> We are gentlemen of Japan:
> On many a vase and jar—
> On many a screen and fan,
> We figure in lively paint:
> Our attitude's queer and quaint—
> You're wrong if you think it ain't, Oh!

I soon sensed that poor Nobu was not sharing in the general merriment. His face was frozen in stony disdain, which turned to a kind of horrified bewilderment when the Lord High Executioner, a rather fetching Canadian lieutenant, sang about "our great Mikado, virtuous man," decreeing that "all who flirted, leered or winked should forthwith be beheaded, beheaded, beheaded . . ."

We returned to the hotel in a painful silence. I was half annoyed with Nobu and half embarrassed for having asked him to come along. It clearly had been a social error. Back at the hotel, he thanked me curtly for a wonderful evening, and made to go straight to his quarters. I couldn't let him go like that, so I asked him what was wrong (as though I didn't know). He turned round and said: "You think we are just joke?" I didn't know what to say. My protestations that *The Mikado* was not meant to have anything to do with the real Japan sounded weak, and to him, no doubt, insincere. So I said: "We must seem very strange to you." This made him even more furious.

For a long time, relations with Nobu remained in deep freeze. He was perfectly polite, of course, and went about his daily round of polishing and cleaning, but there were no more late-night conversations about Baron Charlus and the Princesse de Guermantes. I slipped him extra rations of Ritz and Velveeta to take back to his family, which he only accepted because family obligation (and hunger) took precedence over pride. But all my attempts to thaw the ice invariably met with a sullen silence. Until one day, inexplicably, I found a note slipped under my door. It was a poem, translated into Nobu's English. "For Sidney-san," it read:

> If just a moment, my dear friend,
> I could have watched together with you
> The blossoms of the wild cherries
> On the mountain with the hills,
> I would not be so lonely like this.

It was signed "Gentleman of Japan." Only much later did I realize it was a famous poem from *The Manyoshu*.

5

GENERAL WILLOUGHBY'S OFFICE was unusually sumptuous for an Army officer's. Not only was the floor covered in a thick Persian carpet, but there was a glass cabinet filled with rather delicate Meissen figurines of dancing ladies and shepherdesses. A small bronze bust of the German Kaiser stood on a brightly polished mahogany desk. I thought this was a bit odd, but put it down to the typical eccentricity of a professional military man.

Willoughby spoke softly, with the trace of a foreign accent, like a European aristocrat in a Hollywood picture. He bore a certain resemblance to Ronald Colman. After enquiring after his friend, Mr. Capra, the General wished to know whether I was comfortable in Tokyo. I told him about my arrangements. "Ah, the Continental Hotel," he said. "A trifle basic, I hear, but perfectly adequate, what? And what about your job? Satisfactory?" I told him the truth. Typing and stenography were all right for the time being, but I should very much like to be involved in something a bit more stimulating. "Oh, and what might that be, if I may be so bold?" I said I would like to be in cultural affairs. Perhaps it was the Meissen figurines, but I thought this might fall on sympathetic ears. A slight curl of his reddish lips suggested otherwise.

"Stay away from cultural affairs, Mr. Vanoven. All this talk of giving the Japanese democracy, Mr. Vanoven. Quatsch, I say, quatsch!

They have their own culture, an ancient culture. What is needed—and not only here, I might add—is discipline and order. We should be firm with them, and fair, firm and fair!" Here his hand came down firmly on his desktop, as though giving the wooden surface a thorough thrashing. "But they have their own ways, you know. The Oriental mind is not suited to individualism, and all that sort of nonsense. Unfortunately, we have too many fellows in our midst who are bent on stirring up trouble. These clever Jews from New York, they think they can come here and tell us what to do. Well, I'm telling you, young man, the General will have nothing of it, nothing of it. He is sometimes too kind. He treats the Orientals like his children. But this revolutionary stuff must be crushed at the bud, crushed at the bud! So stay away from culture, Vanoven. That's strictly for Jews and Communists. The Orientals have their own culture, a warrior culture. Perhaps we should do better to learn from them, instead of importing this Jewish rubbish from America."

I did what I always do when the topic of Jews comes up. I looked blank and tried to change the subject. My father's family was Jewish, though all that was left of his Jewishness was his invariable grumpiness on Christmas Day. It meant nothing to me, and I had no intention of bringing my father's background up in front of Willoughby. I told him I was certainly no Communist and would very much like to learn something from Japan. And I would be happiest to do something in culture and education, even if it meant starting at the bottom.

The curled lip was now a picture of utter disgust, as though the General had discovered a cockroach scuttling across his polished desktop. I didn't say so, but couldn't help wondering how this philistine could possibly have been a friend of Mr. Capra. "Well," he said, after rolling his eyes as if bracing himself for a disagreeable task. "If Frank sent you, you can't be all rotten. I promise nothing, you understand, nothing."

Two weeks later, I was in the Civil Censorship Detachment. The official aim of SCAP's new order in Japan was to see to it that the Japanese learned all about the benefits of democracy and free speech, but within certain limits. Our job was to make sure that those limits were observed. But since we didn't like to be called censors, our department was rarely called by its official name. We were simply part of Civil Information. I don't wish to leave the impression that we were cynical. General Willoughby was rather exceptional in his open disdain for the values we tried to impart. We were young in those days, and full of ideals. To lift this defeated nation from its feudal past seemed to us the noblest undertaking in the history of man. Instead of subjugating a conquered people, we would set them free. That is why we gave Japanese women the right to vote in elections, and why we let political prisoners, mostly Communists, out of jail, and encouraged the Japanese to organize trade unions, and made sure that school textbooks promoted democracy instead of militarism. It came as a great relief to the Japanese that we weren't going around raping their wives and daughters, and we were just as relieved that they weren't slashing us at every turn with their samurai swords. So, if we were keen to be their teachers, they were at least equally keen to be our students.

6

ALL THE BIG names in the Japanese movie establishment were there, in the main office of the Information Bureau at the General Headquarters of SCAP. I didn't know any of them then, of course. They might as well have been a group of businessmen, except for one or two who wore floppy hats, as though about to embark on a fishing trip. But if a bomb had been dropped on the former Daiichi Life Insurance Building on that gray September morning, all the most famous directors and producers in Japan would have been wiped out in one blast. After a great deal of formality and smiling goodwill, the Japanese sat down in rows of uncomfortable wooden chairs in front of a desk placed on a kind of dais. From that elevated position, Major Richard ("Dick") M. Murphy, a tall, ungainly man with red hair and pale Irish skin, went through the list of do's and don'ts in the production of postwar Japanese motion pictures. The translator, George Ishikawa, later became a good friend of mine.

The do's included "showing Japanese in all walks of life cooperating to build a peaceful society." Movies also had to reflect the new spirit of "individualism" and "democracy" and "respect for the rights of men and women." Notes were diligently taken by studio secretaries, while their bosses made throaty noises that might well have signified assent, but one could never be entirely sure.

Anything to do with the old spirit of "feudalism," or "militarism," was of course a no-no. Swordfight pictures, long a staple of the Japanese movie industry, were out, since they promoted "feudal loyalty." When one of the directors asked for other examples of unacceptable "feudalism," Murphy paused for a second, to ponder this question, and then mentioned images of what he called "Mount Fujiyama." This caused a degree of confusion in the audience. "But Fuji-san," growled one portly gentleman with oily hair, "is a symbol of our culture." The Major smiled, and said very slowly, to make sure everyone understood, whether or not they had any English: "That is why we are here together, my friends, to change the culture, to foster a new spirit of democracy." When another gentleman pointed out that the Fuji was his company crest, Major Murphy put it to him, with undiminished benevolence, that in that case perhaps the symbol should be changed to something else.

If the Japanese were irritated, or perhaps a little nonplussed, they didn't show it. On the contrary, most of them smiled back at the Major in the manner of grateful students. "Perhaps," said a slim young man in a gray suit, "Major Murphy might be kind enough to suggest a few themes that would best suit the new age of democracy." The Major, who had been a haberdasher in Black Foot, Idaho, in civilian life, was more than happy to oblige. "What about baseball?" he said, looking very proud of himself. "Now there's a splendid theme. Baseball is a democratic sport. We play it, and now you play it too." In fact, the Japanese had been playing it for many years before the war, but the Major wasn't to know that. "Ah," said the slim young man, whom I would soon get to know (it was the young Akira Kurosawa), "baseball." "What did he say?" asked the balding producer. "Baseball," Kurosawa replied, "films about baseball." "Ah, yes," said the producer, "baseball." And everyone smiled.

One of my happiest duties as secretary to Major Murphy was to visit the movie studios, where we spent many hours in smoky screening rooms vetting films for signs of "feudalism." Watching endless reels of Japanese movies was a trial for the Major, who invariably used these occasions to catch up on lost sleep. For me it was an education. George Ishikawa would explain the action, in the way of a traditional storyteller, while I was all eyes. Gradually I began to see patterns in Japanese moviemaking. What had been baffling before started to make sense under George's tutelage. It was a different way of looking, a different visual syntax, as it were: the discretion of Japanese camera angles, for example, keeping a distance even in scenes of great emotion, was actually more moving than the extreme close-ups which we are used to in the West. And stories meandered, following a poetic logic, instead of rushing from one scene to the next, tying up the narrative with a happy little knot. Japanese stories tended to be open-ended, like life.

I'm afraid all this was lost on Major Murphy. Like so many Americans, he had fine ideals but no imagination. A born missionary, he never tired of lecturing the Japanese about great abstractions. I bet he even dreamed about "democracy" and "civic engagement." Every so often, a new notion of how to implement these fine ideals would take hold of him, and become an obsession.

One of these obsessions came to him when a script was submitted to our office about the romantic travails of a young woman. The story was unremarkable. It might have been a remake of many similar pictures. The girl's father wants her to marry the son of his boss. She insists on marrying the man of her own choice. True love prevails. Murphy approved. Indeed, he was over the moon. "At last," he cried, "the perfect expression of the new spirit of equality!" He loved the script so much that he summoned the filmmakers to his office for a special meeting. The director, Ichiro Miyagawa, was a veteran of some distinction. He listened patiently as Murphy gave him advice on how to make the script even stronger. Why, said Murphy, whose face was shining with enthusiasm, did one never see Japanese men and women kiss in public? Wasn't this a sign of feudalism? After all, he said, getting more and more agitated, "even the Japanese must kiss in private, so why be so sneaky about it? Why beat around the bush? Democracy is all about love, after all—open love, wholesome love, love of a spouse, love of family. That's why it's so important to include a scene of the couple kissing!"

Miyagawa, whose previous work was less known for its romantic content than for its deftly staged scenes of fighting samurai, questioned whether the Japanese public was quite ready for such an unusual innovation. People might feel embarrassed and laugh. Murphy waved away these objections, as though addressing a stubborn child. "No, no, no," he said, "it's up to you to teach the public how to change their ways and build a democratic society." Miyagawa's producer, a small man with highly polished black shoes, patted the director on the knee and said something soothing in Japanese. "What did he say?" asked Murphy. George translated that they would do their best to make a democratic film. "Good," said Murphy, "good, very good. Gentlemen, together we'll get there. I just know we will. It's been a pleasure to do business with you."

Less than a month later, Murphy and I traveled through the Tokyo suburbs in an Army car to see the movie actually being shot at the Oriental Peace Entertainment Company. The suburbs were slightly less ruined than the central parts of the city. But in many cases, white concrete storehouses were all that survived of what once had been fine mansions. The charcoal-burning buses were so full that people hung on the outside, like grapes to a vine. Men and women fluttered their paper fans to extract some coolness from the humid air, and swat away the insects that swarmed around the craters filled with stagnant water. Josephine Baker was singing somewhere on a radio set.

The Oriental Peace Studios, located near the Tama River, were the largest in Japan. Men with white kerchiefs wrapped around their heads were running in and out of low gray concrete buildings. Everyone seemed to be in a tremendous rush. It was like watching a speeded-up movie, as though the Japanese couldn't make films fast enough to still the national craving for motion pictures.

To get to Studio A, where *Sounds of Spring* was being shot, we had to pass by a remarkable reconstruction of a ruined Tokyo street, set around a bomb crater filled with water. The ruined houses, made of painted wood, looked disturbingly real. A handpump was inserted into the sump to produce noxious-looking bubbles in the slimy surface of the stagnant pool. An old shoe, a discarded doll, a broken umbrella, and other bits of flotsam had been artfully placed in the water. A man was hunched over a guitar. A fire hose was spraying water over the set to simulate a summer rainstorm. A pan-pan girl with piled-up hair, bright red lipstick, and high heels stood outside the facade of a neon-lit dance hall, from the back of which a handsome young man in a Hawaiian shirt and a white plastic belt came rushing in whenever the director cried: "Start!" A popular ballad was playing in the background. Apart from the large old prewar camera, the sound boom dangling from a bamboo pole, the lights, and the director in his floppy white hat, this scene might have been taking place in any backstreet of Tokyo.

Anxious to get inside the studio building, Murphy strode past the set with barely a glance. I made an awkward half bow at the director, whom I recognized as the slim young man at the meeting in GHQ. He smiled and nodded back. But Murphy told me to hurry up, so I was unable to watch any more of this intriguing scene being shot.

Inside Studio A, the air was even more stifling than outside on the open set. When the lights were on, the heat was suffocating. Miyagawa, the director, stood up when he saw us, and ordered an assistant to place two chairs beside his. The set, bathed in bright light, was a small garden outside a wooden Japanese house. The potted tree and bamboo grove were splashed with water to keep them looking fresh.

In this artificial garden stood a young man in a white summer suit with rather too much makeup on and a petite young woman in a flowered dress and white ankle socks. She looked familiar, but I couldn't place her. To prevent the actors' makeup from running in the heat, a girl was busily dabbing their foreheads with a handkerchief. Miyagawa clapped his hands, called for quiet, and said something to the actors. George whispered that this was a rehearsal. Someone handed us a script in English. The lines went: *Man:* "I love you. For eternity I love you." *Woman:* "You promise me, never let me go." *Man:* "We will always be free."

The actress had remarkably large eyes, which she opened even wider when she spoke her lines, while puckering her lips to receive her lover's kiss. Miyagawa leaned forward in his chair, his face creased with concentration. He clapped his hands again. A sharp word was addressed to the actress, who nodded vigorously, while apologizing for her clumsiness. George explained that she should close her eyes when they kissed. They went through the scene several more times, the young man stooping to take her into his arms, and the girl closing her eyes in blissful anticipation, though always stopping short of actual contact. I was trying to think where I had seen her face before. I asked George who she was. He told me she was very famous and that her name was Yoshiko Yamaguchi. The name meant nothing to me.

"Okay, let's go. *Honban!*" said Miyagawa. This word I knew. It meant something like "the real thing." The actors received a final dab with the handkerchief. Miss Yamaguchi looked toward Miyagawa, clearly disturbed about something. He made a reassuring gesture and barked an order. The girl with the handkerchief rushed to the stage. In her right hand, now encased in a white glove, she held two tiny pieces of gauze, which had a faint chemical odor. Yamaguchi closed her eyes and offered her mouth to the girl, who carefully inserted the gauze between her lips, as though it were a host.

"*Hai* starto!" cried Miyagawa. The actor did his best with the lines. They embraced, his lips briefly brushing against her lips wrapped in gauze. Murphy was smiling, like a benevolent priest. I didn't really appreciate it then, but we were witnesses to a great moment: the first kiss in the history of Japanese cinema.

The release of tension was palpable. Miss Yamaguchi did a little jig on the spot. The actor, whose name was Shiro Okuno, grinned and scratched the back of his neatly coiffed head. Even Miyagawa looked more relaxed, as he introduced us to his stars. "Hi," said Miss Yamaguchi, as she shook my hand. "Nice to meet you. I like Americans." "Well," I replied, slightly taken aback, "I like Japanese." This elicited a nervous titter. "Nooo," she said, in protest. Perhaps she thought I was being patronizing. Murphy then took her hand in both of his and said: "It's sure great to meet you, Yamaguchi-san. Our boys in intelligence know all about you. They all know your song, 'China Nights,' from Japanese class. They love it, just love it."

"Ri Koran!" I said. "You're Ri Koran. I adored your movie." There was a moment of silence, as though I had said something gauche. Perhaps I had insulted her by getting it wrong. But I was sure it was her. How could I have forgotten that face, those eyes? Of course, actors always look larger on screen. Like a starstruck fool, I just stood there, staring at her. "Ri Koran," she said softly, "was indeed my name once, but Ri Koran no longer exists. She died in September 1945. I am Yoshiko Yamaguchi now, and I ask for your kind indulgence."

So the "Chinese girl" Frank Capra had admired was actually a Japanese. Why would she have had a Chinese name? Like so much in Japan, it was all rather baffling. In fact, to me, before I came to Japan, Asiatics were just Asiatics. I couldn't really tell the difference between a Chinese, a Korean, or a Japanese. Now I fancied that I could. But Yamaguchi didn't look typically Japanese. She just looked, well, Asiatic.

7

PEOPLE OFTEN ASK me how the Japanese could have changed so suddenly from our most ferocious enemies, ready to fight us to the death, to the friendly, docile, peace-loving people we came across after the war was over. It was as if some magic switch had been pulled to transform a nation of Mr. Hydes into a nation of Dr. Jekylls. We expected to be met with a hundred million poisoned bamboo spears; what we got instead was the Recreation and Amusement Association offering Japanese girls to Allied soldiers—that is, until our own puritans decided to ban that type of intercourse.

There might be a perfectly practical explanation for this kind of behavior. Aware of what their own troops had done to others, the Japanese wanted to make sure we wouldn't pay them back in kind. To many Westerners this simply confirmed a typically Japanese talent for deception; they were a nation of double-faced liars, thinking one thing and saying the opposite, facing the outside world with masques and phony smiles.

But I don't think so. I believe the Japanese were honest in their own way. They had genuinely believed in fighting a holy war for their Emperor, and now they believed with equal sincerity in the freedoms we promised after the fighting was over. Westerners, believing in one God, prize logic. We hate contradictions. To be authentic is to be consistent. But the Oriental mind doesn't work that way; it can happily contain two opposite views at the same time. There are many gods in the Orient, and the Japanese mind is infinitely flexible. Morality is a question of proper behavior at the right time and place. Since the concept of sin simply doesn't exist in the Japanese mind, it is, in a profound sense, innocent. It was appropriate to die for the Emperor before 1945, and it was just as appropriate to believe in democracy after the war. One form of behavior is no more or less sincere than the other. In this floating world of illusions, everything depends on the circumstances. You might see this as a philosophy of deceit. I prefer to call it wisdom.

None of this came to me at once. It took many stumblings and false steps for me to even begin to penetrate the thickets of the Japanese mind. One thing that struck me almost as soon as I set foot in Japan was the lack of nostalgia, or even regret for the destruction of the visible past. The following story might serve as an illustration.

One day I was walking up the steps of Ueno Hill, the highest point in the flatlands bordering the Sumida River. You could see for miles around, a vista of neatly piled up rubble and cheap wooden houses with the occasional temple roof and stone lantern to show what had been there before that night in March 1945, when much of the city was laid to waste by our B-29s.

One of the survivors, right where I was standing, was the bronze statue of Takamori Saigo, the samurai rebel with the bulging eyes and thick eyebrows. He challenged the guns of the Westernized Meiji Army in a heroic and suicidal last stand in 1877. His samurai troops were armed with nothing but spears and swords. A hopeless enterprise, of course. According to legend (and who would wish to challenge that?), Saigo slit his own stomach in an honorable warrior's death. Japanese still regard their hero with immense affection and respect. He is remembered, among other things, for the extraordinary size of his balls.

So there he was on that cold and blustery day, Saigo of the big balls, standing watch like a sturdy peasant in the short kimono and straw sandals of his native region. At his feet was a swarm of homeless urchins, passing around cigarette butts, and eating whatever scraps of food they had managed to scrounge. The boys were dressed in shorts and tattered T-shirts, despite the cold. A few lucky ones had wooden sandals. And the truly fortunate ones found places to sleep in the warm corridors of the subway station at the bottom of the hill. I saw one little boy, who looked no older than five but might well have been more than ten, hold a rat by its tail, waving it in front of another child's face, to frighten him, or perhaps to show off what they were going to have for dinner that night.

God only knows how these boys had survived the terrible night of the bombings. People who didn't melt or burn in the firestorm choked for lack of oxygen. Women tried to protect their faces from the "Flower Baskets," courtesy of General Curtis LeMay, by wrapping bundles of cloth around their heads. Many of them caught fire and ran around like human torches, their screams muffled by the roaring flames. Others tried to escape by jumping into the river, only to be boiled alive or catch fire as soon as they raised their heads above the scalding water. All that remained of Ueno, or of Asakusa, a few miles farther north, were the concrete remnants of a few large department stores in a vast black hecatomb containing the charred bones of at least a hundred thousand people.

My companion on this walk in Ueno Park was a distinguished old film director, temporarily out of work, because our department didn't approve of the "feudal" character of his movies. He was a specialist in period pictures set in old Edo, stories of doomed love affairs and fatal loyalties. Kenkichi Hanazono was his name. He spoke a little French, since he had spent some time in France as a young art student, and wore a shabby dark blue kimono with frayed sleeves. As we gazed upon the ruins of Ueno, he pointed out some of his favorite places that had disappeared in the firestorms: the graceful wooden shrines of Yamashita; the Buddhist temples behind Kiyomizu Hall; the Sakuraya teahouse, the scene in happier times of illicit love affairs and legendary samurai battles. All gone up in smoke. Like a melancholy stork, Hanazono observed the wreckage. I felt sadness and shame. Should I apologize for what my country had done? I decided against that. It might embarrass him. But I tried to share his grief over what was lost by looking solemn, when, suddenly, I heard a chuckle, then a loud guffaw, then convulsive laughter. Gripping my arm, Hanazono was almost hysterical, tears of mirth streaming down his face, as though the destruction of his city were a great joke. I didn't know what to say, or how to look. I couldn't very well start laughing with him. When the hilarity had subsided somewhat, Hanazono turned to me, and noticed my look of consternation. "Sidney-san," he said, still chuckling, "*c'est pas grave.*" He tapped the side of his head: "You cannot destroy my city. It's all in here."

I admired this man more than I had ever admired anyone before. I grasped the foolishness of our Western illusions, our idiotic hubris of wanting to build cities to last forever. For everything we do is provisional, everything we build will eventually turn to dust. To believe otherwise is just vanity. The Oriental mind, more sophisticated than ours, has grasped this. This floating world is but an illusion. That is why it was of no consequence to Hanazono that the Tokyo of his youth was no more than a memory. Even if every building had still been there, the city would no longer have been the same. Everything shifts, everything changes. To accept that is to be enlightened. I cannot claim to have reached that stage of wisdom. I still craved permanence of some kind.

I decided to track down some of Hanazono's prewar films, especially *Tales of a Woman of Pleasure*, a classic picture admired by all

Japanese lovers of the cinema. Like many prewar Japanese classics, Hanazono's works were hard to find. There were very few copies around. All his films had been made for the same company, called Far Eastern Pictures, whose studios were located in the same western suburbs as Oriental Peace. My contact there was Kashiwara-san, a silver-haired fellow in a blue serge suit. These studio executives always got nervous when they received a call from the Information Bureau, for it could only mean trouble. Censoring any of Hanazono's films was of course the last thing on my mind, but Kashiwara couldn't be sure of that, so he was rubbing his hands anxiously as he came out of his office to meet me.

Kashiwara politely inspected my business card and despite the chilly weather broke into a sweat. His cup of tea remained untouched. Sipping from mine, I asked him about Hanazono's pictures: *Tales of a Woman of Pleasure, Weeds East of the River, Yoshiwara Story.* Kashiwara hissed through his teeth. "Would I be able to see these films?" I asked. Could he possibly arrange a screening? Kashiwara smiled and asked me why I should have an interest in such worthless old movies.

Although he spoke English, I wondered whether I had heard right. "Worthless? But Hanazono is a great director." Kashiwara shook his head. "Very old-fashioned," he said. "Old-fashioned? In what sense old-fashioned?" Kashiwara smiled, with perhaps a hint of triumph. "Not democratic."

I must confess that at moments like this I felt the power of my position as a representative of the victorious Allied forces. The feeling was not entirely unpleasant. It was, after all, rather amazing that I, Sidney Vanoven, a nobody from Bowling Green, Ohio, would be sitting here at a major movie studio in Tokyo, Japan, ordering up film screenings whenever I wanted. On this occasion it gave me license to vent my displeasure.

"Not democratic?" I cried. "Well, I'll be the judge of that." When could Kashiwara-san arrange a screening? Perhaps we should start with *Tales of a Woman of Pleasure*. He dismissed the thought with a wave of his hands. "Please understand that we are abiding by the new rules. We are now a democratic country, thanks to you." He closed his eyes and bowed his head, as a token of his gratitude.

I was wondering why he was so eager to hide these movies. Why the hell wouldn't he show them to me? What was he ashamed of? Was he trying to protect some of Japan's great masterpieces from an American censor? I felt insulted and wasn't going to stand for this nonsense any longer. I'm afraid I lost my patience with this oily little man. I behaved like a boorish American. I shouted at him: "Just show me the damned movie!" Kashiwara stared at me, suddenly very calm, his face a blank slate.

He stood up slowly from his desk, smiled, and said: "Please, let me show you something." At last, I thought, I had got through to him. Now I would be able to see Hanazono's masterpieces. We walked through the long white corridor, past the open doors of offices where men in suits were working away in clouds of cigarette smoke. We came to the back of the building, where I thought the screening rooms might be. Kashiwara invited me to look out the window. I saw a large open space with low gray buildings and bits and pieces of various film sets scattered about: half a Japanese-style house, a castle wall made of plywood. A handsome young man in a white suit and panama hat was smoking a cigarette while a young woman applied makeup to his face. Then they both disappeared into one of the buildings. Farther in the distance was the silvery ribbon of the Tama River. There were puffs of smoke rising from a number of large bonfires near the riverbank.

"There," said Kashiwara, "*Yoshiwara Story, Tales of a Woman of Pleasure*, all the feudal films." For the first time he looked perfectly relaxed, even triumphant. He gave me a thumbs-up sign. "Okay," he said. "A-okay."

8

THE PREMIERE OF *Sounds of Spring*, at the Ginza Bunka Theater, was by Hollywood standards a subdued affair. But Major Murphy thought so highly of the first Japanese film to feature a kissing scene that he wished, as a gesture of goodwill, to contribute something to the party afterwards at the Imperial Hotel. Apart from a gift from the Information Bureau of several crates of Pabst Blue Ribbon beer, Murphy had planned to stage a demonstration of square dancing after the screening. Murphy was an enthusiast of square dancing. A proud son of Idaho, he liked to think that the official dance of his state should be popular, and indeed of great benefit, everywhere. He had tried to introduce square dancing to the citizens of a village in Shikoku, where he had, for a brief time, enjoyed absolute authority as the chief military administrator. Square dancing, in his view, perfectly embodied the new spirit of sexual equality in Japan, and was a fitting expression of democracy. The Japanese movie folks were no doubt somewhat alarmed, but Murphy's good intentions were so patently clear that no one had the heart to protest.

Many of our top brass turned out in full dress uniform. Not "Susan" himself, of course, for SCAP never descended from the Olympian heights of his residence in the old U.S. Embassy, where, rumor had it, the General spent every night alone watching Hollywood pictures. SCAP liked westerns. Especially westerns with Gary Cooper. I had heard it said that the American Mikado watched *The General Died at Dawn* more than ten times. But Willoughby, not generally noted for his love of the movies, was there with a dashing young officer in tow.

Yoshiko Yamaguchi stood out in the crowd like a tropical bird, looking absolutely gorgeous in a red and gold kimono. We all rose to our feet when she made her grand entrance, accompanied by Okuno, her co-star, and an older man whom I didn't recognize. Both men were smartly turned out in tuxedos. The older man acknowledged the presence of various other guests with a slight bow of his silvery head. I tried to catch Yamaguchi's eye as she walked past my seat, but she didn't recognize me. I know I shouldn't have done that. I felt rather disgusted with myself, behaving like some besotted movie fan standing in line for an autograph. Why should she have recognized me? But I couldn't help myself. It's the way I am. Hopelessly starstruck, I'm afraid.

Apart from the divine Miss Y., there was nothing very memorable about the picture itself. I had already seen it anyway, at a private screening for the censorship board. Naturally, the film passed without a hitch. There was, much to my amusement, a sharp intake of breath in the theater during the famous kissing scene, followed, rather curiously I thought, by a round of applause, as if we had been watching a pair of acrobats or performing seals. Kissing, after all, is not *that* hard. Perhaps the audience felt a sense of relief after all the suspense. But after the Great Kiss, the movie rather petered out.

The square dancing, on the other hand, was highly amusing. It took place in the Imperial Hotel ballroom, a huge space furnished with rather inferior copies of Louis XVI chairs. Murphy had trained a number of men and women on the staff of our department for many weeks to make sure they gave a good account of themselves. He had also taken a keen interest in the proper attire. Several Japanese women from our secretary pool were dressed in long wide skirts and peasant blouses. The men wore bright red Western shirts with bolo ties and white cowboy hats. I can't think where Murphy had found this gear, which made the Japanese men look undernourished, since the sleeves were too long and the collars too wide. When everyone had taken his or her place, the band, consisting of a fiddler, a bass player, and a fat man strumming a banjo, struck up a hillbilly tune. As the dancers crossed, and sashayed, and U-turned, Murphy, always the diligent teacher, announced the names of the various dances to his bewildered audience. "This is what we call the California Twirl!" he went, his face a picture of joy, "and this the Box in the Gnat!"

I don't know what the Japanese made of it all. Most of the men stood around in groups, chatting and drinking their beers. Miyagawa, the director, had turned his back on the proceedings. One man, a studio executive of some kind, had gone red in the face after downing several beers, and tried to enter into the spirit of things by shouting "Yeah!" at regular intervals.

"Where is Miss Yamaguchi?" cried Murphy. She was spotted in a corner, talking to the older man who had escorted her into the theater. "May I have the honor?" Murphy enquired with a courtly bow. She opened her eyes wide and graciously declined. "I cannot," she said. "You're a showgirl!" boomed Murphy. "You can learn." "I'm too shy," she protested. He grabbed her by the sleeve of her kimono and said to the older man: "You don't mind if I borrow her, do you?" The man said nothing but smiled indulgently as though appeasing a dangerous drunk. Once more the band struck up a tune, the women hiked up their hooped skirts, the Japanese executive shouted "Yeah!" and Murphy guided, not without skill, the kimonoed Yamaguchi across the dance floor.

"Yamaguchi-san," I said, after she had been released at long last from Murphy's grip. She turned round and this time she recognized me: "Sid-san, isn't it? *O-genki desu ka?*" I replied that I was very well, and added that I had loved the movie. She gave me a radiant smile. "It's so good that we can celebrate together. Japan is such a small place, you know. But this is a real international occasion. Thank you so much for helping us so kindly." I wasn't quite sure what she meant. Helping you to do what exactly, Miss Yamaguchi? My eye was drawn to Murphy, who was busy slapping Yamaguchi's older companion on the back. "To be international. You can teach us so many things. Where are you from, Sid-san?"

I told her that I was from Ohio, but had worked in Hollywood. This made me sound far more important than I was, naturally, but I was keen to make an impression. It looked as though I had succeeded. "Hollywood," said Yamaguchi, gleefully clasping her hands together, "I love Hollywood! Gary Cooper, Charlie Chaplin, Deanna Durbin! Have you seen *Because of Him*?" I replied that alas I had not, but had she seen *The Bride Wore Boots*? "Of course, Barbara Stanwyck! I know we are going to be very good friends, Sid-san."

I felt like dancing all the way back to the Continental, which was actually just round the corner from the movie theater. I couldn't believe my luck. I had made friends with one of the great stars of the cinema, celebrated all over the Far East. As soon as I got into the hotel, I called for Nobu. He had been asleep and was rather annoyed to be woken up.

"Guess what?" I said.

"What?"

"Guess who I met tonight?"

"I don't know."

"You'll never guess."

"Guess what?"

"Yoshiko Yamaguchi."

"Who?"

"Yoshiko Yamaguchi. You know, Ri Koran!"

"Oh."

Nobu was not at all impressed. He wasn't very interested in the movies, preferring French literature and German philosophers. Besides, Ri Koran was a name from the past, a reminder of enthusiasms he preferred to forget. He also thought she was vulgar, or as he liked to put it, "in bad taste," something he regarded with a feeling of horror that I was unable to share. Too much good taste is the enemy of great art, I've always believed.

9

THERE IS NOTHING vulgar or in bad taste about Kamakura. Only an hour away by train, the old samurai capital is centuries removed from the neon-lit garishness of Tokyo. People often find Tokyo intolerably ugly. Well, let them think so. I adore its unashamed ugliness. There is no pretense about Tokyo; the artifice is openly, brazenly artificial. But ever since I was first introduced by my friend Carl to its thirteenth-century temples and shrines, the great Kamakura Buddha, the Zen gardens of Kencho-ji and Engaku-ji, Kamakura has been my refuge from twentieth-century madness. Kamakura was saved from the bombings by its insignificance. It has not played a part in the nation's affairs since the fourteenth century, when the power shifted back to Kyoto, and Kamakura went into a state of aristocratic somnolence. That's why it survived with all its treasures intact. Even General Curtis LeMay, usually so quick on the draw, saw no point in destroying a place that to him was of no consequence at all.

I liked to lose myself in the tart smells of temple incense and pine trees, which bore a curious resemblance to the scented salts my mother used when she bathed me as a child. And I always stopped by Mr. Ohki's store behind Komachi Street, which smelled of camphor wood and old books. Although one might, with a little luck, find a beautifully carved seventeenth-century netsuke there, or a red lacquer bowl of the late Edo Period, Ohki-san specialized in traditional woodcuts. He spoke old-fashioned British English. Before the war, many of his clients had been connoisseurs from Great Britain. "It's hard to make ends meet these days," he told me with a weary shrug. "The Japanese no longer care for these old things." He served me a cup of green tea and patiently answered all my questions. I wanted to learn about everything, from the art of the early monochrome woodblock prints to the painted fans of the Muromachi Period. He would bring out box after box of prints: a perfect set of erotic prints by Koryusai, a first edition print of an early Eisho, as elegant as an Utamaro, but with more delicacy. We talked about art, about literature, about history. Once, to illustrate a point about the Sino-Japanese War of 1895, he showed me prints of battle scenes: handsome Japanese soldiers charging in their black Prussian-style uniforms, bloody Chinese corpses at their feet. "Frightfully vulgar, really," he commented, before gingerly restoring them to their box. "You notice how they no longer used the old vegetable dyes."

This time, however, I had no time to lose, even to see Ohki-san. I had been invited to have lunch with the divine Miss Y., who was staying at the home of a movie producer named Kawamura. The house was in the northern part of town, a plush square mile of traditional wooden houses nestled between the pine trees on a hill. The air was filled with the trilling sounds of early spring—the plum blossoms were just out. It was as if the war had never happened.

Yoshiko (she insisted that I call her by her first name) was dressed in a purple dress and furry pink slippers. We were joined by Kawamura in a freshly matted room decorated with a simple arrangement of camellias and a Chinese-style scroll painting of a bush warbler. I immediately recognized Kawamura as the older man at the film premiere. Something about him, the elegance of his tweed suit, the sheen on his silver hair, the way he discreetly sized me up through his large tortoiseshell glasses, made me feel a little shabby in his presence, as if I were wearing the wrong kind of shoes. Yoshiko called him "Papa," which invited the assumption that there was a "Mama" in the house. As indeed there was. Later, when luncheon was served in the Western-style dining room, a short, smiling lady in a sky blue kimono with cherry blossom patterns appeared. She did not say much, but what little she said was spoken in excellent Oxford English, a little like Ohki-san's.

The dining room was decorated with a few paintings in the Impressionist style. I couldn't make out who the painters were. Delicious Kamakura prawns, followed by tender veal cutlets, were impeccably served by a maid in white gloves. Kawamura was proud of his wines. We drank a German white followed by a French red. "You must excuse us, Mr. Vanoven, for this shamefully inadequate meal," Madame Kawamura purred. "You see, we are living in rather straitened circumstances. Japan is such a poor country now." Her husband, looking grave, added that it was all due to that dreadful war, a terrible error, which ought never to have occurred. "Let's not talk about that," said Yoshiko, "we now have peace. And we're all here happy together, all because of you, Papa." Kawamura murmured something in the way of a polite objection. Madame Kawamura examined the paintings on the wall, perhaps checking whether they were hanging straight.

Since I'm an American, I have never learned to disguise my curiosity in the way the Japanese do, so I asked Yoshiko about the end of the war. Wasn't she in China? How had Ri Koran, the star of *China Nights,* become Yamaguchi Yoshiko again? "I'm sure you'll have some more wine, Mr. Vanoven," said Kawamura, as he picked up the bottle. Yoshiko pulled a tragic face. "It was the worst time of my life," she said, her eyes trained on Kawamura.

"War is just awful," Kawamura interjected, "the way it turns men into beasts."

"That's so right," said Yoshiko. "Let me tell you what happened to me, Sid-san. Me, who was born in China, and loved China as my own country, I was arrested as a traitor. Can you imagine how hurtful that was for me? A traitor, me. Of course, I was a Japanese, but China was my home. And they were going to execute me for being a traitor, for making propaganda for the enemy. I never meant to do China any harm, Sid-san. You must understand that. The date had already been set. In a stadium, they were going to shoot me in front of a crowd. It was a nightmare, Sid-san, an absolute nightmare." She dabbed her eyes with her napkin.

"But how could you be a traitor if you were Japanese?" I said, sounding rather silly, even to myself.

"Of course—" she started, her voice choking with emotion. Kawamura softly patted her knee to ease her distress. I sensed some impatience on the part of Mrs. Kawamura and I felt suddenly embarrassed. It was unforgivably gauche to have brought up these misfortunes. I felt myself breaking into a sweat.

"Of course I am Japanese, but the Chinese wouldn't believe me. They thought I was one of them. After all, I *was* Ri Koran, Li Xianglan." She gazed at Kawamura with her adoring wide eyes. "But thanks to you, Papa, I pulled through."

"I did nothing," he demurred.

"Yes, yes, you stood by me at the worst time of my life. You arranged everything."

I waited for more. Not for long. "Mama had evacuated as soon as the awful war was over, with little Chieko," Yoshiko explained. "Papa, bless his heart, kindly consented to stay with me, to make sure I was all right. Oh, it was a terrible ordeal, confined in that ghastly little house in Shanghai, and later in a prison camp, being insulted by ruffians. I thought I would never survive it."

At this point Madame Kawamura excused herself and said there was something she had to attend to.

With all this talk of Papa and Mama, I couldn't help wondering about Yoshiko's own family circumstances. Again, with typical American brazenness, I asked her. Were her parents also in China at the end of the war? Yoshiko looked down at her feet and said nothing.

"Your father was, was——" offered Kawamura, before giving up on his train of thought. Yoshiko sighed. "Well, thank goodness for the Jewish girl," said Kawamura. As always when that word came up, I felt a slight jolt, forcing me to pay special attention.

"The Jewish girl?"

"Yes. Masha," whispered Yoshiko.

Masha, it turned out, had grown up with Yoshiko in Manchuria. Close to the end of the war, she suddenly turned up in Shanghai, just as Yoshiko was giving a concert. Without her, Yoshiko probably would have been tried by a war crimes tribunal and executed. To prove that she was Japanese, and not a Chinese traitor, Yoshiko needed her birth certificate, but her parents, who kept that all-important document, were stuck in Peking. Yoshiko was imprisoned, and Kawamura wasn't allowed to leave Shanghai. So Masha offered to go to Peking and find the documents that would save Yoshiko from a traitor's death. Somehow Masha tracked down Yoshiko's parents, got hold of the relevant papers, and smuggled then back to Shanghai inside a Japanese doll. A few days later, Yoshiko and Kawamura were on a boat back home. She never heard from Masha again. Kawamura reassured her. "She'll be all right," he said. "The Jews always take care of their own." I paid due attention, but said nothing.

"I felt so lonely," said Yoshiko, her face a picture of suffering, "standing on deck watching the lights of Shanghai slowly disappear. Do you remember, Papa? Nothing but darkness and the sound of the waves. I thought I might never see the country of my birth again. That is when I knew that Ri Koran had died."

"But Ri Koran is still alive in the movies," I ventured. I had meant to flatter, but with sincerity.

Instead of expressing pleasure, Yoshiko bowed her head and burst out: "Stupid, stupid, stupid!" She said this with the sudden passion of a young girl, pummeling her chest. "Why did I allow myself to be deceived by the militarists? Unlike you, Papa. I was a tool in their hands. The militarists, and their terrible war, they made me into an accomplice, forcing me to be in those hateful propaganda films. Do you know how humiliating that was for me, Sid-san? To be an accomplice in that cruel war. Do you understand how awful that was?"

"Now, now," said Kawamura. And turning to me: "Another glass of wine?"

"Perhaps," Yoshiko continued, "I should never be in the movies again." She said this with a look of resolve. Then, smiling: "From now on I am just Yamaguchi Yoshiko, and I will dedicate my life to peace. Yes, that's what I'll do."

"Now, now," repeated Kawamura. "I hear that you have worked in Hollywood, Mr. Vanoven. It's been a long time since I've been there. Tell me, whom do you know in Hollywood?"

I mentioned the only famous name I knew. Kawamura looked at me with interest: "Ah, yes, Frank Capra, a very fine director."

Yoshiko smiled, pleased perhaps that I had made an impression on Kawamura, and said: "Is he knowable?" I wasn't sure if she was addressing her question to me or to her patron. In the event, neither of us gave her an immediate answer.

10

L IFE AS A censor had its small compensations. I had the invaluable opportunity to see many films in their original state, before politics or morality forced us to wield the dreaded scissors. Not that all the movies we saw were really worth seeing, but sometimes we were lucky enough to be the first to witness the birth of a masterpiece. One of them was the picture being made when Major Murphy and I visited the Oriental Peace Studios. Kurosawa's *Drunken Angel* was a revelation: the pathos of the young hoodlum, humanized by his fear of dying, and of the alcoholic doctor, redeemed by his compassion. Above all, the atmosphere I had come to know so well: the dance halls; the black markets; the poor, squalid, violent life in a ruined city that reeked of humanity. What had looked like a chaotic jumble of lights and sound booms and plywood facades on the studio set had miraculously come to life on the screen. I could only marvel at the magic of film, in the way a religious person marvels at stained-glass windows and candlelit saints in a place of worship. That is what the cinema was to me, a kind of chapel, where I worshipped my saints in the dark, except that my saints were not really saints; they were as human as could be. The transubstantiation of light projected through celluloid to reveal life itself, that was the miracle of cinema.

Mifune, as the gangster, is all brutish swagger on the surface, but oh so vulnerable, almost childlike, underneath. It is this quality in

Japanese men that I adore, in the movies and in life. Surrendering my-self to them, worshipping their soft, hairless, adolescent skin, running my hand along their supple thighs, burying my nose in the delicate black tuft above their genitals—this, for me, is a way of sloughing off my adult self and finding my way back to a state of innocence, the natural state of the Japanese, but one that must be regained by us Westerners, corrupted by the knowledge of sin.

Drunken Angel was not the film that caught Murphy's imagina-tion, however. He didn't really see the point of it. Mifune Toshiro, to me, is the perfect Japanese male. But all Murphy could say was: "Who cares about just another dumb gangster." Worst of all, from his point of view, the movie didn't have a message, or not one that he could eas-ily discern. Nor did it have the kind of uplifting conclusion that Mur-phy liked, the happy ending that warmed cold hearts. What stirred his enthusiasm was a different kind of movie altogether. One in particular became a cause célèbre and subsequently left its faded fingerprint on history. The movie was called *Time of Darkness,* produced by a well-known figure at the time, Nobuo Hotta. I came to admire this brave intellectual, with his gaunt, saintly face. He didn't much care for ap-pearances; his suits were disheveled, his hair unkempt. But Hotta was one of those rare individuals who never compromised with power. He stood up for his beliefs, not all of which I shared, but no matter, he was a man of principle. Before the war, he had been a well-known Marxist, and everyone knew how much he had suffered for it once the milita-rists took over Japan.

From the very start, Murphy had taken a personal interest in the picture, to the point of going in to see the rushes and suggesting im-provements. I'm not sure these suggestions were always welcomed, but the Japanese at least pretended to be grateful for his interventions. Hotta was a thinker, Murphy not at all. But somehow the two man-aged to get along. They were both idealists. Although their ultimate notions of the ideal society may not have been the same, a shared commitment to democracy was enough to paper over their differences. Seeing Murphy thump his frail Japanese friend on the back always made me wince, but Hotta didn't seem to mind this at all. He liked the Americans for their "frankness," a word that I always suspected could also be taken to mean a lack of subtlety, or good manners. To be frank was to be unsophisticated.

Murphy was certainly frank. One small matter of dispute still sticks in my mind. Murphy thought the title of the movie was too gloomy. "Sure," he said, "there were dark pages in all our history books, but shouldn't we include something about the present, offer some hope for the future?" His face took on the beatific glow of a visionary. "What about *Light After Darkness,* or *After Darkness, Liberation,* or"—he had to think hard here—"*A Hard Lesson Learnt?*" But Hotta resisted these suggestions, very politely, always making sure to thank Murphy for his excellent advice. He had not resisted the Japanese militarists only to become a toady to the Americans. "Do you know how I got this scar?" he asked us one afternoon, as he pushed out the left side of his face for our inspection. I hadn't noticed it before, but now I saw it clearly, a pinkish stripe running from the corner of his left eye to his jawline. "A little present from our Special Higher Police, just because I wouldn't trample on my deepest convictions." So *Time of Darkness* it was.

Time of Darkness was in fact a documentary picture constructed very much like Capra's *Know Your Enemy,* except that this was even harder-hitting. Using some of the same footage that we selected for our movie—the Nanking Massacre, the bombing of Shanghai, the kamikaze attacks—*Time of Darkness* went much further than we did in blaming the Japanese Emperor himself for the war. In one extraordinary sequence, a photograph of the Emperor in military uniform slowly dissolves into a postwar portrait of him in a suit and tie, looking into the camera a bit sheepishly, like a timid bureaucrat, even as the narrator informs us that the Japanese people want to put their war criminals on trial.

I mentioned Hotta to Yoshiko one night in Tokyo. It was after her concert for Allied troops at the Hibiya Theater. The place was packed, of course. In the first half of her show, Yoshiko was dressed in a red, white, and blue kimono, and sang Japanese numbers like "The Apple Song," then a popular hit, and "Tokyo Boogie-Woogie." But she brought the house down when she appeared after the intermission in a clinging silk dress imprinted with pink cherry blossoms, and sang "I Get a Kick Out of You." The guys just adored her and shouted back: "We get a kick out of you too, baby!" I wasn't too sure about her choice of music, nor did I feel comfortable in a hall full of hollering GIs; mob emotion always makes me feel ill at ease. But the evening was clearly a triumph for Yoshiko, and I was proud to be her friend.

I was invited, as the only foreigner, to join her for dinner at the Imperial Hotel after the show. Kawamura was there, as usual, but there was no sign of Madame Kawamura. Several others, all Japanese, sat around the table, including a well-known and very handsome movie star named Ryo Ikebe. Before we sat down for dinner—Ikebe and myself, that is—we found ourselves standing side-by-side in the men's room, and I couldn't resist a peek. I cannot be entirely sure of this, but I do believe that he was aware of my interest, for he spent an inordinate amount of time shaking his rather formidable member with a trace of a smile on his lips. I found it a little hard after this revelation to concentrate on the dinner conversation. But this is by the by.

"Ah, yes, Hotta-san," exclaimed Yoshiko, when I mentioned his name. "You know we made a film in Russian during the war, a musical. It was never shown. Our military censors wouldn't allow it."

"Frightful vulgarians," muttered Kawamura.

"We had such a lovely time shooting that picture," Yoshiko recalled with a chuckle. "All the men working on the film were in love with me, you know, Sid-san, the Russians as well as the Japanese, the stars, the director. Ooh, it was a new drama every day. But I call it our phantom picture. Do you know, I've never seen it myself. Poor Hotta-san was devastated. He had put so much time and effort into it. Did you know he was beaten by the Special Police?" A frown appeared on her forehead. "The militarists treated him abominably, abominably!"

It is an unworthy sentiment, I know, but I sometimes wished the folks in Bowling Green could have seen me, at the Imperial Hotel, in the company of my Japanese friends. You might well ask why I should wish to impress people I was so eager to leave behind. Perhaps it was my small vengeance for being made to feel like a freak. I was with real friends now, on a much more glamorous stage.

Not that all my friends were so glamorous. Some of my most intimate moments were shared with people who didn't even know my name. In the dark of a Tokyo movie theater I was just like everybody else. If I ate enough rice, I often mused, I might even start smelling like everybody else. It was the smell of the Japanese, that sweet combination of rice-sweat and pomade, that intoxicated me more than anything. It was so good I could almost taste it. Every time I fell to my knees in worship, no matter how squalid the shrine of the moment, a public toilet, the park, the dank room of a short-time hotel, I did so hoping I could possess something of the Japanese; the act of love as a route to transfiguration. But I digress again.

To celebrate the release of *Time of Darkness*, we organized a small party, Murphy and myself, for Hotta and the crew. It took place at Tony's, the first pizza restaurant in Tokyo. The owner was a large New Yorker named Tony Lucca, who had quit his job for SCAP and made a killing on the black markets. Legend had it that he needed a forklift to transport his cash. Tony liked to be driven around Tokyo in the back of his cream-colored Cadillac convertible with his pal, Kohei Ando, boss of the Ando gang, while being entertained by several young women at a time. Rumor also had it that Tony maintained warm relations with the Luchese family in New York, a rumor Tony himself did nothing to dispel. A somewhat dubious character, then, but his pizzas were delicious (and even if they hadn't been, they were the only ones in Tokyo), and Tony, despite his booming voice and crude jokes, had a knack with the Japanese; he knew how to make them feel at ease. Movie stars ate pizzas at Tony's, and so did politicians, businessmen, and, naturally, Tony's gangster friends, the yakuza, who were given pizzas for free.

So there we were, with great slabs of melted cheese and pepperoni laid out in front of us: Hotta, Murphy, the movie's director Shimada, the cameraman, the editor, various others whose names I've forgotten, and me. Murphy, who didn't drink alcohol, raised his glass of orange juice and made a toast "to the success of this great democratic motion picture," and to "my good friend, Nobu-san, if I may be permitted to call you that." Hotta rose to thank him for the kind words. He found it impossible to call Murphy "Dick," no matter how often Murphy invited him to do so, or even "Dick-san," so he compromised, and left it at "Mr. Richard." But he didn't seem in a particularly festive mood that night. In fact, his face looked tight as a clenched fist. Hotta was a fastidious man, and at first I thought that Tony's faintly louche ambiance didn't agree with him. But there was another, more compelling reason for his unease. Although *Time of Darkness* had opened in a small artsy cinema in Shinjuku, the main Japanese film distributors had refused to touch the movie. "Too complicated" was the stated reason; or "Confusing to the general audience." Worse, Hotta had been receiving threats to his life if he didn't withdraw the film.

Murphy dismissed the whole thing as a silly joke: "Now, why would anybody want to kill you? It's a great movie." Hotta thanked Murphy for his support, and said: "Japan is hopeless, Mr. Richard, hopeless."

"What do you mean, hopeless? We're at the beginning of a new era,

Nobu. The Japanese want to be free like everybody else, be free to say what they think, free to vote the rascals out, free to go where they please. That's why we fought this damned war, isn't it? And you fought for it too, right? That's why they roughed you up in prison. But those dark days are over now, my friend. We're building a democracy, and it'll work, Nobu, you'll see, it'll work out just fine."

Hotta took a sip of his red wine and said that Japan was "too complicated."

"Nothing we can't fix," said Murphy, at which point Tony, who fancied himself as an entertainer, gave us his rather Neapolitan rendering of "Slow Boat to China." Murphy led the applause. Hotta's mood did not visibly improve.

11

YOSHIKO HAD NOT kept her word. She did return to the movies. I can't say I was surprised. The reason she gave was that she had to support her family. I'm sure this was true, but I suspect that she had caught the movie bug too badly to stay away from the camera for long. It was all very well singing to a hall full of horny American soldiers, but immortality could only be achieved on the silver screen. To be sure, our dreams are made of flammable material. I remember Kurosawa once saying: "Castles in the sand, Sidney-san, that's all we're doing, building castles in the sand. One single wave is all it takes to make everything disappear forever." Nonetheless . . .

I went to see Yoshiko on the set of her latest film, this time without Murphy, which was a relief. "It's very anti-war," she assured me, "and very romantic. Lots of love scenes, Sid-san. In Japan we call them 'wet scenes.'" This made us both laugh. *Escape at Dawn* was the title. Yoshiko played a prostitute, or as they called them in wartime Japan, a "comfort girl." This had caused some commotion in our Information Bureau. We encouraged love stories, of course, but an admiring portrait of a prostitute came as rather a shock to the Christians in our office. The specter of "feudalism" also hovered dangerously over the project. Questions were asked whether a love story of a soldier and a prostitute really encouraged healthy relations between men and women. The Japanese argument that stories about prostitutes were

part of Japanese culture didn't cut much ice with Murphy, whose respect for cultural tradition ran out when tradition clashed with the
policies of his department—or indeed with the convictions that came
with his upbringing in rural Idaho. But a compromise was found. The
script was revised. The girl was no longer identified as a prostitute but
as a "singer," sent to comfort the soldiers on the battlefront. This way,
everyone was satisfied.

The singer is in fact forced to comfort a sadistic officer, but falls
madly in love with a soldier, played by the gorgeous Ryo Ikebe. The
soldier disgraced himself by being captured alive by the Chinese. That
he managed to escape made no difference at all. His first duty was to
die. Being in love with his superior officer's special girl only made
things worse. So he becomes the sadistic officer's whipping boy; every
day another torment. Until, one day, he cannot stand it any longer, and
the soldier and the singer decide to choose love rather than war—a
sentiment that did much to mollify Murphy's initial reservations—
and plan their escape. The scene to be shot on the day of my visit, of
the escapees falling to the machine gun of the sadistic officer, was the
film's concluding image.

"The role was written specially for me," Yoshiko said, as the camera
was being set up in a kind of sandpit, meant to represent the flat landscape of China's central plains. The director, Taniguchi, told the soldiers to line up. "Everyone in position?" he shouted. "Prepare! Start!"
The sadist, played by a brutally good-looking actor who went on to have
a long career in yakuza pictures, ordered his men to shoot poor Ikebe.
But they just couldn't bring themselves to execute a fellow soldier. So
the brute, quivering with rage, murders the hero himself with his machine gun. Yoshiko, wild with grief, screams the name of her lover and
throws herself on his dying body. The sadist then shoots her, too. In the
last close-up shot, which for some reason took ages to prepare, the
twitching hands of the dying lovers come together in the sand.

It was not the greatest film ever made. But it was a success, not so much because of its anti-war message but more on account of the "wet scenes," which were somewhat bolder than audiences were used to. There is a lot of kissing and thrashing about on army bunks, scenes, by the way, that would never have passed our own Hays Code back home, but with all the absurdities emanating from our office, we were at least spared the censorious eyes of Presbyterian busybodies in Tokyo. I saw *Escape at Dawn* several times in ordinary moviehouses, and was delighted to see that Yoshiko's hot kisses were met with loud cheers and much applause. There were rumors that Ikebe's passion for Yoshiko was not confined to the motion picture screen. If so, she never revealed anything of the kind to me.

Which was a good reason to doubt such rumors. For she did in fact confide much of her private life to me. It wasn't long after my visit to the set of *Escape at Dawn* that she invited me for dinner at Iceland, a fancy French restaurant near the Imperial Palace, one of those dark, oak-paneled places with ancient white-gloved waiters and alarming violinists hovering around the tables. I never found out why it was called Iceland, but such linguistic mysteries abound in Japan. There cannot have been many instances of Japanese ladies paying for the dinners of young American men; but Yoshiko was a movie star, after all, and I was happy to be her adoring acolyte.

The conversation was somewhat stiff in the beginning. She toyed with her food, refused to drink wine, but insisted that I try the red Bordeaux. Perhaps she was self-conscious about the looks we invited. Most people recognized her instantly. Being Japanese, they were too polite to point, or whisper, or come over to ask for her autograph, but the quick glances, designed to go unremarked, made us feel conspicuous.

"Mama and Papa are well," she replied, when I asked after Mr. and Mrs. Kawamura, "but it is time for me to move on." She had found an apartment in Asagaya. And what about Ikebe-san, I enquired, trying not to seem prurient, and perhaps not entirely succeeding, since she gave me a funny look and said, with the hint of a smile, "Ikebe-san, marvelous actor."

I probed no further. We talked about the weather, which had been quite chilly for this time of year, and about films we had seen, or rather, I had seen, for she never had time to see movies. "I wish I did, but it's just work, work, work."

It was, I think, only when we got to the dessert, a baked French custard, that she looked at me intently with those large, luminous, irresistible eyes, and said: "Sid-san, I want to ask you something."

"Of course, anything."

"I feel that I can trust you."

"Thank you," I said, trying not to look too eager.

"Promise you won't tell."

Of course I wouldn't.

"Sid-san, I want to go to America. Do you think that sounds crazy?"

"No, no, but why? Can't you go on holiday in Japan?"

"I can't take a holiday. I have to work."

"All the more reason not to go to America."

She shook her head impatiently. "You don't understand. I want to work in the USA. You see, there is so much good I can still do in this crazy world. I was deceived once by the militarists, so when Ri Koran died, I made a promise to myself that I would never let something like that happen again. Never again would I lend myself to making propaganda for war. It is my duty to work for peace, and for friendship between our countries." She looked very serious when she said this, like a child concentrating hard on a drawing.

"But, honey," I said, "your public is here."

Yes, she said, "but Japan is very small. You know what we Japanese say: to know only your own little world is like being a frog in a well."

I nodded. I had heard the expression before. Since Nobu first told me about it, I kept on hearing it. "Perhaps I can help with some of my Hollywood contacts."

"Oh," she purred, "I was hoping you would say that. I knew I could depend on you." She bowed her head to the crisp white linen table-cloth, almost upsetting the empty crystal wine glass. "*Yoroshiku o-negai shimasu,*" she said, her eyes cast on her plate, meaning something like "I'm humbly asking for your kind help."

A mere two years ago I had been kicking my heels in Ohio, hoping to find some adventure at the Luxor, and here I was, in the best French restaurant in Tokyo, boasting of my Hollywood contacts to a world-famous movie star. I was bluffing, of course, careless of the consequences. But I was young, which, I guess, is a lousy excuse.

"I was thinking," Yoshiko continued, "perhaps you could go back to America as well, to study Japanese, isn't that what you wanted? And then you could be my guide."

I was so astonished that I didn't know what to say, so I said nothing, and just stared at her with my mouth open, no doubt looking rather stupid.

"Think about it, Sidney-san. There is no need to say yes now."

I promised that I would, of course, think about it.

"What an adventure it would be for both of us," she said, her face lit up by a happy smile. "You know why I really want to go to the States?" she said, beckoning with her hand for me to come closer.

"No, why?"

Lowering her voice like a conspirator, she said: "To learn how to kiss." She showed her pretty white teeth and giggled. I noticed that she never covered her mouth when she laughed, unlike most Japanese women.

12

MOVING BACK TO the dreaded United States was of course the last thing I had in mind. It is true that I had thought of studying Japanese properly at a university. I could get a scholarship. Uncle Sam was generous in that way. But I wasn't ready to go just yet. I was having too good a time in Tokyo. Rules against fraternization with indigenous personnel had been relaxed. We no longer had uniformed martinets going around the Mimatsu Nightclub with rulers to make sure there were always six inches of space between Japanese and American dancing partners. Japanese cinemas were no longer out of bounds. We could receive Japanese in our rooms, if we wanted. And oh, how I wanted. I fraternized, and fraternized, and fraternized. I adored Japanese boys, and the great thing was, they were so available: on building sites, in subway trains, in public parks and coffee shops, railway stations and moviehouses, just anywhere, really, where people gathered for work or pleasure. All the straight young men were crazy for sex and didn't much mind where they got it. And they loved Americans back then. Before that inevitable moment that has to come for every Japanese, of marriage and the conventional life, I would service their needs with the greatest of pleasure. I kept a diary in those days, and would mark every new conquest with a little flag. With every new flag, I felt I reached a little deeper into the soul of Japan.

Not a good time to move, then. I was sharing an adorable little

wooden house near the Ebisu subway station with Carl, whose taste for
boys was as voracious as mine. Still, one can't be at it *all* the time.
When we weren't fraternizing, we went to the Kabuki, and the Noh. I
loved opera, so I preferred the showiness of the former, while Carl favored the austerity of Noh. We also spent many hours exploring the
old neighborhoods of Tokyo. The absence of historical remnants added
a peculiar poignancy to the few bits and pieces that we did manage to
find: a charred Tokugawa shrine, a neglected graveyard of Yoshiwara
courtesans, the crumbling gate of an aristocratic mansion, the ruins of
an old garden whose weeds didn't entirely disguise the formal design
of more elegant times. Their sad state left so much to one's imagination. In time, of course, the city was rebuilt. This was all to the good. I
admired the cheerful way the Japanese put themselves to the task of
reconstructing their country. And yet—perhaps I shouldn't say this—
I sometimes miss the wreckage of Tokyo, just as it was when I first arrived. I miss the romance, I guess. I now live in one of the most exciting,
most vibrant, most cutting-edge cities in the world. A man who hasn't
lived in Tokyo hasn't lived in the modern world. And yet, and yet . . .
the city of my imagination is no more.

We would talk, Carl and I, on our long walks through the low city
to the east, about history, the Japanese, the Americans, art, theater,
boys, and books, but also about our luck to be living in a place where
we were treated with deference, but more often with indifference. Indifference is a much-underrated quality. If only the Jews in Europe
had been treated with indifference. Because we were not judged, we
could be whoever we wanted to be, and that, paradoxically, is to be
most oneself. But what I wanted to be, to pile one paradox onto another, was more Japanese. I felt comfortable with Japanese in a way I
never had with Americans. I was figuring out the codes of conduct that
made me feel trusted and accepted by them, and this made me feel
strangely at home.

To claim that General MacArthur felt the same way would be an absurdity. He never saw any Japanese below the ranks of emperor or prime minister, which didn't make for a varied social life. For all his pontification about the Oriental mind, I'm not sure he ever knew much about Japan, or anywhere Asian, but he had an instinctive feel for it. He didn't have to know the place intellectually; books were of no use to him. He knew it in his bones.

It was enough to see him go in and out of his office in the Daiichi Life Insurance Building every day, an operation that was staged with the stylized ceremony of a Noh play. When we were in the area with nothing else to do, Carl and I would go and watch, just to amuse ourselves. It was pure theater. The crowd was held back by MPs, as the limousine pulled up to the front of the building at precisely the same time every morning. A whistle was blown, the ceremonial guards presented arms, the door of the limo was opened, always by the same soldier, always in the same way, facing the back of the car, and SCAP emerged from his black coach, wearing his famous crushed cap. He turned his hawkish profile to the right, then to the left, without ever acknowledging the hushed crowd, even with a brief wave or a half salute, made a quick turn, and walked briskly, though never too fast, to the front door. This fascinating spectacle was repeated every day, except Sundays. "Susan" had acquired the solemn gravitas of a Shogun, every movement of his body an illustration of his lofty aloofness from the people he ruled with the imperious air of a strict but benevolent father.

I was but a cog in the giant wheel of the SCAP's Department of Civil Information. And I would have been quite content to continue in that humble position for a while longer. However, the best plans in life have a way of being disrupted by unforeseen events. I should have sensed trouble when Murphy and I were summoned one day to Willoughby's office, for this was very irregular. Even Murphy never saw

Willoughby, except on official business. Without Mr. Capra's introduction I would never have been able to meet him the first time. It was only after I had joined his staff that I realized what an unusual privilege this had been.

Murphy didn't smell a rat either, even though he, a true-blue New Dealer, detested Willoughby's reputation as a Republican to the right—as Willoughby himself often put it—of Genghis Khan. Ever the optimist, Murphy speculated that we might be singled out for special praise, or, one never knew, perhaps even a promotion. He looked oddly cheerful as he bounded up the stairs in his big black boots and freshly clipped hair, every inch the good soldier. I followed him, with amusement more than apprehension. I was curious to hear what the old monster had to say to us. We were ordered to wait in a separate room. When a young officer told us to proceed, we had been waiting for more than half an hour.

Still entertained, I looked over the familiar objects in Willoughby's office that had struck me the last time I was there: the Kaiser's bust, the porcelain figurines dancing in the glass cabinet by the wall. I noted a new addition to the pictures on the wall; perhaps I just hadn't noticed it before: a small silver-framed photograph of General Franco of Spain, signed with a message of some kind written in neat little letters. I couldn't read what it said, but could make out the name Willoughby quite clearly. "Gentlemen," he said with his elaborate Old World courtesy, "won't you sit down." Murphy looked very pleased to be in this exalted place, this antechamber, as it were, of SCAP's inner sanctum.

Willoughby carefully removed the gold-embossed wrapper from an expensive-looking cigar, and took his time clipping it with an instrument that closely resembled a miniature guillotine. "From Havana," he commented, "best in the world. Have you noticed, gentlemen, the general decline in the quality of cigars? This is no trivial matter. The decline of our civilization is reflected in the steady decline of the good cigar, I always say." He passed the cigar under his nose, lightly brushing the Ronald Colman mustache. I wondered where this was leading. His manner of speaking combined silkiness and pomposity in equal measure, a disconcerting mixture.

"However," he continued, after lighting the cigar, "this is not why I requested the pleasure of your company. Gentlemen, what I wish to discuss with you today is the nature of our mission in Japan, a most delicate mission, to be sure. Winning the war, I believe, was but one necessary step toward a higher goal. As the General observed on the deck of the *Missouri* under the standard born to Japan in 1853 by Commodore Matthew Perry, as the General observed on that great day in our history, we are here to create 'a better world founded on faith and understanding.' We shall 'liberate the Japanese from a condition of slavery' and bring peace for all time. Do you remember those sacred words, gentlemen?"

Murphy, who could not have put it better himself, and was perhaps pleasantly surprised that a crusty old leatherneck like Willoughby would have shared these noble sentiments, confirmed with great enthusiasm: "Yes sir, we surely do!"

"Good," said Willoughby, "good. And we are all agreed that our great mission to bring liberation and peace can only meet with success if we treat our erstwhile foes with the utmost civility. There can be no room for prejudice on the grounds of race or creed. We will show the highest regard for what is best in the tradition of this brave and honorable island race, is that not so, gentlemen?"

"Yes sir, of course, sir!" said Murphy, his voice raised almost to a shout.

"We will not blindly impose our own habits, some of which might be less than admirable, on an alien race. While creating a world of freedom, we will respect our differences in culture and history, will we not? We cannot just act as if the whole world were just another state of America, can we? After all, Japan is not Kansas or Nebraska."

"No sir, it surely isn't," shouted Murphy.

At this point Willoughby paused, peering through the smoke that swirled in the milky beam of the morning sun. "Well, then, if we all agree on these principles, laid out for us with such noble force by the General, would you be so kind as to explain to me how the hell you could have passed a subversive, arrogant, prejudiced, disgusting piece of Red propaganda"—here he spat out a string of tobacco and drew a deep breath, trying to control his mounting rage—"an affront, an affront not just to the fine people of Japan but to the very enterprise we are embarked upon at great expense in blood and treasure. Am I making myself clear, gentlemen?"

Neither Murphy nor I had a clue what he was talking about. Surely there had to be some mistake. Murphy was about to protest, but Willoughby stopped him before he could speak. Willoughby was now hitting his stride, as though he were in a lecture hall, or a church: "I have experienced awkward moments during my time in Japan. How could it be otherwise? This is a strange country. They have their own ways of thinking and doing things. But I have never experienced anything, anything at all, to compare to the mortification I felt after watching that piece of Commie propaganda at the residence of the Japanese prime minister, who is a fine gentleman. When Prime Minister Yoshida objected most vigorously to this frontal attack on our policies, and the gross disrespect shown to the Emperor of Japan, who is worshipped by all Japanese as a deity, what could I say to the prime minister? You tell me, gentlemen. What the hell could I say to him?"

"But . . ." Murphy began.

"No buts," said Willoughby, sounding like a headmaster who has seen discipline go to the dogs. "Don't you know what we're up against? Don't you realize how dearly that bunch of New York Reds would like to sabotage our mission?"

Maybe I was wrong, but I felt as if he were looking straight at me. I had a shrewd notion who "that bunch" might be. Instead of opening that can of worms, however, I asked Willoughby very politely which film he had seen at Prime Minister Yoshida's residence.

This made things worse. By now Willoughby had worked himself into a frenzy, spraying his immaculate desk with drops of spittle. "You dunderheads! You duffers! Don't you feign ignorance! You not only passed this execrable picture, by the title of *Dark Times*, or something of that sort, but from what I hear you even had an active hand in it. What is it you want? A revolution in Japan? A civil war? An insurrection? Is that your idea of peace and progress? Well, it will not pass! It will not pass! The film will be withdrawn from all cinemas and banned forthwith! Murphy, you will be moved at once to another department, where you can do no more damage. I believe they still need men in our postal services. And as for you, young man, I am deeply disappointed. Worse yet, I feel you have abused my goodwill, coming to me with a recommendation from Mr. Capra, then letting your country down in this way. Capra is a fine patriot. Wait until he hears of this. There will be no more place for you in our administration. That will be all, gentlemen."

"But, sir," went Murphy, who was on the verge of tears.

"Dismissed!" cried Willoughby.

And that, I'm afraid, was indeed that.

═ 13 ═

MY FIRST REACTION was one of panic. I felt as though I were about to be expelled from the Garden of Eden. Without a job, it would be impossible to stay in Japan. How would I cope with a life of exile in the cold country of my birth?

My friends, Carl, Nobu, and the others, were sympathetic. Nobu, the dear boy, even wept when he heard that I might have to leave. But there was nothing they could do to help me. Yoshiko was not surprised when I told her what had happened. She had already heard the news through the cinematic grapevine. She wondered whether General MacArthur himself was aware of the situation. She had friends in high places. In fact, she had a thought: Colonel Wesley F. Gunn, he would surely help. Such a charming man. She would invite us both to a party in her new house in Asagaya.

I didn't know Colonel Gunn personally, of course, but was aware of his somewhat fearsome reputation as head of the Special Operations Section, and in a less sinister vein, as a legendary ladies' man, with an endless supply of "kimono girls." Rumor had it that he had even seduced Hara Setsuko, one of Japan's most famous movie stars, also known as the Eternal Virgin because, although many tried, including studio bosses and cabinet ministers, no man had ever managed to lay a finger on her. A classical Japanese beauty, Hara cultivated a wholesome image, which only made her more desirable. But she remained impervious to all men who begged for her favors, until—so they say—Colonel Gunn came, saw, and conquered.

Yoshiko's house was small, but well furnished in a girlish kind of way: thick cushions, fluffy carpets, a large collection of dolls, Chinese scrolls, and photographs of Yoshiko with a variety of people. I recognized Kawamura in several pictures, Ikebe, Hotta, and others whom I couldn't identify. In the Western-style living room hung a portrait of the young Yoshiko, dressed in a high-necked Chinese dress. The artist had made much of her large eyes and red lips, like two burning pieces of coal above a pair of plump cherries.

Major Gunn, who turned up with his executive officer, named Dietrick, was no Valentino. Short and thickset, with a bull neck, he had short blond hair, like pig bristles. Dietrick was by far the better-looking. But Gunn exuded the kind of energy that could easily explode into aggression. He took Yoshiko in his arms and twirled her around, while she shrieked in mock protest, her short legs kicking. Dietrick, a more reserved character, put down some boxes from the PX, filled with bottles of whiskey, sausages, cheese, perfumes, records, and various kinds of ladies' underwear.

Neither Gunn nor Dietrick appeared to be too pleased to see me, and they pretty much ignored my presence for the rest of the evening, which after the first few rounds of whiskey started to get quite wild. Yoshiko had made an attempt to interest Gunn in my case, but without any noticeable effect. He just put another jazz record on the phonograph. Both men took their turns to dance with her, and I was the unwilling witness to a competition in which it was clear who would emerge as the victor. No matter how much Dietrick tried to impress Yoshiko with his somewhat fawning manners, it was Gunn's cruder, more energetic approach that proved more seductive. Yoshiko closed her eyes as he bent her backwards in a tango that upset one of the open bottles, spilling liquor all over the floor. He sat down on the sofa, lifted her up in his arms as though she were a doll, and placed her on his lap. It was getting late. I felt I had seen enough and said I really had to go. But Gunn, who had barely spoken to me, told me to relax; Yoshiko would sing us a song. Yoshiko resisted. She had had too much to drink. "Please," she begged, "please, no. No songs tonight."

"Sure you will!" roared Gunn, while Dietrick, more animated than he had been before, and with a slight air of menace, shouted: " 'China Nights,' 'China Nights'!" Yoshiko, still in Gunn's lap, shook her head and giggled, despite her obvious distress. Gunn put her on her feet, and told her to get up on the goddamn table. "Please, no," she pleaded, still laughing, but with fear in her eyes. Gunn swept the empty bottles and food bowls off the table, grabbed her hand, and lifted her onto the table: "Now sing!" he said. " 'China Nights.' Hubba hubba!" Both men clapped their hands, as though cheering a nightclub act. And she began singing, hesitantly at first, then louder, while the men leaned back, savoring their triumph. At the end of the song, Yoshiko covered her face in her hands and started sobbing. I desperately wanted to protect her, save her from these animals. Gunn grabbed her in his thick, hairy arms. I thought she would hit him, as she had every reason to do. He whispered something in her ear. I saw her arms tighten around his hoglike back.

14

TO SAY THAT I felt miserable would be an understatement. I felt deflated, inadequate, impotent, hopeless. How could we help the Japanese, with monsters like Willoughby and Gunn in charge? There was nothing more to fear from the Japanese militarists. Instead, the Japanese now needed protection from our own people. But what could I do, a nobody about to be sent back to my dreadful country?

Feeling very sorry for myself, I decided to indulge in one of Tony's pizzas. That usually lifted my darkest moods. I've never met a sausage I didn't like, and Tony's pepperoni almost always did the trick. It was after the normal lunch hour on a rainy Thursday afternoon. There was only one other diner, a morose-looking American with thin black hair. He was probably homesick, missing his regular food. Tony emerged from the kitchen, looking big, lumbering, like a retired prizefighter, pressed into a blue double-breasted suit.

"Hiya, fella," he said, as he sat down at my table, nodding at my one fellow diner. "How's tricks?" I don't know why, for I barely knew Tony, and my troubles didn't really concern him, but since I'd already confided in everyone else, I told him my story anyway. He listened carefully until I was finished, and said in his gravelly Brooklyn voice, "Let me tell you something about this country, kid. All this crap about 'democracy' and 'civic rights' and 'social equality' and 'feudalism' is just a crock of shit, to make the Americans feel good. Guys like Willoughby throw their weight around in Japan, because they think they're big shots. And this Gunn fellow? In the end it don't amount to a hill of beans. Japanese have their own ways of doing things, and the more you think you know them, the less you actually know. It's only when you realize you don't know them that you're getting somewhere, do you follow me?"

Though I'd never regarded Tony Lucca as an authority on Japanese culture, I still felt too blue to argue with him. Besides, I wasn't sure what he was getting at. He gave off a smell of aftershave lotion, pungent but not unpleasant.

"I'm not one of your eggheads," Tony resumed, as if I hadn't figured that out for myself, "but I've dealt with enough Mama-sans and Papa-sans to know a few things you can't learn from books. Everything here is about connections, kid. This place is like a huge web of mutual obligations, duties, debts, little favors, big favors, all with consequences. Every favor given is a debt acquired. Haven't you ever noticed how a Japanese won't lift a finger if he sees a stranger being run over by a car, or keeling over in a heart attack, or getting roughed up by a bunch of hoods? Not because he is coldhearted. Quite the opposite: it's out of concern for the other guy. If I help you, you're forever in my debt, see? That's how every Japanese is stuck to the great big web that is Japan. And the spider in the middle, well, let's call him the Emperor. And if some Commie is stupid enough to lob a rock at him, it makes no blind bit of difference, because the spider never moves, he may even be dead, for all we know, or a convenient fairy tale, but he's the God to whom all his subjects feel they owe the greatest debt, that of being born a Japanese."

I was thinking of Hotta. Wasn't he Japanese? He sure didn't worship the Emperor. But I was beginning to get interested. Tony was a rough diamond, but there was shrewdness there, perhaps even a kind of wisdom. "What about us?" I asked. "What about the Americans, SCAP? Will the Japanese owe a debt to us, too?"

Tony looked at me with benign contempt. "Nah," he said. "We're here today, gone tomorrow, a mere ripple in the lake of Japanese history. It makes no difference what we do." So, what were we doing here? "Making money, fucking, surviving, that's all." What about learning from the Japanese? "Learning? Let me tell you something, kid. There are two ways to learn something in life. There's my way, the business way, sticking your hands deep in the common shit. Let me take a look at your hands, kid." He took my right hand, turned it over, and stroked my palm. "It don't look to me that you want to get these babies dirty, so you do it the other way, the way I never could. You go back to school and learn—the language, the history, the art, the politics, everything. You study until you know enough to come back and not just be another American bum. You know what the problem is with these guys who think they're in charge of this place? The problem is that they don't know shit, but they're too ignorant to know that they don't know shit."

15

I T TOOK ME a while to get used to life back "home." Despite my dismissal by Willoughby, I was still able to get a scholarship from the U.S. government, so I had enrolled for a Japanese language course at Columbia University in New York under Professor Bennet D. Wilson, a former missionary who had specialized in Ainu grammar. Professor Wilson was one of the last people on earth to speak Ainu. In the 1920s, he had translated the New Testament, a rather quixotic project, if you ask me, since there were only a handful of Ainu left who could speak their own language, and Professor Wilson's Bible was, so far as I know, the only document ever written in Ainu. His spoken Japanese was not fluent, and rather quaint. I had heard that Wilson had met the Emperor once and impressed him by speaking in the traditional court idiom dating back to the Heian Period. If true, this was indeed impressive, but not much good to us as students.

Us, apart from myself, consisted of two older men who worked for the government and kept to themselves; a loner with terrible acne whose only interest was Japanese prints; a tight-assed fellow who studied eighteenth-century Confucianism; and a homely girl with a ponytail and braces on her teeth, who studied Japanese because she had fallen in love with Arthur Waley's translation of the *Tale of Genji.* I got along best with the homely girl.

But I missed Tokyo so much it hurt: my friends, the theater, the movies, the sound of the cicadas in summer, the cries of the sweet potato vendors, the public baths, the temple incense and pine trees of Kamakura, and the boys, the boys. New York City wasn't Bowling Green, but to me it seemed a cold and joyless city, filled with tight-faced people rushing to and from their work. As for romance, the very idea terrified me. During my first semester at Columbia, a young man was stabbed to death after making a pass at another student. The murderer got off with a minimal sentence. His act of "self-defense" seemed entirely reasonable to most people. In any case, even if I had plucked up the courage to approach them, American men looked so unattractive, with their coarse skin and loud booming voices. And the homos, if anything, were worse. I did once enter one of those depressing bars, somewhere on West Fourth Street, where queens in tight pants and painted eyebrows congregated, screeching away in their peculiar argot. I lasted about five minutes, before fleeing alone into the night.

And so I retreated into my lonely shell, eating box lunches with chopsticks at the university canteen, trying to read Japanese books, perhaps a bit too ostentatiously. But when someone, looking over my shoulder, was foolish enough to ask me a question, I gave them short shrift and crawled farther into my carapace. In short, I was a miserable and no doubt thoroughly disagreeable young man, a prickly show-off, out of place and smug about it. I didn't like myself in my own country.

The hard shell that I had constructed for myself was cracked open just a little bit by a new acquaintance. His name was Bradley Martin, the distinguished art critic and Japanophile. A friend of Professor Wilson's, he would visit the Columbia campus once in a while, partly, I think, to cast his eyes over the latest crop of students. He liked "the young." Well, he cast his eyes on me, evidently liked what he saw, and invited me to have lunch with him.

In public, Martin was a man of great fastidiousness and respectability, his large, fleshy Kentucky body always perfectly encased in dis-

creet custom-made suits and spotted bow ties. The private man was
something else. The suits often gave way to splashy kimonos, of the
kind worn by hostesses at the more disreputable hot spring resorts, or
the full drag of evening gowns and jewelry. Martin actually looked
quite convincing as a graned dame, apart from his waxed mustache,
which, though incongruous, did look rather stylish even with face
powder and lipstick. Not that I was immediately invited to his more
exclusive soirées, where he received a few trusted friends, mostly fellow aesthetes who shared his interest in things Japanese.

At first, our encounters, at a quiet little French restaurant named
Biarritz, or at his apartment on Sixty-seventh and Park Avenue, were
given to discussions on Japanese art. Martin was especially interested
in art of the Kano School. I learned a huge amount from him, not least
by looking closely at his own treasures, scattered around the apartment, while listening to his commentary on each piece. He had beautiful first editions of woodblock prints by Eisen, and three extraordinary
Hoitsu paintings of peonies and cranes. The apartment was a kind of
shrine to Oriental beauty: an Edo Period screen, a lovely dark brown
Korean rice cabinet, walls covered in Chinese silk with flower patterns,
an exquisite penis carved out of stone (Tibetan, eighteenth century).

Our acquaintance advanced from that of avuncular master and
willing pupil to something more intimate one Saturday afternoon. We
were talking about a monthly journal, called *Connoisseur*, which I had
admired, but which was far too expensive for me to subscribe to. After
making some Chinese tea, Martin approached me from behind, laid
his hands on my back, and softly ran a finger up and down my spine.
"It would be my pleasure to let you have it as a gift," he purred, while
subjecting my back to a further exploration. I wasn't absolutely sure
what he was proposing to give me. "*Connoisseur*?" I asked tentatively.
"Mmmm," he said, while deftly opening my shirt. Martin was not exactly my type, but I must confess that being the object of desire

for once, instead of the worshipper, gave me a certain narcissistic thrill. It had been a long time, anyway. I received my first copy of *Connoisseur* through the mail two weeks later.

It was at Martin's apartment, at any rate, that I first met Isamu Noguchi, the Japanese-American sculptor. Martin had not dressed up in drag; it wasn't that kind of occasion. The other guests were Parker Tyler, the film critic; Jimmy Merrill, a rather tense young poet in owlish glasses; and a lady named Brook Harrison, who had a famous collection of Edo Period netsukes. Among his many other talents, Martin was an excellent cook, renowned for his Sri Lankan fishhead curry. We had a Chinese meal that night, which we ate with antique black lacquer chopsticks (late Edo).

Noguchi was without any doubt the most beautiful man I had ever seen; delicate without a hint of girlishness, penetrating Oriental eyes, long sensitive fingers, a smooth ivory-colored forehead. He had just returned from Tokyo and was keen to show us some Japanese art magazines featuring his latest work. It seemed that Isamu had made a bit of a splash in the exclusive pond of Japanese art. Even as Japanese artists were turning their backs on the classical tradition, tainted in their eyes by "feudalism," Isamu had introduced a startling new range of sculptures that showed the influence not only of Zen rockeries but of ancient Haniwa funeral ornaments. The Japanese, he told us, were shocked and fascinated at the same time. This was a place they daren't go themselves, even if they felt so inclined.

Isamu spoke fast, in bursts of feverish enthusiasm, as though there wasn't enough time to express everything he wanted to say. "There is so much richness there," he explained, "and all the Japanese want to do is imitate the kind of modernism that went out of style here years ago. They refuse to see that their own tradition is way more modern than anything produced in the West. Zen is avant-garde—"

"Ah, Zen," remarked Jimmy Merrill, "the sound of one hand clapping—"

"Those Kamakura Buddhas, aren't they just the most adorable things you've ever seen?" gushed Mrs. Harrison. "I do believe that Unkei is a genius. I think I'm pronouncing it right. Do you know his work, Mr. Noguchi?"

"Of course," said Isamu, a little brusquely, I thought.

"The space not filled, pregnant with meaning," said Parker Tyler, who was beginning to feel left out. "You see this in Japanese film, Mizoguchi, and so forth."

"And in Naruse, too," I chimed in, not wishing to be outdone, "especially in *Spring Awakening*."

"But," said Tyler with a flicker of annoyance, "even more so in *A Man with a Married Woman's Hairdo*."

I was defeated. I had never heard of this movie. So I just nodded my agreement and tried not to notice Tyler's smug little smile.

Isamu, however, was not a connoisseur but a young artist in a hurry. He couldn't wait to get back to Japan, he said. There was so much work to be done there. He felt the urge to reinvent the Japanese tradition because, as he put it, "it's in my blood." His training, he said, was in New York, Paris, Rome; but his instincts were Japanese. That is where he had spent his early childhood in the 1930s with his American mother. His Japanese father was a poet, whose famous ode to the Japanese martial spirit was banned after the war. I later learned that Isamu and his mother had been more or less kicked out of their home by his father, and had been forced to return to the United States pretty much destitute. During the war, Isamu had actually volunteered to be interned in Arizona with other Japanese-Americans, even though, with a Caucasian mother, this was not really required. He soon came out again, apparently after seducing half the women in the camp. Isamu

rarely talked about this part of his life. He rarely talked about anything that didn't concern his art, about which he talked a great deal:
"You can find the spirit of a people in their soil, in the rocks, if you
know how to dig it out. That's my mission, to rediscover that spirit, before the Japanese forget who they are."

I was impressed by Isamu's enthusiasm, slightly put off by his manner, and I must confess, a little bit envious. How marvelous it must be,
I thought, to be Western and Japanese at the same time, to fuse his
sharp analytical intellect with the natural sensibility of the East. He
had the very best of both worlds. He was born with everything I had
to acquire by learning, painfully, frustratingly, a little more every day.
The Japanese have an expression for mastering a difficult skill, so that
it becomes second nature, like the Zen archer who can still hit his target with a blindfold: "Learning with the body." I wish I could have
learned Japanese with my body.

16

I HADN'T HEARD anything from Yoshiko since I left Tokyo. Typical of her. Out of sight, out of mind, I'm afraid. I hadn't rated her chances of coming to America very high. Only one movie actress had managed it since the war: Tanaka Kinuyo. She was a very grand lady, and rumor had it that General MacArthur himself intervened.

So I was astonished, to say the least, to open my *New York Times* one morning and read about the arrival in Los Angeles of none other than my beloved Yoshiko. "Madame Butterfly Flies into Town" was the headline. Madame Butterfly had actually changed her name a little; she was now Miss Shirley Yamaguchi. She told reporters that she had always been a huge fan of Shirley Temple. She also told reporters that she had come to America "to learn how to kiss." Whereupon the photographer from the *San Diego Union* offered his cheek and shouted: "Why don't you start right here, honey." The photograph of Shirley planting a kiss on the grinning snapper's mug was reprinted all over the country, even in the august pages of the *New York Times.*

I still didn't see Yoshiko (I couldn't bring myself to call her "Shirley") for several months. She was busy touring California and Hawaii, giving concerts for her Japanese fans. Then, a short note, in English, which read:

Dear Sidney-san,

Long time no see. Weather in California so sunny. Arriving New York on 5 June. Meet me at Delmonico's for lunch on 6th.

Thank you. So long.

XX Shirley Y.

Once again it was she who invited me. I couldn't possibly have afforded Delmonico's, anyway. I arrived there first. When I told the maitre d' that the table was booked under the name Yamaguchi, he looked at me a bit curiously, as though I were some kind of imposter. Japanese names were not yet so commonly heard in New York in those days. Thank God she soon came sweeping in, every inch the diva, in a high-collared crimson Chinese dress with a pattern of silver chrysanthemums. "Yoshiko!" I cried, glad to see her finally after such a long time.

"Sid-san, I'm Shirley now, we are in the States, no?" She was bubbling over with excitement. There was so much to tell. Oh, the people she had met! Charlie and Yul and King! I had no idea who she was talking about, so I asked her to elaborate, while carefully avoiding the use of her name. By the time we got to our porterhouse steaks, I was firmly in the picture. She had met Charlie Chaplin; Yul Brynner, an actor; and King Vidor, the director who happened to be an old acquaintance of Kawamura. Charlie, apparently, adored Japanese culture and showed a great interest in her views on world peace. "And Yul is such a sweetheart, Sid-san. You know we might star together in *The King and I*, on Broadway. On Broadway! I'll be a Siamese princess, and Yul the King of Siam. Yul loves my singing. Can you imagine, Shirley Yamaguchi in a musical on Broadway! And after Broadway, I want to be in a Hollywood movie." Oh, how she loved "the States," its openness, and its businesslike manners. "Sid," she squealed, "I think I feel at home in this country. You know something, it reminds me of China."

I was pleased for her, of course, but curious to know how she had managed to come to America at all, despite all the travel restrictions. After all, Japan was still an occupied country. "You remember Major Gunn?" I did, with a great deal of distaste. "Well, he fixed it for me. He's a good guy, really. He makes sure my family gets enough food from the PX." I didn't wish to know what price he had exacted, nor, quite understandably, did Yoshiko volunteer any such information.

Instead, she gushed on about Charlie and Yul. Charlie loved Japan. They had met at the house of Richard Neutra, the architect, and Charlie had entertained the guests with his version of a Japanese country dance. And she had sung Japanese folk songs. She was so glad no one had asked her to sing that vile "China Nights" again. She refused even to sing it for her Japanese fans in L.A. and Honolulu, no matter how many times they requested it. That's why it would be so great to do *The King and I*. It would be a new beginning, a rebirth, as it were, the launch of Shirley Yamaguchi on a world stage.

"Yul is half Asian, you know," she said, as her plate of half-eaten porterhouse steak was efficiently removed by the waiter. "The first time we met, it was as if we had known each other forever. Like me, he is a citizen of the world, a Western man with an Asian soul. His real name was Khan, you know, and he was raised in Harbin. His father was a Mongolian and his mother a Romanian gypsy. He invited me for dinner at Charochka's Russian Restaurant. It brought back so many memories of home, of Masha, who saved my life, of the phantom film we made in Harbin, of Dimitri and the Harbin Opera Company." Here she paused, drying a tear with her little finger. It was no more than a second, though, before the words came tumbling out again: "Then Yul took me to his house in Santa Monica and played his guitar and sang Russian songs for me. He understands my feelings, like no one else before . . ." And then what happened? She giggled and slapped my arm. "Sid-san, you're so naughty."

"Oh, honey," I said.

"But," she burbled, "you can't meet him, I'm afraid. He's very jealous, you know."

"But," I began.

She didn't wait for me to finish. "I know," she said, "even though you're not that kind of man. I know you're not interested in me as a woman, but . . ." It was not quite what I had been meaning to say, but I decided to leave it at that.

17

W E SPOKE A few times on the phone, but the next place I saw
Yoshiko was on television. She had landed a spot on *The Ed
Sullivan Show.* This came just at the right moment, for auditions for
The King and I had not been a success. Perhaps Yul had tired of her,
but the coveted part as the Siamese princess failed to materialize. She
had decided to practice her English-language skills, and hired a teacher
to straighten out her pronunciation, the "l's" and "r's" and all that.
The Ed Sullivan Show, meanwhile, would launch her career in America. She was tremendously excited. "You know," she said, "that I'll be
seen by everyone in America?"

I watched the show at the Upper East Side apartment of Mr. and
Mrs. Owada, friends of Brad Martin's. Judging from his art collection
(including a rare Hokusai scroll painting, and several stone sculptures
by Ken Ibuki), Owada-san was a very wealthy man. He wrote essays
about literature and politics for a prestigious Japanese journal and
prided himself on being, as he put it, "very progressive." The Owadas,
too, had been put in touch with Yoshiko through Kawamura, who
seemed to know everyone worth knowing.

Isamu was at the party, looking intense as usual. So was Brad, who
had gone cool on me after I declined to continue our physical relations.
I noticed how my subscription to *Connoisseur* had suddenly come to a
halt. Brad was in a sour mood from the beginning and made sarcastic

comments as soon as the program started. The first guest to appear on the show was a man with a singing saw. Then came Joe DiMaggio, wearing a loud checkered suit. "My God," exclaimed Brad, "just look at that nose!" He proceeded to chatter all the way through the interview with DiMaggio, which didn't bother us much, since none of us was particularly interested in baseball, except Mr. Owada, but he was too courteous to complain.

I knew, as soon as the studio orchestra struck up the overture from *Madama Butterfly*, that Yoshiko's moment had come. Sullivan announced: "All the way from Tokyo, Japan, land of Mount Fujiyama and the Geisha girls, ladies and gentlemen, the descendant of a long line of Cho Cho-sans, my good friend, the beautiful, the talented, the mysterious—Shirley Yamaguchi!" And there she was, *my* good friend, in a striking lemon yellow kimono bound with a burnt orange obi, smiling to the camera and bowing to Sullivan, who bowed back in elaborate fashion, whereupon Yoshiko bowed once again, a little deeper this time, to which Sullivan responded by falling to his knees to loud laughter from the studio audience. "Oh, my God!" said Brad. "Will you just look at that kimono. I haven't seen anything like that since I was in Atami. She looks like a hot-spring entertainer."

"They drink a lot of tea in Japan," said Sullivan. Yoshiko laughed and said that was indeed so. "But they don't drink tea like we do, do they?"

"No, we don't, Ed-san."

"The Japanese are a velly velly porite people," said Sullivan. Yoshiko tittered. Brad groaned. The Owadas looked on blankly.

"Miss Yamaguchi-san here will show us just how her people drink tea, ceremoniously."

"Yes, I will, Ed-san," Yoshiko said, as the various utensils of a traditional tea ceremony were produced. She sat on her knees and stirred the bitter green brew with a bamboo whisk, explaining to Sullivan and a grinning Joe DiMaggio just what she was doing. When the tea had been prepared, she offered the bowl to DiMaggio, who sniffed at it with suspicion, kept grinning, and passed it on to Sullivan, who turned the bowl, bowed to Yoshiko, took a sip, cleared his throat as though he had swallowed poison, bowed to Yoshiko once more, and thanked her for the delicious cup of tea. "Jesus," said Brad. "Well, what can you expect," said Madame Owada. The only one who had said nothing throughout the proceedings was Isamu. He stared at the television screen with the intensity of an artist contemplating a blank canvas or a pristine slab of stone.

The orchestra struck up another tune, a jazzier one with odd Chinese flourishes. I could hear a gong being sounded. Shirley got up behind a microphone, and Sullivan announced that she would sing us a song entitled "Cha Cha Cho Cho-san." Gently swaying with the rhythm, smiling, continuously smiling, Shirley sang the song, which went:

I'm Cho Cho-san, Cho Cho-san, butterfly from Japan,
I'll sing and I'll dance and I'll cha cha cha cha,
I'll please you any way I can.

When it was all over, none of us knew what to say. Brad rolled his eyes. The Owadas refrained from comment. I was about to denounce Ed Sullivan for his crassness. Finally it was Isamu who broke the awkward silence: "She's extraordinary," he said, "absolutely remarkable. I must meet her. It is essential that I meet her . . ."

"But of course," cried Madame Owada, as she pressed a little bell for the maid to bring in some Japanese snacks. Watching television had made us all hungry.

18

ONE YEAR HAD passed at Columbia University. A relatively faultless conversation in Japanese was now possible, even though my reading was still at a basic level. Part of the problem was our textbook, which was of a somewhat specialized nature, since it was designed for intelligence officers during the war. I can still tell you exactly what a howitzer gun is in Japanese, or a sergeant second class in the Kanto Army. Typical textbook sentences like "Father has been shipped out to Manchukuo to join the Kanto Army as a lieutenant" held no mysteries for me, but were of limited use. Still, it was a start. A more vexing problem was finding people to practice my Japanese on, short of returning to Japan, something I intended to do as soon as I possibly could.

Reading books I actually wanted to read was still a challenging, not to say frustrating, enterprise. I tried to decipher some Kawabata short stories, and understood just enough to guess what was going on. But it was like watching a movie in an unknown language, something I was quite used to, of course, and following a story by deduction had its own small satisfactions. Even the most banal sentences (not that there are many of those in Kawabata) contained deep mysteries for the semi-literate.

I tried out some of my new linguistic knowledge on the Owadas, who were kind enough to praise every stumbling effort as though I spoke with extraordinary eloquence, but my military jargon, mixed with my teacher's archaic manner of speech, did sometimes reduce these kindly socialists to helpless laughter. I felt rather like a half-trained seal, performing tricks to catch a fish from my grateful audience. Oftentimes, this made me into a shameless ham, raising my snout to land yet another fish, and another.

The Owadas were indeed very wealthy (his grandfather had invented a new type of silk-weaving loom; she came from a family of soy sauce manufacturers) and they used their money generously. The guests at their parties fell into distinct categories: the Orientophile aesthetes; the activists for "progressive" causes; and the artists, some "progressive," all fashionable. I belonged to a category of my own: the amusing nobody. Madame Owada found me entertaining and trusted me enough to treat me as part wayward son, part father confessor, a role I often ended up playing for my lady friends. Many little problems of marital life were poured into my always sympathetic ears; his furtive infidelities, her unfulfilled desires, his disinterest in her "ideas," her disdain for his political hypocrisies. I felt I knew Mr. Owada rather more intimately than he was aware. It gave me a sense of power over him, the minor power of the spy, which, I must confess, shamefully, I rather enjoyed. Since I had neither money nor fame, secret knowledge was my only capital.

I was there, at the Owadas', on the memorable evening when Yoshiko met Isamu for the first time. There were many of us already in the room, talking about the ghastliness of Senator McCarthy, no doubt, since this was a common topic of conversation at progressive gatherings in those days. "The way they are hounding poor Charlie Chaplin," said Madame Owada. "I don't know how we can tolerate living in this country anymore."

Isamu said he no longer felt American and couldn't wait to go back to Japan. "In the New Japan," he said, "even Communists are free to express themselves any way they want. I never thought I'd say this, but I'm proud to be a Japanese. There is so much hope there, and people are so eager to learn."

"Quite right," said Brad, and raised his glass of champagne to make a toast to "the New Japan."

"And to dear Charlie Chaplin," exclaimed Madame Owada.

"To Charlie," we all went.

At that moment, Yoshiko came sweeping into the room, looking lovelier than ever in a lilac kimono and a navy blue sash. "Charlie Chaplin?" she said. "Oh, I love Charlie. No one is more dedicated to peace than Charlie. He loves Japan. You know, he's always talking about his trip to Japan before the war. He says that the Nara Hotel has the best bathrooms in the world. Charlie is very particular about bathrooms. One of his men always checks out the bathrooms, even in private houses, before he'll set foot in them."

Isamu was looking at Yoshiko intently, soaking up her presence with those large, hungry brown eyes. When Madame Owada introduced them, it was clear that Yoshiko had no idea who Isamu was. Informed that he was an artist, she asked in her innocent way: "So are you very famous?" Whereupon Madame Owada showed her the Japanese art magazines with pictures of his work. This seemed to impress Yoshiko, and she asked him how old he was. "Why should that matter?" said Isamu, who knew a great deal more about her. He folded her small white hand into both of his. "You're one of us, aren't you?" he said. "The battered children of history, me in the camps here in the States, you in China. We come from different places, but belong to one place alone, the only place that matters, our real home, the land of art."

I watched with fascination how a fuse had been lit that promised to be hotter than mere seduction. I could see nature taking its course: her eyes widened, her mouth slackened.

"You were exploited, weren't you," he said, "by the militarists."

She sighed. "Yes, I was."

"It must have been very hard for you."

"Yes, yes, it was," she whispered, as tears made little tracks down her white powdered cheeks.

19

SAMU AND YOSHIKO got married in Tokyo on a cold day in December 1951, three months after Japan and the United States signed
a peace treaty in San Francisco, and the occupation was formally declared over. I had managed to come back to Tokyo in the spring of that
year, as the movie reviewer for the *Japan Evening Post*. The job wasn't
particularly well paid, but it suited me fine. The arrangements had
been made by my dear friend Carl, who knew the editor, a pipe-smoking
man with a stammer named Cecil Shiratori. Cecil's British childhood,
of which he was tiresomely proud, still showed in his fondness for
tweeds, and in his bottomless fund of well-worn anecdotes about long-
dead literary figures, whose exploits in London's clubland were a
source of enduring fascination to him. You mentioned Max Beerbohm,
and a wistful look would appear on his narrow face. "D'you know what
B-B-B-Beerbohm said about f-f-f-feeling like exercise?"

"No."

"He s-s-said: 'You lie d-d-down until the f-f-f-feeling wears off.' Ha
ha hmmm."

But listening to Max Beerbohm stories was a small price to pay for
being able to return to my beloved Japan.

Even after an absence of little more than a year I could barely recognize parts of Tokyo. The Ginza area especially. The rubble had made
way for spanking new buildings. People were better dressed and moved

about town in a less resigned, brisker, more businesslike manner. The black markets were no longer the only places to get food and other necessities. Stores now had stuff you could actually buy for reasonable prices. Young toughs still roamed the main strips in Shibuya and Shinjuku, but sharkskin suits had replaced the Hawaiian shirts in vogue in the late 1940s. Above all, I felt a difference in the way Japanese treated foreigners, especially Americans. Too polite, and still no doubt too fearful to be openly hostile, the old deference was fading. No more "Japan no fuckin' good," and more "USA no fuckin' good." Less "Tokyo Boogie-Woogie," more "Tears of Nagasaki" (the big hit of 1951).

Being able to read the billboard advertisements was exhilarating and disappointing—exhilarating because they no longer held any mystery for me, and disappointing for the same reason. Those beautiful calligraphies in neon and paint lost all their exotic allure once I knew that they signified nothing more than a brand of beer or hair tonic.

I practiced my Japanese on anyone who would listen, sometimes in my half-trained seal mode, fishing for compliments or laughs, but mostly because there was no other way to communicate. Some Japanese pretended not to understand, rendered deaf and dumb by the assumption that no foreigner could possibly speak Japanese. And so even the clearest, most basic statement—"Take me to the Ginza, please, driver"—would be met with blank stares of incomprehension, as though one had said it in Swahili. The more common reaction was a theatrical show of utter disbelief. I often felt like a conjurer who had just bamboozled his public with a particularly good trick, which, I guess, is a variation of the performing seal act.

My comprehension of Japanese movies was far better than before, though not yet by any means perfect. I would still spend many daylight hours in dark halls, figuring out what was happening on the screen by deduction, while savoring my favorite odor of rice-sweat and pomade. Afterwards, I would take a stroll around Ueno Park, where the workingmen lolling about the lake with time on their hands were a constant temptation. Sometimes my conversations with likely prospects ended there, as pleasant conversations, which was just fine, since my vocabulary was invariably enriched by such encounters, replacing my repertoire of military terms and stilted court language with a different and earthier patois. And sometimes they resulted in more intimate encounters, where I would pay silent tribute. Anonymous, on my knees, in rapture; there is no greater feeling of ecstasy, or, indeed, of freedom.

The wedding, as I said, was in December, on the 28th, to be precise. I accompanied Isamu to Haneda International Airport for the arrival of his bride. Isamu hadn't seen Yoshiko for several months, and was frisky as a colt. Yoshiko had been busy with her first American picture, playing the wife of an American GI, returning home to California from the Far East. The picture was shot in and around Los Angeles. News of her casting in a real Hollywood movie had made the headlines in Japan. So her reception at Haneda was almost as spectacular as Charlie Chaplin's had been: reporters from all the main newspapers and magazines were there, creating such a scrum that Isamu and I could get nowhere near the spot where she would emerge from the Customs area. Announcements on the public address system told us how far she was still from the airport: thirty minutes, fifteen minutes, ten minutes—"Landed! Shirley Yamaguchi has come home to her native soil all the way from Hollywood, USA!"

That Haneda was in fact very far away from her native soil was a minor detail that bothered no one, least of all Yoshiko, who finally appeared to an explosion of flashbulbs. It was such pandemonium that we could barely see her at all. Bug-eyed pressmen were trampling over each other just to catch a glimpse of her, shouting questions in her general direction. A wooden platform decorated with flowers had been prepared for the press conference. Yoshiko, looking every inch the Hollywood diva in her large sunglasses, white gloves, and flowered dress, stepped up to the microphone, waved her arms at the crowd, and said in English: "Hello, boys, long time no see!" More pandemonium. More questions: What did she eat in the States? Did she get used to American bathrooms? Were the houses very big? Whom did she meet in Hollywood? What did the Americans think of Japan?

Isamu tried to press his way through the melee. Reporters violently resisted his progress, assuming that he was just another pushy shutterbug trying to barge to the front. However, a critic from the *Mainichi*, craning his neck to see what was going on, recognized Isamu and called out his name. All of a sudden Isamu was propelled forward by many arms, while people called for a photo. Spotting Isamu, Yoshiko cried out: "Hey, Isamu-san! Come over here!" "Kiss kiss!" went the reporters, as Yoshiko helped her bridegroom, looking a picture of misery, onto the podium. "Kiss kiss!" went the crowd. To Isamu's visible discomfort, they kissed. When he made to pull away, Yoshiko pulled him back toward her cheek, giving photographers one more chance to record the moment of young bliss for the early morning editions.

After that, I did not see the happy couple until their wedding day. They were ensconced in the bridal suite of the Imperial Hotel, or perhaps I should say they were besieged, with photographers lying in wait all day and night. The curtains of their room remained drawn for three full days.

I was reminded of this time many years later, when I met a paper craftsman who had known the young couple, when Isamu was designing Japanese-style lanterns in Gifu Prefecture. The craftsman would pick up Isamu in the mornings from an old Buddhist temple, where he was put up with Yoshiko.

"I learned about the power of love," said the craftsman, looking rather solemn. I asked him what he meant.

"In Japan," he explained, "men and women don't show their sexual feelings openly. But Noguchi-sensei and Yamaguchi-san couldn't get enough of each other. They'd disappear for hours into the temple. Even in public, they'd be touching and kissing and stroking, like young cats. Americans are more frank and open, you know. This is good. We Japanese should learn from that."

Isamu and Yoshiko were even late for their own wedding reception. It was held at the Manyo'en, an old aristocratic mansion which had somehow escaped undamaged from the war. The garden, dated around 1700, is one of the most famous in Japan. Designed to evoke in miniature the imaginary landscape of an ancient poem in the *Chinese Book of Songs*, it has miniature mountains and miniature lakes and miniature trees, miniature temples and shrines, and a tiny teahouse for contemplating the poetic vistas, brightened in their seasons by rows of cherry blossoms and azaleas. Since the wedding was in winter, the trees were protected from the snow by bamboo umbrellas. I had never seen trees with umbrellas before.

Before the banquet, the bride and bridegroom sat formally in front of a gilt screen, Isamu in a gray kimono with rather odd-looking black pantaloons, and Yoshiko in a white kimono with a thick golden sash. They were like two beautiful sculptures, sitting absolutely still, blending Western practicality and Oriental beauty in a perfect mix, quite literally, since Isamu had designed the clothes himself and even applied the makeup to his bride's face. Isamu's *hakama* was a kind of Westernized version of the skirts worn by courtiers on the Kabuki stage. Yoshiko's kimono was actually constructed like a Western evening gown, with hooks and buttons. And her makeup was highly unusual; Isamu said that he was inspired by the *Tale of Genji*. She looked like an exquisite Japanese doll, her face painted white, with bright red lips, like rose petals, and her eyebrows painted high on the forehead, like twin moths, in the style of a tenth-century court lady.

Apart from myself, there were no other foreigners at the wedding, certainly not Murphy or Colonel Gunn. But I saw several of Yoshiko's Japanese admirers. Ikebe was there, and Hotta, looking as emaciated as a martyred saint, and Mifune, splendid in his dark kimono with a large white family crest. Kurosawa, never one for small talk, made polite little bows when people addressed him. Yoshiko's father was absent. So Kawamura, looking suave in his *hakama*, presented the bride in loco parentis with a flowery speech about their mutual love of China and Yoshiko's lifelong dedication to peace. Hotta also referred to China in his speech and expressed his joy that peace and justice had finally come to "the New China, under the leadership of Chairman Mao, the greatest Asian of the twentieth century."

After the speeches, Isamu hopped from table to table, looking like a big bird with his long sleeves and black pantaloons flapping wildly behind him. He spoke to me in something resembling formal Japanese, with a thick American accent, and I replied as best I could. Kawamura, who overheard, chuckled and said: "You both speak perfect Japanese."

"Better than us Japanese," said a venerable old painter, Umehara Ryuzaburo.

To which Mifune, with his usual barking laugh that expressed goodwill rather than mirth, added: "We are international now. That is good. That is very good."

There was only one brief moment that threatened to blight the festive air. When we filed out of the main hall, called the Crying Deer Pavilion, and were met by a phalanx of photographers asking a smiling Yoshiko and a scowling Isamu to look this way and that, a man in a well-cut but very shabby suit suddenly made a dash toward Yoshiko. It happened very quickly, so I didn't get a close look at his face. But I remember his wild eyes, like those of a hunted animal. I remember Yoshiko's face more clearly, a picture of sheer astonishment. "Sato-san!" she cried, before turning away. All he could shout back was "Yoshiko-chan, I must talk to you!" He was swiftly dragged off by a burly member of the Manyo'en staff, who scolded him as if he were a bad dog.

I asked Yoshiko afterwards who this gentleman was. For a moment I thought he might have been her father. She said that it had all been so long ago. What was? She didn't reply for some time. Then she said that she had known him slightly in Manchuria, during the war, but it was all so long ago. She didn't wish to talk about it now, maybe some other time. Since she was still in visible distress, I didn't probe. Not a word appeared about this incident in the following day's papers, which didn't stint on other details, including a full guest list. Once again I marveled at the way Japanese ignore what they choose not to see. The frantic look on the man's face stayed with me for a long time. He seemed to be persecuted by something or someone. The extraordinary thing was that the next time I asked Yoshiko about him, she claimed to have no recollection of the incident. She even joked about it: "Maybe you saw a ghost, Sid-san!"

The common Japanese verdict on the wedding was summed up in the headline of the social pages of the *Asahi Shimbun:* "American avant-garde artist marries Japanese movie star in a beautifully abstract wedding party." I was not sure quite what was meant by "abstract." I meant to ask Yoshiko later.

20

THE HOUSE IN Kamakura was almost too perfect—a picture of traditional rustic beauty, a scene from an Edo Period scroll, a modern Japanese-style painting expressing a dream vision of "Old Japan," or a set for a historical movie. The main house, nestled between emerald green rice paddies and the purple Kamakura hills, belonged to a distinguished Japanese-style painter (as opposed to the Western-style kind, who typically goes in for ghastly sub-Impressionism with academic earnestness) named Nambetsu Ogata. He was so famous that people dispensed with his family name and just referred to him as Nambetsu. His pictures of birds and fish in black ink or rock pigments on Japanese paper were highly prized by wealthy collectors. A spry little figure, with long pepper and salt hair and a wispy beard, Nambetsu looked quite benign, like an old Chinese sage, but he had a reputation for being difficult. Money, as such, didn't impress him. He once threw a cabinet minister out of his house for calling a picture "pretty," a picture, moreover, that the said politician had fully intended to buy for a very large sum. The man was, as Nambetsu put it, "too vulgar to own a painting of mine."

More than for his pictures even, Nambetsu was known in Japan for what people nowadays would call his "lifestyle," which was entirely traditional. The eighteenth-century farmhouse with its lovely thatched roof was featured frequently in the weekly magazines. Dismantled before the war in a remote village in western Honshu, the house had been carefully reconstructed by carpenters in Kamakura. Not one nail had been used; every piece of timber, sliding screen door, plastered wall, or bamboo fence, every rafter, brace, girt, and purlin, had been joined together like a gigantic puzzle of cedar, cypress, plaster, and teak. The bath, made of solid iron, was heated from below by a wood fire. Even the toilet, of camphorwood filled with boughs of fragrant cedar, was a work of poetry. Squatting in the semidark, listening to the insects buzzing and the rain softly dripping from the eaves, was worth the trip.

Not only did Nambetsu use only traditional pots and bowls—some of them priceless antiques, and some from Nambetsu's own kiln, constructed for him by Bizen potters from Kyushu—but he also manufactured his own paper in the Tosa style. His *Tosa Tengujoshi,* "Wings of Day Flies" paper, was especially fine. He was a superb cook, too. In his traditional country kitchen, two great wooden vats, one filled with seawater, the other with sweet water, contained live fish, which he would scoop up with a net to prepare for dinner with freshly cut vegetables and homemade pickles. To watch Nambetsu tackle a fish was to see an artist at work, cutting and stripping the scales with his favorite knife, made by a famous Kyoto knifemaker, whose family had been forging knives since the early sixteenth century.

Nambetsu never wore Western-style clothes, of course. At work, he wore a traditional indigo cotton artisan's smock. On the rare occasions that he set forth from his house, he wore only kimonos of the finest cottons and silks, all woven in Kyoto. The only concessions he was prepared to make to modern life were electricity—even though he often stated that the beauty of Japanese lacquer and ceramics could be appreciated only by candlelight—and an eccentric fondness for Pepsi-Cola—not Coca-Cola, God forbid, but always Pepsi, which had to be served to him at exactly the right temperature as soon as he emerged from his scalding iron bath. A few degrees too warm or too cold could provoke a ferocious rage. He would scream at poor Tomoko, the maid, and send the unwanted glass crashing to the wooden floor. Once he even struck her in the face, so viciously that she needed stitches, which, full of remorse, he applied himself, without anesthetics, naturally ("new-fangled rubbish"). It must have been excruciating. She didn't utter a sound.

I mention all this because the old rice storage house, opposite the main house, was where Isamu and Yoshiko started their married life (and ended it, too, but we'll get to that later). Much smaller than the main house, though just as old, this too was a rustic place of great traditional beauty. They called it their "love nest." To get to it you passed through an Edo Period gate bearing a plaque in Nambetsu's grass-style calligraphy that read: *Land of Dreams.* The gate was as far as a car could go. From there you had to walk along a narrow path through rice paddies, and up some very steep steps for several hundred yards, past an old disused shrine guarded by stone foxes covered in thick velvety moss, thence up the hill for another hundred yards or so, and finally, panting with exertion, especially on a humid summer's day, you would reach the love nest. Looming behind was Nambetsu's farmhouse. And behind Nambetsu's house was a small hill, with a cone not unlike that of Mount Fuji. This was Taishan, or rather a replica of the sacred Chinese mountain, constructed by Nambetsu as part of his private landscape garden.

Nambetsu had taken a shine to Isamu in a way that was quite uncharacteristic of the old misanthrope. Isamu was perhaps the only person who was never subjected to his famous rages. They first met when Isamu showed his new sculptures, inspired by sixth-century burial figures. Nambetsu's attendance at a Tokyo gallery was such a rare event that it was reported in the national press. Nambetsu never took the trouble to see anyone's show, no matter how distinguished. But he had been a friend of Isamu's father before the war. Or perhaps he was just curious to see how this American had reworked the Haniwa style. Whatever the reason, there he was, in his dark blue kimono, scrutinizing the pieces through his Harold Lloyd glasses, while others gazed at him with great reverence, to see what he would say. His only comment was *kekko*, fine. That was enough. Isamu was launched. And the offer of a place to live was made, for as long as Isamu wanted.

Isamu and Yoshiko had settled into their new life by the time I went to see them. The weather was sublime, a blue spring day, when the birds sang their hearts out and the cherry blossoms floated from the trees like pink snowflakes. Isamu's huge lilac Buick convertible— his one concession to American life, a more grandiose version of Nambetsu's fondness for Pepsi—stood at the gate, as though it had been abandoned by its owner. Isamu was still working in his studio at the back of the house when I arrived. Yoshiko, looking the perfect country woman in her light blue cotton kimono stenciled with a pattern of Xs, greeted me with a wave of her hand, followed by a bow, and then, as an afterthought, since I was, after all, a foreigner, a handshake. I complimented her on her kimono. "Kisses," she laughed, as she pointed to the Xs. "Isamu designed the fabric for me. We had it made in Kyoto." As she poured hot water on the tea leaves from an ancient-looking iron pot, she said, "You know how much Isamu loves Japanese culture." I asked her how she was liking her new life. "Oh, it's most interesting. I've never lived on tatami mats before. In China, we always had Western-style houses. And since I left home I've only really lived in hotels. So I have to learn how to live like a Japanese. But Isamu knows so much about Japan. He's my *sensei*, my teacher."

But it was soon clear to me that she was missing Hollywood already. Everything was so much more efficient there, she said. Things worked in the States, and the enthusiasm of the Americans was so inspiring. "Here in Japan," she'd often say, with a deep theatrical sigh, "it's always, can't do this, can't do that, that's not the way we do things here. It's almost as if they're proud of it." Besides, playing a Japanese war bride was so much more interesting. Here she was typecast as an "exotic," asked to play Korean prostitutes, or Chinese nurses, and once even a native Taiwanese. In America, she felt she was being taken more seriously. "But I'm poor, so I have no choice, Sid-san. I'll take anything I can get." She was in a new picture now, entitled *Lady of Shanghai*, playing a Chinese singer. It was fine, but "I feel a bit like a circus monkey, a monkey that can sing in Chinese."

I wondered how she got to the studio from this remote place. "Oh," she said, "a limousine arrives every morning, to pick me up at the gate. It's a bit of a walk up and down, but it's so beautiful, and Isamu's so happy here. You've seen the sign over the gate?" She giggled. "You know, it really *is* like a Land of Dreams." She kept rubbing her feet. I suggested that it must be painful *clip-clopping* up the hill in her tight wooden sandals. "It's okay," she said. "Isamu loves to see me in traditional clothes."

Isamu was looking pensive as he came out of his studio, wiping his hands on a pretty cloth of indigo cotton. The studio was actually more like a cave hewed out of the rocky hill behind the house. "Tea," he said, without looking at his wife. "Japanese green tea, the one from Shizuoka." "*Hai, hai,*" she answered, and *pitter-pattered* on her blistered feet into the kitchen to go fetch the iron pot.

The difficulty with Isamu, or, indeed most artists of my acquaintance, is that you never knew whether he was listening to what you were saying. One would talk and talk, and he nodded, but his eyes were on some distant world, deep inside himself. The more he lapsed into silence, the more one heard oneself babbling away, like some garrulous housewife.

It was like that on this occasion. I was chattering on about topics that I thought might be of interest, the Buddhist sculptures I had just seen at the Engakuji Temple, a new movie playing in Tokyo, the modern Japanese art scene. He nodded, as always, and said, "That's right," or, "I quite agree," sometimes in English, sometimes in his heavily accented Japanese, but I could tell he wasn't really there. Yet he wasn't oblivious. When Yoshiko said, "Oh, you two, always talking about difficult things," he turned to her with a smile of great tenderness, and said: "You're quite right, we should be talking about what's in front of us, the birds, the sun, the cherry blossoms, the stones. All the answers are right there. You just have to know how to find them."

"What about some lunch?" said Yoshiko, full of good cheer.

And so the afternoon passed, sitting on the tatami floor, by the open screen wall, gazing at paradise. Nothing in this landscape of bamboo groves, cherry blossoms, rice paddies, and fish ponds suggested that we were living in the middle of the twentieth century. Nambetsu had banned telephones, so the vision of loveliness was not disturbed by unsightly telephone lines. If the eye couldn't detect the modern world, nor could the ears: no radio, no loudspeaker, nothing of the mechanical noise that blighted Japanese life even back then. The room we were sitting in was empty except for a single scroll of a laughing monk. "Ah," said Isamu, "this is where I belong. I never want to leave this place as long as I live."

"But darling," said Yoshiko. "What about New York, Paris, and all those other places? Don't you want to stay in touch with the art world?"

"There is nothing to stay in touch with," snorted Isamu. "The art world in New York is without interest. They're like a bunch of mindless dogs chasing each other around the track. Round and round they go, faster and faster, without a clue why they're running. No, this is the real thing." He sniffed the air in a rather exaggerated manner, like a wine connoisseur: "The smell of my childhood." He pulled Yoshiko toward him, hugging her from behind. "And the smell of a beautiful woman."

"Oh, you Americans!" she squealed with full-throated pleasure. He grinned. I felt rather relieved when the gong rang from the main house to summon us to dinner. I adored both of them, of course, but the happiness of friends can be endured only in small doses.

We sat on the floor at a beautifully carved table under a large wooden fish suspended from the ceiling. The fish provided a counter-weight to a suspended cooking pot, in which a stew of vegetables and wild boar meat was bubbling away over a charcoal fire. Nambetsu had also prepared the most delicious-looking sashimi, including large translucent prawns that were still so fresh that they quivered nervously to the touch of our chopsticks. "So what does he do, your friend?" Nambetsu asked Isamu, without looking at me. This was one of those Japanese courtesies I've never quite gotten used to. Why couldn't he have asked me directly?

"He's a"—Isamu paused. "He's a film critic," interjected Yoshiko, "a very distinguished film critic, for the *Japan Evening Post*."

"Ah, a film critic," replied Nambetsu, who did not look very impressed. "For the *Japan Evening Post*? So, which film directors does he like?"

Wishing to show him that I could understand his Japanese perfectly, I jumped into the conversation: "I think this young director, Akira Kurosawa, is very fine. But I also love the films of Keisuke Kinoshita, especially *Carmen Comes Home*, so funny, and yet so poignant . . ."

Nambetsu's wizened head slowly swiveled my way. He examined my face, not with disgust, or even disapproval, but with a hint of surprise. "He speaks Japanese, your friend."

Yoshiko picked up an earthenware bottle and made to pour cold saké into our cypresswood cups. Nambetsu growled again, took the bottle from her hand, and poured it himself. "From Aomori," he said, "the best." He then poured a glass of Pepsi for himself, after testing the temperature and finding it satisfactory.

"So you can eat sashimi, eh?" It was the first time Nambetsu had spoken directly to me.

"Delicious," I said, as I dipped a flesh-colored piece of bonito into a tiny bowl of garlic and soy sauce.

"Fresh from the market," Nambetsu said. "Tomoko went to fetch it early this morning. What do you think, Isamu?"

Isamu nodded approvingly. "It is very good indeed, *sensei.*"

"Isamu loves our food," said Nambetsu, "but then he's got a Japanese spirit. It must be different for foreigners. I know I couldn't eat hamburgers all the time."

"We don't just eat hamburgers," I said, feeling a little defensive. Nambetsu ignored me.

"What about Ozu's pictures? I think he's the best director we have. Still, like sashimi, you have to be Japanese to appreciate him."

I knew I was in danger of being rude, but couldn't stop myself: "Oh, but I like Ozu very much. His films may be about Japanese, but he expresses feelings that we can all share."

I sensed that Isamu was getting irritated. Nambetsu was not used to being contradicted, especially not by a young foreigner like me. Perhaps to appease the old man, Isamu said: "I agree with *sensei.* Some of the feelings may be the same, but the nuances are impossible for foreigners to grasp."

He used the word "foreigner" (*gaijin*), as though he himself were a full-blooded Japanese. Now it was my turn to feel irritated. I didn't much care whether I was being rude. "But I'm a foreigner, and I understand Ozu's films perfectly."

Nambetsu examined me again at leisure, but this time with amusement sharpened by malice: "Ah, what we have here is a crazy foreigner who knows our ways."

Yoshiko, darling Yoshiko, thinking perhaps to save my face, said: "Well, I'm Japanese, and I think Ozu's films are a complete bore."

Isamu stared intensely at the lovely plate in the middle of the table, lined with slices of silvery sashimi, a plate crafted by Nambetsu's own masterly hands. It had a shiny chocolate brown and dark green glaze. Nambetsu looked at Yoshiko, almost pityingly, and said: "Yes, yes. Well, I suppose Ozu would be hard to understand in China."

He took a sip from his glass of chilled Pepsi. Perhaps sparked by Yoshiko's remark, he began to hold forth. "Chinese culture is like a thick, spicy sauce; rich, heavy, a blend of many tastes: sweet and sour, hot and mild. Think of their elaborate traditional dress, the many layers of cotton and silk, the intricate embroideries, the violent colors. Our Japanese kimono is simpler, but more refined. We pare things down to the essential. Look at this piece of raw bonito. To smother it in sauce, the way the Chinese do, is to kill its essence. Our crazy foreign friend here talks about feelings shared by all men. He is right, there are things we all feel, but to express the universal you have to go for utter simplicity. As Basho said: 'The whole world is in a blade of grass.' To savor the pure taste of the bonito is to understand the fishness of things."

At least, I think this is what he said. I'm not sure I understood "the fishness of things." Isamu gazed at his host with a look of sheer adoration. "Tofu!" he shouted, as though he was onto some great new discovery in Japanese culture.

"What's that?" asked Nambetsu, distracted from his train of thought.

"Tofu," cried Isamu. "Japanese culture is like cold white tofu, dipped in a tiny splash of soy sauce and lemon."

"Exactly!" said the old man. "Very well put. Isamu-kun understands us perfectly, even as most Japanese have drowned themselves in an ocean of American vulgarity. Look at our artists, running after every foreign fad like dogs sniffing shit. Ever since the war, we've been trying to snuff out our own culture. We're a nation of suicidal maniacs, that's what we are, stabbing our own hearts, strangling our spirit."

"I don't see why we have to choose," said Yoshiko. "Why not have the best of Chinese culture, American culture, and Japanese culture? I like all of them. Why not mix them up?"

Isamu, looking at Nambetsu, said: "But first you have to know who you are." Even I could hear the grammatical mistakes in his Japanese. It came out sounding something like: "But the first time you must see who I am."

Nambetsu declared that Isamu was absolutely right, that it was no use discussing culture with women, and that Tomoko should hurry up and bring some new bowls (beautifully crafted with a mud-colored glaze of simple bamboo patterns) for the fish stew.

21

EVERYONE WHO LIVES in Tokyo has his favorite district for nocturnal mischief. Some like the raffishness of Shibuya, or the dives
of Ueno. Others prefer the equally seedy but more international atmosphere of Roppongi, where Tony Lucca holds court in his pizza place.
Partial as I am to the plebeian low city along the Sumida River, my
usual hunting grounds are in Shinjuku, once an entrypoint to the city
of Edo, where the horses were fed while their weary masters visited
the brothels. The brothels are still there, though not always in the
same places they used to be. After the war, the areas to the east of the
station were divided into so-called blue lines and red lines, one li-
censed, the other not, run by different yakuza gangs, which regularly
came to blows. The alleys in these warrens, smelling of vomit and
blocked drains, were so narrow that one could almost touch both sides
of the street at once. Actually, one would have had little opportunity to
indulge in such experiments, since the girls lined up on either side
tried their best to drag you into their lairs by clutching your tie, or
other more intimate parts, screeching: "Boss! Boss! Come, come. I'll
show you good time." When they spotted a foreigner, the ones who
didn't instantly recoil in horror shouted: "Hey you, Joe! America number one."

One of the attractions of the blue lines was the offer of so-called
live classes in "art academies." For a fee, girls would pose in the nude.

Pencils for sketching and cameras without film were provided on the premises. After all, these were respectable establishments and the proper forms had to be observed. What the art lovers did afterwards with their models was of course their own affair, and subject to various complicated financial negotiations.

Having no intention of sketching these painted trollops, let alone doing anything else with them, I still liked to sit myself down in one of the bars and watch the action with a beer in one hand and a skewer of pig's heart in the other. My eyes were drawn less to the girls, of course, than to their pimps, tough-looking boys in white pants and dark shades, which they wore even at night. Once in a while I got lucky and one of them allowed me to be used for his pleasure, in a nearby hotel room, or, if I really struck gold, in one of the rooms of the brothel, which reeked of sweat, sex, and cheap cologne. Even then, as I knelt reverently at their feet, they sometimes refused to take off their shades.

There were some establishments, near the blue lines, that catered to gentlemen of my persuasion, but they tended to be filled with young screamers of the kind that I loathed with a passion. Who needs a mincing little assistant hairdresser pawing the hair on your arms like some cheap harlot? I like men, not fake girls, or "sister boys," as the Japanese called them. Men were to be found lurking in the grounds of the Hanazono Shrine, a tradition that goes back at least three hundred years and, I'm happy to say, still persists. Truck drivers, construction workers, and the like went there to get quick relief from the old drag queens, who made up in technique for what they might have lost in looks. They were also much cheaper than the whores in the red lines. If they were drunk, or horny enough, the men would allow me to pleasure them for nothing.

I had to be careful, though, for the drag queens could be vicious. Getting a beating from one of the men was never a serious concern. This was Japan, after all. But I did have to duck more than once from a sharp high heel. One venerable queen of the night even pulled a knife on me once. It happened very quickly. She hitched up her skirt, reached into her garter, and flashed a switchblade, missing my face by inches. Mostly, though, we got along. As long as I didn't get in the way of their business, the drag queens regarded me with amused tolerance. With a few of them, Fellatio Yoko and Shinjuku Mari, I even became quite friendly. Fellatio Yoko had been a soldier on the Burma front. God only knows what she had been up to in the jungle. She told me a story once about her platoon getting stuck during the monsoon rains in the Irawaddy delta. When the water rose, the men had to climb the trees to escape from the crocodiles. Debilitated by hunger and fatigue, many failed to hold on, and you heard them screaming while the crocs feasted. Such reminiscences were rare, however. Usually we just discussed tricks. Fellatio knew a hundred different ways to make a man come, without even bothering to take her clothes off. When doing what she was best at, she always made sure to remove her dentures. "More better," she assured me.

I loved those Shinjuku streets, especially at night, when the neon lights threw a purplish haze over the city, and the promise of adventure hung in the air like the heady smell of magnolia in summer. Even the most depraved pleasures were offered innocently, as natural parts of life, like eating and drinking. Shinjuku was my turf, as much as the shrines and temples of Kamakura, or the moviehouses of Asakusa. One was for the body, the others for the soul. I did, naturally, venture out into the more respectable areas of Japanese society, too. I knew how to be a good boy. But nothing delighted me more, before attending some important social function, than a little wallow in the Shinjuku mud. There I was, fresh from a hot encounter with a rough young hood behind Hanazono Shrine, bowing to the president of the Japanese Motion Pictures Association, or discussing the tea ceremony with the Dutch ambassador's wife.

There were times when social or professional obligation forced me into straighter forms of entertainment. These occasions were endurable if one took an anthropological interest in them. One of my more memorable nights of this kind was spent in the company of none other than Nambetsu-*sensei*. After several more dinners in the Land of Dreams, he had decided that I was all right after all, a crazy foreigner who truly did have some understanding of Japan. I was honored to have earned his approval and had warmed to him, too. Since he did not get up to Tokyo very often, I was particularly honored to be included in his party at an exclusive and no doubt absurdly expensive hostess bar in the Ginza, called *Kiku no Shiro*, or "Kiku's Castle." O-Kiku was the Mama-san, who ran the place with the discipline of a first-rate military commander. If any of her girls slipped up, dropping a tray or even just a napkin, or failing in any way to burnish the egos of the pampered customers to a bright enough sheen, the Mama-san made sure they paid the full price of her fury. A slap in the face, I was told, was the least they might expect. Always dressed in an immaculate kimono, O-Kiku, an elegant woman in her forties, treated her loyal customers with the elaborate manners of a royal courtesan. As the recipient of countless intimacies, she knew more secrets behind the bland facade of Japanese politics and business than the prime minister himself. Although there was never any hint of this in public, apart from a certain air of familiarity between them, Yoshiko had told me that Nambetsu was in fact O-Kiku's patron. I found her as terrifying as I often found him.

We sat around a black lacquered table in a rather too brightly lit fawn-colored room, with soft jazz playing in the background. There was not much decoration apart from some hideous flower arrangements of camellias in shiny pink vessels. Our party consisted of Nambetsu himself, of course, and his business manager, a thin man in pince-nez glasses named Tanaka, who asked me the occasional question about Paris, where he had been several times, and I never. Then there was a young gallery owner, whom I suspected of being a gentleman of my persuasion. Nambetsu was flanked on either side by kimonoed hostesses, who tittered annoyingly, while feeding him little snacks with their chopsticks, and making sure his glass was regularly topped up with Pepsi-Cola mixed with an expensive brand of French cognac. Sitting back in the soft-cushioned sofa, smiling away as he opened his moist lips to receive another morsel of dried cuttlefish or raw tuna, this often ferocious man, on this occasion, looked oddly babyish and wholly benign. The two other men, the manager and the nelly gallery owner, said very little, but, like the hostesses, laughed at all the *sensei*'s jokes and told him how right he was whenever he expounded on any subject that took his fancy.

My own role in the proceedings was not entirely clear until many hours had passed, and we all had had too much to drink. I was still enough of a foreigner to believe that silence was bad manners, so I offered my opinions on this and that, which were received by the old man with indulgence. Once in a while, he would look at me with mock severity and say: "Always remember that I'm the *sensei* here." As if I could forget. The longer the evening wore on, however, the more it became clear that one of Tanaka's professional duties was to be the butt of Nambetsu's cruel jests, not all of which were amusing. "Tanaka here knows less about culture than our crazy foreigner." The hostesses tittered. Tanaka grinned awkwardly. Not wishing to be left out, I laughed along with the rest of them. "Tanaka is like the proverbial frog in the well, quacking with pleasure at the shadows in the dark. *Quack, quack, quack,* he goes . . ." Tanaka's smile froze on his face. "Go *quack, quack, quack,* frog!" Nambetsu ordered. Tanaka began to perspire and reached for a napkin. The hostesses told Nambetsu to open his little mouth wide and fed him more snacks. The gallery owner, sensing danger, tried to humor Nambetsu. "Oh sensei," he said, "you are too severe. Not all of us can be men of the world like you."

"Men of the world?" Nambetsu shouted. "What do you know about the world? The crazy foreigner, he knows. He's traveled all over the world. He's international. That's why he has something to say, unlike you bumpkins."

From then on, the two men, Tanaka and the gallery owner, were ignored altogether, and Nambetsu addressed himself exclusively to me. The Pepsi and cognac had worked their effect. His speech was slurred, as he beckoned me to move closer, which meant that Tanaka, doubtless with a certain sense of relief, had to change places with me. "Sid-san," Nambetsu said confidentially, breathing brandy fumes into my face, "it's time for me to branch out, to break away from this narrow little island country, in short, to become international. I know that foreigners like my art. After the war, the Americans bought my paintings. I even sold some to General MacArthur, you know. But the Americans have gone home now. It's time for my art to cross the ocean. You know people in New York. I'm appointing you to be my representative. I want you to introduce my art in foreign countries."

Although flattered by his confidence in my connections abroad, this request made me feel deeply uneasy. I knew I couldn't just refuse. That would be taken as a snub. I wondered whether he had asked Isamu first. He was much better placed than I was to help Nambetsu get established in Paris or New York. Or did he respect Isamu too much as an artist to make such a request? I was just a critic, a movie critic for a local English-language paper, so I could be asked for such favors without any danger of causing offense. Indeed, I should feel honored. And so I did, to be sure. But how could I possibly deliver on any promise I might make? When Yoshiko asked me for a similar favor, she saved me from embarrassment by employing her own entrepreneurial skills. She was prepared to go out and promote herself, in Hollywood, Chicago, or New York. I was let off the hook. As for Nambetsu, I could see trouble looming.

When I finally got to bed that night—alone, I might add—I had resolved to write a letter to Brad Martin and possibly Parker Tyler. They might be able to give me some pointers on how to deal with this unwanted burden. I fell asleep and dreamed that I was walking through Yasukuni Dori, the avenue running through the most crowded part of Shinjuku, dressed in nothing but my underpants. This was a disconcerting experience. I don't remember how or even whether I resolved my predicament.

22

TO SAY THAT Yoshiko was happy when she was offered the part of Mariko in *House of Bamboo* would be a grotesque understatement; she was ecstatic. This would finally launch her Hollywood career, she would be an international star: "Oh, my gosh, Sid-san, Twentieth Century–Fox! In Japan! I will show the world my country. I will show how we have changed, how we have become a beautiful, peaceful country." When I heard that *House of Bamboo* was to be a remake of a gangster picture, set in Tokyo instead of New York, and directed by Sam Fuller, master of film noir, I wasn't so sure that Yoshiko's vision of peace and beauty would turn out quite the way she imagined. But who was I to spoil her party.

Isamu failed to share his wife's joy. The thing is, he wanted her around all the time. He didn't even like it when Yoshiko took off in her limo to be at the Oriental Peace Studios. Fortunately, however, Isamu too had been blessed by a stroke of good fortune, which took his mind off his domestic worries, at least for a while. Kenzo Tange, the architect, asked him to design the Peace Memorial in Hiroshima. Tange said Isamu was the perfect artist to "heal the wounds of war," an opinion shared wholeheartedly by Isamu himself. On his return to Japan after the war, he had told reporters that he had come not just to make art, but "to reshape Japan." Here was his chance to do just that, in Hiroshima, in the middle of Peace Park, right above which the fateful bomb had exploded. With this task in hand, he would be more than just an artist in his father's land; he would contribute to its legacy. His creation would be there for centuries to come, an expression of emotions that were not just Japanese, or American, but universal. That, give or take a word, is how Isamu put it.

I, too, benefited from fortune's sudden largesse, for the producers of *House of Bamboo* had asked me to be the liaison man between Hollywood and Tokyo, to smooth over cultural frictions, make sure no Japanese feathers were ruffled overly much, keep Sam Fuller happy, take care that the right people were paid off to let us work on location—the right people usually being the local yakuza gang. My friendship with Tony Lucca proved to be invaluable when it came to these practical matters.

The first person to arrive in Tokyo, on a kind of reconnaissance mission, was the main producer, by the name of Maurice "Buddy" Adler. I was bracing myself for boorish behavior: failure to take off shoes in Japanese homes, using soap in Japanese bathtubs, shouting at waiters, that sort of thing. We met at his hotel, the Imperial. Thinking I'd hit the right note of American familiarity, I addressed him as "Buddy," which did not go down well. An eyebrow was slowly raised: " 'Mr. Adler' will do fine." I should have known better. Silver-haired and beautifully turned out in custom-made English suits, Adler looked like a high-powered banker. On his first night in Tokyo, he invited Yoshiko and myself for dinner. It had to be Japanese food, he insisted. We went to Hanada-en, where they were used to serving distinguished foreigners.

"Are you a Jew?" asked Yoshiko. It was perhaps not the happiest opening gambit at dinner with a perfect stranger who was producing her next film. I froze. Up shot his right eyebrow again. He pursed his lips and ran his right hand down his silk tie, as though to smooth away any creases. "Madam, may I enquire why you ask?" I was beginning to have second thoughts about my role as the cultural mediator.

"Oh," said Yoshiko, childlike in her undisguised joy at dining with such an eminent man, "I thought all producers in Hollywood were Jews. You know, I used to know many Jews in China. They were such cultured people, and so clever. I love Jewish culture: Mozart, Einstein, President Roosevelt, George Cukor . . ."

"That's quite a formidable group," Adler said, "but I rather think some of them would be surprised to be included in that company. As for myself, since you kindly asked, my father became a Lutheran in Vienna around the turn of the century."

"Vienna!" cried Yoshiko. "I knew it. Jewish culture, in music, in theater, wonderful."

"Madam," said Adler, who seemed quite ready to move on to another topic, "I have been fortunate enough to meet many cultured people, some from Vienna, some Jewish. But Jewish culture is not something I recognize, except of course in the synagogue."

"There used to be a beautiful synagogue in Harbin," said Yoshiko. And that, to my intense relief, rather exhausted the subject.

Adler in a display of his perfect manners took Yoshiko's innocent remarks with good humor. I was thankful that much of the rest of the dinner conversation revolved around her role in the movie. She had to feel free, Adler told her, to make comments if the lines didn't sound correct. It was most important to get the cultural details absolutely right. Her role was a pivotal one, since she had the only major Japanese part in the film. There was one other Japanese, the good Tokyo cop, to be played by Sessue Hayakawa. But Mariko was the more important role, for she was at the very center of the story.

The tale of betrayals and double betrayals had a typical B-movie plot. It opens with a botched heist in Tokyo by a gang of discharged

GIs. A fellow named Webber is shot by one of his own gang. Just before he dies, he tells the Japanese cop (Hayakawa) that he has a Japanese wife, Mariko. He also discloses that his best pal, a convict named Eddie Spanier, will come to Japan as soon as they let him out of jail in the States. Instead of the real Spanier, however, a military cop (Robert Stack), pretending to be Spanier, joins the gang, and takes Mariko on as his "kimono girl" for cover. Sandy, the gang boss (Robert Ryan), likes the new guy. Unfortunately, this makes Sandy's "number one boy," a young punk named Griff, jealous. Mariko falls in love with Eddie. Eddie tells her he isn't who she thinks he is, and that he's after the gang that killed her husband. Sandy hears of the double-cross. He tries to kill Eddie. Eddie kills Sandy instead, in an amusement park. Eddie and Mariko walk off, arm-in-arm, down the Ginza.

Simple enough. But there was trouble even before the shooting began. Hayakawa, arriving at Haneda from Hollywood dressed in an absurdly lavish kimono, like a Kabuki actor a hundred years ago, was furious because the Japanese press wasn't there to meet him, whereas Robert Ryan merited a full press conference. Off he went to his hotel in high dudgeon. The star's mood didn't improve when he found out that he had to share a studio dressing room with three other actors, instead of having one to himself. "I'm a Hollywood star," he protested, "and I deserve respect!" Sam Fuller told him to talk to the studio people, and they told him to talk to me. Since there was nothing I could do, he went back to the studio people, who went back to Sam Fuller, who told Hayakawa that he was indeed a major star, and he would talk to the studio people, et cetera. Hayakawa finally got a room to himself.

The set on the first day of shooting was supposed to be Mariko's house in Tokyo. Stuart Weiss, the set designer, had come up with something that bore very little resemblance to a Japanese room. It looked more like a lavish restaurant in Chinatown, with odd red lanterns and

other bits of Oriental frippery. The Japanese set builders were too polite to say anything. If this is what the foreigners wanted, this is what
they would get. Yoshiko told Fuller that the set looked very strange.
Fuller replied that it looked just fine to him. "Shirley," he said, "don't
you worry your pretty little head over these details. This picture has to
play in Peoria, not Yokohama."

"But Mr. Adler said . . ."

"I don't give a damn what Mr. Adler said. He isn't making the
movie. I am. And I say it's fine."

To say that Yoshiko and Bob Stack didn't warm to one another
would be putting it mildly. She couldn't stand him. I never quite figured out why. He was a bit on the dull side, to be sure, talking endlessly
about his mother back in L.A. Although he had made a splash earlier
in his career as the first man to kiss Deanna Durbin on screen, he was
not the romantic type. Yoshiko liked men to make a fuss over her. Bob
Ryan certainly did. She complained to me that Bob had quite fallen in
love with her, which didn't seem to overly bother her. Quite the contrary, I should say. In fact, Bob, a strict Catholic, and a married man,
was not known as a Lothario. But he followed Yoshiko about like a dog
in heat. I once caught him banging on her dressing room door, shouting: "But Shirley, I love you!" It was all most unseemly.

But Yoshiko was a pro. I watched her shoot the famous scene with
Stack in the Chinese restaurant that was supposed to be her apartment. He was on his stomach, dressed in a kind of funereal black kimono, his shoulders bared, as she, in a bright red kimono, more
appropriate for a bar hostess than a demure young woman, kneaded
his spine. "Where did you learn how to do that?" he purrs.

Yoshiko: "In Japan, every girl learn from early age how to please
the man."

Stack: "So what is it in a man that attracts a Japanese woman? Broad shoulders? Muscles?"

Yoshiko: "Nooo . . ."

Stack: "So what makes a Japanese woman want to . . . ?" (Yoshiko whispers something in his ear) "What?"

Yoshiko: "His eyebrows. In Japan, woman finds eyebrows so romantic."

Stack: "That's traditional, too, eh?"

No wonder Yoshiko found her Hollywood debut rather a disappointment.

23

I T WAS DURING a rare break in the shooting, between locations, on a Saturday morning, that the phone rang in my apartment in Azabu. "Hellooo," said a reedy voice, clearly American, probably Southern, almost certainly female. "How are you, Sid? It's meee." Who? "Meee, Truman." Funny name for a girl, I thought. I had no idea who I was talking to. Who? "Ooh, Sid," came the reply. "Truman, Truman Capote. Parker gave me your number. I thought you might be my Cicerone in this garden of vice, or should I say my Mephistopheles?"

Of course I had heard of Truman Capote. I had actually read his *Other Voices, Other Rooms*. I admired his writing, but I had never made his acquaintance, and certainly hadn't expected a phone call. I must admit that the voice threw me. Still, I would soon get used to it, since for the next eight days, he called me at all hours; where to buy drugs for his migraine, where to have lunch, where to drink cocktails, or buy American magazines or a pair of socks. But mostly he called to tell me he was bored: "Bored, bored, bored, darling. Is there really *nowhere* in this ugly town where a boy can have some fun?" I told him about the attractions of Asakusa and Ueno. But he showed no interest.

Truman had come to Tokyo on an assignment from *The New Yorker*, to write a profile of Marlon Brando, who was shooting a movie with Josh Logan in Kyoto. Unfortunately, Logan had banned journalists from the set, and told Brando to reject all requests for interviews. He knew just what a literary bitch like Truman might make of his Japanese venture. So Truman chose to be cooped up like a fuming prisoner in his room at the Imperial ("A retirement home in Akron, Ohio, my dear"). If he couldn't have his interview with Brando, he would sulk: "Hell isn't hot enough for that old Jewish queen Logan."

I decided that the only way to snap him out of this mood, which wasn't doing anyone any good, was to make sure he found some romance. So I took him on a little tour. He was mildly amused by the drag queens at Hanazono Shrine, but dismissed the boys in the blue line bars, even though some of the boys certainly showed an interest in him. They couldn't get enough of his light blond hair, which they stroked as though he were a Siamese cat. On and on we went, from bar to bar, ending up in a place called *Bokushin no Gogo,* Japanese for *L'Après-midi d'un faune.* A photograph of Clark Gable gazed at us from the wall. The furniture was a kind of fake French Empire style, made of cheap wood painted gold. Truman held forth amusingly on grisly murders in the American South. Whenever I pointed out some promising Japanese youth, he turned away after a perfunctory glance and said: "Too small." What did he mean, too small? "Too small down there." How did he know? He held up his thumb, as if to hitch a ride: "Just look at their thumbs, honey. It never fails."

At two o'-clock in the morning, groggy from too many watered-down whiskeys, no longer amused by the murder stories, tired of trying to pimp for the great young American novelist, I said to him: "Is there really nobody you like?"

"Yes, there is," he mewed.

"Thank God for that. Who?"

He glanced at me slyly from the corner of his eye: "You."

Time to go home, I thought, though I managed to extricate myself a little more politely.

I thought I would never hear from Truman again, after my attempt to find him some romance ended in disappointment, and more sulking on his part. But two days later, the phone rang just as I was trying to write my weekly movie review. It was about two o'clock in the afternoon. The crows were making a terrible noise outside my window. Not only was there no trace of his earlier funk, he sounded positively delirious: "Honey, I'm in heaven!" I asked him where he was. "In heaven. Why didn't you tell me about this place, Asakusa! All the pretty things you can buy around the temple . . ." But I *had* mentioned Asakusa to him. "No, you did not. I had to find it all on my own."

As with much of what Truman said, this turned out to be a falsehood. Sam Fuller had invited him to come and watch the last scene, of Bob Stack shooting Bob Ryan in an amusement park on the roof of an Asakusa department store—gunshots and merry-go-rounds, carnival music and murder, the kind of thing Orson Welles did so well in *The Lady from Shanghai*. Bored with waiting for the action to start, Truman had gone wandering around the Kannon Temple market, with its rows of little stalls filled with touristy gewgaws. "Oh, those lovely artificial flowers, those gorgeous gold Buddhas, those adorable dwarf trees . . . And I bought myself a beautiful silk kimono, jade green, with the most marvelous chrysanthemums in gold thread. It was just as I remember it from Aunt Marie's parlor in Alabama. You know, as a boy, I would spend hours with her Oriental menagerie, imagining I was in Japan. Now I know it's all true. Oh, Sid, I wish you could have been there."

24

EVERYTHING SEEMED TO be going so well with Isamu's project in Hiroshima. While Yoshiko was out filming, Isamu worked on his designs from morning till night, alone in his cave, like a hermit monk possessed by a vision that had to be realized at all costs. When he emerged from his cave in the evenings, all he wanted to do was talk to Nambetsu about atonement, historical memory, the aesthetics of war, and other lofty subjects. Yoshiko, exhausted from long days in the studio, was a silent witness to these intellectual exchanges. Once she actually fell asleep at Nambetsu's table, her head falling into one of his exquisite bowls filled with a particularly choice selection of raw sea urchins. Nambetsu was beside himself. Isamu, to placate his mentor, immediately shook his wife awake and told her to apologize for her appalling manners. She broke down in sobs, rushed into the night, lost her footing in the dark, and fell into a rice paddy, yelping with pain as she twisted her ankle. (If you look very carefully in the scene of *House of Bamboo* where she meets Bob Stack for the first time, you can see a flesh-colored supporting bandage on her right leg.) The men continued to drink saké and discuss art until well past midnight.

Isamu's design for the Peace Memorial, to be called the Arch of Peace, consisted of a squat dome, like a huge Haniwa funeral ornament, with an underground vault. This somber space, Isamu explained to me, was meant to be a kind of traditional tea ceremony room, where people could reflect on matters of life and death. Inside would be a black granite slab engraved with the names of all the Japanese victims of the atom bomb. There were victims who were not Japanese, of course, but it was decided by the Hiroshima Peace Memorial City Construction Committee that for the sake of "public coherence" (I think I have the translation right) they would not be included. This was no fault of Isamu's. Thousands of Koreans, many of them slave workers, had died from the bomb, instantly if they were lucky, or slowly, in terrible pain, if they were not. When representatives of the Japanese-Korean community protested some years later about the exclusion of Korean victims, there was a typical municipal row, with demonstrations, and harsh words in the press. In the end Koreans were permitted to build their own memorial just outside the borders of Peace Park.

But this was not yet an issue when Isamu, after many months' work, for which he wasn't receiving a dime, submitted his plans to the Hiroshima Peace Memorial City Construction Committee, consisting of various notables from the government and the architectural profession. Tange had praised Isamu's plans for their boldness and clarity. Both men were itching for the construction to start. Surely nothing could go wrong now. But something did, of course, go wrong. A formal letter from the committee was passed on to Tange, who had to break the news to Isamu. His design had been turned down, because the proposal, in the words of the gentlemen of the committee, "although no doubt admirably suited to foreign countries, such as the United States, was not appropriate for Japan." As the letter explained, such a delicate project could only be entrusted to an artist "who understands Japanese feelings."

Isamu was devastated, but much too proud to say anything in public. Privately, I could see his earlier zeal to change Japan slowly turning sour. This might explain the notorious plastic shoe incident, notorious that is among those of us who found ourselves entangled in the life of

Yoshiko. I happened to be there, in the Land of Dreams, when the actual incident occurred. It was one of those sultry summer evenings, when you work up a sweat just sitting still. Isamu and I were drinking cold saké from wooden cups. Yoshiko was still out filming somewhere. She had left around five-thirty in the morning, in the studio Packard. She rarely returned before nine or ten at night.

Isamu was in one of his intense moods, brooding over the lack of understanding in Japan of his art. First he was hailed as a savior, the famous American artist who had come all the way from New York to teach the Japanese how to be modern. Now they resented it when he tried to convince them that their own tradition was actually closer to the modern spirit than all their third-rate imitations of Western trends. "I'm not in the slightest bit interested in exoticism," he said, his dark eyes burning with the passion of his conviction. "I'm just telling them to look into their own souls. You know, the problem with the Japanese is that they're the only ones who won't learn from Japan."

The last rays of the sun were painting the landscape pink, as though the rice paddies were covered in cherry blossoms. A small speck of white in the distance was moving slowly in our direction. The speck turned out to be Yoshiko's Packard. She sighed with relief as she stepped onto the veranda after taking off a pair of light blue plastic sandals: "Home at last. It's been such a long day. I'm exhausted. My feet have been killing me. Is there any cold barley tea?" Isamu stared at her feet and didn't reply. He didn't even respond to her greeting. I assumed he was still sunk in his thoughts about Japanese art.

Yoshiko neatly arranged her plastic sandals at the entrance to the house, and was about to fetch the tea from the kitchen herself. I offered to help her. No need, she said. Then something snapped in Isamu's mind, like a spring that had been coiled too tightly: "Oi!" he shouted at Yoshiko. "Come back here!" First I'm getting some tea, she said. "Come back here right now!" he screamed. I had never seen

Isamu in such a rage. It was as if he were mimicking, in exaggerated fashion, Nambetsu's tantrums.

Yoshiko, looking pale and flustered, stepped back onto the veranda: "What?"

He answered in English: "What the fuck do you think you're wearing?"

"What do you mean? My usual summer kimono. The one you like. What's wrong with it?" Despite her visible exhaustion, she smiled, still eager to please.

"I mean this junk!" Isamu stooped to pick up the plastic sandals and tossed them in a high arc far away into the rice paddy, where they slowly sank into the mud. "How dare you come into this house wearing this vulgar plastic rubbish! Have you no taste at all? It's an abomination, a desecration! An attack on everything I'm trying to accomplish in this wretched country of yours."

First she looked bewildered, then she was speechless, and finally it was Yoshiko's turn to be furious. "Oh, so now it's just my country, is it? What about your boasts of being so Japanese? If you're just a foreigner, what do you care about my sandals? Plastic is American, no? Well, let me show you something . . ." She took a pair of traditional Japanese straw sandals out of her bag; they were covered in splotches of red. "I've worn these to please you, Mr. Japanese Tradition. Well, look what they did to my feet!" She peeled off a Band-Aid from the side of her left foot and showed us a nasty gash with pus oozing at the edges. "Unlike you, I *am* Japanese. Why should I have to ruin my feet to prove it? I'll tell you one thing, you're just a typical American, you'll never understand our feelings."

I wish I could have disappeared, but there was no chance of that. "Stay," said Yoshiko, quite firmly, when I mumbled something about it being time to get back to Tokyo. I didn't wish to hurt her feelings, so I stayed, a mute and uncomfortable witness to their marital distress.

"You think you lost your precious commission in Hiroshima because of discrimination," said Yoshiko, whose anger was far from dying down. "It wasn't discrimination. It was your bad manners. I told you to take gifts when you went to see the committee members. They were very hurt. I know. I was there, remember?"

Isamu, still panting from his fit of hysteria, snorted with contempt: "What do you mean, gifts? This is a professional job. I'm not asking them for a favor. What do you expect me to do? Bribe them? That's all nonsense."

Calmer, but still speaking with a steeliness I had rarely seen in Yoshiko, she replied: "You'll never understand, will you? We're not talking about bribes. We're talking about goodwill, about custom, about *tradition*. You're always spinning theories about our traditions. But you don't understand it in your heart. You only think with your head, like a typical foreigner."

If all had been well in the Land of Dreams, I guess this storm would have blown itself out, so to speak, in the conjugal bed, followed the next morning by apologetic smiles. But that's not the way it was. Yoshiko retired to the bedroom, Isamu went back to his studio to work, and I spent the night drifting in and out of dreams, one of which I can recall because it was so utterly peculiar: I walked into a bar stark naked. It resembled the *Après-midi d'un faune* in Kanda; or at least the fake antique French tables did. The place was full of men, wearing kimonos. One of them was Nambetsu, who was leading them in a tea ceremony. I wanted to take part. But nobody listened. They totally ignored me, as if I wasn't even there.

25

THE PARTY FOR *House of Bamboo* in Tokyo was more like a wake. *Le tout Tokyo* was in attendance, of course, dressed in all their finery, even though everyone knew it was an absolute stinker. This being Japan, no one openly said so, but word had traveled at lightning speed. Remarks after the premiere screening were carefully chosen. "Most remarkable," murmured Mr. Kawamura. "Quite so, quite so," added Madame. "Very interesting," was Hotta's verdict, "Japan seen through blue eyes." "The costumes were very nice" was the opinion of dear, loyal Mifune. And Kurosawa just looked amiable and said nothing at all.

Since none of the American actors had bothered to come to Tokyo for the premiere, poor Yoshiko was left to face the disastrous reception of her Hollywood picture alone. Well, not quite alone. There was always Twentieth Century–Fox's man in Tokyo, a preposterous figure named "Mike" Yamashita, who sported large gold cufflinks engraved with his initials, wore striped suits in the style of a Chicago mobster, and thumped every foreigner on the back. Mike was of little help in a crisis.

So there was Yoshiko, at the official press conference in the Hilltop Hotel in Kanda, dressed in her kimono, fielding questions from a largely hostile press about flaws in the film for which she could hardly be held responsible. The many errors—only the *Yomiuri Shimbun* was

kind enough to call them "misunderstandings"—were not just regarded as regrettable mistakes by the Japanese reviewers but as deliberate insults to Japanese honor. The fact that minor Japanese roles
were played by Japanese-American immigrants with only a rudimen-
tary knowledge of their ancestral language; the fact that Japanese
rooms looked like Chinese restaurants; the fact that a man running in
the Ginza turned a corner to find himself almost climbing the slopes
of Mount Fuji. These were all taken as American slaps delivered
firmly, and quite deliberately, on the national face.

Mr. Shinoda of *Kinema Jumpo:* "What do you feel about being in a
movie that will make the whole world laugh at us?"

Mr. Horikiri of the *Asahi Shimbun:* "Do you agree that *House of
Bamboo* is a typical example of U.S. imperialist arrogance?"

Mr. Shindo of *Tokyo Shimbun:* "Do you still think of yourself as a
Japanese?"

Forget national face; every question landed like a stinging blow on
Yoshiko's own face. Although nobody actually used the word, the im-
plication was quite clear: Yamaguchi Yoshiko was a traitor.

She managed to keep her composure during the press conference,
but broke down as soon as we were alone. Tears flooded down her
cheeks, making a terrible mess of her makeup. Black lines streamed
like little rivers down the craggy pink valleys of her face. How could
they do this to her? Why did they say these terrible things? Didn't they
know how hard she had tried to improve the image of Japan in the
outside world? She had done her very best to tell Sam Fuller about the
errors in the film. Why didn't people appreciate her more? I tried to
console her as best I could, as we sat in the back of the Twentieth Century car, an absurdly large, lemon yellow Cadillac Eldorado, rolling
past the moat of the Imperial Palace, where only a few years before a
GI had been lynched by a Japanese mob after it became known that
the United States would be keeping its military bases in Japan. There

was no mob there now, just people rushing to and from work in the gray drizzle, and provincials lining up in front of the palace gate to have their souvenir photographs taken.

My own review in the *Japan Evening Post* did not come easily. I found a way, though, of maneuvering around the danger areas while remaining essentially honest. I decided to treat the movie as a fairy tale, an American fairy tale set in Japan. To take it as an attempt to show the real Japan would be a grave misunderstanding. Shirley Yamaguchi, I wrote, "brilliantly acts out the Occidental fantasy of the Oriental woman. Not since Madame Butterfly has the loving innocence and gentle submissiveness of this iconic figure been conveyed with such consummate skill."

The next time I saw Yoshiko, for lunch at a tempura restaurant in the Nishino Building, she didn't mention my review, which I took as a silent acknowledgment of my friendly intentions. She was wearing a mauve kimono, and a pair of large sunglasses, presumably as a shield against prying eyes. When she took them off, I noticed that her eyes were bloodshot and puffy. I thought it was the torrid reception of her movie, and was about to commiserate, telling her what unthinking idiots journalists were, but her anxiety turned out to have a different source. Yoshiko had been asked to be in a musical on Broadway, *Shangri-La*, a musical version of James Hilton's *Lost Horizon*. It is a variation of the Rip van Winkle story. A plane carrying Westerners from the war in China crashes in the Himalayas. The survivors wake up in a mysterious place where time doesn't exist and peace lasts forever. One of them, a British novelist, falls in love with a beautiful Oriental woman (Yoshiko). They decide to elope. But the moment they leave the timeless zone of eternal peace, the beautiful young woman becomes a wrinkled old crone.

I had seen Mr. Capra's *Lost Horizon* before the war, with Ronald Colman as the novelist and Sam Jaffe as the High Lama. For months

I dreamed of Tibetan temples, Oriental wise men, and snowcapped mountains. It fed my loathing of the world I lived in, its addiction to material wealth and violence. I'd have accepted a one-way ticket to Shangri-la anytime.

"My dear," I said, "the part sounds perfect for you. You must do it, of course." She nodded vigorously. Starring in a Broadway musical had always been her dream. She couldn't have asked for anything better, she assured me. But she didn't look happy at all. She kept readjusting her collar, as the truth emerged in bits and pieces. Apparently Isamu didn't want her to go. He wanted her to stay in Kamakura, and anyway, he said, the musical was just "mediocre American rubbish." But that hurdle had been negotiated, though not without a few paper doors being torn and crockery smashed on the way. Isamu gave in. He had to. As Yoshiko said: "My career was on the line. We're both artists, but he doesn't understand that I work for the public. I need an audience. It's different for Isamu-san. He just works for himself."

Then a second, far more formidable barrier arose: her visa application was denied. No reason given. Strings were pulled. Kawamura wrote to a friend at the embassy. Letters went back and forth between Tokyo and Washington. It took several months before an answer emerged from the American consul in Tokyo: Yoshiko was "a threat to U.S. national security." This sounded quite mad. But still no stated reason. More letters were sent, and contacts asked to intervene. It turned out that Yoshiko was suspected of Communist activities. But why? More time, more letters, more interviews. The name of Colonel Wesley F. Gunn came up in the files. He had marked Yoshiko as a suspected Communist agent in wartime Manchuria. Her childhood friend, "the Jewess Masha," was known to be working for the Soviet government. And besides, hadn't Yoshiko been conspicuously friendly with Charlie Chaplin, even as his "un-American" activities became known?

Just as life's misfortunes ambush a person without warning, help too can come from the least expected quarters. There is a certain rough justice in this, I guess. A year or so before Yoshiko's visa problem, she had played the part of a mistress of a British merchant in Yokohama in an utterly forgettable Japanese picture called, for some reason, *Autumn Wind*. Ikebe was in this movie as well, playing the merchant's handsome Japanese servant. The foreigner is cruel. The mistress falls for the servant. They try to elope. The foreigner is about to kill the servant. She threatens to kill herself. The foreigner hesitates. The lovers get away in the fog.

A forgettable picture, as I said, but a fateful one. For the British merchant was played by a fellow by the name of Stan Lutz. I knew him slightly. He had held a position in Willoughby's intelligence section. A shady character, with straw blond hair and thin lips, Lutz had stayed on in Japan after the occupation ended. I spotted him once or twice at Tony Lucca's place, eating pizzas with Japanese men with big necks and flashy neckties, the kind one doesn't pick a quarrel with. I didn't much care for Lutz. But Yoshiko appears to have got along with him all right. He played in a few other Japanese movies, many of them a trifle louche, the kind of thing we would call "soft porn" today, all pretty bad. There were other ventures, too, in businesses of one kind or another.

Lutz was not unusual. I knew the type. Japan offered rich pickings for men who weren't too fussy about the way they made their money. As Lucca would say, it was all a matter of connections, and Lutz had more powerful ones than most. One of them was a man named Yoshio Taneguchi, an indicted war criminal who had written a well-known memoir while awaiting his trial. The Allies arrested him for crimes committed in China during the war: torture, assassinations, looting, that kind of thing. Rumor had it that he was very rich. During the war, the Imperial Japanese government had been grateful enough for his services to give him the honorary title of "Rear Admiral." The translator and publisher of Taneguchi's memoir was Stan Lutz.

Anyway, Taneguchi never had to stand trial. Willoughby had him released, because of his wartime reputation as an avid hunter of Japanese Communists, just the kind of man the Americans thought they needed when China fell in the late 1940s and Japanese trade unions were beginning to get troublesome. It turned out that Taneguchi had a soft spot for Yoshiko, whom he remembered from her Ri Koran days in China. When Lutz told him about Yoshiko's visa problem, he said something about having been a member of Ri Koran's "fan club" in Manchuria. He promised he would have a word with friends in the U.S. government. The visa came through in a week. What Lutz got out of the transaction, I don't know. Perhaps he had acted purely out of friendship. But neither "purely" nor "friendship" are words I would normally apply to an operator like Lutz.

To thank him for his kind help in this personal matter, Yoshiko hosted a small dinner for Taneguchi at a discreet Japanese restaurant near the Hattori Building in the Ginza. We had a private tatami room. Lutz came. Kawamura had been invited, but when he heard the name Taneguchi, he suddenly remembered a previous engagement. Isamu was there, reluctantly, one felt. The party was never going to be convivial. It was one of those ceremonial occasions without which Japanese society could not function. Yoshiko made sure only the most expensive dishes were served. The service was impeccable and the food tasted, well, expensive. Yoshiko, as a token of her gratitude, handed a beautifully wrapped gift to Taneguchi, a short porcine man with a crooked mouth and little, shrewd eyes. I noticed that he was missing a finger on his left hand. "This is from my husband and I," said Yoshiko. "No, it's not," said Isamu, pulling a face like a stubborn child, "it's just from Yoshiko." Yoshiko laughed, flashed him a look of anger that pretended to be mock, and said something to the effect of "Pay no attention to him." Taneguchi grunted and put the parcel aside without opening it. Grunting was in fact his main contribution to the conversation. Lutz would sometimes translate a grunt, which put Isamu in an even worse mood. "I know," he said, "I speak Japanese."

26

SOME COUPLES THRIVE on frequent separations; absence sharpens their passion. Others can't bear to spend even one night apart. Myself, I wouldn't know. I'm just an observer. I can't say I've ever really been in love. I've been in lust many times, of course. In Japan, that is my normal state. But love, living with a person to the exclusion of others, having a soulmate who shares my bed, making love to my most intimate friend, that is something I've never experienced, nor ever wished to. In love, the self of one person is transformed into another self, a collective one, the self of the couple. In lust, I too lose myself, but, satisfied after possession of the other, I like to have myself back again. So I have lovers, and I have friends. I am content to observe how others attempt to become couples and fail, only to attempt the same thing all over again with new partners. I admire their fortitude, or should I say, foolhardiness. I have learned to live without illusions myself, but cherish them in others.

An added complication is the particular nature of my lust. In Ohio, I could be arrested for what I like to do. In Tokyo, I am free to do as I please. Not that I didn't arrive with all the baggage of my American Puritan past. Since that glorious first day in ruined Yokohama, I've managed to throw some of that overboard, but not all of it. I sometimes wish I could be like those married couples, happy as cows grazing in the fields. And sometimes I wish I were Japanese, taking my

Japaneseness for granted, soaking in the huge warm communal bath
of my collective self, along with millions of others who look and talk
and think just like me. That, too, is a way of losing oneself.

But I'm not Japanese and not a happy breeder. One of the great
blessings of living in Japan is that the sexual deviant is not placed in a
neat little box. There are certain obligations, to be sure. But as long as
a Japanese acquires a wife and starts a family, how he finds his sexual
pleasure is his own business. As a foreigner, there are no boxes, except
for one very large one that is very clearly marked: *gaijin*.

In the case of Isamu and Yoshiko, I could see the end of their happy
coupledom approaching some time before it actually occurred. The
plastic sandals incident already revealed cracks that would soon widen
to serious rifts. Isamu's notion of the perfect Japanese life was a fantasy
that Yoshiko could never have shared for long. She was a movie star.
She needed more than one role. The one Isamu had written for her
couldn't hold her forever. Broadway and Hollywood still beckoned. It
was time for her to move on from the Land of Dreams. Some couples
drift apart, like two rivers parting ways. With Isamu and Yoshiko, the
break was more like the culmination of a series of storms that brought
the crumbling edifice of their marriage down in a heap of rubble. The
night of the biggest storm was also the last time I visited the house in
Kamakura.

A Hollywood producer named Norman Waterman had come to Tokyo. He was considering Yoshiko for a possible role in a movie, something about GI wives. Yoshiko had invited him down for dinner in
Kamakura without asking Isamu first. I was to accompany him.

Waterman was not exactly my type. A small, compact man with a
loud voice, and a taste for expensive shoes, he half expected me to
match him up with a local "cutie." Girls were very much his thing. He
didn't actually use the phrase "kimono girls" (he said "cutie"), but
that was what he was looking for. I put him in a taxi with the address

of a well-known massage parlor scribbled on a piece of paper. Tokyo taxi drivers have to be given precise instructions to get to most places. Not this place, however. Everyone knew it. Waterman came back with a wide smile on his neat little face, like a frisky dog wagging his tail after having had a nice juicy bone to chew on.

But Waterman wasn't so bad, really. We shared a taste for Preston Sturges movies, especially *The Beautiful Blonde from Bashful Bend,* in which Waterman had played a minor part as assistant to the assistant of the producer. As long as we stayed off the subject of "cuties" and talked about the movies, we got along fine.

It was a sultry night. The last of the cicadas were crying lazily under a starlit sky. Isamu, who had no interest in Preston Sturges, or movies, or Yoshiko's prospects of a Hollywood career, hated Waterman on sight. He barely acknowledged his presence, as Yoshiko told stories about her good friends Charlie Chaplin, Yul Brynner, King Vidor, Ed Sullivan, and so on. Waterman was charmed. "You'll love working in L.A.," he said, his voice booming all the way across the rice field to Nambetsu's house, where the sensei was cutting our sashimi. "I hope you like our Japanese food," said Yoshiko. "Like?" said Waterman. "I love it! Sukiyaki, tempura!" Isamu stared at him as though he were a wild ape.

Nambetsu, to my relief and, it must be said, surprise, behaved well for once, even when Waterman mispronounced his name. Nambetsu just smiled, exuding benevolence, in the manner of a grown-up at a children's party. Waterman was the kind of American Japanese know how to handle, not like those crazy foreigners who try to be just like them. Waterman actually behaved like a foreigner. There were no surprises there. Nambetsu, like all Japanese, cherished predictability. He poured saké into Waterman's cup. Waterman protested mildly: "I'm not much of a drinking man, Mr. Nambis. If you keep pouring like that, I'll get bombed in no time."

"Bombed?"

I explained the meaning. Nambetsu waved his hand. "Oh, no," he said, "all foreigners are strong. Have more."

Waterman's face soon became alarmingly red, as though he were overheating. And his voice grew even louder. Like many people not used to drinking, he drank too fast, prompting Nambetsu to pour more saké into his cup. Isamu, just to be difficult, refused to speak English, so that Yoshiko and I were obliged to translate what little he said in his broken Japanese. Not as insensitive as his booming voice might have suggested, Waterman was quite aware of Isamu's hostility and tried, in his American way, to defuse the tension: "Hey, Isamu, lighten up. I hear you're a famous artist. Have you had any recent shows in the States?"

Isamu's face darkened. There was an awkward pause, filled by the tired-sounding cicadas. "That's just what I've been telling him, Norman," said Yoshiko, making an effort to sound bright. "He's getting so stuck here in Japan."

Nambetsu was in the kitchen, preparing the next course. The smell of grilled mackerel wafted into the room. "I'll go to the house," said Yoshiko brightly, "and get a catalogue of Isamu-san's last show in Tokyo." Isamu told her to stay right where she was. Waterman said he'd love to see it. Sensing another storm brewing, I said nothing. I knew when to keep my head down. Yoshiko left the room and stumbled into her sandals in the dark.

"So, when are you coming back to the States, Isamu?" insisted Waterman. "I mean, it's great here, beautiful, but you can't bury yourself in the boonies like this forever. You've got to have a show in New York, L.A. That's where the action is. Look at Yoshiko. She knows the score."

Isamu looked at him aghast. "What do you know about art? You're nothing but a vulgar, money-grubbing idiot. You're the reason anything of value in America gets swamped by junk. Junk culture, that's you. You're a peddler of junk, a rubbish merchant, an enemy of art."

"Take it easy, fellow!" shouted Waterman, his face the color of beetroot. "You may not rate my movies—"

"I've never seen your lousy movies, and I doubt I ever will!"

"I produce quality products—"

"Products?"

"Listen here, you damned snob, I work my ass off to produce art for real people, while you . . . you just sit here in your little cave in Japan, thinking you're too good to get your hands dirty in the only place that counts, where the public decides what's good and what's lousy. You talk about art. I know about art, pal. This is the way it's always been, in Renaissance Italy as much as in Hollywood, USA. Michelangelo didn't sit around jerking off in Rome. He made . . ."

It happened in a flash. Waterman was howling, as the scalding tea from Isamu's cup streamed down his face. This was the moment Yoshiko chose to return from the house, carrying the catalogue of Isamu's Tokyo show. Waterman was whimpering on the floor, covering his face with a napkin. "Ice!" he cried. "For Chrissake get me some ice!" I was just sitting there, numb with shock. Yoshiko slammed the book on the floor and shouted at her husband in Japanese: "What's going on? What have you done?"

She looked at me, but I didn't know what to say. In a fury I had never seen before, Yoshiko screamed: "I can't believe what's happening here. You've assaulted my guest!" Isamu told her to shut up. The man had insulted his intelligence. Nambetsu, quietly serving the fish, nodded his head in agreement.

"Insulted your intelligence? Who do you think you are? He's our guest!"

"Shut up, woman," said Isamu, replying in English to her Japanese.

"You don't know what you're talking about. You've already insulted me by bringing this vulgar Hollywood shyster into my home!"

"Shyster? What do you mean shyster. I . . ."

Isamu had picked up an ashtray and hurled it at his wife, only just missing her face. It crashed through Nambetsu's sliding door of the finest Shikoku paper, and thudded into the cypresswood wall, making a nasty crack. I was hardly aware of what I was doing. I was still a numbed observer, but this time a mad impulse jerked me out of my passive state. I did what one should never do, intervene in a conjugal fight. Absurdly, I lurched to my feet, the knight in shining armor, the protector of the gentle sex, and shouted the first thing that came into my mind: "Don't you dare throw things at a lady!" Isamu's eyes, hot with rage, swiveled my way. Even Yoshiko, the object of my chivalry, looked shocked. I had deflected the storm by turning it toward myself. Waterman had stumbled to a tap, splashing water on his face, with quick frantic movements, as though he were on fire. Nambetsu looked at me with contempt, perhaps even loathing. I will never forget his words: "You're just an ordinary foreigner after all."

27

I SAW YOSHIKO only once before she left for America. We had coffee at our usual table in the Imperial Hotel. The Waterman incident was left unmentioned. But she did say that her marriage with Isamu was over. She had been foolish to think that she could live with a foreigner, she said. The cultural differences made it impossible. "Isamu thinks he knows Japan, but he's a typical American. He never even learned to speak proper Japanese. You are different, Sid-san. But Isamu lives in a world of his own imagination. I admire his purity as an artist. But I can't sacrifice myself for his art."

The breakup must have been hard on her. When she removed her sunglasses to rub her eyes, I could see that she had been crying. "Divorce is a terrible thing," I said, sounding fatuous even to myself. "But you'll soon get over it. Time is a great healer. Think of all the movies you'll make in America, and the Broadway show."

"It's not that," she said with a slight air of irritation. "Believe me, getting divorced is a relief. I just had some distressing news today, but it's okay. There's nothing to be done about it."

When I insisted, as her friend and confidant, that she tell me the bad news, she shook her head. The fey-looking waiter came over and asked if we would be needing anything further. I ordered another coffee, and settled into my seat. A young woman in an evening gown was tinkling away on a white piano. Yoshiko began talking about her father. He had always been a feckless type, she said, a gambler, incapable of taking care of his family. But he had been a good man in China, a true idealist. He had genuinely loved the Chinese. China was his world, his reason to exist. But after the war, back in Japan, he couldn't cope with life. He was barely able even to take care of himself, let alone his family. It was as if there were nothing left to live for. So he became a bum, stealing his own daughter's money, only to gamble it away. At first Yoshiko felt sorry for him. He too, she felt, had been a victim of that terrible war. But enough's enough. Though she continued to bear his name, she wanted nothing more to do with him.

Again I offered my sympathy. It must be very hard to lose a father like that. No, she said, it wasn't that either. So what was it? She looked so helpless as she cast those big dark eyes up at me. A solitary tear rolled down her cheek. "Sid-san," she said softly, "do you remember that man who came up to me after the wedding?" I thought back for a moment, and said, yes, of course I did. Well, his name was Sato, Sato Daisuke. He had been more of a father to her in China than her real one, always looking out for her, helping her when she was in trouble. Sato had loved China as intensely as her father had. To be sure, he had a weakness for Chinese girls, and was always getting into scrapes, but he had a good heart. Here she paused, dabbing at her eyes with a silk handkerchief. "He deserved better," she sobbed. What happened to him? Who was Sato?

I received only fragments of information: how he had worked for the Japanese army, and been lucky to have escaped arrest by the Russians after the war. But, Yoshiko said, perhaps there was a fate even worse than dying in a Siberian slave camp. Back in his own country, Sato had no more reason to live. His world, like her father's, had vanished. So he drifted like a ghost, appearing from time to time without warning. She had given him money. He promised to stay away. But he couldn't carry on, and committed suicide. His headless corpse was discovered by a farmer in Yamanashi Prefecture. He had tied himself to a tree, after taking an overdose of sleeping tablets. It was at the height of summer. A red mountain dog must have found him several days later and made off with his head. The dog was spotted by a local girl just as it was gnawing on its prize in an abandoned shed.

As I was listening to this horrifying story, my mind drifted back to my first glimpses of Japan, in those cinemas in the east side of the city. Dimly perceived story lines came back to me of shabby figures arriving at ruined homes they no longer recognized, finding their wives living with other men. The pianist in the evening gown was playing a Cole Porter song, skillfully and devoid of any human feeling.

"Well," said Yoshiko, smiling through her tears, "there is no point dwelling on the past, is there? There is nothing we can do about it anymore. You remember that song that everyone sung a year ago?" She sang the words: "*Que sera sera*, whatever will be, will be . . ." Still smiling, she said: "I believe in that. The world is sure to become a better place one day. That's what I want to dedicate my life to. You know that, don't you, Sid?"

I wasn't quite sure what she meant. "Dedicate it to what, darling?"

She softly squeezed my arm. "To peace, of course," she said.

And so Yoshiko went off to the United States, where a glittering future awaited her, or so she hoped. Isamu went off on some tour of the world, paid for by a big American foundation, to investigate art and religion, or perhaps it was culture and spirituality. Nambetsu went on, without my help, to have a big commercial success in New York. The Japan Society organized a huge exhibition of his works, and one of the Rockefellers bought all his paintings.

Shangri-La got off to a decent start. Reviews in Boston and Baltimore were respectful, though not exactly effusive. Still, there was time for improvements. The costumes were much praised and Sam Jaffe, older and even more like a wizened old grandma than in the movie, was said to be terrific as the Grand Lama. Yoshiko certainly looked the part, from what I heard. "Pretty as a tropical flower," declared the *Baltimore Sun*. Yoshiko gave an interview to *Time* magazine, reflecting with proper modesty on her role as an Oriental ambassadress. Her photograph, showing her dressed in a Tibetan-style costume, was published as a full spread in *Life*. She was consulted on *The Ed Sullivan Show* about the spiritual wisdom of Buddhism. Bob Ryan came round to see her backstage in Philadelphia. He assured her she would be a triumph on Broadway. Tables at Sardi's were booked for the opening night. Flowers were ordered, stars invited, crates of champagne stacked up high. All of New York would be there.

And it failed. Not just failed, it bombed. The costumes were praised once more, and Sam Jaffe was again lauded as a superb Grand Lama. Yoshiko looked "as pretty as a peony," declared the *New York Times* critic. But the music stank and, as the *New York Herald Tribune* put it, "the story was as soggy as a piece of cardboard left in the rain." *Shangri-La* limped on gamely for three weeks. Party invitations were canceled, lunches postponed. Yoshiko was suddenly in the big city all alone.

She never heard from Waterman again. But the doors of Hollywood had not yet entirely closed in her face. Yoshiko was cast in a comedy called *Navy Wife*, directed by a fellow named Ed Bernds, who started off as a soundman for Mr. Capra, and went on to have some success with the Three Stooges. I never saw *Shangri-La*, but it must have been a masterpiece compared to this mawkish little confection. Joan Bennett is the wife of a U.S. Navy commander based in Japan (and the actual wife of the film's producer, Walter Wanger, hence her appearance; I can't think of any other reason why she would have bothered). Her name is Judy, or something, and the Navy man is Bud, or Bob, or Jack—I can't recall. The point, if there is one, is that a Japanese housewife, played by Yoshiko, observes how Judy, or Debbie, or whatever, bosses Bud or Jack around, and not just in the house. So Yoshiko wants "equal rights" too, just like the American wife. It all comes to a head at a military Christmas party, a scene that is supposed to be humorous but is in fact deeply depressing.

Since the movie was assumed to be of special interest to the expatriate community in Tokyo, I was compelled to review it. I wrote: "Too talented to be in this turkey, Shirley Yamaguchi's beauty is still worth the price of a ticket. Given the severe limitations of the script, she makes the most of a part that is so ludicrous it isn't even funny." Not the most stylish piece of writing, I know, but I too had to struggle with unpromising material. My charming editor, Cecil Shiratori, had adored the film and asked me why I had to be so "b-b-bloody negative." I don't think the movie played for more than a week in Japan. The Japanese critics politely ignored it.

It can't have been long after her appearance in *Navy Wife* that Yoshiko announced to the world that she was retiring as a movie actress, and would marry a promising young Japanese diplomat. I was stunned. A failure on Broadway and one dud movie shouldn't have fazed her, let alone sink a budding international career. She was still Japan's best hope. Perhaps it was "true love" that prompted this mad, impulsive act. If so, it confirms my doubts about true love. I fear the promising young diplomat made his move when she was feeling most vulnerable. Alas, however, by marrying an older actress with a somewhat checkered past, he ensured that his youthful promise would go unfulfilled. He wasn't exactly fired from the Foreign Ministry, just sent to Rangoon. What the hell Yoshiko would do in Rangoon was anybody's guess. I felt caught in a tangle of emotions: abandonment, loss, even a certain sense of betrayal. A great legend had died before her time. A bright star had suddenly gone dark. It felt as if I had been yanked roughly out of a wonderful dream.

I still adored Yoshiko, of course, and had hoped to resume my role as mother confessor as soon as she came back to Tokyo. Surely her husband wouldn't mind me. He must have heard that I was no threat. I was dying to hear all about her adventures in New York and Hollywood. She did call me once, from her husband's apartment. We gossiped and laughed, just like old times, and then I made my fatal mistake. The subject of *Navy Wife* came up and we happily agreed that it was an awful picture. She said: "And let's face it, I wasn't much good in it either, was I?" "Truthfully, darling, you were not." I heard a sharp click as she put the receiver down. I've not heard from Yoshiko since.

28

THE RAINY SEASON of 1959 seemed never to end. Everything in my apartment, from the tatami floor to the clothes in my closet, had the rank smell of old mushrooms. My shoes in the hall had turned a gangrenous green. The covers of my precious books were bent out of shape, as though they had passed through the hands of a circus strongman. Yet I had little desire to venture out into the gray drizzle, or the sheeting showers, or the never-ending *drip-drip* of warm spring rain. No wonder the Japanese have so many words for rain. I wish they had had as many words for principle, or spontaneity. I was bored with my job as a movie reviewer, tired of hearing my own voice, week after week, pronouncing verdicts on the work of others. I was trying to write a novel set in the occupation years, but realized with a steadily sinking heart that it was going nowhere. The words remained abstractions, without the smell of life. Opinions kept intruding. Perhaps I had written too many reviews. Frankly, I was getting bored with Japan.

Precisely the things that had delighted me when I first arrived, the strangeness, the childlike innocence, the courtesy, the attachment to form and ceremony, all these things had begun to grate on my nerve ends like a file. Now, instead of exoticism and formality I saw insularity, conformism, and narrow-mindedness. The obsessive politeness was really a form of social hemophilia, the terror of pricking a person's self-esteem lest he or she bleed to death.

These moods can pass, I know, and the odd, unexpected encounter with a beautiful young man with a gap-toothed smile and sturdy thighs would lift my spirits, but never for very long. I should have rejoiced at the revival of Tokyo from a charred wasteland to a prosperous city. It was good to see the disappearance from the streets of young children fighting over cigarette butts and eating out of garbage cans. It was a blessing that millions of ordinary Japanese were beginning to lead civilized lives once again. Every new neon sign and concrete building was surely a sign of progress. And yet I couldn't help feeling that the hope of something more inspiring than material comfort had been dashed. Thinking of the indomitable spirit of those defeated people gathered in the cinemas in 1946, their openness to new ideas, their honest stoicism, I felt a sense of loss, of promise unfulfilled and hope abandoned. Something great could have come from the catastrophe. What the Japanese acquired instead was the worst of the American way of life, imported wholesale with much greed and no understanding. We gave them democracy, and what did they do with it? They elected a prime minister who had been arrested for war crimes just a few years before.

I complain about the Japanese. But my own country was largely to blame. We had taught them to mimic us in every way, and they were our all too willing pupils. We instilled the idea of our superiority, and they believed us, poor lambs. We released Kishi Nobusuke, slave driver of Manchuria and wartime minister in General Tojo's cabinet, from prison, just because he was an anti-Communist. Did anyone protest? Not a bit of it. The Japanese were willing to forget the past, and be corrupted by the promise of riches. More than willing. Like a submissive pan-pan girl, Japan spread her legs for us to impregnate her with the seed of our own shallow mediocrity. She got her chewing gum, her Hershey bars, her perfume, and her silk stockings, but she lost her soul. And now she hated us for it.

The loathing of the seduced for the seducer, of the hooker for the john; I saw it in the movies: the endless succession of sour-tempered stories set around U.S. military bases, or the films about Hiroshima, one of them featuring a group of gloating American tourists buying souvenir bones of their incinerated victims.

I am often tempted to see the election of Kishi, that weak-chinned, buck-toothed, scheming bureaucrat, as the beginning of everything that went wrong with Japan, but I should have seen the signs of rot much earlier, back in those days when I was blinded by the innocence of my ideals. Perhaps the transformation of Japan was doomed from the beginning, doomed by arrogance and false expectations. How could Americans ever have believed that they could take an ancient culture and remake it in our own image by waving General MacArthur's magic wand? Only a people lacking any sense of history or tragedy could fall into such hubris. Perhaps Tony Lucca was right: our presence in Japan hadn't amounted to a can of beans. The occupation was no more than a ripple in the ocean of Japanese history.

And yet, to my surprise, my old friend Nobuo Hotta, whose face was lined with all the sorrows of his country's twentieth-century history, was strangely optimistic in those Red-baiting years of Kishi's rise. Normally the most taciturn of men, he was actually quite animated when we met one night for drinks at the Paloma, his favorite little bar in Shinjuku, near the Hanazono Shrine. It was one of those magical Shinjuku nights. The air was hazy, like fine gauze, after the rains, and neon lights shimmered in the alleyways lined with bars. A strolling musician was strumming his guitar behind the public toilet. It was early still, and only one or two other people were sitting at the bar, chatting to Noriko, the Mama-san and keeper of many secrets.

"Kishi?" said Hotta. "I knew Kishi back in Manchuria. He was a member of the Ri Koran Fan Club, you know. A perfectly nice man, with beautiful manners, always smiling, and he had the softest of hands, almost like a woman's. You'd never have guessed that he was responsible for thousands of Chinese slaves being worked to death in the steel mills and coal mines of Manchukuo. But don't you worry. He's overplayed his hand this time. The Japanese people won't be deceived again. You'll see, the people will rise against him. You Americans may think you can get away with forcing a security treaty down our throats. You think we will allow you to keep all your bombers on our soil, and aircraft carriers in our ports. Well, think again. Kishi doesn't seem to mind signing away our birthright for a pot of gold. He doesn't care if Japan becomes one huge military base for Yankee imperialism. But the Japanese people won't take it. Not this time. If Kishi signs this treaty, there will be a revolution. This is the most important moment in our history, the moment I've been waiting for all my life. We can be rebels too, you know. Just you watch, the revolution is finally going to come."

I didn't like the way he said "you Americans," and told him so. I was against the security treaty, too. I hated the arrogance of the Americans. First we preach peace and democracy and make the Japanese into a nation of pacifists, and now we tell them it was all a mistake, and we must be allies in another war, against the Communists. I was as outraged as Hotta. He immediately apologized. "I'm sorry, Sidney. I know you're really one of us." We drank another whiskey to that, and another, and another, until we walked into the velvety light of a Shinjuku dawn, arm-in-arm, like old comrades, singing the *Internationale* in Japanese.

To dispel my gloom, I did what I always do when I'm depressed: I spent more and more time at the movies. I had discovered the charm of Japanese gangster pictures. Rather than face another sleepless night in my apartment, I would sit through the all-night shows, with the movie addicts and the drunken bums watching my yakuza heroes taking on the modern world. One night it was Kensuke Fujii in his *Sword of Justice* series. Fujii was handsome in a dark, brooding way (much later I found out that he was a gentleman of my persuasion with a liking for big American boys who would rough him up on his holidays in Honolulu; it was a good thing the fans never found out).

The story line was always the same: the bad guys wore suits, like bankers or Chicago mobsters, and killed their enemies with guns. Fujii and his gang were kimonoed traditionalists, whose weapon of choice was the Japanese sword. The bad guys made their money in crooked real estate deals, financial scams, and the rough end of the construction business. The good yakuza deplored these practices. In the inevitable last scene, Fujii, provoked beyond endurance by the bad guys, set forth with his sword on the always suicidal mission to restore justice to this world by taking on the baddies alone. This was the moment when the fans, who had been slumbering in the stale air of cigarette smoke and clogged toilets, stirred in their seats and shouted their encouragements at the screen: "Go and get them, Ken-san!" or, "What a guy!" or, "Die for Japan!" But more and more, in the spring of 1960, I heard variations on these themes, which had little to do with Fujii's yakuza stories, except perhaps in spirit: "Scrap the Treaty!" "Down with U.S. Imperialism!" "Go and get Kishi!"

Perhaps wise old Hotta was right after all. Perhaps there really would be a revolution this time, staged from below by the Japanese people themselves. I welcomed it. God, how I welcomed it. In my excitement during those magical few weeks in May, I jotted the following notes in my diary.

May Day: Workers and students demonstrated in a carnival spirit, carrying huge effigies of Kishi, an ogre with dragon eyes and monstrous fangs.

May 19: Socialist members of the Diet barricade the entrance to the plenary session to stop Kishi and his fellow conservatives from voting for the new Security Treaty. Kishi orders the police to clear out his opponents with force. The speaker of the house is pushed toward the rostrum. The treaty is passed without the Socialists.

June 10: Eisenhower's press secretary James C. Hagerty and U.S. Ambassador Douglas MacArthur II are mobbed in their car on the route from Haneda Airport. They have to be evacuated by military helicopter.

June 15: Students bearing long wooden poles, like medieval lancers, tried to break through the South Gate of the Diet Building, while others, tens of thousands, perhaps even hundreds of thousands of students, workers, and ordinary citizens, streamed toward the Parliament from all directions. Some moved in a festival spirit, carrying banners and grotesque puppets of Kishi and Ike, chanting: "*Washoi! Washoi!* Scrap the treaty! Kishi out! Kishi out! Down with the foreign invasion!" Others were more like an army, marching in strict order of hierarchy, senior students before sophomores, sophomores before freshmen, with grim-faced officers of the Zengakuren student federation shouting slogans through their megaphones. Others still, linking arms, formed part of a great impenetrable snake dance, coiling through the avenues leading to the Diet, where the riot police were waiting for them, helmeted, like samurai warriors, with batons and shields.

It was more exhilarating than any Shinto festival I had ever seen, more thrilling even than the naked festivals in the rural northeast. Here was a people on the move, their excitement kept from boiling over by a cultural talent for ceremony. Several hundred thousand delirious young people felt their power as they approached the rulers of their nation. This could so easily have erupted in massive violence. But on the cusp of total mayhem, the surging crowds were held back by a sense of discipline that made their show of power all the more awe-inspiring.

I was dying to join in, to merge with the demonstrators, to lose myself in their collective delirium, my sweat mixed with theirs, my body submerged in the zigging-zagging dance of rebellion. Here, at this moment, in this crowd, I felt fully alive. There was no way I could have joined the snake dancers; they were as tightly packed as a football scrum. If you got in their way, you would be swept away as if by a tidal wave. I tried to join the marchers, but where could I fit in? With the sophomores, or the seniors? With the Tokyo University students, or those from Waseda, each with their own banners? On and on they went, marching right past me, shouting: "Foreign invaders, go home!" Individual faces, contorted not in rage but in ecstasy, got lost in a whirl of bodies and faces, but my eyes met, just for an instant, with those of a handsome university student, just as he was denouncing my country. He suddenly looked apologetic, even embarrassed, as he swept by me, and shouted over his shoulder: "I am sorry!"

I should have gone after him. I desperately wanted to tell him to stop feeling sorry. His cause was just. I was on his side. But he had already been swept along by the tide, to make way for the next churning wave of chanting, dancing, marching, running crowds. I tried to keep pace, by following the sea of people to the Diet, cheering them on all the while. I was excited by the force of this rebellion, which contained a real hope of change, of reviving that sense of limitless possibility that I felt when I first arrived in Japan. But I also felt a sense of impotence and frustration, like a lone spectator at a massive orgy.

Near the South Gate, the picture became fuzzier. Battering against police barricades, discipline appeared to be breaking down. Even as some of the students were crashing the gate with their battering rams, others were throwing their bodies at the riot police with a kind of recklessness that had to end badly. It was the first time that I saw fresh blood, washing down the young faces of people who had got too close to the police batons. One policeman, trapped in the midst of a group of students wearing headbands that read *Victory or die*, was in danger of being lynched. A young woman was trampled on, screaming for help. A new group I hadn't seen before joined in the melee. Young men with thick peasant faces, dressed in army fatigues, hacked their way through the student ranks with wooden kendo swords. They did so with the angry relish of country boys who couldn't wait to teach those pampered students a lesson. I didn't know it then, but they were the "patriotic" hoodlums working for Yoshio Taneguchi, the same man who had helped Yoshiko with her visa problem.

Whether it was one of Taneguchi's thugs, or one of the students, I will never know. My memory is a blur of disjointed images. I remember the trampled girl screaming and I tried to reach out to her. I remember someone shouting, "Down with the Anglo-American devils!" I remember it because it seemed like a strange thing to say. Why Anglo-American devils? What did the British have to do with any of this? And I remember seeing a black car passing the demonstrators in the direction of Hibiya Park, away from the Diet. A woman, sticking her head out of the window, was calling out to the students. "Keep going," she cried, "students of Japan, keep going! We are proud of you!" So many things were going on at the same time, and happening so quickly, that I can't be sure of this, but I could swear that that woman was Yoshiko.

The next thing I remembered was waking up with a splitting headache in the St. Luke's International Hospital in Tsukiji. I hadn't felt the blow to the back of my head. I must have lost consciousness instantly. Dr. Ivanov, a tall Russian doctor, smiled down at me, as though to a wayward child. "That'll teach you never to get involved in Japanese business," he said in a faint Russian accent. "You'll end up being crushed." I was hardly in the mood for lectures of this kind, and was disposed to dislike this Dr. Ivanov. But as I slowly recovered from the blow to my head, and he told me stories of his life, I began to like him. Born in Harbin, ten years before the Japanese took control of Manchuria, Ivanov had come to Tokyo as a medical student in 1940. "I've done very well in Japan," he said, "but that's because I've always known my place. I'll probably die in this country, but I know I'll always be a guest, an interloper, a permanent outsider. That's the way it is, and that's the way I like it. I don't want to belong anywhere. I don't bother others, and nobody bothers me. If you wish to stay here, you'd better remember that, my friend."

I thanked him for his advice. He laughed. "You're an American, right?" I confirmed that indeed I was. He began to chuckle. "I was a kind of American once," he said, laughing more loudly. "I died many horrible deaths as an American." He was laughing so much, I thought he would choke. It turned out that he used to earn his school fees in Tokyo during the war by playing Americans in Japanese movies. "I was very good as a bad guy." I asked him which films. "Oh," he smiled, "you wouldn't know. Even the Japanese have forgotten most of them." I wanted to know whether any of them starred Ri Koran? "Ri Koran," he shouted, "she was my idol, already in Harbin. Oh, I can tell you a lot of stories about Ri Koran. She had a Russian lover, you know?"

I didn't know and was about to ask him for more details. I wanted to hear all about the things she had refused to talk to me about. Whenever I mentioned the war, or China, or the Japanese puppet state in Manchuria, she would say something about the need for peace and switch the subject. After several attempts, I simply gave up asking. But Dr. Ivanov was hardly more forthcoming. Instead of answering my questions, he started to sing, very softly, staring out of the hospital window at the tiled rooftops of the Tsukiji fish market. A blue neon advertisement for a cigarette blinked on and off on a tall building in the distance.

" '*Shina no yoru,*' " he sang in his Russian baritone, " 'China nights, ah China nights . . . the junk floating upstream . . .' " I recognized the words. It was one of my favorite Japanese songs, even though Yoshiko hated to sing it. So I joined in: " 'the ship of dreams, China nights, nights of our dreams, ah, China nights, I dream of my homeland, so far, so sweet, I dream of you . . .' "

PART THREE

1

THE ONE THING I can't stand is the coffee, that thick Arab coffee which sticks to the palate like liquid mud. Not that the prison food is much good in general, a dull routine of watery lentil soup and stale Arab bread, and, with luck, once a week, a kebab of skinny meat from who knows what animal; the Arab prisoners call it Roumieh rat, after our present abode in the fragrant pine-forested hills east of Beirut. We can't actually see the city from where we are. We can't in fact see anything at all from our cell. The window is too high, letting in just a tantalizing sliver of light which, late in the afternoon, casts a reddish glow on the ceiling while leaving us in the·dark. If one were able to climb up and look through the window, one might catch a glimpse of the courtyard where they shoot the poor wretches from death row. You know when it's about to happen when the cries echo around the prison: *Allahu akhbar! Allahu akhbar!* Sometimes you'll hear the man about to be executed cry out, begging for his life. Then, a volley of gunfire, followed by silence, complete silence, one of the rare moments in this hellhole when there is no sound at all. One savors it, like a cigarette after a good meal.

The food, as I said, is pretty miserable. But more than anything, I miss a decent cup of coffee, the weak tasty kind we call "American" in Tokyo, not the sweet mud that the Arabs like. I'm convinced that taste is a reflection of national character. And national character is shaped by the weather. Our crisp climate gives us Japanese a taste for limpidity and subtlety which foreigners often mistake for blandness. That's why Japanese love the plain unadorned taste of tofu, soft and white, like a woman's breast. It matches the mildness of our four seasons. The Arabs are a desert people, used to the pitiless sun beating down on them. They aren't blessed with the clarity of our seasons, and so they find comfort in the opaque, the secretive, the cloying, just like their coffee.

Still, I musn't complain. After the first eight months, our conditions were much improved. Roumieh was built in 1971—one year before our triumph—to hold about fifteen hundred men, including the boys in the juvenile wing. We now share our temporary address with five thousand men. Being stuffed into a cell so full of guys that there is no room at night for everyone to lie down on the concrete floor is pretty unpleasant, especially if you're a newcomer, or *pissoir*, as the new boys are called here. They are called that because they have to sleep sitting upright, knees drawn up, next to the toilet. This is actually just a stinking hole in the floor, which gets slopped out twice a week, by the *pissoir* of course. If it overflows, as it almost always does, the *pissoir* is held responsible by the cell boss and gets a beating. To avoid this punishment, the *pissoir* will have to mop up the slimy muck with his own shirt. Hence also, possibly, my allergy to Arab coffee; it reminds me of my first months in Roumieh. And my cell boss wasn't as bad as some. Khalil al-Beiruti had murdered a family of eight in Saida—some matter of family honor. He wasn't a bad sort, more the elder brother type who would take care of you, if you didn't cross him, and did what he wanted, like washing his feet or massaging his hairy back at night. Other cell bosses were worse. Morioka's boss used his underlings as footstools. Another notorious lifer, Mahmoud, insisted on having his ass scrubbed.

They were a mixed bunch, the hundred-odd guys in my cell: professional hit men, drug smugglers, rapists, forgers, kidnappers, bank robbers, murderers; and then there were the "politicals," revolutionaries of various stripes, some religious, some not, a few Palestinians, usually picked on by the other Arabs, an Australian of Lebanese descent who had hijacked a bus, and so on. The addicts were the worst, for they screamed at night. I was lucky in a way. Japanese were exotic, and as members of the Japanese United Red Army, the victors of the battle of Lydda Airport, we were treated with a certain respect. But rules were rules and we too had to pay our dues as *pissoir*s.

Things are better now. I share my cell with three other Japanese commandos: Morioka Akio, Nishiyama Masaki, and Kamei Ichiro. We try to keep ourselves as clean as we can, picking the lice from each other's hair, giving each other rubdowns with a wet rag. The scorpions can kill, so we take care not to lie down without careful scrutiny of the floor. The fleas are the worst. You just can't get rid of them, however many you manage to kill. This takes a certain finesse: you maneuver the little pest between your thumbnails, and crack its hard little spine, producing a trickle of human blood. Satisfying, to be sure, but insufficient. Fleas resist extermination. My legs are red and swollen to twice their normal size because of the fleas, which drive me half mad. Strangely, Kamei and Nishiyama are plagued by lice, but are left alone by the fleas. I don't know which are a greater torment. But catching the lice is a little easier.

We try not to talk about women. Actually, no matter what anyone outside may think, hunger trumps sexual desire anytime. We close our eyes, and each of us imagines the perfect menu for lunch or dinner: yellowtail sashimi or succulent sea urchin wrapped in seaweed, or juicy red cod's roe, followed by shabu shabu of thinly sliced prime Kobe beef, accompanied by crisp light tempura of Ise lobster and sweet potato, and a thick red miso soup with freshwater clams. This would typically be Morioka's choice. He's a traditionalist. Nishiyama went to Tokyo University and has Westernized tastes. We tease him that he reeks of butter. He can go on for hours about the perfect pâté de foie gras, or steak garnished with fresh truffles, washed down with a 1970 Château Something or Other. Kamei is crazy about Korean food, so he'll dream of barbecued ox tongue and red-hot stews with tofu and pork. Me, I'm a country boy at heart, so my perfect meals are not so refined. My dream is to have a bowl of rice with a slice of salmon drenched in Japanese tea, or Sapporo noodles in a dense brown stock of soy sauce and scallions. It's amazing what the human imagination can do. If you concentrate hard enough, you can even make a crust of Arab bread taste like a delicious white tuna sashimi, but only for a few seconds, after which the hard stale bread just tastes like hard stale bread again. But those few moments are priceless.

When we're not imagining great meals, we remember the good times, when we were back home, or in Beirut, celebrating the battle of Lydda Airport, when we got twenty-six enemies for the loss of two of our soldiers. One was shot by the Zionists, and the other, Okudaira, blew himself up with a hand grenade. We were sorry to lose our comrades. But in May 1972, we were the kings of the Middle East. People would come up to kiss us in the street, and offer us gifts. Women looked up to us as war heroes, and named their babies after us. Okudaira is a common name now in the Palestinian camps.

When we remember the good times, we sing the old songs of our student days. Morioka has a beautiful baritone voice and a real gift for singing Japanese ballads: "Nagasaki Blues," "Tears of Shinjuku," "Mother's Farewell," "Tears and Sake" . . . A few of these, and we're all blubbering. Another favorite is the "Song of the Japanese Red Army": "United for victory, we must fight on . . ." My favorite song, however, is "Let It Be," by the Beatles. Nishiyama always makes fun of my faulty pronunciation. But who cares? I'm Japanese: "When I find myself in times of trouble, Mother Mary comes to me, Speaking words of wisdom, Let it be, let it be . . ." Some of the Arabs in the other cells know the song too and will join in. This feels so good! You know you're not alone in the struggle. United for victory, we must fight on!

2

THE TOWN OF my birth was known for two things: horses and bombers. To these one could possibly add a third, the foggy weather drifting in from the Japan Sea. Otherwise it is a place without interest. I regard having been born there in May 1945 as a mistake, a quirk of fate, or history rather, in which I played no part.

The bombers roaring over our heads when I grew up belonged to the United States Air Force: B-29s, the same steel vultures, gleaming with malevolence, that destroyed our cities in the war. I had a toy gun when I was a child, made of two pieces of wood, which I would point at the bombers pretending I was shooting them down. What right did these bastards have to lord it over us in our own country? Did their pale skins give them a special authority to rule the world?

Not that I felt any sympathy for the previous occupants of the base. Quite the contrary. It always was a blood-soaked place. During the war, the Japanese Imperial Navy flew kamikaze raids out of there. Before that it was a base for Imperial Army bombers on their way to China. Before that it was a stud farm, where they bred horses for the cavalry. The warmongers got what they deserved. They were no better than the Americans, possibly even worse. But why should the Japanese masses have to suffer for what a bunch of militarists and their wretched Emperor had wrought?

The reason for my unfortunate birth in this place all the way up in the foggy northeast of Japan can be summed up in one word: hunger. I never knew my father. All I have to remind me of his existence before I was born is a fuzzy brown photograph of a handsome man dressed in a white suit. I can see some resemblance between him and myself, but I look more like my mother, the same round face and thick eyebrows. She hails from Hokkaido. We probably have Ainu blood running through our veins. I like to think so. My father was in China during the war. We don't know what happened to him. If he was captured after the war by the Russians or the Chinese, we would surely have known, for they kept meticulous records. Perhaps he did return to Japan, but just didn't want to come back to us. I've heard of such cases. My mother didn't seem at all bitter about it. Bitterness wasn't in her nature. She just got on with life. "No point in brooding," she'd say. "There's nothing we can do about it." I loved my mother. But sometimes it would drive me crazy, this refrain of "nothing we can do about it." And yet, I didn't know what to do about it either, whatever "it" was.

You might have thought that I should have been more curious about my father, what he was like, what he did before the war. In fact, I couldn't have cared less. My mother hardly ever mentioned him, and I never asked. As far as I was concerned, he had never existed. Maybe he was a war criminal, or one of those crazy idealists who thought that the Emperor was God. Who knows? To me he was an old photograph, nothing more. The past was a blank. I wasn't interested. You could call this a failure of my imagination. But there was enough to worry about in the present.

As a woman alone in bombed-out Japan, with a hungry baby to feed, my mother found work where she could get it. Although she never talked about it, I have reason to believe that she worked in a bar catering to the Americans and may even have struck up a relationship with one of them. Later she managed a movie theater in the center of town. It was a shabby place, with painted pictures of movie stars stuck onto a gray stucco front. Inside, it smelled of urine and stale smoke. Yanks used the place to feel up their local floozies and drink beer, tossing the empty cans at the screen when they got angry at something, or just bored. I noticed how they would stick chewing gum under the chairs when they kissed their girls. That is if they were considerate. Most wouldn't even bother to take the gum out of their mouths. The girls didn't seem to care. They had a Yank, and that meant goodies from the PX, or straight cash. I don't blame them really. Like Mother, they had to survive. One of my tasks was to scrape the gum off the wooden chairs with a penknife. The more disagreeable task of scooping up used condoms under the back seats was left to an old lady named O-Toyo, whose toothless grin conveyed that she had seen it all in her time, as no doubt she had.

Occasionally there would be a brawl in the theater between local toughs and the Yanks, usually provoked by the latter when their fooling around with the local girls became too blatant. These fights could get out of hand, especially if a local boy had caught his own girl in the arms of a Yank. To keep me away from trouble when I was small, my mother would park me behind the movie screen, where I would be left alone for hours while she tended to her business. This was the start of my cinematic education, sitting behind the screen in a movie theater that smelled of piss, trying to make sense of the flickering shadows of Gary Cooper or Joan Crawford, speaking in muffled voices in a language I couldn't understand. But to me they were like family, these foreigners in black and white.

Most people see the movies as an escape route from reality. For me it was the other way round. To me, the movies were real. I once read something about small children whose parents leave them for hours in front of a TV. Soon they start jabbering to the TV screen. To cope with the confusion of talking to people who fail to respond, they develop a private language, inventing conversations with imaginary people. Perhaps I was a little like those children. Confronted with people of flesh and blood, I was hopelessly tongue-tied, and around the age of five or six I developed a stammer. I imagined that everyone around me, apart from my mother, was a faker of some kind, a hypocrite, wearing a mask. I was especially afraid of older people who wore benign masks, smiling grotesquely as they tried to press me in their clammy embrace. All my life I've wanted to rip off those masks, and expose the bloody reality hidden behind them.

I loathe pop psychology, but I need to make one confession. Although I hated the Yanks, and their bombers, their hard clots of chewing gum, and the arrogant way they treated my mother, holding her around the waist, trying to kiss her and calling her "Mama-san," I secretly admired them. I couldn't help noticing how cool they looked in their pressed uniforms and shiny shoes, their sunglasses and leather jackets, a Lucky Strike dangling casually from the corner of their mouths, speeding around in their jeeps, one leg outside the door, nice and easy, shouting, "Come on!" or, "Let's go!" or, "Hi baby!" Compared to them, our men looked pathetic: craven, scrawny little guys bowing and scraping to their white masters. I should have been on their side, and felt sympathy and even rage on their behalf, but I didn't; I wanted to be like those superconfident, long-legged, suntanned, laughing Yanks. I, too, wanted to wear those cool aviator shades and leather jackets with a picture of a nude woman or a map of Japan on the back, and shout, "Come on, baby!" They may tell you otherwise now, but most of us felt the same way. Most boys of my age weren't even ashamed of their hero worship. They loved to hang around the entrance of the base, hoping for handouts, a stick of gum, a Hershey bar, a movie star photograph, or just a pat on the head. The difference between me and them was that I wouldn't admit it. I would stammer out my protest against such abject behavior. The other boys, almost always stronger than me, would just laugh, or beat me up. And they were right, for I was more contemptible than they were. I was the hypocrite.

The biggest worshipper of Uncle Sam at our school was a boy named Muto, spelled with the same Chinese characters as the famous general's name. Muto was a tall, wiry fellow, good-looking, with a mean grin on his face. In spite of my stammer and general awkwardness, I wasn't one of his usual victims. My ability to smuggle the boys, including Muto, into our movie theater offered me a degree of protection against bullying. Neither a victim nor an accomplice, I always observed Muto with horrified fascination.

One thing about Muto, he had an imagination. He was always inventing new games to torment the younger kids. One day he arrived in the school playground with a short, chubby boy named Inuzuka, or "Inu," as we called him. Inu was a fat, placid, smiling sort, not too clever, but full of goodwill. In this latest game, Muto had figured out a new way to inflict pain. By squeezing the two sides of Inu's palm together, Muto made him yelp and jerk forward as though he were bowing. They became an inseparable pair, Muto and Inu, casually going about the playground. "Meet Inu, my pet dog," Muto would say, before squeezing his slave's hand. "Aaaagh!" went Inu, as he made his bow, much to the amusement of the other boys.

Behind our school, on the far side of a field where we played baseball in the summer, was a small wooden hut, used to store various bits of equipment: brooms, pails, baseball bats, that kind of thing. Late one afternoon, strolling along the field on my own, as usual, I heard a wailing sound. It came from the hut, and it sounded like Inu. I watched from a distance, wondering what was going on. Once in a while older boys opened the door of the hut and came out with grins on their faces. I made sure they couldn't see me. Then there was more wailing, and boys going in and out. I was transfixed by the scene and couldn't move until it had reached a conclusion. Finally, after about an hour, Muto emerged from the hut. He was followed by three of his comrades, slapping him on the back and laughing. After they had gone, Inu came out, patting his clothes, which looked dirty. He didn't seem too unhappy. I waited for him to pass me by. "Hello," I said. He looked at me, with his round doggy eyes. I don't know what possessed me, but I grabbed his hand and tried to squeeze it, as I'd seen Muto do so many times. Furious, Inu pulled himself away. "What the fuck do you think you're doing, you idiot!" he hissed, and walked off with a look of total disgust. I broke into a sweat and looked around to see if anyone had noticed this shameful encounter.

I can't remember a time when I didn't want to leave my hometown. I knew very little about the rest of the world, but it had to be better than this, or if not better, at least more interesting. Two classmates from my high school, one named Kaneko, the other Kaneda, went "back home" to North Korea with their parents. It wasn't really home to them, of course. They had never been anywhere outside our hometown. I didn't know either of them well. They kept to themselves. Kaneko was the victim of a certain amount of bullying. Once, Muto made him eat an earthworm, one of those slippery pink ones. "A Korean snack," Muto called it. The other boys laughed. I walked away. A few days later, Muto was badly beaten up by a gang of boys, led by Kaneko's elder brother. His jaw was dislocated, and he wasn't able to speak for a month. Many of us observed this with quiet satisfaction. After that Kaneko was left alone. The boys were not missed when they left for North Korea. But I felt a pang of envy. Lucky bastards, I thought, leaving school and going abroad like that. We never heard from them again.

People say my native country is beautiful. I suppose it is. We have plenty of lakes and snowy mountains and rice fields. But natural beauty still leaves me cold. I prefer neon to sunlight, concrete to wood, plastic to rock. Only one place still haunts my dreams, even here in my prison cell in Beirut. Every Japanese has heard of it. It is called the Mountain of Dread, a sulfurous volcano not far from our home, where blind women talk to the spirits of the dead, and pilgrims lay flowers at the Buddhist temple to comfort the souls of aborted children. My mother would take me up there in July, during *O-Bon*, when we feed our ancestral spirits. Even in broad daylight, the mountain seemed to be shrouded in darkness. It was altogether a gloomy place. Large black ravens caw from the branches of leafless trees. Yellow vapor drifts across the rocky landscape, leaving a smell of rotten eggs. My mother told me to stay put as she wandered off with one of the old crones dressed in a dark gray kimono. I couldn't hear what the blind woman was muttering while she fingered her beads. After about fifteen minutes my mother came back to me, her eyes red from weeping.

What little I did know about the world outside came from the movies; the skyline of Manhattan, the palm-tree boulevards of Los Angeles, the streets of Tokyo, these were familiar to me, as though I had actually been there. One film in particular changed my life. I must have seen James Dean in *Rebel Without a Cause* at least a dozen times. I would go in the afternoon and again in the evening. Alone in my room, I practiced all James's mannerisms and could recite every line, in Japanese of course. I would spend hours in front of the mirror trying to get my hair to sit like his blond ducktail, but my stiff black bristle always proved too stubborn for the task. I tried to walk like him, smile like him, sit like him, frown like him, and wave like him when I saw someone I knew, or even someone I didn't. Where I lived, guys didn't wear red jackets like James's, so I got a girl's jacket, which didn't look remotely like his, but was the closest thing I could find in our country town. No doubt I cut a ridiculous figure. Girls giggled behind my back and boys jeered, calling me "Jaymu": "Hey, Jaymu, where's your jackknife?" But I didn't care. I knew that James would understand me. I felt closer to him than I did to anyone else, including my mother. He was, in a way, the elder brother I never had. I often dreamed that James would come swooping down on my hometown to take me away with him, me riding on his back.

I didn't tell any of my schoolmates about my dreams. I knew they would just laugh. Except for one kid, Mori-kun. I would sometimes confide in him, because I knew he wouldn't mock me. Mori's father owned a men's clothing store. It was a modest store, nothing fancy. Out of school uniform, Mori was always better dressed than the rest of us, in neatly pressed gray pants and soft sweaters. This might have made him a target of Muto's torments. But Mori was good at baseball, and blessed with enough self-confidence to escape that fate. His good manners made him seem older than he was.

We talked one afternoon, after school, about our hopes in life. He said he would stay in our town and one day run his father's store. I must confess I was rather baffled by this. He wasn't even the eldest son, and under no obligation to enter the family business. "Don't you want to see the world?" I asked him. "Even Tokyo? Do you really think this is it? This dump on the Japan Sea coast?" I looked at him, with a queasy mixture of pity and disdain. "Aren't you interested in what the world is like?"

He just smiled. "But this is the world too. Our world. What's wrong with it?"

"Well," I said, "we'll never find out if we don't know what the rest of the world is like, will we?" I kicked a loose stone in the sidewalk, a little harder than I intended.

"I think I'll try the one I know first," he said with a placid smile. "The rest of the world can wait. It'll still be there, if I decide to take a look."

Perhaps there was wisdom in his words, but I never understood Mori's attitude. In fact, I had a terrible impulse to kick him in the shins, to punish him for his complacency. I suppose I wanted life to be like the movies. Not that I even dreamed of making movies myself. I had no idea what I would do. I just wanted to get away.

My mother worried about me. She wanted me to be a respectable citizen, join a company, get married, build a home, have children. She thought I was a hopeless dreamer, especially when I talked about the movies. I think she associated movies with the lowlifes smooching in her theater. She had to serve this riffraff to survive, but the idea of her only son getting carried away by that kind of thing would have horrified her. She had put enough money aside for me to study at a university. One day, she said, I would come back and take care of her. She wept as I boarded the train, and I watched her receding figure through the window as she waved a white handkerchief and called out my name, over and over, until I could no longer see her. I was sad too, in a guilty sort of way, but the sadness was overwhelmed by a much more powerful feeling of excitement, and relief. Away at last! To Tokyo, to Tokyo!

3

OUR UNIVERSITY WAS like many others in the capital, a campus of shit-colored brick buildings from the 1930s, dull and rather forbidding—functional fascism, I call it—and a hideous library built sometime in the 1950s. The original campus was badly damaged by the Great Kanto Earthquake in 1923, and some of the later buildings hadn't survived the bombings. The entrance to the reading room was sealed. Students had occupied it during the protests in 1960 against the U.S. Security Treaty. Getting a book out was a cumbersome process, involving an endless trail of stamped and sealed permits. Only foreign exchange students were allowed in the library. There were two. I think they were Americans. Only in Japan would foreigners be accorded such special privileges. Why do we have to grovel as soon as a pale face hovers into sight?

I slept through a few classes on law, and after a couple more months of tedium, without telling my mother, I took up philosophy instead. I don't really know why I chose philosophy. Perhaps it was just that, like many young men, I wanted to find a key to unlock the mysteries of life. During the war, the philosophy department had been a nest of fascism. All that rubbish about uniting Asia under the benevolent rule of our Emperor—Japan was propagated from this same place. Our university founded a sister institution in Manchuria, no doubt to indoctrinate the natives with the blessings of our fine Imperial System. After the war, as though to make up for its past mistakes, the university established a reputation for radicalism, especially in the 1950s, when it became known as the "Red Fort."

By the time I arrived, however, the defeat of 1960 lingered on our campus like a permanent hangover. Even the professors spoke bitterly about Kishi and the other war criminals who cynically undermined the constitution to please our American masters. The older students who had taken part in the demonstrations were like soldiers in a vanquished army. They had lost all hope of change. Others got entangled in doctrinal battles between this faction and that. Disputes over the correct line on democratic socialism, or anarcho-syndicalism, or whatnot, raged between the Revolutionary Communist Faction and the Revolutionary Marxist Faction and the Revolutionary Marxist-Leninist League and the Central Committee for Mao Zedong Thought. These disputes sometimes resulted in murders. A fellow I knew slightly was killed one night on his way back home. His skull was cracked open with a lead pipe.

But I didn't care about these political fights. I was still a rebel without a cause. Too late for the 1960 revolt and not interested in democratic socialism or anarcho-syndicalism, politics seemed pointless. On the wall of my dorm was a slogan painted about ten years before: *World Revolution!* Attempts had been made to scrub this graffiti off the wall, but it always came back, no matter how many times they tried to wipe it out. The slogan had an almost antiquarian feel to me, like something from a lost age.

So I fell in with the theatrical crowd instead. The undisputed leader was a baby-faced student from a rough Tokyo neighborhood. His real name was Yoshimura Tadayuki, but he changed it to Okuni Tojiro, which had the raffish sound of an old-time Kabuki actor, when Kabuki was still a theater of outcasts and prostitutes. I immediately recognized a kindred soul in Okuni. Like James Dean, he was touched by a spirit of rebellion, but like me was turned off by the factional squabbles of organized revolt. His eyes were his most striking feature, burning with passion, quick to shed tears or flare up in anger. His fiery temperament suggested that he might be Korean. There was something of the gangster in him, and something of the poet. I had never encountered someone like Okuni in my hometown. He was my first real friend. Like me, Okuni lost his father in the war, killed somewhere in the Philippines, I believe, just before the Japanese surrender.

Okuni was amused by my passion for Tokyo. I really felt as if I had landed in a circus that never stopped: the movie theaters, the bars, the cabarets, the streetgirls, the hawkers around the Shinto shrines, the markets under the railway tracks, the old soldiers playing melancholy wartime ballads in the subway stations. I had no money, but I was all eyes, taking everything in like a child at a fairground. Who needed theater? The streets were my theater. Okuni and I would roam around the city, from the backstreets of Asakusa, where he grew up, to the cheap bars in Shinjuku, where we got drunk and argued about theater and movies and Jean-Paul Sartre. Okuni was crazy about Sartre. "The situation," he would shout, his eyes bulging like shining black marbles, "that's what it's all about. Nothing is determined. We change by reacting to new situations." He was always dressed in black sweaters, of course. And when he started his theater troupe in his last year at university, he called it the Existential Theater.

But Okuni's theories, or rather the theories of Jean-Paul Sartre, interested me less than his endless supply of stories of growing up in the ruins of Asakusa. I had never seen a ruined city. Where I grew up was too remote for bombing raids, except for the air base, which had been hit a few times. There was something extraordinarily romantic about a ruined metropolis. You could still see the scars in some parts of Tokyo, but much of the wartime damage had already been cleaned up for the Olympic Games in 1964. We Japanese were like a nervous housewife, terrified that the esteemed foreign guests would notice even a speck of dust in our parlor. Okuni felt a deep nostalgia for the city of ruins. Tokyo used to be a fantastic playground, he said. Since everything was wrecked, the city had infinite possibilities. He remembered how you could see all the way from Asakusa to Mount Fuji. He told me stories about characters I couldn't even have imagined: the transvestite prostitute who made his home in a public toilet; the kamikaze survivor who became a dancer in a burlesque theater; the gang of young pickpockets led by a Buddhist priest.

"You know," Okuni said, as we sat in a Shinjuku bar drinking beer one steamy night in August, "I envy you." A half smile played around his lips as he stared into my eyes, as though challenging me to be the first one to look away. To say I was astonished is to put it mildly. Okuni *envious* of me? Surely, it had to be the other way round. He explained: "Growing up in Tokyo is like being in a great stew with everything thrown in, Western, Asian, Japanese. We have nothing really local, of the soil, reeking of mud. While you, who grew up in the country, have something much richer running through your veins. You may not be aware of it, but it's in your subconscious."

This was way too deep for me. How could he know what was in my subconscious? So I protested: "But it's a culture without interest, narrow-minded, provincial . . ."

He shook his head: "Provincial is good."

". . . But why be a frog in a narrow well? I came to Tokyo to escape from that. I can always go back to my country. First I want to see the world."

"That's where you're wrong," said Okuni, pouring the last drop of beer into my glass. "Once you leave, there is no way of going back. It'll be too late. Hold on to your native soil and guard it like a precious jewel. You want to know what I think?"

"What?"

"I think an artist should never leave home."

I must confess that his words struck me like arrows, me who had been doing my very best to drop my slurred north country accent and talk crisply like a true-born Tokyoite. I felt that Okuni was patronizing me, pressing me into the role of the country bumpkin for his amusement. "What about Sartre?" I said.

"What about him?" said Okuni.

A certain edginess had entered the conversation. Raw nerves were being exposed. "Sartre says that a human being is never determined by situations," I urged. "You make your own choices. People who live in good faith transform themselves all the time. You yourself are always saying that. How can you now claim that creativity is determined by the place we happen to be born in?"

"Who said determined? I said you have to cherish it. That is the opposite of being a frog in a well. Only by expressing what is local, specific, personal, can you express something of value to other people. Call it universal, if you like. All good artists understand this instinctively. Traveling around the world, learning other languages, that's for people who lack the talent to express themselves in their own. I hate those show-offs who jabber away in foreign languages, as though that makes them so superior. They're just mimics, phonies with no talent. Perhaps you're not an artist after all, but just a tourist."

I felt cornered. My stammer got worse. I should have just left it at that. But I couldn't resist arguing, raising my voice: "If it hadn't been for Japanese learning French, you wouldn't have been able to read Sartre."

"So become a translator. That's not the same as being an artist. Maybe that's what you should do, be a translator of other people's ideas."

I stammered that he was full of shit. The next thing I knew, I was sprawled out on the wooden floor with a salty taste in my mouth. I tried to get up, but he was stronger. Strange hands attempted to separate us. After a few more blows to my face, Okuni stomped out of the bar. I lay there cursing him. But he was not the real object of my rage. It was my own sense of impotence. Okuni had his theater. What did I have? I needed to do something, make my mark, leave a dent in the world, so people would know I'd been around. But what?

4

EVER SINCE THE whore beckoned men to Babylon, great cities have been marketplaces of human flesh, cornucopias of erotic possibilities, promising every imaginable sexual pleasure known to man. Tokyo was no exception. What really attracted me to the metropolis, like a fly to a Venus flytrap, was not discussions about Jean-Paul Sartre, or libraries full of books, but girls, girls, girls. Tokyo was like a great juicy carrot tempting the hungry man at every street corner: the billboards of girls licking creamy ice creams; the pink cabaret girls tempting customers with a menu of perversions; the department store girls in their pillbox hats and high-heeled shoes bowing low as you sampled the goods; the girls in miniskirts hovering round the Fugetsudo waiting to be picked up by a foreigner; the pictures plastered outside the porno cinemas of girls tied up in ropes, voracious divorcées and demure office ladies pressed into orgies, beautiful housewives pleasuring gangsters; the short-time hotels offering spankings administered to naughty maids, air hostesses begging to be taken, sex in suits of armor, sex in cowboy gear, sex in military uniforms, sex in swings, baths, massage beds, railway carriages, long-haul trucks, subway cars, French castles, ocean liners, Chinese palaces, Japanese tea ceremony rooms, American saloons, Arabian tents. All that, and much much more. And I wasn't getting any of it.

Apart from my stammer, I blamed our culture. We Japanese prize hypocrisy in girls. No, we demand it. We love them to be so damned coy. Girls want sex as much as men do. So why do we want them to resist, or at least pretend to put up a fight, as though they can only give in to superior force? In fact, resistance breaks down quite quickly in the face of power and money, which comes down to the same thing of course. Japanese love to submit to power. Only when they can claim to be overwhelmed do they feel free to do as they like. That is why girls can never say no to a foreigner. Foreigners, in stupid Japanese eyes, are too powerful to resist.

Okuni never seemed to have trouble with girls. He radiated such confidence that women melted in his presence. It was all too easy for him. That is why he usually treated them with contempt; but the more he abused them, the more they would come back for more, like addicts. Myself, I turned into a stammering wreck as soon as I tried, in my polite, tactful, diffident, roundabout way, to signal my intentions to a girl. Yet it was me, not Okuni, who provoked outrage and disgust, as though I had offended their dignity with my disgusting intentions.

This may come as a surprise, but it's actually easier here in Beirut, as long as you stay out of prison, that is (although even in Roumieh pretty much anything imaginable to man does go on, for a price). The Arab mind is less hypocritical about these matters. Girls who want it are Christians and make no bones about their desires, if they like you. And most of them like Japanese men. Muslims are different. You know they are not available to anyone but their husbands. But they are never coy. The juicy carrot isn't dangled in front of your face, only to be withdrawn the moment you reach out to have a nibble.

Anyway, this is all a roundabout way of introducing the next stage of my career: assistant director in pink movies. I should explain something about the pink movies. Though they were churned out cheaply at a fast rate to titillate a lot of sad old bastards in backstreet cinemas, some of them were actually pretty good. Because the old movie studios were like sclerotic old men grimly holding on to life by regurgitating the same old shit over and over again, the pink industry attracted some of the brightest talents around. There were rules to be observed, to be sure: one sex scene every six minutes (not five, not seven, always six; I never figured out why, but the industry was full of such arcane practices). In between the sex scenes, however, we could insert all sorts of ideas. The sex itself, by the way, was also bound by certain unalterable conventions: most sex acts, including rape, torture, even murder (strangulation with a kimono sash was popular for a time), were permissible, but the sight of even a single pubic hair was strictly forbidden. Genitals, male or female, were absolutely banned from the screen.

The director I had the immense good fortune to assist, a tall bearlike figure named Sugihara Banteki, but known to everyone as Ban-chan, was also known as "the King of Rape." He cut his teeth on all the different genres, from schoolgirl pictures to housewives-molested-by-gangster vehicles, but his specialty was Yankee base movies, a popular subgenre of pink movies at the time. His greatest successes were: *Red Light Zone Okinawa, Violated Angels of Atsugi Air Base, GI Rape,* and *Rape Camp Zama.* The last movie, especially, was a big hit among Japanese students. The heroine, acted by the late great Takano Fujiko, a former stripper from Osaka, is infected with syphilis after being gang-raped by five American GIs. Her vengeance, plotted with her Japanese lover (Osano Toru in an early role), is to have sex with as many Yankees as she can, so they will all die of the disease.

Ban-chan's most personal movies were all political like that. Politics was his lifeblood. A proud native of Osaka (unlike me, he never disguised his accent; on the contrary, he cultivated it), Ban-chan first made his name as a student leader in 1960. He was a natural leader, broad shoulders, long hair, booming voice, a big drinker. There is a famous Dutch painting called *The Laughing Cavalier.* That's what he was like, always laughing, always the center of attention in any crowd.

Like Okuni, he never had trouble attracting girls, who would do anything to please him. So did the men around Ban-chan. Everyone just
adored the King of Rape.

I should confess that the reason he took me into his group had nothing to do with my artistic talent, such as it is, and everything with my
birth. He even called me Misawa, after my hometown. My real name,
Sato Kenkichi, never passed his lips; not even Ken-chan, as my friends
called me. The fact that I grew up around a U.S. military base was my
most attractive asset, as far as he was concerned. "Misawa," he would
say, "you had the most precious education imaginable. You saw the
imperialist oppression with your own eyes. You lived in it. Now the
important thing is to turn that experience into praxis."

I had read my Marcuse, of course. But I wasn't quite sure what sort
of "praxis" he had in mind. Ban-chan was a little vague on this score.
He never told you directly what to do, but liked to lead by example and
let you draw your own conclusions. After a day's shooting, in or around
Tokyo, he would take a bunch of us assistants to his favorite bar in
Shinjuku, named Pepé Le Moko, after the French movie with Jean
Gabin. He was like a father to us, or an elder brother, always paying for
our beers and food, teaching us how to think. He drank whiskey himself, White Horse, neat, without water or ice. And he would talk, talk,
talk, the words flowing like a river, about life, and art, and politics.
Once he talked for two hours and a half without stopping, except to
sip from his glass, after holding it up for one of us to replenish with
whiskey.

Once, after a particularly long drinking session, he did something
that struck me as humiliating at first, but turned out to be of great sig-
nificance to my life. "Misawa," he boomed, as he peered at me intently
through eyes that the drink had reduced to tiny slits, "are you angry?"
Angry at what, Ban-chan? "Angry!" Yes, but at what? "That is the
question, isn't it?" he said, and struck me hard in the face. I felt a sting-

ing pain in my cheek. But worse than that, I didn't know how to react. I was too stunned. The other guys were staring at Ban-chan too, waiting to see what he would do next. I could only stammer: "What, what, why did you do that?"

"React!" he screamed. "React! I've slapped you! Hit back!"

"But why?"

"Are you angry at the American oppressors?"

"Yes."

"Are you angry with them for destroying our freedom, for corrupting our boys and raping our girls? Angry with capitalist society for turning our people into soulless slaves of consumerism? Angry with our bourgeois morality that stifles our natural desires?"

"Yes," I said, as tears welled up in my eyes, "yes! yes! yes!"

His voice suddenly grew softer, soothing me, like a mother comforting her baby: "Then cherish that anger and channel it into action. Find a way to change the world. Value your desire for vengeance, put it in a drawer, and use it constructively one day for the sake of justice, freedom, and peace. We tried to change Japan in 1960. We failed. I blame myself as much as Kishi and his gang. Now I can only try to change the false consciousness of the masses through my films. I still think this is worth doing, but it'll be a very slow process. You, on the other hand, you are still young. You still have a chance to really make a difference. Wait for that chance. Be patient. And when it comes, you will know. Don't think. Just act."

5

OKUNI, IN THE meantime, was getting a lot of attention with his Existential Theater. Like the old riverside beggars who started the Kabuki, he traveled all over the country with his troupe, pitching the yellow tent wherever he could get a permit, and sometimes even where he couldn't: in empty car parks, disused railway yards, temple grounds, riverbanks, old cemeteries, abandoned aerodromes, and most famously, at the Hanazono Shrine in Shinjuku. That is where he had put up his tent when we filmed him and his actors in a movie about youth rebellion, entitled *One Night in Shinjuku*.

Okuni and I had patched up our differences long before then, of course. In fact, even before *One Night in Shinjuku*, he had acted in one of Ban-chan's pink films, for which I had written the script. Ban-chan encouraged all his assistants to write scripts. I had written several already, all of which I showed to him, none of which he even acknowledged with a word of praise or criticism. Things could be worse. Sometimes he showed his contempt for a scriptwriter's work by tearing the manuscript up in front of his eyes. On one occasion he took a fresh script into the toilet and used it to wipe his ass. But not this time. Finally I had written something that met with his approval. "Not bad," he declared, "let's do it." That's what he was like, Ban-chan. He never hung about. Decisions were made on the spot. I guess that's how he was able to crank out two pink movies a month for so many years.

Anyhow, I was delirious, and at the same time filled with dread: would it really be good enough? Wouldn't this show me up? *Wet Desire,* the title of my film, was about a bourgeois young woman, about to go through with an arranged marriage to a respectable young banker. The opening scene is of the two families, dressed in formal kimonos, meeting at a restaurant to exchange gifts. The ceremony is filmed in a stylized way, in a long panning shot, to illustrate the manners of the Japanese bourgeoisie: unsmiling patriarchs exchanging formulaic pleasantries, wives on the lookout for the smallest lapse in decorum, and the young couple staring ahead without showing any emotion, still as Noh masks.

Cut to the bride (played by Kujo Junko) visiting her dentist. While she is pinned down in the leather chair, the dentist slips a hypodermic into her mouth, and then a drill. Cut to a shot of her eyes closing, imagining all the things the dentist could do to her, while his drill dissolves into a giant dildo probing her in every orifice; and not only the dentist, for as her fantasies become more lurid, she imagines being raped by a gang of construction workers, and being used by a black GI who sticks a gun in her mouth, and being suspended in ropes in a roomful of yakuza, who spin her round and round and round, laughing at her helplessness. The dentist was acted brilliantly by Okuni.

It was a pink movie in form, of course, but also an attempt to strip away the hypocrisy of Japanese society. My model was Jean-Luc Godard. The point was to show how bondage is the only way for Japanese to find liberation. But it is not true liberation, for it exists only in the mind. It would take a revolution for Japanese to throw off their chains and act on their desires. And revolutions, as Chairman Mao said, are not dinner parties. Japanese simply weren't ready for it. They still aren't. Nor was I, if truth be told. But if praxis was still a way off, at least I was edging toward an understanding of the problem.

For *One Night in Shinjuku* we took a more documentary approach, mixed with fantasy sequences. We interviewed people, some famous, some not. Dr. Horikiri Tsuneo, who wrote a bestseller about sexual life in contemporary Japan, spoke about the main reason for male impotence (to do with the extraordinary size of our prostate glands apparently, unique to the Japanese race). A former student leader, and current chairman of a large trading company, Suzuki Muneo, talked about the defeat of 1960. And we spent a week with Okuni's troupe in Shinjuku. Some of the actors were kids from the provinces, looking for a Tokyo home. But the leading figure in the Existential Theater group, apart from Okuni himself, was Yo Kee Hee, his half-Taiwanese wife. She was a typical Chinese woman of fierce temperament, who once broke an empty saké bottle over her husband's head when she suspected him (quite rightly) of fooling around with a young actress. Things changed after that. Girls still turned up for auditions, but Yo always found fault with them. So the main female roles were shared between Yo and Nagasaki Shiro, who dressed in women's kimonos, and spoke like a woman, but was in fact a very tough guy, who once smashed the nose of an obnoxious boxer who was giving Okuni trouble in a Shinjuku bar. (We were all a little afraid of Nagasaki.) The handsome young male roles usually went to an actor named Shina Tora.

The play we recorded on film, *The Ri Koran Story: Asakusa Version*, was one of Okuni's best, and certainly most successful. In typical Okuni fashion, he had taken ingredients from the life of the legendary wartime movie star Ri Koran, cooked them together with his childhood memories of Asakusa, and peppered them with references to old movies, current comic book heroes, and old Japanese myths. In a nutshell (as if Okuni's dreamlike stories could ever fit into a nutshell), the play is about Ri losing her memory when she returns to Japan after the war. Wandering through Asakusa, trying to find her old self, she has strange encounters along the way: the actor Hasegawa Kazuo (played by Okuni) appears as a character in a popular detective story; Captain Amakasu

(Shina Tora), the notorious spy, makes a comeback as a rockabilly star; a well-known Asakusa stripper turns out to be none other than Kawashima Yoshiko, the Manchurian princess who worked for the Kempeitai, played by Nagasaki, of course. There is a stunning scene at the beginning of the second act where Amakasu appears as a puppetmaster, holding the other characters by a bunch of strings. But the puppets slowly come alive at the end of the act, running out of the master's control. Amakasu turns out to have been a ghost all along.

We filmed the whole play, but ended up using just the final scene, where Ri discovers that she and Kawashima are actually the same person. As the ghost of Kawashima fades into the background through a neat trick of lighting, Ri stands alone on the Asakusa stage, stripping her clothes, layer after layer, like peeling an onion, without ever revealing her naked self. The audience went wild, shouting Yo's name, tossing gifts onto the stage.

Every performance would be followed by a drinking session inside the tent, with actors and friends. Okuni and Ban-chan did most of the talking, while the actors poured their drinks from large bottles of cold saké. Ban-chan talked politics. Okuni argued with him. "My revolution," he said, "is here inside this tent. This is where I create my situations." Ban-chan insisted that more was needed. He didn't want to isolate the action inside a tent, or, for that matter, on the movie screen. "We must create new situations," he said, "in the streets, in the parks, on the beaches, and turn the whole world into a stage."

There was an American there too, a tall, dark-haired guy, Vanoven-san. For a Yank, he was all right. Like most foreigners, he spoke Japanese like a woman. I had seen him before, at movie openings and the like. Vanoven-san was a crazy foreigner who liked everything about Japan, and knew more about our country than we did. He was also a homo. This didn't bother me. I don't think I was his type, anyway. He showed a flicker of interest once, but when I tried to talk to him about

Sartre, his eyes glazed over. From then on, he never paid much attention to me.

The subject of Ri Koran came up, the real one as well as the one imagined by Okuni. Nagasaki did a hilarious puppet theater routine, imitating the jerky movements while doing the falsetto woman's voice. "Good," said Ban-chan, who was already halfway through a bottle of whiskey, "very good, but who were the real puppeteers? It was surely Amakasu and his gang of Japanese Fascists." Okuni, dragging thoughtfully on his usual Seven Stars cigarette, suggested that, on the contrary, Amakasu's power was an optical illusion. Ri herself was pulling the strings of the men around her. "She was an artist," he said. "Her power was her imagination. Art is the ultimate power." Ban-chan shook his head. "That, my friend is the illusion. You forget about the politics. Ri Koran, Hasegawa, they were just pawns in a much larger game which they barely understood. The real source of Fascist power was the Emperor System." He paused, then suddenly turned to me: "Misawa, what do you think?"

I dreaded this more than anything. I felt I was being compelled to make a speech, or take my clothes off, or dance in public. But Ban-chan wouldn't let me off the hook: "I want to hear what Misawa thinks. Let's hear what Misawa thinks." By way of encouragement, he poured some saké into my glass. My face was dripping with perspiration. I stammered that maybe no one was in charge. Maybe that was the "Emperor System." "Hmmm," went Ban-chan, "interesting," and turned away.

At which point Vanoven joined the discussion with a short lecture on Japanese politics. "Japanese politics," he said, in his feminine Japanese, "is a system of irresponsibility. In the middle is the Emperor, pushed this way and that, like a portable shrine, by a group of anonymous men. Since none of them guides the shrine personally, no one is responsible. Ri Koran was a typical portable shrine, pushed around by invisible hands . . ."

"Hmm," said Ban-chan, "a portable shrine, very interesting." To which Okuni, eyes twinkling with enthusiasm, added that Vanoven knew so much more about us Japanese than we did ourselves. Vanoven looked pleased at this, and began to tell us about his friendship with the real Ri Koran. "It was still during the war," he began, before being interrupted.

"You're all wrong," said an emaciated old man with bad teeth and a receding chin, wearing a dark blue kimono. He was a regular guest at Okuni's post-performance parties. Professor Sekizawa Chu was a distinguished scholar of French literature. He had translated several works by the Marquis de Sade. The remarkable thing about him was that in all the sixty-six years of his life, he had never once been to France. I'm not sure he even spoke French, although it was rumored that he could speak eighteenth-century French quite fluently. I don't mean to suggest that he was a dry old stick. On the contrary, Chu-sensei was actually a remarkably jolly fellow who could drink with the best of us, and when in his cups would sometimes get to his feet to do a country dance, pulling grotesque peasant faces.

"You're all wrong," he said. "I was born and bred in Harbin, and though I've never met Miss Ri Koran, I know one or two things about her. On the surface it may have seemed that we Japanese pulled the strings in Manchuria, and most of us were naive enough to think so. Not surprising, really, when you think of the way the Kanto Army strutted around for all the world as though they owned the place. But in fact, behind the scenes, it was the Jews who held the strings. They had the money and the connections. Did you know that Abraham Kaufman, head of the Jewish community in Harbin, knew Victor Sassoon, who owned half of Shanghai in the 1930s and had close relations with President Roosevelt? Sassoon, Kaufman, Roosevelt—all Jews, looking after their own people's interests. Can you blame them? The Russians knew this. The Chinese knew it. The Europeans all knew it. Only we Japanese didn't know it, because we're a gullible island people, too innocent in the ways of the wider world to realize that we're a nation of puppets ourselves."

There was a moment's silence, as we let Chu-sensei's words sink in. Ban-chan nodded, and Nagasaki made an appropriate sound to register his surprise. We looked at Vanoven. Surely he would have a view on this. He peered into his glass, and said nothing. Okuni laughed, took a swig from his glass of saké, asked one of the actors to hand him his guitar, and began to sing a song from a popular yakuza movie. We all joined in, clapping our hands. Shina Tora was asked to sing an old student song, and Nagasaki crooned a chanson by Edith Piaf. Ban-chan began a song from the 1960 anti-treaty demonstrations, and then one of his favorites, "Song of the Japanese Red Army." As he sang, in his booming voice, of the martyrdom of fallen comrades in the struggle for justice and freedom, I suddenly felt his loneliness. Always surrounded by people, Ban-chan seemed terribly alone in this world. Perhaps that is why he was so eager to change it.

6

WHEN I RECALL those sunlit days now from my dark Lebanese prison cell, I am both touched by the confused, anxious, stammering person I was back then, and a little embarrassed. Perhaps most people feel that way about their former selves, sloughed off along the way like snakeskins. It is sometimes claimed that one remembers the good times and forgets the rest. I don't know about other people, but I think with painful vividness of all my missteps, my shameful gaffes, the maladroit remarks, the unintended hurts inflicted, the shallowness of my views on the world. Then, of course, I didn't really know the world as well as I thought I did. I just knew a tiny sliver of it, my hometown in the north country, the pink movie industry, Okuni's tent. In the bright neon lights of Tokyo, I felt small and insignificant. Who would notice the difference if I suddenly died?

I was floundering like a blind man, spending all my time in the cinema, when I wasn't working on movies with Ban-chan. My favorite place was the National Film Center in Kyobashi. I sat through festivals of Mizoguchi, Naruse, and Kurosawa. I sat through all the films starring Jean Gabin. It was as though I were living a hundred different lives in the dark, only to go home feeling like a man who was still in search of his own life. I saw revivals of wartime movies, movies about heroic Japanese mothers, samurai movies by Uchida Tomu, Hollywood movies of the 1930s, French movies by Duvivier and Clouzot, and even one or two wartime films with Ri Koran. My memory of them is hazy. One was called *China Nights,* I believe, and another was about a native girl in Taiwan who falls in love with a native man who joins the Imperial Japanese Army.

The real Ri Koran, who was actually called Yamaguchi Yoshiko, never came to see Okuni's play that bore her name. I don't think anyone really expected her to. The world of underground theater wasn't exactly hers. She was supposedly married to a diplomat, and had retired from the movie industry years ago. For all we knew, she was living abroad at some foreign posting. Someone mentioned Burma. Once in a while, her name would come up in some nostalgic article in a weekly magazine about the good old days in Manchuria, usually illustrated by a still from an old movie. People still knew who she was, but her star had faded to a distant glimmer. What little I knew about her didn't exactly endear her to me, anyway. She had, after all, been a collaborator with Japanese fascism, a propagandist for our war in Asia. And quite frankly, the nostalgia among certain Japanese for those days made me sick.

The idea that I might actually meet her in the flesh one day would never have occurred to me even in my dreams. And yet that is precisely what happened. This had nothing to do with Okuni's play, or indeed *One Night in Shinjuku.* The film wasn't a major commercial success, but it achieved a certain cult status. Ban-chan established his reputation as a political filmmaker and not just a director of interesting pornography. But this made it harder for him to get new projects off the ground. The people with cash didn't like political filmmakers. Nor did they always like his pink stuff, but at least it made more money. So we went through a bit of a trough, and all of us had to cast around for other jobs to tide us over. I decided to try my luck in television.

A new documentary show was about to start up on one of the independent television channels, called *What a Weird World,* not the most promising of titles, I must admit. All I knew was that most of it would be shot in foreign countries. I wanted to travel, so I applied for the job. The interview process was long and unnecessarily complicated, or so it seemed to me after the world of pink movies, where everything was done at maximum speed. First I had to meet an assistant to someone's assistant in a coffeeshop. Then I found myself in a haze of smoke with a number of men in suits, only one of whom asked me questions, while the others took notes. A week later, I was finally summoned by the producer, a sleek man in a blazer, with a mustache that made him look vaguely like that British actor, David Niven. He smelled of aftershave lotion and cigarettes, which he chain-smoked. His office was small and without a trace of character. A few gilt-framed diplomas—or perhaps they were prizes for television shows—were tacked to the wall. A female doll in a kimono stared out blankly from a glass case. On the desk was a gold pen—another prize, perhaps?—lodged into a stand of magnificent ugliness, with a rim of gold babies holding up flower baskets.

"Congratulations," he said, "you're on board. We'll put you in the scriptwriting department." I expressed my gratitude, while hoping that he would take my stammer as a sign of enthusiasm. "You know President John F. Kennedy?" he asked, as he lit a fresh cigarette with his half-finished one. I replied that I'd heard of him, of course. "Remember what he said about America? Well, we like to apply the same thing to our outfit. Do that, and you'll be fine." I waited for a further explanation. Noticing my bewilderment, he laughed and told me what President Kennedy had said, or almost said: "It's not what the company can do for you, it's what you can do for the company." This didn't sound much to my liking, but I nodded, as though it were a matter of course. "And by the way, can you drink?"

The next thing I knew, we were sitting in a bar, somewhere on the sixth or seventh floor of a building near the Azabu subway station. A young woman in a velvet evening gown was playing cocktail music on a piano in a narrow room that was empty apart from us. Since it was only four o'clock in the afternoon, this was hardly surprising. David Niven proudly had his personal bottle of whiskey taken from the cabinet above the bar and he fully expected me to share its contents. "Johnnie Walker Black," he insisted. "Always go for the Black."

When I probed him on the exact nature of the program, what it would be about, who would front it, and what my role as a writer would entail, he became oddly evasive. "You'll soon find out," he said, as the Mama-san behind the bar picked up the bottle with a practiced hand to refill our glasses. As dusk began to fall outside, one or two more men in dark suits came through the door. I judged from their nods that they were Niven's colleagues. Without glancing at me, they asked him who I was. After I was introduced as the new writer, they acknowledged my presence and slunk off to the other end of the bar.

Niven, meanwhile, became steadily more inebriated and, despite my protestations, made sure I kept up with him all the way. Still no word about the program. Instead, he talked endlessly about himself, moving his head uncomfortably close to mine. He had been "very political" as a student at Waseda, he confided, "but, you know, 1960 and all that, we were young and innocent." I indicated that I understood perfectly. He had had ambitions once to make serious films, serious art films, like that Frenchman. I tried to be helpful. Did he mean Jean-Luc Godard? "That's the one. But, you know, in Japan, there is no chance of that. You'll soon find out. We all start with fine ideals. Then you grow up, and you see just what the real world is made of. You'll find out soon enough yourself. Before that, my advice to you: have a ball." When he launched into a mawkish account of his recent divorce I nodded to show that I was still with him, while trying hard to think of other things, far removed from that dreadful bar.

I left him at about two o'clock in the morning, slumped over the bar in a stupor, occasionally waking up with a jolt, murmuring "Mama" to the woman behind the counter. I felt depressed as I walked into the street. It had been raining and the asphalt under the expressway was giving off steam, which reminded me in a curious way of the Mountain of Dread. The idea of working for this hopeless producer, after my heady days with Ban-chan, was too awful to contemplate.

But it turned out that I had underestimated him. A week after our drunken encounter, I was finally introduced to the presenter. Niven had organized a lunch in one of those stiff little French restaurants in Azabu Juban. In came a small, shapely woman in a yellow miniskirt. Her hair was puffed up in a permanent wave, like a luxuriant fur hat. She sat down. Niven explained my presence. She removed her sunglasses, and fixed me in her gaze. She had the most extraordinary eyes I have ever seen in a woman: large and luminous, more Thai or Indonesian than Japanese. They looked so foreign that I assumed she had had them fixed by a plastic surgeon. "Meet Yamaguchi-san," said David Niven, beaming, like a conjurer who has just pulled a rabbit out of a hat.

After I had been scrutinized, she turned to the producer and told him how excited she was about the show. "Do you know," she said, bubbling over with enthusiasm, "I've always wanted to be a journalist, ever since I was a little girl in China. I always wanted to show people the real world, what it was actually like, what was really going on." She sighed. "But . . . the movies intervened. I never wanted to be a movie actress. It was foisted on me against my will." She brightened up, all smiles. "But now, at last, I'll be able to do what I've always wanted, to be a real journalist. Are you a journalist?"

She addressed this question to me. No, I said, alas not. I made movies. "Oh," she said, with a note of disappointment. Niven quickly explained that I would be responsible for shaping the programs, writing the scripts, making everything coherent. She would be the reporter. "Yes," she said, full of enthusiasm once again, "I'll be the reporter. That's the important thing. You take care of the rest."

I asked what precisely we were going to be reporting. Niven looked at Yamaguchi-san, who had taken a smart-looking black reporter's notebook from her shiny white leather purse. She put it beside her plate, as though she were about to take notes of our conversation. Niven said: "The program, which will be aired in the afternoons, is aimed at the intelligent housewife, the housewife who wishes to be informed about important events in the world."

Yes, Yamaguchi-san confirmed, that was exactly right. Housewives were the perfect audience, for they represented the best hope for mankind. "You see, Sato-san," she explained, "men are addicted to violence and destruction. They are forever going to war. But women are different, don't you agree, Sato-san? Women have to protect their children. That's why they are our best hope. I'm quite sure of that. Only the women can stop our men from blowing up our beautiful planet. Our first program will be about the Vietnam War."

David Niven nodded. "I couldn't tell you this before," he said, again with that air of the professional conjurer, "because we had to keep it confidential, but now I can divulge the full title of our new show: *What a Weird World: Yamaguchi Yoshiko Reports from the Front Line.*"

7

I HATED SAIGON on first sight. It was only May, but I felt as if I were being choked inside a warm wet blanket. Every time I stepped out of the hotel, I was accosted by Chinamen with gold teeth trying to sell me things: fake antiques, local currency, girls. The food tasted like soap, and there were Yanks everywhere, treating the city like their private whorehouse, big guys with red faces, like hogs, wrapping their fat pink arms around one or two or three girls, yelling and hooting to one another like savages. It brought back all the worst memories of my native town. But I was older now. I no longer admired these barbarians, not even secretly. I could see them for what they were, and I hated them for raping an Asian country, corrupting the people with their mindless greed. The sooner the Viet Cong took over this city and kicked out the foreign imperialists, the better.

I tried to convey this to Yamaguchi-san, but she warned me not to be "too political." The program had to be suitable for television. Forget about all that "theoretical stuff," she said. We had to find a way to get the Vietnamese people to communicate their feelings straight to the hearts of our viewers.

This was typical of her approach. Although my first impression of Yamaguchi-san was of an airhead out of her depth, I soon began to regard her with more respect. On the flight from Tokyo to Bangkok, she told us about her experiences in China during the war. We Japanese should learn from the past, she said, and be on the side of the common Asian people against foreign aggressors. Her heart was clearly in the right place, even if she was politically naive. There was a purity about her that I hadn't expected. All she needed was a bit of education.

She was certainly a diligent reporter, going about in her light blue safari suit. Her first port of call was the Foreign Correspondents Club, where she interviewed Japanese journalists. But political or not, I felt it was vital to get some shots of the front lines, and an interview with an actual Viet Cong. She agreed. The Japanese Embassy, represented by a nervous little man named Tanaka, said it would be far too dangerous to leave Saigon. Especially at night, he warned us, the Viet Cong took control of the villages, and you never knew what might happen. Several Japanese reporters had already been shot. The Japanese government would not vouch for our safety. I thought this was rubbish. And Yamaguchi-san, bless her heart, wouldn't take no for an answer either. We had to talk to ordinary Vietnamese, she insisted, and find out how they felt about the war.

So in the end, after much protestation from Tanaka, a trip was arranged to a village about fifteen kilometers out of Saigon. The embassy provided us with an interpreter and we hired five security guards. I went ahead to organize the shoot, along with the cameraman, a silent type named Shino, and Higuchi, the soundman, who loved to talk. Yamaguchi-san followed in a separate convoy. She was dressed in a long silk Vietnamese dress and a straw rice planter's hat. The children touched her sleeves, as though they were made of gold. The adults also looked as though they wanted to touch her, but were too shy to do so. I found it all rather embarrassing, but David Niven had insisted on the costume. "Good TV," he said.

As we were setting up our equipment, we were surrounded by children, who were gibbering at us like monkeys. "They think you're Chinese," explained the interpreter. Higuchi shook his head vigorously and said in English: "No, no, Japanese. Japanese!" He proceeded to fold bits of colored paper into bird shapes to distribute among the children, who immediately picked them apart. Yamaguchi-san confused matters further by speaking to the villagers in Mandarin Chinese. A toothless old woman in simple black pants was dragged out from one of the huts to meet us. She spoke a few words of some Chinese dialect. Yamaguchi-san spoke to her very slowly. The old woman bared her betel-stained gums in a blood red grin and reported back to the villagers that we were Japanese. The interpreter said, a little sourly, that she had told them that already.

Villagers, all dressed in the same simple black clothes as the old woman, surrounded Yamaguchi-san. Whenever they spoke into her microphone, they turned solemn. No, there were no Viet Cong here, they insisted. The Americans? Yes, they saw the foreign soldiers sometimes. A thin man in glasses and a wispy beard—a schoolteacher perhaps?—spoke up: "Foreigners have tried to conquer our country for thousands of years. The Khmer, the Thai, the Chinese, the French, the Americans. What's the difference? They always leave in the end. It makes no difference to us. This is our land, the land of our ancestors. We stay here. They will go." But surely, said Yamaguchi, war was a terrible thing. The thought of all the innocent people getting killed, the women, the children . . . The man in glasses shrugged his shoulders, and quickly slipped away. Shino, the cameraman, stopped for a change of film. Yamaguchi-san waited until he was ready, took a little boy with holes in his shorts in her arms, and said: "I pray that this child will live in peace."

The program was a great success. I wasn't entirely pleased with it. Too many questions remained unasked. But it was better than most programs of this type, and that was entirely due to Yamaguchi-san. She was a professional actress, of course, who knew all the tricks of her trade—the costumes and all that. But she was sincere. Her feeling for the people she interviewed was real, and this, somehow, came across. I even managed to make a few political points about U.S. imperialism. We used some powerful newsreel footage of Americans bombing Hanoi. All in all, not too bad for a daytime TV show for housewives.

I can't remember who first suggested doing a program about the Palestinians. But I found it quite strange that everyone was talking about Vietnam, while ignoring the Palestinian struggle. This would have been round about the time that an old acquaintance from university came back into my life. His name was Hayashi, and he used to be in Okuni's theater crowd. We lost touch after he dropped out of school. I heard rumors that he had become "political." But I had no particular interest in his life, until we met again, by sheer coincidence, one night at Pepé le Moko's.

Ban-chan was treating me, as usual. He was holding forth about politics and art and life. There were three or four other people drinking at the bar. I didn't recognize any of them. "Misawa," said Ban-chan, already swaying on his barstool, "when are you going to do something big?" I protested that I was writing programs for a popular TV show. It was as if he hadn't heard me. He simply repeated: "When are you going to do something *big*? If you don't do something big soon, you'll be old, fat, and finished before you know it. In fact, you're well on your way already, wasting your time on rubbish. If you haven't done something big before you're thirty, you might as well be dead."

This was typical of Ban-chan. Perhaps he was just sour that I wasn't working for him anymore, that I'd flown the coop. I sensed someone stirring at the other end of the bar. A man was lumbering toward us, holding a bottle. "Hey!" he shouted at Ban-chan. "This guy's my old friend." I didn't recognize the man at first. His hair had grown very long, and he wore dark sunglasses, like a gangster. "What the fuck!" screamed Ban-chan, as the bottle crashed over his head. I was about to punch the guy, when he turned to me: "Sato, don't you remember me?" It was Hayashi. I was furious, but had no idea what to do. Ban-chan lay on the floor with blood all over his face. I should have tackled Hayashi right there. But I was never any good at fighting. So I stammered that we had to get Ban-chan to the hospital. To his credit, Mizoguchi immediately took charge, carrying Ban-chan out of the bar, into a taxi, and to the nearest hospital, where he was quickly patched up. I felt useless, even a little treacherous. What saved my face was Ban-chan's generosity. An hour later we were back at Pepé le Moko drinking from his whiskey bottle. "Loyalty to an old comrade should be rewarded," he declared, and raised his glass to Hayashi.

Hayashi liked drinking in the Korean bars in Asakusa. Though not, as far as I knew, Korean himself, he seemed to feel comfortable with Koreans. While drinking that thick milky saké they like, he told me that he had joined an action group fighting against police harassment of the Koreans. "Discrimination against the Koreans," he said, "is the core of our rotten, oppressive Emperor System." This was one of Hayashi's favorite riffs: the Emperor System. "If we don't smash the Emperor System, our country will never be free," he said. I nodded my agreement, peering into his dark glasses. Not that I felt so strongly about the Koreans, or indeed the Emperor System, but I nodded to humor him, without wishing to give him too much encouragement to ride on this hobbyhorse. Hayashi finished his drink and locked arms with the Korean barman, who smiled indulgently and poured us another round of drinks. Hayashi assured the barman that the revolution would surely come.

"You know," he said, after we sat down on a park bench near the Kannon Temple, "I talk about the Emperor System in our country, but the problem is really much bigger than that." His breath smelled of garlic, from all the kimchi we had just eaten at the Korean bar. A few homeless men were settling in for the night on the benches beside us. There was a distant murmur of traffic crossing the Azuma Bridge. One of the men was already snoring. A flickering streetlamp was reflected in Hayashi's dark glasses. "We, too, are part of a discriminated minority."

"We?" I said, genuinely surprised.

"Think of it this way," he went on. "Oppression is a matter of concentric circles. Koreans are oppressed by our Emperor System, but all Asians, Africans, Latin Americans, and Arabs are oppressed by the capitalist American system. Our government is just a slave to American imperialism. That's why it's not enough to have a revolution in Japan. We must think like internationalists. To smash the American system, the revolution has to be international. We must stand shoulder-to-shoulder in the armed struggle with the oppressed peoples of the world." Hayashi dropped his voice and drew closer, breathing more garlic into my face. "Sato," he said, "even though we didn't know each other very well at university, I always figured you were serious. You should join our struggle. Why don't you come to our meeting next week?"

Armed struggle. All the peoples of the world. This was heady stuff. I asked him what group he belonged to. He looked around, in case there were spies lurking in the bushes of Asakusa Park. There was nobody except for the sleeping men surrounded by empty bottles and broken glass, twinkling like diamonds in the neon light. "The Japanese Red Army," he whispered, as he grabbed my hand in the same way he locked arms with the Korean barman. I was suddenly reminded of Muto, our school bully, squeezing the hand of his willing slave.

I never went to that meeting. As usual, I chickened out. I guess I wasn't ready for armed struggle. In fact, I was afraid of it and avoided meeting Hayashi for a long time, feeling mildly disgusted with my own timidity. But his words had had an effect on me. They kept churning in my head. What he said about internationalism made sense. At least Hayashi dared to think beyond the narrow confines of our island country. When he told me on a later occasion that he was born in Manchuria, I wasn't surprised.

Which brings me back to Yamaguchi-san. The more I saw of her, the more she impressed me. Perhaps it was she who suggested doing a program on the Palestinians. In any case, we discussed the idea as soon as we heard the news of the September hijackings in 1970. You had to admire the gumption of those guys who managed to take over four civilian aircraft, divert them to the Jordanian desert, take the Jewish passengers as hostages, and blow the planes up in front of the world press. The commandos were from the Popular Front for the Liberation of Palestine, or PFLP, an acronym I would get to know well.

David Niven was not at all keen on our plan to interview the Palestinian freedom fighters. He told Yamaguchi-san that she would never be able to resume her movie career if she made such a program. Didn't she know that Hollywood was entirely owned by Jews? Or that all the international film distributors were Jews? They would never forgive her. But she bravely stood up to these pressures. "I don't care," she said. "My movie career is over, anyway. I'm a journalist, and a good journalist should go where the story is. We must get to the Palestinians." She said this with an air of impatience, as though we had an immediate flight to catch.

So off we went, to Beirut, three months after the hijacking. High above the clouds, Yamaguchi-san reminisced, as usual, about her China days. She had always admired the Jews, she said. In fact, her best friend at school was a Jewess from Russia, whose father ran a bakery in Mukden, but later turned out to have been a Soviet spy. "Didn't the Jews really pull all the strings in Manchuria?" I asked. Her lips parted in astonishment. "No," she said, "we did. Our Kanto Army was in charge." I repeated what I had heard from Professor Sekizawa, that the Jews had manipulated the great powers behind the scenes. "Well," she said. "They had to survive, didn't they? The Jews suffered a lot, after all. The Germans even put pressure on us to arrest the Jews. But we didn't." I said that perhaps we should have. That would have spared the world a lot of trouble.

The first time I stepped into the street from our hotel and smelled the heady melange of coffee, shwarma kebab, and popcorn, I fell in love with Beirut, this city of cities, where you ate the best food in the world and saw the most beautiful women: Maronite girls with olive skins and short skirts; long-haired Iraqi girls; Iranian girls in tight jeans; and Palestinian beauties in keffiyehs. Beirut belonged to the world. Lebanese, Syrians, Palestinians, Iraqis, Europeans, Russians, and Asians freely mixed in the hotels and bars along Hamra, the main boulevard. But there was another city too, just under the surface glitter, and just as international, a revolutionary city where the future of the world was forged by men and women of all races. On any given day, you could meet Latin American comrades, freedom fighters from South Africa or Chad, French anarchists, Danish Maoists, German revolutionary Leninists, Iranian Marxists, Kurdish nationalists. But all the Marxist theory, which had always bored me in Japan, was just so much talk. The important thing was the Palestinian armed struggle. This was not just a local struggle, of no concern to others, but internationalist to its very core. By taking on the Zionists, the Palestinians had taken on the whole Western world and its capitalist imperialist system.

Beirut reminded Yamaguchi-san of Shanghai. "This city smells of freedom," she said, sniffing the air as we raced to our first appointment through a maze of streets in a suicidal taxi drive. The PFLP office was on the sixth floor of a white apartment building in West Beirut, an area that was policed by the Palestinians, so we felt quite safe. The first thing I saw, as we entered the PFLP office, was a large poster of Chairman Mao. I despise racial chauvinism, and I know that what I'm about to confess smacks of bourgeois sentimentalism, but this poster of the greatest Asian of the twentieth century gave me a sense of ethnic pride, as though something of the heroic Chinese revolution had rubbed off on me, as a fellow Asian. We were greeted by a stout man with a thick mustache and a friendly smile. His name was

Abu Bassam. He kissed me on both cheeks in the Arab manner and took my hand into both of his, which were warm and soft. These were the hands of the man who had pulled off the hijacking of four planes, including a TWA plane full of Jews.

"You are my good friends," he said in a deep, warm voice which made one feel at home at once. "What can we do for you?" We told him that we would like to interview Leila Khaled, the hijacker of the TWA plane. She had just been released by the British in exchange for a Zionist prisoner. Abu Bassam made a clucking sound. "That might not be so simple," he said. "Look." He pointed out the window, where a vapor trail was painting an elegant white streak in the clear blue sky. "The lives of our commandos are never safe. The Zionists are observing us all the time." I heard a few shots outside and white puffs like bits of cotton wool drifted slowly upwards. "Useless," said Abu Bassam. "Just for show, to boost our morale." Yamaguchi-san looked disappointed. "We will be very careful," she promised. Abu Bassam stroked his mustache and invited us to have some of the sweets presented on a round silver plate.

After taking one himself and slowly licking the sugar off his finger with a remarkably pink tongue, he pointed at Yamaguchi-san's black and white Palestinian scarf. "You are wearing our keffiyeh." He laughed. "We have many Japanese volunteers helping us in our struggle against the Zionists. Why don't you make a film about them? That would be more interesting for Japanese television, no?"

We told him that the Japanese volunteers would surely be of interest, but what really interested us much more was the life of Palestinian guerrillas. Perhaps someone could show us around a refugee camp. The world should know about the heroism of the Palestinian people. Abu Bassam chuckled and said: "We are not heroes, but ordinary human beings. All we want is to live like other peoples, in freedom and peace." He then told us that we should talk to one of the Japanese volunteers first. They could put us in the picture. We expressed our gratitude for his kind consideration. But what about Leila Khaled? "Comrades," he said, "our home is your home. Your film will help us in our struggle. And I will help you to make it a good film. We will stage a military exercise for you. You can shoot that." But what about Leila Khaled?

Yamaguchi-san was clearly not going to take no for an answer. She was turning into a first-rate reporter. I would never have dared to insist as she did. I don't want to sound sexist, but she was also a beautiful woman. Who could refuse her anything, once those great dark eyes had cast their spell? Abu Bassam shouted something in Arabic and stood up from his desk. I had not even touched my coffee. He kissed me, turned to Yamaguchi-san, and touched his chest in a gesture of respect. "Patience, my friends," he said. "If you can walk, why run?"

We found a message at the hotel. We were told to wait the next morning at the Café Balthus, in Jeanne d'Arc Street. After sitting there for about half an hour, a skinny young man in a light blue shirt came in, greeted us, and told us to follow him. We took a taxi to the outskirts of West Beirut, where we stopped, and after the young man had looked around to make sure we hadn't been followed, he hailed another taxi to drive us to a white apartment block a little farther west. A man in aviator shades stood outside the door, greeted us, and took us round the back, where a battered blue Renault was waiting to take us to yet another place, about twenty minutes away. In the car, Yamaguchi-san told us stories about Harbin in the 1940s, how risky it was to get around the city. Japanese were always in danger of being kidnapped or killed by Chinese guerrillas. "We used to call them bandits," she explained. "How stupid we were. Now I know that they were simply fighting for their country. Just like the Palestinians."

Leila Khaled was the most beautiful woman I had ever seen. Rather petite, with delicate hands, she had the sweetest smile, pure, like a child's. A keffiyeh was wrapped around her head, almost like a hijab. But her most striking feature were her eyes—dark, narrow, catlike, like those of a lynx. Even when she smiled, revealing a row of perfect white teeth, her eyes expressed a bottomless well of sorrow. Like all Palestinian refugees in Beirut, she had been expelled from her home by the Zionists. Her longing for home was so great that she forced the pilot of the TWA plane to fly low over Haifa, so she could see where she was born.

The interview did not last long. Leila's time was limited and to linger put her in unnecessary danger. But Yamaguchi-san and I were so moved by her sincerity that we barely spoke a word on the way back to the hotel. There was a gentleness about her that made it almost impossible to imagine her as a commando, armed with hand grenades and a Kalashnikov. Leila talked to us about her hatred of killing and war. She didn't hate the Jews, she said, just the Zionists, for they had taken away her home and expelled her people. Unfortunately, she explained, armed struggle was the only way to regain the freedom of her people. Yamaguchi-san asked her about the lives of innocent people. Was it fair to put them in danger? A slight frown swept like a shadow over Leila's delicate features. "All death is terrible," she said. "I even cry over the death of a bird. But unfortunately you cannot fight a war without casualties. We are weak. Our enemy is strong, with a large army, backed by the Americans. Still, we have to fight. For there is no other way to make the world pay attention to our suffering. You see, I'm prepared to die. I would even welcome it. Dying for your people is the most beautiful thing a person can do. Sacrifice for the sake of justice is what separates humans from the wild beasts."

Her words made me feel unworthy. I had never been prepared to sacrifice myself for anything. Instead, I had fretted about my career in the movies, about my sex life, about money. While Palestinians were dying for their freedom, I was making pink movies for dirty old men in cinemas smelling of piss.

Yamaguchi-san appeared for dinner that night with her keffiyah wrapped around her head in Leila's style. We had a Lebanese meal, with delicious red wine from the Bekaa Valley. I could see that she was still shaken by the day's events. We spoke about Leila's bravery. I told her about my sense of unworthiness. She looked away. I could see tears welling up in her eyes. "To lose your home is the worst thing that can happen to a human being," she said. "I lost my home, too, you know. And I betrayed my people."

I said: "But you are Japanese."

"Yes, I'm Japanese, I know, but Japan was never my home. My home is in China. Once you lose your home, you're a rootless wanderer. People call me a cosmopolitan. They say that the world is my home. I've often said so myself. I like to think that it's true. But in fact, in my heart, I'm homeless, like a Jew. Which makes the suffering of the poor Palestinians even more astonishing to me. How could the Jews do something like that to another people, the Jews who have suffered so much from persecution themselves? How could they do it?"

I said that it wasn't just the Jews. I tried to explain to her that it was the whole system of Western imperialism, led by America, and manipulated by the Jews. The Jews may have suffered in the past, but they had blown their suffering out of all proportion, as an excuse to behave just like the Nazis. This was their revenge. The question is whether they were manipulating the Western powers into carrying out their vengeance on an innocent people, or whether the Western powers were using the Jews to control the Middle East. Without Arab oil, the capitalist system would collapse.

Yamaguchi-san was observing the other people in the restaurant while I spoke. She gently admonished me for being too much of an intellectual. "All that theory," she said, "is too difficult for me. I just think of all the human suffering. The politics is for academics. A journalist must show the lives of real people, their bravery, their love, their dreams."

I understood her feelings. That is the way I had felt myself. But was it enough? Wasn't there a danger of lapsing into bourgeois sentimentalism? What are feelings, if they are not followed up by action? Leila Khaled had stirred something in me that I couldn't quite put in words, but there was something in her manner that conveyed an accusation, not just of the Zionists but of all those, like myself, who refused to help, who turned their backs, who went back home to write their articles, or make their little TV programs, without the guts to help in a cause crying for justice. I knew this may have sounded impertinent, but I put it to Yamaguchi-san that we Japanese had a special responsibility to fight against colonial oppression, since we had once been oppressors ourselves.

She put her glasses back on. She didn't like people to see when she had been crying. I felt a little guilty, like a trespasser of some kind. But then she said something that I'll never forget: "I hate violence and war. I've seen enough of that when I was in China. All I've ever wanted was peace. I don't understand why people want to kill each other. I'm a journalist, not an activist. But you're young. You still have a whole life ahead of you. You're right. We Japanese have to make amends. You must do what you think is right. Don't just obey the authorities. Don't be a frog in the Japanese well. You must think internationally. All the time we have been here, I've been thinking of China, the China of my student days in Peking, when my dearest friends were talking about resistance against Japan. It was all so confusing for me. I couldn't see clearly what we Japanese were doing. Now I do. The Jews, who have suffered themselves, have become the new oppressors. But we Japanese, who were the oppressors once, must help the oppressed. This time, we must be on the right side."

I don't believe in coincidence. Everything in life happens for a reason. My meeting in Beirut with one of the Japanese volunteers came about because I was making a TV program with Yamaguchi Yoshiko, but this event had such important consequences for me that I know it was meant to be. As soon as I saw Hanako's sweet round face, her silky black hair falling halfway down her back, her kind eyes, I knew that she was unlike any woman I had ever seen, even in the movies. If I had been a Christian I would have described her face as that of a Madonna. Like Leila's, Hanako's beauty came from her faith. Her strength was her beauty. She radiated a kind of inner glow that drew me to her instantly, like a helpless child.

Yamaguchi-san interviewed Fujisawa Hanako in the same office where we had met with Abu Bassam earlier. Indeed, Bassam was there, sipping coffee under the poster of Chairman Mao. "One day," he said, shining with goodwill, like a roly-poly Buddha, "when we have reclaimed our beloved homeland, we will live in peace with everyone, Jews, Christians, Muslims. That's the way it always was in our culture. People say we hate the Jews. They're quite wrong. Hatred of the Jews is a European invention. We Arabs always treated the Jews with great respect, as a people of the Book."

Yamaguchi-san nodded as he spoke. Then she sighed, as though burdened with a great sorrow. Why, she asked Hanako, why did she believe in armed struggle? Couldn't we fight for our ideals without violence? This time it was Hanako's turn to nod. She understood how Yamaguchi-san felt, but, she said with a warm smile, "guns are good." Yamaguchi-san shifted uncomfortably in her chair. There was an awkward silence. Still smiling, Hanako continued: "Without guns, we can't have real democracy." Yamaguchi-san, astonished: "What can you possibly mean by that?" Hanako looked at Bassam. "Bassam, did I ever tell you the story of the guns of Tanegashima?" He shook his head.

"Let me tell you, then. In the middle of the sixteenth century, several Portuguese ships landed on the island of Tanegashima. They brought many things, Bibles, spices, sponge cakes, silk, wine, atlases, telescopes, and matchlock guns, two of which were presented to the Lord of Tanegashima, who was deeply impressed by these priceless weapons and promptly used them to go duck hunting. We Japanese were always good at copying and then improving foreign inventions. So it was with guns. Soon the smiths of Tanegashima were making better guns than the Portuguese. Europeans didn't know how to make matchlocks work in the rain. We Japanese figured out a way to do it. The feudal lords started supplying huge armies of conscripted peasants with muskets and went to war against one another. Great land battles took place in the central Japanese plains. Soldiers from both sides marched into storms of gunfire, and died by the thousands.

"Swordsmanship didn't count for anything anymore. For the first time in history, a peasant soldier had the means to kill the highest-ranking samurai. Even a general in full armor was helpless against a musket-wielding peasant. When the most powerful Shogun, Hideyoshi, unified our country, he decided to put a stop to this. All weapons not belonging to samurai were confiscated. Samurai went back to their swords. Guns became obsolete. In a few years, Japanese no longer even knew they had ever existed. We achieved a state of absolute peace in Japan, which only came to an end when the Americans arrived in the port of Shimoda two hundred years later on their notorious black ships, loaded with firearms and cannon. So innocent were the Japanese of such destructive force that they believed the American guns were a kind of white man's magic."

Yamaguchi-san clapped her hands in delight. "But that's a wonderful story!" she cried. "It shows that it's possible to get rid of murderous weapons. That's why we must support our peace constitution. We must show the world that there is a better way to solve our problems than going to war."

Hanako shook her beautiful head. "Just a moment, Yamaguchi-san," she said, with a quick glance at Bassam, who was slipping a nugget of treacly baklava between his lips, "there is more to this story. Yes, the Japanese managed to get rid of firearms, it is quite true. But at the price of living for over two hundred years in a police state ruled by a military clique. We had peace at the cost of our freedom, of being at the mercy of any man of samurai rank who felt the urge to cut down a commoner, simply to practice his swordsmanship. Abolishing guns made us into a nation of slaves, and an easy prey for foreign imperialists."

I was overwhelmed by the sharpness of her mind, the logic of her thinking, the purity of her conviction, the sound of her voice, so compassionate, and the sweetness of her manners. I loved this woman in a way I had never loved any woman before. I had always thought that the expression "love at first sight" was ridiculous, something in cheap novels for teenage girls. But I can't think of another way to describe my feelings. That's what it was. A spark had flown, a dart had penetrated my heart. I wanted to kiss her, hug her, hold her, there and then. I wanted to be with her forever.

Of course I didn't kiss her. We were Japanese, after all. When she suggested, after the interview was over, that we should visit one of the refugee camps the following day, I was like jelly, stammering my thanks. I must have been perspiring. She asked me if I was all right and handed me her handkerchief. I thought I would melt from embarrassment, but also from the sheer delight at having encountered an angel.

The camp was really a slum of low brick houses with roofs made of plastic bags or, in the more fortunate cases, sheets of corrugated iron. There was uncollected garbage everywhere. A pack of filthy dogs was feeding on the refuse from an open bin. The camp had been targeted many times by the Israelis. Children dressed in rags were splashing around in filthy waterlogged craters where the Zionist shells had exploded. It looked, in fact, like hell on earth. And yet the people were smiling. Everyone we interviewed was convinced that victory would one day be theirs. The spirit of these people was so extraordinary that it put us to shame. Here, every man, woman, and child was a soldier. Women did their laundry with Kalashnikovs stacked up against the wall behind the washtubs. Children from the age of five were trained to be freedom fighters. We saw these brave little souls practicing drills with wooden rifles.

Yamaguchi-san was taking notes in her reporter's notebook when a young couple was brought over to talk to her. They were dressed very simply, and welcomed us in the formal Arab manner, asking where we were from. Hanako said we were all from Japan, which seemed to please them. Both had been born in a village near Tel Aviv, they told us. Although they were still children when they were brutally expelled, they had never forgotten their homes, and would pass on the memory to their baby boy, named Khalid. The father, Abu Mohammad, glowed with pride as he fingered his boy's short dark hair. "He will fight for our freedom," he said. When Yamaguchi-san asked the parents whether they weren't worried that he might get hurt, they looked at their child with deep tenderness. The boy's mother, Aisha, then handed him to Yamaguchi-san, who placed the infant on her lap. "Please accept our little boy as yours," said Aisha. "You come from an ancient culture of warriors. Your blessing will ensure that he will grow up to be a kamikaze and bring honor to all of us."

Yamaguchi-san, moved by their gesture, hugged the child before handing him back to his mother. "I will always be there when he needs me," she said. They scribbled down their address in her notebook. Ten years later, the little boy and both his parents would be dead, murdered by the Christian Fascists doing the Zionists' bidding. And by the time we got back to Tokyo, Abu Bassam, that smiling Buddha of a man, addicted to coffee and sticky baklava, would be blown to pieces by a car bomb in a quiet backstreet of West Beirut.

When we made our tearful farewells from him, and Hanako, he kissed me and said that I was welcome to come back anytime. Even more precious to me were Hanako's words in parting. She looked at me intently and said: "I know you'll be back here soon." I knew that I would, too. I knew I had found a home at last.

8

AFTER BEIRUT, I was utterly disgusted with the country of my birth. Sure, the streets were cleaner, and the trains ran on time; they always do in Fascist states. The millions of salarymen, teeming through the stations like gray-suited rabbits, returned every night to their little suburban hutches, where their wives tucked them into bed, safe and snug. This was a society addicted to security, where the salaried rabbits had learned to stop thinking; a society that prized mediocrity, without a sense of honor or higher purpose; a society grown soft and selfish; a place from which the only escape was the false consciousness of pornographic fantasy. And the rabbits looked content. That was the worst of it. They had exchanged their brains, and their souls, for— what? *Comfort.* Since political resistance was now useless in Japan, the few remaining revolutionaries who still retained some vestige of their souls had turned on one another, like rats trapped in a sack.

Again, nothing in life occurs without purpose. Of that I remain firmly convinced. It all happened only a few weeks after our return to Tokyo: Twelve soldiers of the United Red Army murdered by their own comrades. Cops in a shoot-out with five survivors of the purge in a Karuizawa mountain lodge. Manager of the lodge taken hostage. Round-the-clock television coverage, watched by eighty-five percent of the Japanese population. Two cops killed. Hostage released. Five arrests. The "United Red Army Incident"!

It was clear to me from the very beginning that Japanese TV had become the voice of the oppressors, making a sentimental melodrama out of the woman taken hostage, presenting the police as national heroes, and the Red Army as criminals. The people had been thoroughly brainwashed by the ruling class. But the way Japanese minds had been colonized by the authorities was interesting: it was done by turning news into spectacle. The Karuizawa shoot-out was just another cop show, with good guys triumphing over the bad guys. Politics had turned into soap opera, and armed struggle into a samurai drama. The Red Army warriors had played their parts to perfection, looking like stage villains, poking their guns through the windows of their mountain lodge.

And I felt complicit. Wasn't I working for the same TV station that licked its chops over the siege in Karuizawa? What was our program about the liberation struggle of the Palestinian people if not another kind of entertainment for the rabbits glued to their flickering shrines? To them, it was a travelogue, political porn, pictures for the armchair reveries of the petty bourgeois. Even so, after the United Red Army Incident, David Niven had got cold feet about broadcasting the show. He was afraid that the Red Army fighters for Palestinian justice were portrayed too sympathetically. He was right. They were. But he needn't have worried, because the showbiz-hungry, brainwashed Japanese rabbits showed no interest in the Palestinians. All they cared about was the glamorous presence of Yamaguchi Yoshiko, in her miniskirts, her shiny white boots, and her keffiyeh, which she wore on the show. Her face was everywhere: on the covers of fashion magazines, on subway posters, in department stores, and on TV chat shows. She won a prize as Journalist of the Year. Yamaguchi Yoshiko's star was reborn in Beirut. And I was disgusted.

But I didn't blame her. Her intentions were sincere. When we talked about her new fame, she told me, as she so often did, that I was being "too intellectual." Her star status, tedious as it was, could only help to promote the matters we believed in. She even asked me to help her write a book about the Palestinian struggle. And there were other things we could do. She was brimming with ideas. What about a program about Colonel Gaddafi, Libya's wonderful revolutionary leader? Or an interview with Kim Il Sung, the Great Leader of North Korea? And who knows, we might even get permission to go to China and meet Chairman Mao.

I didn't want to let her down. But the truth of the matter was that I was wasting my time in Japan. I felt so powerless there. I couldn't wait to get back to Beirut, for that was where I was needed. There, everything felt real, important, vital. It was impossible to erase the images from my mind of the children's faces in the refugee camp, the pride of Khalid's parents, the resolve of the freedom fighters in the PFLP office, and Hanako, of course, Hanako with her sweet Madonna smile, her total dedication, her love of the poor and the oppressed. Hanako, who knew that I would soon be back.

After Beirut, even Tokyo, the city of my dreams, seemed flat. Ban-chan was away, making another pink film, something about sex and student politics in Kyoto. Talking to most of my old friends was impossible. Their eyes would wander when I told them about Beirut and the Palestinian struggle. Perhaps I shouldn't be too hard on them. They had their own lives to live and Beirut was far away. But wasn't this just how the Japanese had behaved during the war? Pretending not to know, when innocent Chinese civilians were being massacred by our soldiers. Nanking must have seemed far away then, too. Why do people never learn the lessons of history? Do we never change? Is change impossible?

I didn't think so. I didn't want to think so. And this is why I will always be grateful to Yamaguchi-san. Her enthusiasm was the one thing that kept my hopes alive. She was different from most Japanese, no doubt because she grew up outside Japan. Maybe Okuni was right, and the landscapes impressed on our minds in early childhood do shape our perspectives. Just think of the difference between growing up in the vast empty plains of Manchuria, and being trapped on a narrow little archipelago filled with rice paddies, volcanic mountains, and over-crowded cities. A child raised in Dairen or Harbin would have been exposed to people from all over the world, while we saw only other Japanese, just like us. Unless you happened to live near a base. Even then, the only foreigners I ever saw were Yankee soldiers, and they were country boys themselves, still reeking of cow dung.

I finally took Yamaguchi-san round to meet Okuni. We went to see his latest play in the great yellow tent, pitched on a vacant spot beside the lily pond in Ueno. It was on one of those humid summer nights when the cicadas rasp and the fireflies set the pond alight. The tent was full, with no standing room left. A solitary electric fan valiantly displaced some warm air, and even that stopped when a fuse blew half-way through the play. Sitting on the dirt floor, packed together with hundreds of sweating young people, was uncomfortable. But I didn't mind. Good theater shouldn't be comfortable. People must sacrifice comfort for art. I noticed Vanoven, the American homo. When he spotted me, he smiled and held up his thumb. I felt rather sorry for him, though I don't really know why. There was something sad about the crazy foreigner in the Japanese crowd. When I asked him whether he was staying for a drink later, he shook his head. "Another time," he shouted.

Yamaguchi-san, noticing my exchange with Vanoven, asked me how I knew that foreigner. I explained that I had met him in Okuni's tent and asked her whether she had ever come across him. "I've not had the pleasure," she said.

The play was a fantasy based on the movie *Lost Horizon*. In Okuni's version, the survivors from the plane crash in the Himalayan mountains were not British, of course, but Japanese, one of them a famous character from a popular movie about a detective with seven faces. Shangri-la was not part of Tibet, but Asakusa after the bombing raids. The Grand Lama was a popular singer of Japanese ballads, who was also a serial killer. In the last scene, the back of the tent opened up to reveal the entire cast singing a wartime ballad about kamikaze pilots. Their faces were white and streaked with blood, the ghosts of those who died in the Asakusa bombings.

Yamaguchi-san said she didn't understand the play at all, but loved it all the same. Okuni laughed and asked her why she hadn't come to see *The Ri Koran Story*. She pulled a face and said: "I suffered too much in the past. I don't want to remember. Ri Koran is dead." Okuni's eyes widened. I could tell he was fascinated. To him she was still Ri Koran, whatever she said. She would always be Ri Koran. Yamaguchi Yoshiko didn't interest him.

"But we can't just slough off the past," Okuni said. "We are made of our memories. And besides, Ri was a great actress."

"But I'm no longer Ri, and I never wanted to be an actress in the first place. I wanted to be a journalist. An actress does as she is told. I was fooled. It's different being a reporter. A reporter is free. An actress can't do anything to change the world."

Okuni shook his head and said: "Journalism is just about facts. It's the truth of accountants. We artists can show a higher truth."

"Well, I prefer reality." Yamaguchi-san then talked about our trip to Beirut and the Palestinian struggle. I could tell that this bored Okuni. I could see it in his face. It was how most of my friends reacted when I spoke about these things. One detail, however, caught his imagination: Khalid's mother asking Yamaguchi-san to raise her boy as a kamikaze. "Amazing," he said, his little dark eyes shining. "Can you imagine such passion in Japan today? Here, when the students occupied the campus in protest against the Security Treaty, mothers threw candies over the wall, ha ha."

Yamaguchi-san suggested that "maybe we don't need heroes anymore."

"But we do," said Okuni, "we do. In the movies." He was still laughing, and asked one of the actors to bring his guitar. We clapped along as he sang a song from his latest play: "On the far side of the Sumida River is the Land of No Return, Where lovers roam and home fires burn, On the far side . . ."

"Did you know," said Yamaguchi-san, "that I was in the musical version of *Lost Horizon?* On Broadway, in New York." Yo Kee Hee, who hadn't said much all evening, asked her to sing a song from the musical. Yamaguchi-san swatted this idea away. No, she couldn't possibly. It was all too long ago. She had lost her voice. But Yo wouldn't be denied. After a bit more coaxing, Yamaguchi-san sang a song called "The Man I Never Met." Her soprano voice was as beautiful as ever. Okuni wiped a tear from his eyes. "Ri Koran is still alive!" he shouted, giggling with excitement.

"She is dead," said Yamaguchi-san quite firmly. "That was Shirley Yamaguchi, anyway. And she's no longer with us, either."

"What about singing 'China Nights'?" suggested Yo, not without a note of malice.

I froze, hoping Yamaguchi-san wouldn't be offended. "Never," she said, with a firmness that closed the matter at once. "I will *never* sing that song again." Changing the subject, she asked Okuni where he was going to pitch his tent next. He mentioned Osaka, Kyoto, Fukuoka, and Kumamoto. Something extraordinary always happened in Osaka, he said. "We usually pitch our tent in Tennoji, near the Zoo. At night you can hear the wild animals howling, and once an escaped sea eagle flew right into the tent, just as Yo was singing a song about a ghostly captain roaming forever in his submarine."

"Perhaps," said Yamaguchi-san, "you should think of going abroad, pitch your tent in other countries, become more international."

Okuni's eyes lit up. "But not America or Europe," he said. "What about Asia? That would be good. In Seoul. Or Manila, or Bangkok—" He reached for the saké bottle. His high-pitched giggle sounded almost like the shriek of one of those wild animals in Osaka Zoo. "Sato," he roared. "What about Beirut? Why don't we put up the yellow tent in the middle of a Palestinian camp?"

"Too dangerous," we all said in chorus. "Crazy." "Never get permission." "We don't have the money" (Yo Kee Hee). "What about the food?" (Nagasaki). "And the language?"

"We'll do it in Arabic," shouted Okuni, with a beam of madness in his eyes. "Next stop Beirut. The Existential Theater for the Palestinian guerrillas. That'll be some situation!"

Yes, I thought, and a tuna fish will one day climb Mount Fuji.

9

F THE TARMAC hadn't been melting in the heat on the day I arrived, I would have gladly kissed the ground of Beirut International Airport. A week later, I was in a training camp learning how to fire a Kalashnikov and throw hand grenades. The hand grenades, frankly, left me cold. But the gun was something else. I'm not a military type. So in the beginning my shoulder felt sore from the kick, and I burned my fingers on the gun metal. But there is nothing, nothing at all, more satisfying than holding a warm Kalashnikov and letting it rip. We used pictures of Moshe Dayan and Golda Meir for target practice. I didn't kill them that day, unfortunately.

There were people from all over in the training camp, from Argentina and Peru, from Africa and the Philippines. At night, sharing the flatbread and hummus with our Palestinian instructors, we felt like an international family, a family of revolutionaries. My English was poor, and some of the South Americans spoke it even worse, but I loved listening to their stories, about fighting the white Fascists to liberate the peasants. I was embarrassed when they asked me about the Ainu or the Koreans in Japan, for I had never given them much thought. Sure, I had envied my schoolmates when they left for North Korea, but not for any political reason. Their lives just sounded more interesting than ours. I went along to the Korean bars with my friend Hayashi, because he liked going there and I quite liked the kimchi, but that was about the extent of my involvement with the Koreans. Hanako, who visited the camp from time to time, had lectured our comrades on the discrimination of minorities in Japan, so they may well have known more about the subject than I did. I had to be careful. I made sure to look serious and nod in agreement when they talked about racism in Japan. What else could I do, without looking like a complete hypocrite?

I felt closest to the Germans, especially Dieter and Anke, commandos in the German Red Army Faction. Like me, they had had no military training before. Dieter was a philosophy major from Tübingen and Anke was a high school teacher. They were both tall and skinny. His bony face and thin blond wisp of a beard always reminded me of Don Quixote, a Nordic Don Quixote. Anke had straight dark hair and dreamy brown eyes. She loved German literature. She told me all about Heinrich Böll, and Günter Grass. I hadn't read either of them. We also talked a lot about the Second World War and the failure of our parents to resist fascism. I even talked about my father, but only because they went on about their parents so often. I felt I had to reciprocate, to be fair to them. Anke's father had been a member of the Nazi Party, and she was terribly ashamed of him. Dieter's father, like mine, had gone missing in the war, somewhere on the Russian front. Although they were foreigners, I felt closer to them than anyone, except Hanako, of course. We understood one another on a profound level, in our minds, but especially in our hearts. Our friendship went deeper even than my friendship with Okuni. There was no idle chatter among us. There was no time for that.

The camp closed down early. The streets were too dark to hang around in. The electricity supply was limited and most people went to bed as soon as the streetlights were turned off. All you heard was the sound of crying children and, in the early morning, the call to prayers. Our instructors took little notice of this. They were socialists. The Arab revolution was their creed. Dieter, Anke, and I often talked until late at night, by candlelight, when everyone else was asleep, about history, politics, art, and literature. We agreed about almost everything and they opened up a whole new world for me of German writers. Apart from Böll and Grass, I learned about Novalis, Hölderlin, and Rilke.

Just once did we have a serious quarrel. Perhaps I shouldn't call it a quarrel. It was more like a misunderstanding, about something I said, inadvertently, which put my friends in a rage. But I didn't really argue with them. I didn't have the words in English. We were discussing strategies in our armed struggle against Israel. I favored hijackings, while they saw more hope in bombing raids on Israeli targets. Dieter was convinced that "every Israeli citizen should be made to feel the pain of the Palestinian people." I didn't disagree, but added, rather matter-of-factly, "So here you are again, fighting against the Jews."

I thought Dieter was going to explode. His bony face went horribly pale, making him look more than ever like a Nordic Don Quixote. He banged the hard mud floor with his fist and screamed something at me in German. Anke was shaking, and stared at me with a look of horror, as though I'd swallowed a live rat. Dieter was beside himself: "We are not fighting the Jews! That's what the Nazis did! How dare you insinuate that we are like the Nazis!" I protested that I wasn't doing anything of the kind, but with my stammer and my broken English, perhaps I hadn't made myself clear. "You were clear," shrieked Anke. "Quite clear!" Then she started to sob: "We thought you were our friend and comrade, so why do you have to insult us?"

People sleeping around us were beginning to stir. A light was switched on. One of the Peruvians asked what was going on. "He insulted us," said Dieter. "He called us Nazis." An Italian Red Brigadist called Marcello, who had been woken up by the commotion, asked me why I said that. I suddenly felt very alone, and horribly misunderstood. I stammered something about fighting the Jews. Marcello, a peaceful, friendly guy, tried to calm the German comrades down. He said that as a Japanese I might not understand the historical nuances. We weren't fighting the Jews, he said, only the Zionists. And I should apologize to our German comrades.

So I apologized, bowing to my friends, asking them to forgive me. Dieter said okay, and accepted my handshake. Anke was still sobbing, tugging at her straight dark hair with both hands. But I wasn't satisfied. Something wasn't right here. I couldn't leave the subject dangling like this. So, just as people were lying down to sleep, I said: "But what about Jewish capital?" "What about it?" said Marcello. Well, I said, clearly Jewish money was pressing the Western powers to support the Zionists. "Tomorrow," said Marcello, "we'll talk about it tomorrow." No, said Dieter, who was very calm now, "we'll talk about it *now.*" And he gave a typical Dieter-like lecture, concise, logical, about the subject at hand. "Jewish capital," he explained, "is USA capital. We must resist the USA in our struggle against fascism. But that doesn't mean we fight the Jews. On the contrary, the Jews were victims of fascism. Our resistance against fascism now is part of our solidarity with the Jews, to make up for the cowardice of our parents. *Gute Nacht.*"

I didn't sleep much that night. I kept arguing with Dieter in my mind. There was something wrong with his logic. But I decided to leave it at that. We all have to live with the burdens of our own histories. Dieter and Anke have to live with a German past that is hard for us Japanese to understand. I still don't see why the suffering of Jews in the Second World War should be an excuse for them behaving like Nazis today. We should be fighting the Jews precisely because they are like the Nazis. That is the honest way to resist fascism. I actually believe that Dieter and Anke secretly agreed with me, but couldn't bring themselves to say so. For the sake of our friendship and the success of our cause, I decided never to bring up the subject of the Jews with them again.

10

HANAKO BELIEVED IN free love. As did I, in principle. But I savored every second we could be together. I wished our nights in the top-floor apartment on the rue Sanayeh could have gone on forever. I thought I knew all about making love to a woman. In fact, I knew nothing. She was my teacher, my mentor, my guide through the portals of paradise. I had never imagined that such pleasure was possible. But she also made me aware that I was still a reactionary at heart. As we lay together, smoking, gazing at the starlit sky over the old city, she made it clear that I could never possess her, since she was a free human being, who gave me her love freely. She didn't belong to any man. Her only master, she said, was the revolution.

Of course, I knew I was being a hypocrite, no better than those Japanese salarymen who go home to their faithful wives after jerking off to a pink movie about raping hot schoolgirls. But I wanted to have Hanako to myself. The idea of her melting into the arms of another man, offering herself to his passion, filled me with jealous rage. I knew that she had slept with Abu Bassam, and continued to sleep with Abu Wahid, the chief of propaganda, a thick, dark-skinned man, who took women as his lovers as though it were his natural right. When I told Hanako that I loved her, she said that she loved me too, but not just me. Once, when I argued about this, she got angry. "Who do you think you are?" she screamed. "What do you think we're doing here? This isn't a girls' high school, you know. We're fighting for our freedom. Not just the freedom of Palestine. Freedom for all of us."

I knew I couldn't honestly disagree. So I tried a different tack. "But Abu Wahid is a bully," I said. "He *does* want to possess you." She walked away in a fury. Days later, when we were back on speaking terms, she said: "Abu Wahid is a hero of the revolution." Quite why this gave him a special right to Hanako was not immediately apparent, but I stopped arguing. I learned to live with the idea of sharing her. Better a fishtail than no fish at all.

Not that I saw all that much of Hanako, for she was usually working on various missions, moving from one safe house to another, often with Abu Wahid, who was effectively my boss, since the PFLP cadres had decided that I would best be employed as a maker of propaganda films. I liked the work, even if all the scenes I shot—of commandos shooting at Zionist targets, women working on the home front, children singing revolutionary songs—were staged to show the Palestinians to their best advantage. But this didn't bother me at all. Bourgeois television was staged as well, to promote consumerism, and the capitalist imperialist system. I saw myself in the same mold as the early Soviet filmmakers. Like Pudovkin. Art is never neutral. Everything is a reflection of power relations. My films, shot on sixteen-millimeter stock, were made to empower the powerless.

I didn't miss Japan much. The one thing I did sometimes pine for was a steaming bowl of Sapporo ramen swimming in miso soup. They have Chinese noodles in Beirut, but they don't taste the same. And sometimes I missed my friends. Once, Hayashi visited us in Beirut, but he felt homesick after three days, couldn't stomach the food, and flew back to Tokyo. I received a long letter from Yamaguchi-san, full of enthusiasm as usual. She was proud of being the first Japanese TV reporter to interview Kim Il Sung in Pyongyang.

She wrote:

It was an unforgettable experience to meet this great man, who had fought so bravely against us as a guerrilla fighter, suffering so many hardships for the sake of his people. Do you know, Sato-kun, when he wrapped his firm hands around mine, I felt his great strength. It was like standing in front of an open fire, so warm and powerful. His piercing eyes seemed to go right through me. I apologized for what our country had done to his nation, but he wouldn't hear of it. He said he had always admired me and that my songs had given him and his comrades comfort during the war. I couldn't help myself, Sato-kun, I was so moved that I couldn't stop myself from crying tears of joy. Then he said he would give me all the time I wanted, on one condition, that I sing "China Nights" for him at the official banquet. You well know how much I hate that song. It's as if the ghost of Ri Koran will never stop haunting me. But how could I turn down his request? I felt I owed it to the Korean people, as a token of my friendship. Will we ever have peace in this world, Sato-kun? I hope so with all my heart.

Reading her letter, I was close to tears myself. There was such sincerity in her feelings, so rare among Japanese. Here, among the Palestinians, it was different. There was no time to think selfishly, for everyone was dedicated to the same cause. Perhaps it takes extreme hardships to bring out the best in a people. Peace had weakened the Japanese, made them soft and self-centered, like babies.

There was no chance of us going soft. Some of my comrades, including Dieter and Anke, had left Beirut to continue the struggle in Europe and elsewhere. Their names would sometimes crop up in the newspaper headlines. When that happened, you usually knew it couldn't mean good news. Our commandos prefer to stay anonymous. Those of us who stayed behind were kept busy in the camps, lecturing on world politics, practicing rifle drills, learning how to detonate car bombs, working in the free clinics, making propaganda. If I had any complaint in those days, it was that I grew tired of training. I longed to practice the skills I had acquired. Making films was fine. But films don't change the world. Films can't deliver a direct blow to the enemy. Films can't kill.

I was reassured by the men in the PFLP office. "Your time will come, Comrade Sato," Abu Wahid said one day, when I'd pestered him yet again for a more important job. "We have plans for you." But he didn't tell me what they were, and I knew it wasn't my place to push him for more information. Secrecy was essential. Hanako always knew more than I did, because of her proximity to the leaders. "One day we'll be very proud of you," she said with her sweet smile that never failed to get my spirits up.

11

MY DAY DID indeed come. But first I should relate an extraordinary event that came as a complete surprise to me. In the late summer of 1972, I received a letter from Okuni. It was written in his typically feverish style, coming straight to the point, dispensing with mention of the weather in Tokyo or other pleasantries. While reading his letter, I could picture his face in my mind, his eyes blazing. He was ready to come to Beirut, he wrote, with Yo and the others. They would perform *The Ri Koran Story* in a Palestinian refugee camp. Would I quickly prepare the way and organize a proper venue? The play had been rewritten somewhat, he explained, and was translated into Arabic. A team of language coaches was already teaching the actors to speak their lines phonetically. With luck and application, they should be ready in another month.

The idea sounded so absurd that at first I didn't know how to respond. What was he thinking? Didn't he realize how serious the situation was in the camps? These weren't playgrounds for theatrical experiments. We were at war.

Still, I felt duty-bound, for the sake of our friendship, to at least put Okuni's proposal to Abu Wahid. We had a meeting in an office at the Shatila camp in central Beirut. Hanako was with us. I tried not to notice Wahid's dark hairy arm brushing her left thigh. They had coffee. I had mint tea. I told him of Okuni's plan, and tried to describe the

play, which, in Tokyo, was unusual enough, but sounded utterly preposterous in Beirut. A Manchurian movie star trying to find herself in
the lower depths of Tokyo. What could this possibly mean to an Arab
people fighting for their lives? There was a painful silence. Hanako
looked at Abu Wahid, shaking her head in disbelief. Feeling embarrassed and a little guilty, I looked out the window at a bunch of children in dirty T-shirts playing in the street. One tiny boy was aiming a
sling at something. Another was shooting off a plastic gun. I was fully
expecting Abu Wahid to say no. Then I heard a slow chuckle, which
quickly grew into bellows of laughter. Wahid's outburst of honking,
hooting, hiccuping mirth gathered such steam that the children
stopped playing and looked in our direction. Hanako, clearly relieved,
started giggling as well. "Why not?" he shouted between spasms of
coughing and knee-slapping. "God knows our people need entertainment. A Japanese theater! About a movie star in China! Why not? Why
the hell not?"

And I must confess, on second thoughts, that even though I failed
to see what was quite so hilarious, the idea of Okuni's theater in a Palestinian refugee camp did have a certain surrealistic appeal. The question was where to stage it. There were few open spaces in the camp,
and they were vulnerable to Israeli attacks. Their Phantoms were constantly streaking over Beirut, like little silver birds of death. Nothing
escaped from their prying eyes.

Various spots were considered—a disused cinema in West Beirut, a
marketplace in Sabra—and rejected as too impractical. It would have
to be outside Beirut, thought Abu Wahid. Then he hit on an idea. Why
not go where the enemy would least expect such a thing? There was a
camp near the front lines in southern Lebanon which had an abandoned school playground in a fairly secluded place. The Israelis had
bombed the camp several times, but the rubble had been cleared, and
there had been no attacks for almost a year now. If the Japanese actors

didn't mind taking the risk of dying in a bombing raid, they were most welcome to set up their stage in there. This thought, too, filled him with helpless mirth. The hand that had been squeezing Hanako's thigh was slapping the wooden table with merriment.

When I saw my old university friend emerge from the Customs Hall at Beirut International, with his beady eyes and his broad grin, I thought I would cry with happiness. This was only his second trip outside Japan. He had visited Taiwan once with Yo. And I must say, even in cosmopolitan Beirut, Okuni and his actors, with Nagasaki in a purple woman's kimono, and Shina Tora wearing high Japanese clogs, like a sushi chef, looked like a very odd bunch indeed.

As we sat around in his room, drinking Suntory Whiskey, eating Japanese rice crackers (I hadn't realized how much I had missed those), and gossiping about old friends, even I felt a wave of nostalgia for the world I had left behind. In the thick blue smoke of their duty-free Seven Stars cigarettes it was as if a little part of Tokyo had come to life in a dreary business hotel in West Beirut.

Even though it was his first time in the Middle East, Okuni had no desire to be shown around our splendid city, which he treated with an air of total indifference. When I suggested a tour, he said: "If Tennessee Williams came to Tokyo, do you think he'd go sightseeing?" The analogy struck me as far-fetched, but still, Okuni wouldn't be persuaded. When he wasn't drinking with his actors, he was working on his next play, alone in his hotel room. Still living in his own head, I thought, not without a twinge of envy for a man who could be so self-contained. I had always admired his intensity, the way he concentrated on his actors during rehearsals, silently mouthing every word of the lines he had written, his eyes locked onto the stage. I wondered whether I would ever be capable of such absorption.

The trip south, in a hired bus, through some of the most stunning scenery in the world, left him equally cold. Okuni barely even glanced at the lush green vineyards and ochre-colored hills. Only Nagasaki peered out the window from time to time. Okuni, Yo, and the others talked about the play, and rehearsed their lines in an Arabic that made Khalid, our driver, laugh out loud. And after this improvised rehearsal in the bus, Okuni strummed his guitar and sang songs from his older plays, while the others sang along with him. We might as well have been traveling from Osaka to Fukuoka, for all they cared.

And yet there was not much that escaped Okuni's attention. He observed, without appearing to be looking, and what he saw was not usually what others would have seen. The public toilets, for example, held a peculiar fascination for him. He came up to me, soon after we had arrived in the camp, to comment in his high-pitched giggle on the interesting differences between Arab and Japanese shit. "Our turds," he pointed out, "are small and hard, whereas theirs are softer but with more body. Do you think we're different inside? Or is it just the food we eat?" I honestly told him that I had never given this any thought. He walked off, unsatisfied, sniffing his finger, the question still very much on his mind.

He insisted on shooting a Kalashnikov. The Palestinians were amused by Okuni and happy to take him to the shooting range. He was like a child with a new toy. I warned him not to burn his fingers on the barrel, and watch for the kick. "Fantastic!" he shouted to Yo, as he took aim at a target marked with the star of David. "Fantastic! Do you think we can smuggle one of these through Haneda? Ban-chan would love it! What do you think, Yo?" Yo told him not to be ridiculous. He pursed his mouth, a child deprived of his new toy.

Meanwhile, the stage was set up on the abandoned playground. The actors were followed by hundreds of wide, hungry eyes of children in rags, who stood there watching their every move as the yellow tent took shape. Old people, too, observed the proceedings, looking tired and uncomprehending. There was a small concrete building that had somehow survived the Israeli attacks, which the actors used as a dressing room. We had to start at four, because it would be too risky to perform at night; the lights would attract too much attention. Besides, electricity was at a premium in the camp, and blackouts were a constant nuisance.

A slight afternoon breeze took the edge off the daytime heat when the play began inside the tent, which was packed with people of all ages, people who had never seen a play before, let alone a Japanese one. They seemed to enjoy the music, and the lighting effects. At least some of the words must have got through, and even if they didn't, the actors hammed it up so much that they made the Palestinians laugh anyway. They laughed and they laughed, more than I'd ever seen a Japanese audience laugh, as though these Arabs had been starved of laughter, and their natural joy came gushing back through a broken dam.

I didn't recognize much from the original *Ri Koran Story*. The play had been changed almost beyond recognition. Ri Koran went looking for the key to unlock her amnesia in a Palestinian refugee camp, instead of Asakusa. The evil puppetmaster, Amakasu, played by Shina Tora, wore an eyepatch, like Moshe Dayan's, and a star of David was pinned to his chest. When the evil puppetmaster is overthrown, the actors sing the Palestinian guerrilla anthem, with Ri in the middle, dressed as a Palestinian commando, brandishing a gun.

All went well until about halfway through the last act. No one who was there will ever forget it. Okuni couldn't have staged a more dramatic effect if he had tried. The stage went dark. A sinister blue spotlight was switched on to the tune of the Israeli anthem; Shina Tora, as Moshe Dayan, stepped onto the stage holding Ri as a puppet on his string. The arch enemy had entered the camp. First the children screamed, then they pelted poor Shina Tora with gravel and stones picked up from the ground. Yo, as Ri, tried her best to stay cool, but I could see panic in her eyes. Shina Tora ducked, while pulling evil faces at the audience, which agitated them even more. Near the edge of the stage was Abu Wahid, waving his big hairy arms, trying to calm people down, telling them it was just a play. But the crowd was far too excited for such niceties. They were ready to lynch the Jewish villain with the David star. This was the moment when Okuni showed his genius for improvisation. Standing behind Shina Tora, as one of his henchmen, he ordered the actors to duck behind the scenery. The stage went dark once more, and a minute or two later Yo reappeared, dressed as a Palestinian commando, holding the villain's star in one hand and a Kalashnikov in the other, while the cast sang the Palestinian anthem.

It was a master stroke. Every man, woman, and child in the tent joined in, some of them crying their hearts out. A few of the younger guys blasted a few rounds with their guns. I had learned the song too, during my training, and could hear myself screaming the words: "Howling storms and roaring guns, our home soil soaked with martyrs' blood, Palestine, oh Palestine, my land of revenge and resistance." Tears were streaming down Abu Wahid's face. I had never experienced anything like it: theater had broken through into real life at last. Yamaguchi-san would surely have loved it. I filmed the whole thing, but the movie stock got lost in an air raid. Most of the Palestinians who were there that night are dead.

12

GOOD NEWS USUALLY comes when you least expect it. Perhaps I should have known something was up when Hanako spent a whole night with me without a moment's sleep. Always a passionate woman, on this particular occasion she just couldn't stop. She was like a love demon. I was totally exhausted, and she was still begging for more. When I asked her what had got into her, whether she had been drinking some love potion, she just tightened her legs around me and whispered that she loved me, that she was mine, all mine. When I asked her about Abu Wahid, she put her finger to her lips and went: "Shhh."

I felt as though I had suddenly grown a few inches. Beirut never looked more beautiful—the sky a glorious Kodachrome blue; smiling faces everywhere; the smell of kebabs. I didn't even mind when the taxi driver asked me about China, as we wound our way through the streets of West Beirut to the Abi Nasr café, where I would be picked up by another driver who would take me to a rendezvous with Georges Jabara and Abu Wahid.

Jabara was a shadowy figure, whom I seldom saw, and even when I did, it was hard to make out exactly what he looked like, since he was always sitting in the darkest corner, behind a screen of smoke from the pungent French cigarettes that he favored. Since he never took off his sunglasses, I don't recall ever seeing his eyes. Jabara was the only person to whom Abu Wahid was abjectly, even slavishly, deferential. I could smell his fear as he groveled to his master. I know it was unworthy of me, but I wished Hanako had been there to see it.

I was shown into a private room at the back of a small, dingy café. There were a few old men silently smoking their waterpipes, making soft bubbling noises. The backroom was dimly lit with one desk lamp. Abu Wahid offered to bring coffee and sweet snacks for Jabara, who waved him away as though he were an annoying fly. Jabara, dressed in a black leather jacket, spoke so softly that I had to lean forward to hear him. Since he also spoke slowly, in perfect grammatical sentences, I had no trouble understanding him, however.

"Comrade," he said, "do you know the story of Lydda?" I said I did not. "Then let me tell you, my friend. Lydda was a beautiful Palestinian town, between Yafa and Al Quds. The first settlement was built by the ancient Greeks. They called it Lydda. We Arabs call it al-Lud. It was occupied for a time by the Crusaders because they believed it was the birthplace of St. George. My name was chosen by my parents for that reason. Our family lived in Lydda as Christians for many centuries. As you know, comrade, we Arabs are hospitable people and we made no distinction between Muslims, Christians, or Jews. All lived in peace in al-Lud. Until that day of catastrophe which no true Arab will ever forget, April 11, 1948.

"I was a young medical student, visiting my parents on that day of catastrophe. We were sitting in the garden of the house of my birth, eating figs, and enjoying the quiet beauty of the olive trees that my father had planted with his own hands. We were proud of our olive oil, famous all over Palestine for its subtle flavor and heavenly fragrance. Many tried to imitate it, none succeeded. Anyway, comrade, it was around two or three o'clock in the afternoon when I heard the first screams of terror, which came ever closer to our house, like a rolling tide. I rushed to our front gate and saw a cloud of dust at the end of our street. The screaming was joined by the sharp cracks of gunfire and the roar of engines. The youngest child of our neighbors rushed into the street, followed by her mother, who shouted for her to come back. I heard the stuttering noise of a machine gun and the little girl dropped like a floppy doll caught in a gust of wind. Her mother, howling like an animal, tried to reach her child, when another shot cut her down as well. A pool of blood spread like a fan around her covered head.

"Then I saw the column of armored vehicles speeding in the direction of our gate. In the front car stood a man, whose cold killer's countenance I shall not forget until my last day on earth. He wore an eyepatch. I did not know it then, but this was Lieutenant Colonel Moshe Dayan. As they raced through our town, the soldiers fired their guns at innocent people, as though they were on a hunting expedition. In the wake of this caravan of death, comrade, lay the first martyrs of Lydda, like beasts of prey. We were not even allowed to gather our martyrs and give them a dignified burial. The men were rounded up and sent to camps, and the women and children were herded into churches and mosques, assured that they would be safe there, while the Jews stripped our town of everything that took their fancy.

"The women and children suffered, but at least their lives were spared. Until July 12. Two Jews were shot in a firefight by our Jordanian comrades. That is when the monster bared its fangs once more and the Zionists demonstrated to the world that they could be worse than the Nazis. Like killer rats, their soldiers entered the churches and mosques and murdered the women and children in cold blood. Some of us, including me and my parents, who survived the massacre, were forced to march across the fields for many miles in the blinding sun, until we got to the nearest Arab town. Children were the first to die, of thirst and exhaustion. I saw one child drowning in a fetid well, while others tried to lick the slimy moisture off the inside wall. Stragglers were shot or beaten to death. My dear friend, Salim, was carrying a pillow. It was the only thing he had been able to salvage from his home. The soldiers, thinking perhaps that he was hiding money from them, shot him in the head. Right where I was standing, comrade. He slumped to the ground with a sigh, his eyes rolling in his head, like a slaughtered animal. I tried to hold my friend, but the butt of a rifle crashed into the small of my back, and I was forced to leave him, to rot in the sun.

"There were foreign witnesses to these atrocities. One was an American reporter. He described the 'Death March of Lydda' as a wave of humanity leaving a long trail of detritus: first the pathetic bundles of abandoned possessions, then the corpses of children, then of old women and men, and finally of the younger people who had been murdered simply because the soldiers were annoyed with them, or bored, or drunk with the feeling of their own power."

Abu Wahid was in tears as Jabara related these sickening events. Jabara himself seemed strangely unmoved. The words were vivid, but he spoke them softly, rhythmically, as though reciting a poem. Myself, I felt a deep anger welling up inside me, an anger that only needed focusing on a clear target for it to explode.

"Now for the good news," said Jabara, in the same low voice. "We are ready at last to pay the murderers back for what they have done. The ancient Arab town of al-Lud, known to the Greeks as Lydda, is now the site of an international airport which the Zionists call Lod. On May 30, a Jewish scientist will be arriving there, with plans to build a Jewish bomb that will threaten the lives of all the Arabs. We will have to stop him for the sake not just of the Arab people but of humanity. And you, Comrade Sato, have been chosen for this sacred task. You, and Comrade Yasuda, and Comrade Okudaira.

"You will arrive from Paris on an Air France flight, dressed as Japanese businessmen. They will not suspect you of anything. You will carry attaché cases, which will contain hand grenades and light automatic weapons. You will have a few minutes to assemble them in the restroom. You will then walk over to the Customs area, where the Jewish scientist, Aharon Katzir, will be picking up his luggage from his El Al flight. You will know where to find him and eliminate him and anyone who stands in your way. Remember that in this war all Zionists are enemy combatants. Armed struggle is the only humanistic way to advance the cause of all the oppressed peoples."

I knew we would almost certainly die, but death was not real to me, even when we disembarked at the enemy airport, from which there could be no escape for us. Even at this moment of supreme peril, I found my own death unimaginable. It was as if I were a spectator in my own movie, deeply involved yet strangely detached. I wonder if it had been like this for our kamikaze pilots? They were so young when they died. What went through their heads, as they drank their farewell saké with their comrades? Much the same things, I guess, that went through mine. That is to say, very little, except for the task at hand. The future is a blank. I have heard it said that the proprietress of a well-known bar near a wartime kamikaze base would sleep with the young pilots on their last night. I have even heard it said that this last favor was sometimes granted by the pilots' own mothers. Hanako performed this service for me, in Paris, in a hotel room near the airport. I remember thinking that I would never forget it, and then realizing that I would, for there would be no memory to remember. I would be gone. My time would be up. Extinguished. But others would remember me, as one who had helped to blaze the trail of freedom. As long as my name was remembered, something of me would survive.

It all happened so quickly that my memory of the battle itself is a blur. I remembered what Ban-chan had once said to me: when the moment comes, don't think, just act. I can't recall who first began the shooting. Okudaira, perhaps. Or it could have been me. The noise was deafening. I saw people falling all over the place. I felt a rush of excitement, so powerful that it is beyond my ability to express in words. People have compared the thrill of combat to sex, but that doesn't quite describe it. It's more intense, better than sex. In those few moments of total power, you lose all sense of fear. In a way, you lose yourself, you merge with the universe. Maybe it is like dying, except that I wouldn't know, since I didn't die.

I didn't see Yasuda die, but can remember him shouting that he had no more bullets left. He died a soldier's death at the hands of the enemy. Okudaira—again I didn't see this—ran out of the building onto the tarmac and managed to kill a few enemies coming off an El Al flight before dying a warrior's death by holding his hand grenade to his chest and pulling the pin. He was the bravest of us all. I don't know whether I would have had the courage. I often think about whether I would have passed the ultimate test. It tormented me for some years after, the fear that I might not have passed. Would I blow myself up rather than surrender? Would I lead a suicidal charge? If I saw armed men about to rape Hanako, and they hadn't spotted me, would I hide, slink off, run away, or risk getting cut to pieces?

In any case, I fell into enemy hands. When the battle was over, we had killed twenty-six people. My only regret is that not all of them were Jews. A number of Christian pilgrims got caught in the crossfire. This was regrettable, but in war the innocent suffer along with the guilty. That's just the way it is. We can regret this, but that doesn't change anything. In prison, the Zionists did everything they could to break me. I won't dwell on this, except to say that on many occasions I was close to losing my mind. For three days and three nights they tied me to a chair in a dark room, pumping terrible noise into my ears, shaking me until I thought my head would explode. I was put in the "refrigerator cell," after being made to stand naked in a barrel of ice-cold water. They shackled me to the wall and blasted me with freezing air. They made me squat on my toes—the "frog position"—until I passed out, and they revived me with more icy water. They forced me to lick up my own mess after I had vomited or shitted myself. I had lost all sense of time. Sleep was rare and always short, and made a torment by nightmares. Not that I always knew whether I was awake or not; delirium was an almost constant state. I had visions of Hanako being ravished by a huge Arab male, while I was tied to a chair. She was screaming with obscene pleasure, a helpless tool in his thick hairy arms. I tried to escape from my bonds, but couldn't move. Hanako turned her face toward me, laughing at my impotence, but it wasn't Hanako. It was Yamaguchi-san, whose laughter still rang in my ears, as I woke bathed in sweat in a cold, stinking cell.

I came close to dying, but I didn't break. Even in the worst moments, I still felt I was holding on to a fragment of myself, just large enough to survive. I don't want to sound mystical, or sentimental, but there was another image of Yamaguchi-san that played through my head, over and over, like a cinematic loop, an image that was the opposite of the Satanic one in my nightmare, telling me that I was making up for the errors of her generation. My resistance was a way to redeem the honor of the Japanese people. She was proud of me. She was my guardian angel. We modern Japanese don't have gods anymore. Unlike the ancient Greeks, we don't believe in divine intervention. Yet she was there, when I needed her most. Her spirit surely saved my life.

═ 13 ═

THE JAPANESE PRESS called us "terrorists." That is not how we were treated in the Arab world. In Beirut, Damascus, Amman, or any other Arab city, we—Okudaira, Yasuda, and myself—became legends. I had the solitary distinction of being a legend in my own lifetime. Everyone knew us as "the Japanese victors of Lydda." Arab children were given the names of our martyrs, Okudaira and Yasuda. Proud parents asked me to bless the innocent souls of these Okudaira Yussufs or Yasuda Al Afghanis.

I was released in an exchange for an Israeli soldier. Almost straightaway, still weak and more than a little confused by my sudden change of fortune, I was taken on a tour through the Middle East. I remember when the Beatles came to Japan in 1966. That's what it felt like when I landed in Damascus, or Amman, or Beirut. Total strangers would come up to me in the street and thank me for what we had done. People went home happy to have held my eyes for just a second, or touched my sleeve. I was proud of what we had accomplished, of course. Ours was the first real victory in the armed struggle for Palestinian freedom. But I also felt uncomfortable, even embarrassed by all the adulation. I was treated as though I were a deity. It was as if I was no longer a living human being. Besides, like the first men who landed on the moon, what could I do to top our moment of triumph? I was too famous now to go back to making propaganda films. The PFLP would support me for life. But what could I possibly do? I wanted to live again.

During my season in the Zionist hell, I had tried not to think too much about Hanako, for it was just too painful. To dwell on the past or think of the future would have driven me mad. I had to take every minute as it came. But of course I did think of her. How could I not have? Only always in terms of the past. I couldn't afford to have illusions about the future. As a result, perhaps, we drifted apart without wanting to. She became a distant image more than a living presence. When I was with her once more, in Beirut, it was as if an invisible wall had grown between us. Too much had happened. I could not share my experiences with her. She wouldn't have understood. What was perhaps most painful was that she too treated me as a public figure, a hero. She wanted me to describe what it was like on the front lines, at Lydda. I said that I couldn't remember exactly what it had been like. It all happened too fast. I tried to convey the sense of power that I felt. This confused her. It was not supposed to be like that. She asked me whether I meant the power of the Palestinian people. I replied that I was Japanese. Yes, she said, but it was the cause that gave me power. I said that it wasn't quite like that. I didn't want it to end this way, but it was clear that we couldn't resume where we had left off, as lovers. And even if we could, it was not possible. She was with Georges Jabara now. He didn't share his lovers with anyone.

I never saw Yamaguchi-san again. She had come to Beirut twice, while I was still in captivity. The first time was right after the battle of Lydda, when she interviewed Hanako, as the senior Japanese Red Army commander on the spot. To get to see Hanako at all was considered to be a great journalistic coup. For a while, Hanako was number one on the most wanted list of Interpol. Yamaguchi-san was the envy of her colleagues. Her program won the top Japanese television award that year. She came back just once more, this time for an interview with Chairman Arafat. The PLO people seemed pleased with it. I never saw the program myself.

But I did hear from her, for she was a loyal correspondent, and one of the few friends who kept me informed on Japanese affairs. Not that we were altogether cut off from the news in Beirut. People sometimes spoke of us as if we were living on the other side of the moon. In fact, we led quite normal lives. It's perfectly true, however, that Japanese news rarely reached the Beirut newspapers or television broadcasts. What happened in Japan didn't affect us much. But what happened here did affect Japan. When the Japanese government slavishly followed the West in supporting Israel during the 1973 war, provoked by the Zionists, the Arab powers quite rightly punished Japan with an oil embargo. The weak have to use every weapon at their disposal. It was only a few months after the embargo that I received the following letter:

Dear Sato-kun,

Winter in Tokyo has been colder than usual. Heavy snow fell in February. The first plum blossoms are yet to be in bloom.

I hope you are well on your way to recovery from the difficult times you have endured. I think of you often, always with affection and gratitude. Without your talents as a writer and a political analyst, I could never have had so much success. I feel that much of the credit for the prizes I was lucky enough to receive, despite my deep unworthiness, really belongs to you. It was a privilege to work with you, and it would have been such a pleasure to do so again. However, we must move on in life, and do whatever we can to achieve our goals. My main aim has always been to foster peace and international understanding. You have done so much to help me understand the tragedies of the Arab world, especially of the Palestinian people. As for peace . . . well, I'll never understand why men have to go on fighting wars. Perhaps it's in their nature. That is why I believe that we women must take a more active part in public affairs.

As you may have heard already, my days as a journalist have come to an end. I have no regrets about that. Being a journalist was always one of my great ambitions. But, as I said, we must move on, and I know that my next step will give me an even better chance to accomplish the tasks I have set for myself in the short time allotted to me. Life is a fleeting thing, and we must make the most of it.

You would naturally have been very critical of our government's policies during the Israeli war. I understand your feelings perfectly. Indeed, to a large extent, I share them. But we are a small island nation without natural resources, entirely dependent on oil for our survival. We are also a weak Asian nation, dedicated to peace but living in a dangerous world. That means, alas, that our security has to be guaranteed by the United States. Since Jewish opinion is highly influential in that country, we were forced to support Israel in the last war, whatever our private feelings may be, and are now paying the price for it. It can't be helped.

If I were still a journalist, without any responsibility for the politics of our country, I would be as critical of our government as you are. Thinking freely is the writer's prerogative. I have seen myself, in the dark days of my foolish youth, what happens when governments take that freedom away. We should be grateful that Japan is a free country now, and writers must continue to think as they please, even if their thoughts are irresponsible, which of course they often are. That can't be helped either.

However, now that I am a politician, I have to think more about the consequences of my words. People's lives may depend on it. As a politician, it is no good just to be critical from the sidelines; we have to deal with real problems in the real world and come up with solutions. I can no longer afford to be carried away by my heart. As a politician, I have to keep a cool head, weigh different interests, and come up with policies that are practical, as well as beneficial to our country. I believe that I have enough experience to undertake this task. So, when our prime minister asked me to run for the Lower House as a candidate for his party, how could I possibly turn him down? Duty called, and I had to do what is best for our country.

I know you think our party is reactionary, but if you hear me out, you might not think of your old friend too harshly. The first thing our government must do is to make friends with the Arab countries, as well as other parts of the Third World. This is not just a practical matter of natural resources, which we sorely lack, but also a question of making amends for our past mistakes. After more than a century of trying to please the West by imitating its ruthless system of competing for power, we must now take a softer, more spiritual, more Asian approach, and express our solidarity with our friends in the developing world. Power politics led us down the road to catastrophe once. We must make sure that this error will never be repeated. Here, I believe, my credentials are better than those of most of my colleagues. My home was in China. I have lived with my husband in Burma. I have made friends with Kim Il Sung, and other leaders. And I have experienced the plight of the Palestinian people at first hand.

Since you have chosen the path of armed struggle, you may call me naive, but in my view our military weakness should be our greatest virtue. Westerners, whose cultures are not as deep or ancient as ours, cannot help but think in terms of military force and economic expansion. They are rationalists. This makes them more efficient than us Asians, perhaps, but they lack a spiritual dimension which we should use to make friends in the world. Asia has a glorious past. Now Japan must lead the East to an equally glorious future. The power of culture is so much greater than the power of the gun.

Unfortunately, you were still in prison when I visited Beirut to meet with Chairman Arafat. He left a deep impression on me. What a wonderful person! The modesty of his personal habits. The dedication of his life and soul to the cause of liberating his people. The warmth of his personality. His frankness. And the sincerity of his feelings of friendship for the Japanese people, feelings to which I like to think I contributed a little bit. I truly regard the Chairman as a great man, perhaps one of the greatest men in human history. I feel confident that you share my feelings in this regard.

I have also had the great privilege to meet with Colonel Muammar Gadaffi to celebrate the sixth anniversary of his Green Revolution. Of course you know all about his heroic efforts to help the Palestinians. They call him their "star of hope." I must confess to feeling a bit nervous when I was introduced to him in Tripoli for the first time. I guess I was expecting a fierce revolutionary type, who would have little time for a simple woman from distant Japan. He comes from such a man's world, after all. His sharp, hawkish features are intimidating enough. And although I had studied his Green Book, I found much of it very hard to understand. So my poor heart was racing when he cast his piercing gaze upon me.

But my apprehensions couldn't have been more groundless! He was absolutely charming, with a warm handshake and friendly dark eyes, full of sincerity. First he gave a press conference for journalists from all over the world. They wanted to know when the oil embargo would be lifted. And he answered: "When Israel gives up its occupation of Arab lands." Then he took me aside and guided me to his personal tent, where we sat on cushions drinking sweet fruit juices. He looked so handsome in his green uniform, and even though I was old enough to be his elder sister, he treated me as though I were the most important woman in the world. Don't get me wrong. Despite his revolutionary credentials, Gadaffi is a very religious man, and behaved like a perfect gentleman. He asked me about my religion. This caused me some embarrassment. I suppose I am a Buddhist, but I tried to explain to him that we Japanese are not a very religious people. Unlike the Muslims, our daily lives are not usually linked to one faith. He looked at me with a mixture of severity and genuine concern: "A human being must believe in God. Without faith in our hearts, we are lost."

I thought about his words all the way back to Tokyo. And in fact I still think of them today. Perhaps he is right. We Japanese are so caught up in the material demands of modern life. We lead such superficial lives. I think that we have lost something of deep value that the Arabs have retained. I believe in my heart that we have much to learn from the simplicity of the Arab mind. Anyway, these were some of the random thoughts that sprang to the mind of this silly woman on her way back from Libya to Japan.

By the way, one of the other guests at Gadaffi's party was Idi Amin, the president of Uganda. My goodness, he is a big man! Standing beside him, with the top of my head reaching no higher than his mighty chest, I felt like a little Oriental doll. The president was built like a heavyweight boxer, but he was not at all frightening. More like a sweet black bear. I adored him. And he seems to have taken a shine to me too, for he instantly invited me to visit his country. I had always wanted to visit the dark continent and was delighted to accept. Sato-kun, you won't believe how pretty the capital city of Kampala looks. Blessed with a lovely climate, there are flowers everywhere. The president told me wonderful stories about the culture of his people. "My people love beauty," he said. "They love beauty too much." Then he pointed at several young women in the room and roared with laughter. (I believe they were his wives, but was too shy to ask.) We were served with a whole chicken. I was a little startled by the president's table manners. He ate everything, even the bones, which made a crunching sound as he sunk his teeth into them. I guess that's why he had such dazzling white teeth. But despite the differences in our cultures and traditions, our hearts were one. We Japanese should really study African cultures more diligently. They are so much richer than people think.

So now you know what I've been up to of late. I think our prime minister was pleased with the results of my travels, and he has made me his special envoy to the Third World. There is even talk of organizing a Japanese-Palestinian Friendship Committee, and I will be the first chairman! This must please you, surely. I know that Prime Minister Tanaka has his critics. They say he uses money too freely in elections, and so on. But I know for a fact that Prime Minister Tanaka is a good man, who sincerely wants to live in peace with our Asian neighbors. His dream—and mine—is to visit China one day and be friends again with the people to whom we owe our civilization. When that day should come, my dearest wish is to go with him, and shake hands with Chairman Mao, the greatest Asian leader of the twentieth century. For me, it would be like going home at last.

Please be safe and take care of your health. I don't know when we will be seeing one another again, but you will always retain a special corner in my heart.

Yours,

Yamaguchi Yoshiko

I didn't know whether to laugh or cry. Poor, poor Yamaguchi-san. All her life she had been exploited by cynical men who used her for their own nefarious ends. Tanaka Kakuei, that most corrupt of all politicians, the man who would cover Japan in concrete, the former black marketeer who had bought his way to the top, the party leader who invented the term "money politics," the friend and associate of Fascists and gangsters, had now, like his predecessors, exploited the very qualities that made Yamaguchi-san so special: her sincere wish to do good, her internationalism, her purity. He is just the latest in a long line of puppetmasters playing her like a Bunraku doll. And for what? Well, I'll tell you what: oil. That's the only reason why he cares about the Arabs. I hope OPEC never sells a drop of oil to Japan again. May Tanaka and his gang rot in hell!

I wrote her back. When I didn't hear from her, I wrote again, and again, until I realized it was no use. They must have got to her. I was too dangerous, even as a harmless correspondent. And yet I didn't feel bitter toward her. I knew her intentions were good. I was even pleased to read in the papers that she had been granted her wish. She did return to China, with Tanaka, to shake Chairman Mao's hand. The Chinese received her like a long-lost child. There was a photograph of her, in the Great Hall of the People, toasting Zhou Enlai. They must have had their reasons. The revolution works in mysterious ways. And so do the Chinese.

There was one other news item that caught my eye not long after Yamaguchi's "homecoming." A friend from Ban-chan's production company had sent me a clipping from the *Asahi Shimbun*. The headline ran: "Right-wing Actor Crashes His Plane in Suicide Attack." It happened in Tokyo. A right-wing nut had crashed his plane into the house of Taneguchi Yoshio, the war criminal and Fascist fixer. This in itself was not of particular interest. Tokyo is full of right-wing nuts, and Taneguchi richly deserved to be attacked. What arrested me instantly, however, was the madman's name: Maeno Mitsuyasu. I had known him as an actor in Ban-chan's pink films. Maeno was not handsome, and had no acting talent, so far as anyone could see, but he did have an unusually large penis—if he could put it to the purpose for which it was designed, which was by no means guaranteed. Maeno was a serious type. Once, when nothing, and I mean nothing, could prod his member into the required state of readiness, not even the most sophisticated techniques of Yuriko-chan, our most desirable star—techniques involving a double-headed vibrator, ice cubes, and her own oral ministrations—he still tried desperately to get some kind of tumescence through a punishing round of hand-jerking. Finally, the crew couldn't take it any longer and burst out laughing. Beside himself with rage, he screamed: "Silence while I'm at work!"

This Maeno, then, this loser from the porno circuit, had dressed up in a Second World War kamikaze pilot's uniform, probably swiped from some movie studio, hired a single-engine Piper Cherokee, and blew himself up in a ball of flame after crying: "Long live His Majesty, the Emperor!" Taneguchi, alas, remained unscathed. According to the report, Maeno's extreme right-wing politics had been identical to Taneguchi's. Both wanted to restore the Emperor's divine authority and rebuild the Fascist state. But Taneguchi did one unforgivable thing in the eyes of his fellow ultranationalists: he had taken bribes from a Yankee aircraft company on behalf of his friend the prime minister, Tanaka Kakuei. The middleman was an American named Stan Lutz, identified in the press as a "former movie actor."

Maeno was probably mad. But even madmen are sometimes worth taking seriously. I felt a twinge of sympathy for old Maeno. Everyone with any moral sense is disgusted by the corruption of modern Japan. Being bribed by American businessmen to buy their aircraft is just a symptom of a deeper sickness. Our entire system is rotten to the core. Maeno should at least be commended for his courage. He gave his life for what he believed in. How many of us would do the same? Who can claim that their lives have any meaning? The modern Japanese is nothing but a blind consumer of goods he doesn't need. In the consumer society, even death loses its redemptive force. The death of a consumer is as meaningless as his life. We have lost our honor. Maeno, in his confused way, tried to get some of it back.

But what good did his act of self-sacrifice do? None at all, I'm afraid. For nobody cared. People just went on, living in darkness, for their eyes were blinded to reality. In Okuni's play on Ri Koran, the puppetmaster turns out to be a ghost. But this was an exercise in wishful thinking. The evil puppeteers are not dead at all. Nothing has changed since the war. The same criminals are still running the show. The great temptation is to believe that things would be better if only the puppets took over and became the new puppeteers. But this is just another illusion, another exercise in wishful thinking. All we would get is another generation of puppetmasters in different uniforms. For the revolution to succeed, we must not only kill the puppetmasters, but destroy the puppets, too. Only then can we get rid of the illusions, fed to us by the powerful to keep us enslaved. To find our way back to the real world of the living, we must kill the movies, and all the fantasies they feed. They are the opium that makes us powerless to act, to take hold of our own destinies. We must reclaim reality from the masters who colonize our minds.

14

I THOUGHT BEING locked up in a Lebanese prison cell might at least have the virtue of isolation. I had hoped that I could reach some core of authenticity, somewhere deep inside myself, stripped of all worldly illusions, like a mystic or a monk. I tried so hard to kill the movies inside my own head.

The fact that we were locked up at all was utterly absurd. When the Soviet Union collapsed in 1989, the Lebanese government was put under pressure by the Western imperialist powers to arrest us. So we, who had been leading ordinary lives in Beirut for more than twenty years, were suddenly the targets of the special armed police. I was wrestled to the ground in my own apartment by three gorillas with machine guns, who shouted at me: "Where's Sato?" Even with a hirsute hand wrapped around my throat, I managed to squeak that I was in fact the man they were looking for. They charged me with all kinds of fabrications: assassination plots against so-and-so, plans for terrorist attacks on this or that embassy. It was too ridiculous even for the prosecutors, who were ordered to convict us, so they got us on a detail: forging an exit visa in our passports. Since our actual passports had been forged for years—mine was Brazilian; Morioka was, I think, a Costa Rican—this was technically true.

People say that prison is the ideal breeding ground of religious faith. Two of my comrades, Nishiyama and Kamei, were living proof of this notion. They decided to convert to Islam. A great deal of fuss was made over this in the Lebanese press. TV crews and newspaper journalists were never allowed inside Roumieh, but an exception was made on this occasion. It was a complete circus, with the entire press corps of Beirut turning up to witness the conversion ceremony conducted by a sheikh, who arrived in a white Mercedes-Benz.

Six months later, Morioka married his Arab girlfriend and decided to convert to her Christian Orthodox faith. This too drew public attention, and once again the press turned up at the gates of Roumieh Prison to witness the conversion of a Japanese war hero. But this time the prison authorities wouldn't let them in. Perhaps they were biased against Christianity, or perhaps they didn't want a repeat of the media circus. In any event, the camera crews and radio reporters were left outside, to file their reports from the main gate, until a tank was sent by the army to force them out of the area. But this was not the end of the affair. Religion is a sensitive issue in Lebanon, so the priest refused to carry out the ceremony without the presence of the press. If the sheikh could have all the publicity, then why not the Christian priest? And so Morioka had to wait for another occasion, when a less fussy priest could take him into the bosom of Christ.

As for myself, I thought about religion, the meaning of our fleeting existence, and all that. But I found nothing. Perhaps I lack a necessary component, a religious gene. Maybe I don't have the human impulse to believe in gods. I'm incapable of religious worship, even of the primitive faith that my mother had in the powers of the old crones on the Mountain of Dread. I envy my friends sometimes, who have gone inside themselves and found God. I too, as I said, tried to go inside myself, since there is nowhere else to go in prison. But all I managed to dredge up from the depth of my soul were ghosts of a kind. I found images flickering inside my head, as though my brain were a kind of cinema. In the isolation of our prison, I'm transported back to my childhood, trapped in my chair on the other side of the movie screen. I remember dialogues, monologues, long shots, close-ups, in Technicolor or black and white, grainy or knife-sharp, pictures of compliant women molested in dentist chairs, of Belmondo making faces at the mirror, of Jean Seberg selling the *Herald Tribune*, of Okuni's tent in Shinjuku, of Okuchi Denjiro flashing his samurai sword, of Jean Gabin as king of the casbah, and so on and so on, until I think I'm losing my mind. Once I spent a whole day mimicking Katharine Hepburn, endlessly repeating one line that struck me as hysterically funny: "Ah, London," I would go. "Ah, London." I don't know why I thought it was hilarious. I think I must have been a bit mad. It certainly drove my comrades crazy. The colonization of our minds by the movies offers a certain solace (one is never alone), but it is terrifying too, for their voices drown out your own.

Every Japanese knows the story of Amaterasu, the Sun Goddess, from whom we are supposed to be descendants. My mother used to tell it to me, before I ever saw a movie screen. Although I regard that idea of divine ancestry as total rubbish, promoted in the past as racist propaganda, I have always loved the story of Amaterasu's cave. Susanoo, her brother, the God of Wind, had created a storm in her realm, smashing the rice fields and pissing during the sacred rites for the Sun. Furious, the Sun Goddess retreated into her cave, plunging the world into darkness. Desperate about what to do, the gods convened a conference, and devised a plan. A tub was placed at the entrance of the cave, and the Dread Female of Heaven climbed on top of the tub to perform a dance. Slow at first, the dance picked up speed, with a great deal of stamping and rolling of the eyes. Finally, the Dread Female, cheered on by the deities, bared her breasts and revealed her private parts, whereupon the gods screamed with laughter. The Sun Goddess, still in her cave, couldn't bear it any longer, and poked her head out to see what had provoked so much mirth. Instantly, a mirror was placed in front of her, and the Dread Female announced that a new god was born. The Sun Goddess, in a jealous rage, reached out to the mirror image, trying to touch her own reflection. Her arm was grabbed by the Strong-handed Male, who pulled her out of darkness and once more there was light in the world.

Perhaps my love of this story reveals my peasant roots, deep in the soil of the Mountain of Dread. Okuni may have been right about that, after all. Just as the sun comes up every day to give us light, and just as the seasons will always come and go long after we're dead, the images we make have a kind of permanence. They are our only shot at immortality. That's why I cannot kill the movies in my head, however much I try. I've wrestled with the angel and lost. For they are part of me, they are what made me. In the isolation of my prison, I finally made peace with myself. For I, too, have a capacity for worship. I worship what religious people call the craven image. This is why Ri Koran will never die. Nor will Yamaguchi Yoshiko, or even Shirley Yamaguchi. Long after my Yamaguchi-san turns to dust, they will live on, wherever there is a film, a screen, and a projector of light.

ACKNOWLEDGMENTS

This is a work of fiction based on historical events. Some were invented, others took place, though not always quite in the way they appear in this book. I owe a great debt to Otaka Yoshiko, formerly known as Yoshiko Yamaguchi, who graciously allowed me to interview her on several occasions in Tokyo. Her memoir, *Ri Koran, Watashi no Hansei* (*Half My Life as Ri Koran*), (Shincho Bunka, Tokyo, 1987) was an invaluable source of information on her extraordinary life in China. It was a conversation I had with her admirable co-writer, Fujiwara Sakuya, whose own memoir, *Manshu no Kaze* (*Manchurian Winds*), (Shueisha, Tokyo, 1996) was also of great use to me, that first planted the seed of this novel in my mind. For this I owe him my thanks.

Donald Richie, novelist, critic, and the most distinguished foreign writer on Japanese cinema, lived through much of the Allied occupation of Japan. His book, *The Japan Journals: 1947–2004* (Stone Bridge Press, 2004), offers the best personal account of that period. A mentor, and beloved friend of many years, he taught me much of what I know about Japan.

Thanks, too, for the excellent guidance of my editors, Vanessa Mobley in New York and Toby Mundy in London. My friend John Ryle was a careful reader of the manuscript and prevented several infelicities from going into print. Jin Auh, Jacqueline Ko, and Tracy Bohan, of the Wylie Agency, have provided constant, much needed support.

My dearest critic and supporter throughout the process of writing the book was Eri Hotta, my wife, whose encouragement kept me going at all times, especially when writerly anxieties threatened to halt the momentum. I cannot thank her enough.